Betrayal, Malt Whisky, & A Toilet Brush

IRA PHILLIPS

ISBN: 978-1492240563
ISBN-13: 1492240567

Praise for

Betrayal, Malt Whisky, & A Toilet Brush

"I really enjoyed this book by Ira Phillips! Funny, witty, and yet sad in parts, I loved the heroine of the story and could definitely sympathize with what she went through, and I loved the ending!"

C.J. Pinard, Author of *Patriotic Duty*

"Ira Phillips portrays one woman's betrayal with great skill, artistry and compassion."

Jill Moffat, Exhibition Exhibitor

"While reading this book I found myself on a journey - a journey with Jen. One minute I was laughing out loud, the next I was wiping away tears. Phillips has a special talent for creating character and accentuates all the nuances in a genuine and poignant way."

Jennifer Brisk, Musician

"Ira Phillips's first-person narrative is flowing, emotional and insightful. Her main character is so real, so human as she shares her experience of what it's like to be betrayed and start again."

JoAnne Keltner, Author of *Obsession*

For Elsie

Always believe in your own magic.

The Prelude

I wouldn't say I was scared of heights, but I wasn't that comfortable with them either. That poster of the workmen on top of the Empire State Building, that you see – men eating their lunch on a steel beam, their feet dangling onto thousands of feet of nothingness? It makes my stomach contract and flip over. Yes, just by looking at it. Obviously three floors up, where I was, did not compare, but letting my eyes drift downwards, I could visualize myself on a shrieking descent. The thought of it was exhilarating: the ability to just let go of everything, allowing myself to do something reckless and completely irresponsible. I closed my eyes and felt a sense of freedom just anticipating it. I've had similar sensations when on cliff-tops over a rocky beach or above deep water, that compelling voice telling me to keep walking. I felt it that afternoon.

The window was wide open. It's one of those huge, old-fashioned hinged windows that open inwards. I've already pulled it right back and sat on the windowsill, balancing by leaning against the side and pulling my legs into my stomach. The sun felt warm on my chestnut hair, which fell haphazardly around my shoulders, framing my petite features. Nothing to stop me, I stretched my left foot out farther, probing the distance. What would it feel like?

The buzzing vibrations of my phone against the table interrupted my musing. Sighing, I pulled my leg back and swung myself round into the sunlit room. I probably wasn't high enough to kill myself, only high enough to sustain a nasty injury. However, I was not thinking about ending it all by jumping; not then anyway – that came later.

It began on Saturday, June 18. At least it did for me. Prior to then I am only aware that Clive (before he became *he*) was stressed. Presumably, this was because he was juggling two jobs: the old one, finishing in a month, and the new one, which he had started but was still unsure about.

It was a hot day, and he went off for a cycle. He was testing a friend's bike to see whether he wanted to buy it.

"I'm going to be a while," he had announced, flashing me a huge grin with his azure eyes. Oh yes, I always caved easily when he looked at me that way. At five feet, ten inches, slim with a good physique, he had literally swept me off my feet, when I had met him as a young student. His boyish face had matured well during the years we had been together, but his red (I wasn't allowed to call it ginger) hair still hung the same way it always had, across his left eyebrow, sometimes obscuring his eye.

He left me at home in our flat and I was lonely. It was the last weekend before we moved away from this town, the place I've been desperate to escape for so long. To be honest, I only came here because he accepted a lecturing post at the University. I had reservations then, but it was time to leave London and all its craziness, so I ignored my doubts and made the journey north with him. I did not expect the grey winter days with fog that never lifted all day and the ever-present icy drizzle, which left my hair constantly damp and frizzy. Yes, it was "driek" (a great Scottish term meaning grey and miserable), and after ten years, I constantly craved warmth and more sunshine.

So although we both had some concern about the permanence of the new job, we both agreed that a move south would be good for us. As a self-employed hypnotherapist, I would start up my business again in a new location. It would be hard initially, but we had his excellent salary to cocoon us and I would enjoy the challenge.

I had thought we'd be doing something together. Celebrating a "This is the last time we'll do this, go here," or perhaps a final walk round the park. Here we had shared so many dreams and fabricated plans together. We should have been waving goodbye to the irate golfers, who were only too keen to hit balls at the walkers crossing their course. (It was a public right-of-way.) Mainly it would have been to see the rabbits for one last time. To walk so silently up to their labyrinth of burrows, surprising them and catching a glimpse of their lives, before they magically disappeared.

No, it wasn't to be.

He took forever that afternoon, and in the evening there was a football match on. He had invited friends round. That's when one of them noticed something wasn't quite right. For me, he was just distant.

It wasn't until Sunday I asked him about it. He was evasive and said, "I just feel confused."

"What about?" I nervously tucked some loose strands of my long hair behind my ears, touching the silver hoops, hanging in my pierced ears.

"I think I'm having some sort of mid-life crisis. I have concerns over where I'm going and what my life should be about. I'm worrying about the new lecturing position. I'm not sure I chose the correct career."

"What else would you do?" I tried to curb the instinct to laugh. "Let's talk about it then."

He shrugged, tugging at his goatee. "I'm not sure I want to."

Now he had my attention because this was unusual, as he loves to talk about himself. We had been together for thirteen years, and his next comment so casually thrown out had my chest tightening as a throbbing pain began.

"I don't know. I'm not even sure I want to be with you." It was a flippant comment that hurt.

"Well," I replied, far more calmly, than I felt, "now would be a good time to make a decision. We're moving in two weeks, flat sale and house purchase, both in place."

"Of course we'll go and buy the house," he had grinned. "I'm just very unsettled. It's very difficult to focus with everything going on. We'll settle in, meet new people, and we can look at it all in a few months and see how we feel - if we like it there."

"But you do want me to go - to help you through it all?"

He nodded, playing with the frame of his John Lennon glasses.

"Are you sure?" I asked, looking for reassurance.

"Yes, I'm sure." He turned away.

That was it. All he was prepared to say.

Then we did go for that walk. I reached for his hand as we walked passed the ornate park gates, but he ignored my gesture, instead pulling out a tissue and blowing his nose. I wanted to touch him, share some closeness, but he was not really there. As we walked by the huge oak tree, he finally put the tissue away, but as I attempted to put my arm around his waist, he jogged to one side to retrieve a football for some small boys. We stopped to sit on a bench in the evening sun, watching a couple and a friend kick a ball around. The couple seemed more interested in each other. We sat in this awful silence, which was not right, and I commented on it.

"I don't want to talk about it, I've said it all." He got up, pushing his hair from his eyes. "Let's go."

The following week was not easy for me. I don't like pretending. I've always been a "get things out into the open" kind of a girl; always wanted to discuss issues. I couldn't shelve all this until we'd moved houses; pack it all up with the boxes of recipe books and selection of odd cutlery from the second kitchen drawer.

I had this week off; a couple of days to make a dent in the packing. Then, we had planned a long weekend away, just the two of us, to slow life down before the stress of moving home. I was looking forward to this week.

Isn't it odd sometimes how things turn out? I hardly saw him that Monday or Tuesday. He was so busy at work, coming back late, and without any conversation. For the first time ever, I packed his suitcase for him, choosing his clothes, putting in his bathroom necessities. I'd never done that for anyone before, and it felt weird. Admittedly we – no, that's wrong – I was packing light. Carrying unnecessary baggage had never made sense to me and my neck and shoulders thanked me for it. Nevertheless, it just seemed so peculiar to pack a suitcase for someone else, and for that someone to either trust me to get it right, or not actually care.

Looking back, I have to wonder if he knew. If he had prior knowledge that the plane would be cancelled and we would not be going, advised to get our tickets refunded because there would be no flights out for two days. How could he have known that? Not possible, just an incredible piece of good fortune for him, because if that flight had indeed left, he would have never lasted the week. As it was, he only just did anyway.

So I was not busy that week. I just thought he was, trying to run two departments.

I saw my friend Lucy on Wednesday, an ex-social worker, who now worked as a Hypnotherapist in Glasgow, whom I'd trained with several years ago. Many years older than me, I had been drawn to the self-confident manner, which she had displayed during our classes. Tall, broad and determined, she never let our teachers forget about our breaks or allowed them to overrun lessons.

"Clive's been acting really strangely."

"How, and what has he said?" Her blue eyes looked intrigued.

"He's not really telling me things. I think he's concerned about his new job."

"Could it be anything else?" She paused before suggesting, "Another woman? – No, I doubt that! I can't imagine him conducting an affair. He hasn't got the initiative!" We both laughed, instantly dismissing the idea.

"He did have a wobble about everything: his career and me. I think this overlapping of two jobs is crazy, but at least he'll get two wages!"

She dissolved the conversation with a shake of her bobbed, highlighted hair. "Sounds like he's finally had to work like an average person does."

Thursday evening I had arranged to see my friend, fun-loving Mhairi. In her thirties, a married mother, she also did part-time, freelance Colour Consulting. She always had plenty of interesting stories to impart. A dark-eyed, dark-haired Scot, she was down-to-earth and tolerated no nonsense. Her two boys were well disciplined and growing into unique individuals. Having previously planned to stay at her home and return the next morning, I was regretting the decision a little already. Sleeping with someone else, for me preferably a man, is so much nicer than sleeping alone. I know many of my friends would disagree and I understand why. Sweating, farting, snoring males, forever grabbing the covers off you does seem to lose its appeal sometimes. Ever since my first experience of sharing a bed at seventeen, I'm lonely on my own – even if I do get to read, keep the light on for as long as I like and stretch out diagonally across the bed. There's just something about waking up with someone else in the morning that I enjoy so much.

Before I left that evening, Clive gave me this look, which at the time, I read as mournful: The "I wish you weren't going, I'll be lonely" look. He would laugh if he knew how I had misread him. Now, I presume it was more, "How stupid are you; you still trust me?"

We had a great girls' night in. We didn't do that often. Mhairi's husband was away on a course with work, and after putting the boys to bed, we just chatted over a superb bottle of wine. Again, I confided to her about Clive's out of character behaviour, and again, the idea of him having an affair was totally dismissed.

"Och! You've got to be kidding, Jen!"

This was Clive we were talking about.

The next morning I was to go into work with him to begin packing his office. I was surprised when he called me early, saying he was awake and raring to go. We put in a good morning's work and at lunchtime we played badminton for the last time with two colleagues. We did not play well as a team. When I mentioned it, he said, "What's wrong with you? Will you stop obsessing?"

This was all before.

That evening we caught a train into Glasgow. Having planned a Chinese meal, I was caught off-guard when he guided me into an Indian restaurant. Not such a big deal, you might be thinking, but for me it was. I have an extreme allergy to fresh coriander: Extreme being a violent eruption of all stomach contents from both ends simultaneously. It's a very purging experience, and one I prefer not to repeat too often.

Normally, I'm quite confident and not the sort of girl who has a history of being easily led or influenced by others' decisions. However, obviously something was not right, as I allowed myself to be seated at a table inside the restaurant and found myself ruminating over a menu. Hey, there must be something I could have, right? So he placed his order, a dish for two to share. I felt vulnerable, uncomfortable in a situation I did not recognize. Was this some kind of test? Since when had he ever presumed to order for me? I intervened; well I wasn't about to poison my system. The chef promised me he could cook the food without coriander. A great deal of trust is required in this situation, as on another occasion, I have trusted a chef to do just this and then found myself presented with a garlic and coriander Naan bread alongside the meal. What part of *coriander allergy* do they not understand?

Slightly still in shock over the whole bizarre episode, I sat back in my chair only to hear him object and say, "But I want coriander in my food."

Quite belligerent when they brought the meal out and the poor waiter, sensibly taking the decision to omit the offensive herb, announced that it was, indeed, coriander-free.

I think perhaps my head was caught up in one of those misty days we experienced so often in Scotland, with poor visibility due to the constant haziness. Despite the huge cavity growing between us, and his obvious attempt at subterfuge, I persisted in ignoring all signs and even had the stupidity to thank him for a nice time out.

Saturday morning, oblivious of what would happen later that day, I left for the gym.

"How long are you going to be?" he'd asked sulkily.

"No longer than usual. Why?" I pulled him into an embrace, tilting my head upwards to look into his eyes.

"I'll time lunch so we can eat together if you tell me when." He almost smiled, but then pushed me gently away. "Get going then!"

As it was, I was half an hour late, which I did not consider a problem. He was at home, not waiting in a restaurant for me. Our flat was in the centre of town so on my way home, I called into The Vegetable Cave to buy some salad and their deliciously creamy coleslaw, which I just couldn't resist. I collected some more sturdy cardboard boxes as I was there. When I did get in, I was greeted with a grumpy look. "You're late!" His anger was apparent.

"I just picked up some more packing boxes." I frowned, bemused by this unreasonableness.

"I expected you earlier," he replied in the same belligerent manner. "You shouldn't tell me one time and just arrive whenever you feel like it!"

"I'm sorry," I said to his back as he stormed upstairs. I checked in the kitchen. Lunch was only soup so no spoilt food. At the time, I just shrugged this uncharacteristic behaviour off and cleared up the mess he'd left in the kitchen.

Looking back, I can't believe how tolerant I was with all his intolerant conduct. I've obviously changed.

So there I was, serving lunch upstairs for him. He did not talk to me except to say that the food was tasty and that the football was to resume on the TV.

I suppose football has always played a part in my life. My father and brother are both fanatical about it. I remember the lounge, where the TV was situated, having to be darkened for important matches and how no one was to make any noise and disturb my father when football was on. It was all rather puritanical, but I guess at the time I knew no different. One of my earliest memories of my relationship with my father is sitting in his lap, cheering on England.

"Come on, boys!" I would shout each time they got the ball, my large brown eyes sparkling with excitement, as I bounced up and down.

I got to stay up late to watch the match to the very end, and amazingly, England won, and I was jubilant. My mother, who had thought that the game was live, saw that I was enjoying it so much, and let me stay up to the end. She was rather annoyed when she discovered my father was just watching a rerun of the 1966 World Cup final.

As I got older, I enjoyed attending the local teams' matches, the sense of community spirit. I was a teenager with plenty of time on my hands, and although most of the players were older than me then, it didn't hurt to fantasize a little about them. There was often a good supply of decent legs on show, and plenty of testosterone. I had crushes on one or two of them. It still makes me smile to remember.

However, after I left home, and having good football knowledge was no longer needed to score me brownie points with the opposite sex, football lost its attraction for me. You could say I sold out, but quite honestly, I don't think I ever sold in. See? Now you hate me. It is strange the relationship we have here in the UK with football. It is a kind of religion, isn't it? By this stage of my life, I no longer followed it. I either did my own thing when football was on, or would watch it for the sake of a friendly gathering – but I no longer professed to be a fan.

The strange thing about it and Clive was how he hated his own father vehemently. One of his few memories of him, before his parents' divorce, was how obsessed he was, putting football on a pedestal above his relationship with his wife. Ah well, only too common in this beloved, footballing nation of ours, but Clive had objected to this attitude and hated football as he grew up, only to embrace it when he was older and become obsessive about England matches. Too bad 1966 was before his time, because let's face it, it's been downhill ever since.

On this particular evening I chose to absence myself. Plugging in my earphones, I sat on the window ledge alone.

I see it all so differently now, so the way I'm writing this is tinged with what I know now. Then I just felt sad. For the first time in thirteen years, he wasn't telling me everything about how he felt. He wasn't confiding his worries to me, and I wasn't sure why.

I had been sorting out my music as I packed it up and had made a compilation entitled "When I was 17." That's what I listened to now. Music has always played a big part in my life. It's not that I am musical – far from it. My mother, her sister, and her mother all sang in choirs, even performing in the Royal Albert Hall. I was probably a disappointment to them all. No, I wasn't musical in that sense. I had played recorder and guitar at school but never progressed. Fortunately for me, my fingers had been too small for the piano when my mother had decided piano lessons were a good idea. She had obviously forgotten by the time they'd lengthened out, so I had avoided that one. No, by saying that music was important to me, I meant listening to music.

I'm a lyricist; it's the words that are the most important. The same could be said for my brother, although most of the styles of music we choose differ. We shared this growing up together and could never understand someone, for example, who commented, "That was a good tune." Music touches your soul, helps you to express yourself and transports you away from the present. I guess that evening on the window-ledge, that was what I was doing, transporting myself back to when I was seventeen and life was so much simpler. The lyrics were sad and relevant, so the tears just rolled and then cascaded down my face. I just sat with my eyes closed "in the music," my grey top becoming saturated. He just sat and watched football. Finally, my bottom and mind numb, I got up and went to the bathroom.

A little later I prepared pasta in the kitchen, and he came out to open some wine, which I refused, preferring water, as I'd had plenty of wine the previous evening. Again, my head was bitten off, for no apparent reason, and as I started to eat, I realized I couldn't. Putting down my plate, he asked if I was going to eat it.

"I'm sorry," I said, "but I'm a little upset by all the biting comments being aimed at me."

That led to an explosion about it all being in my mind, and, "What is wrong with you?"

I went upstairs. He ate my food.

No understanding, incredible denseness on my part, no recognition. So cold, so I ran a bath. More tears. Silence as I sat in the water, hugging myself, because let's face it, no one else was going to. Amazing really, how the body knows, even when the mind is in denial.

Eventually he came in, probably to use the toilet, I don't recall. He didn't notice my sogginess for a while. When he did, instead of saying anything, he just touched my back, kissed my head, and quietly returned to the football. It wasn't us anymore.

Once I was cosseted in my dressing gown, I headed upstairs to the bedroom. He commented that I had been moping all day.

Unbelievably, at this point, we sat and watched a film. He put his arm around me and held me, which is really what I'd needed all day. Why so late? We both escaped into the film. I have no memories of what it was or who was in it, the last one.

It finished. That memory of us sitting on that small Ikea couch in the bedroom is etched on my brain. It's the end of thirteen years and the beginning of the rest of my life.

We got into bed. Now I don't know about you, but I can't go to sleep with unresolved issues. "Never go to sleep on an argument" that's the saying, isn't it? Although I think I knew even then that it wasn't a good idea to push it, that's just the way I am. I couldn't pretend any longer. So from 10 p.m. to 2 a.m., I pulled. It's like slowly unravelling the threads on an old jumper. You don't want to do it, but once you start, it becomes compelling.

"I don't want to talk about it now."

Hey, I think I knew that, but I could just see an end of a thread hanging loose, by the seam, so I gave it a little tug.

"What is the 'it'?"

No matter how hard I tried to tug, that thread was not giving, so I decided to live dangerously. Why, oh why, do humans like hitting the self-destruct button so much?

"I'll ask French Tart then," I finally broke the silence.

This, of course, is written from the now perspective, because then, she hadn't become French Tart (short for French Tart, Shit Beneath My Shoe) the term I adopted for her. She was just a "her" and at the time of my utterance, I did not really even believe she was a "Her" with a capital H, but anyway, that did it; the thread came loose and the jumper began to unravel.

Yes, with me mentioning her, I guess then he had to talk. He was all over the place, repeating, "I'm sorry," being pathetic when he hadn't told me anything. Betrayal is an odd beast. Looking back I cannot believe *(oh, but I do!)* I was the one who has to do all the work on this, digging into something I knew I wouldn't want to hear.

It was dark, thank God. My body lay rigid. Each of his replies slashed open more muscle and sinew, until I lay there split completely down the middle, like one of those murder victims you see on the autopsy table. It hurt – and hurt because I was still alive, and yet, I continued to probe.

Once I had pulled out the first row, beginning with that stubborn first thread, I would not be satisfied until the whole jumper lay in threads. I needed to know it all. I just was not prepared because I never expected the size to be an XXL.

I started the interview and he lied. (I know anyone else would expect this, but don't forget I was thirteen years into an honest relationship and even though something was terribly wrong, I still expected honesty. *Stupid girl.*)

"Well, have you been sleeping with her?"

Even as I asked this, I told myself that this was a ridiculous question and maybe I should take it back, as it seemed too hurtful an accusation. I lay there, wrestling with this to complete silence. As I slowly awoke to the realization that this extreme question had produced only a silent reply, I acknowledged that unbelievably, the reply must be a "yes."

Eventually he answered a quiet, "Yes."

"Well, for how long?"

Silence.

"Six months?" I questioned, my ripped insides recoiling, as sharp, dagger-like swipes slashed at me as I prodded.

It's interesting, looking back, that at this point, all the knife attacks are aimed at me. Later all I can visualize for months when someone mentions *him*, is a blade, slashing horizontally through his entire body.

"Three months?" I interrogated, and getting no answer, followed up with, "One month?"

"One month," he finally answered sheepishly.

My head screamed at me, *Liar. Liar. Liar!* I calmly enquired, "So what are you going to do about it?"

I don't remember now how long it took for him to reply or how many times I had to ask the same question, my insides quivering, cramping, and twisting in spasm, as I lay there, completely motionless.

All seemed too surreal; the faint light from the street filtering through the curtains, the clock gently ticking, and the distant sound of a car. This was my world, my safe place, where I could hide away from life and recuperate. When you receive news so shocking that you simply cannot accept, do you feel yourself outside of your body, looking on like an observer? Do you jolt yourself back to reality by thinking: *It's me here. This is happening to me?*

It is akin to knowing that a close relative has a serious illness or has died: A fact that won't go away, yet you can go to sleep and forget it. It is only in the cold light of morning that you awake with an unnerving feeling in your stomach before you acknowledge that you know that fact and nothing you do can dismiss it. All you can do is accept it and continue with your life.

That was all familiar to me, and yet, I could not accept this violation.

As he finally answered, I saw it all disintegrating before me. Everything that I have known for the last thirteen years, all that I have put my complete and utter trust in. The shock began.

"I think I want to take her with me next week. Not you."

I didn't believe what I heard, so I questioned the "I think." Was I grasping at linguistics? That the "I think" is a possibility that this was not happening, that it was not real, that all could be rectified?

Of course the reason for the "I think" rather than "I know" wasn't because he was uncertain; he wasn't sure what he wants. No, it is quite the opposite. There was nothing to be salvaged, nothing to be rescued, after thirteen years, for that poor, unloved woman lying next to him in the darkness. It was just purely an "I think" because he had not asked her yet. So the use of "think" was just in case, God forbid, she might say no. Then he might reconsider and fall back on all that is familiar and take me because he would not go alone.

I have to hear it three times before galvanization kicked in. I got out of the bed, ran downstairs to the bathroom and lost control of my body. The professional term is "Cockcrow Diarrhea" due to the early hour of the morning. He tried to follow me and come into the bathroom. I pushed the door against him with my feet.

He waited silently for me in the hallway.

I had, until this point, been ridiculously controlled and calm (bowels apart). From an outsider's perspective it would look like I was the one in charge of the situation, delivering the news and blows to him. He had been a complete wimp, a coward, cowering in the corner, capable only of short utterances such as "I'm sorry" and "What should I do?" As if I should provide an answer. It was too late to ask for my support and my assistance. That way of life was over, and no, it wasn't my choice. It might have been me evacuating the physical "crap", but from an emotional standpoint – and ten times more – the "crap" had come from him.

I told him that I had to go. I had to go and collapse somewhere safe. Somewhere safe was no longer there, with him in the flat, which was no longer our home. I had enough self-dignity to know that I needed to leave, exit sharply, to be somewhere on my own where I could break down and let go of all the tension in my body. I had enough self-respect that I wanted to walk out still standing; to show that, despite everything, I could still hold my head up. I wanted to know that I did not mess up, did not rant and rave, but in a controlled, calm way, removed myself from his messed up life, his uncontrolled behaviour.

As I unlocked the front door, he was moaning, "What do you want me to do?" repeatedly. Anyone looking on would see him as the victim. *Pathetic.*

So I turned and looked him in the eye, which was difficult because I only just had control, and I was walking away from a long history. He finally raised his eyes to meet mine.

"The one thing I couldn't stand is that once I go, you phone her and go round there. If you really want to do something for me now, please don't do that."

Obviously he didn't want to do anything for me anymore, as I was no longer important, because after I left, of course, he went to her.

Unfortunately it was early in the morning and all my friends happened to be away this weekend. Isn't that generous of life? So, I had no choice. I could not stay much longer. For my own self-preservation, I had to get out and go somewhere that wasn't here. Our close friend lived downstairs in the block of four flats. This should have been the ideal solution, but really was not, because although he is our close friend, he is Clive's best friend and work colleague. However, time was running out for me if I wished to leave in the manner that I wished to leave in and not witness my legs collapsing from under me. I had no choice and phoned ahead to announce my arrival at his door – in the middle of the night.

Nancy was there, a former student of his, who fell for him, the older lecturer, but that's another story. She did not live there, but often stayed over.

I arrived, still in a cloud of astonishment. How could Clive do this to me? Leaving me alone with no income and no home?

Kyle was ashen as he pulled the door open, his blonde hair sticking up in tufts at odd angles from where he had been sleeping. Nancy accused him of knowing. Very fair with a 'lacking in lustre' skin tone, she appeared even paler than usual tonight; her raven black hair accentuated her tired eyes. My resolve of not collapsing, teetering on the edge, drew out its last little piece of strength. I now faced the fact that obviously, as Clive's best friend, Kyle may well have known. Had I just walked from one form of danger to another? I watched as if from somewhere outside myself, I observed him squirming, as he answered, "I kind of knew last week. Clive told me that he'd been having a difficult time considering whether he still wanted his career, was having a fling, being rather stupid and would sort it all out before he moved next week."

"A fling?" I heard my voice as if from a distance, high-pitched, it didn't sound at all like me. "Yep. He's sorted it out. He's taking her and leaving me!"

I could see by the widening of his brown eyes that Kyle was almost in as much shock as I was. Younger than Clive, he had always seen our relationship as golden, something to be exalted, an example of all that is good and of how life does work out. Nancy further removed from us, reacted better and offered me some kind of support. "Sit down, Jen. I'll make you a drink."

After what seemed an eternity (but was probably less than half an hour), Kyle could not contain his desire to go upstairs. "I'll just check that Clive is okay." Yes, you can see where his loyalties lie.

A couple of minutes later he returned, which is why I know Clive went immediately to *her*. Another punch in my stomach. I knew I should have expected it, but it didn't hurt any less.

With Clive gone, I was safe to escape from Kyle, wearily ascend the flight of stairs, and return to collapse in familiar surroundings.

DAY 1

"Walking on the shore's edge, I search for sea glass. I imagine the sharp edges of these glass shards softening over time; the brightest of colours fading and becoming cloudy. These pieces are broken, shattered and fragile, yet with time, they become more beautiful than they were originally."

I wait until five o'clock in the morning to phone my friends. All asleep, I leave messages. I watch the clock, time passing, until seven, and call my brother. I wake him up.

"Are you okay, Jen?"

"No."

He can't really help me as he lives so far away.

It is now that the obsessing about lists begins. My logic takes over, which is less painful – or maybe it is a survival instinct – as my first listed item is a bolt, so that he cannot get back in.

Once a relationship is ending, I remember vividly all those others I've experienced and what happened when they ended. The bolt being the most important thing is a result of my first long-term relationship. This guy, after it ended, used his key to walk back into my apartment unexpectedly. Fortunately, I wasn't in a state of undress, sat pontificating on the toilet or happily in bed with a new guy. In retrospect, perhaps it would have been better if I had been with someone else. Being alone, I was in considerable shock at his sudden entrance and felt tentacles of fear rising from the pit of my stomach as he approached me. With him over six feet tall and myself a rather petite individual, it could have been worse than it was. Mercifully, he seemed in a dazed state, and despite having to fend off a couple of lurching embraces, I took control and evicted him without too much difficulty. I suspect his visit was due to an inebriated state of forgetfulness and need, rather than malicious intentions. I did, however, learn a lesson about safety, which I haven't forgotten. This memory resurfacing and not wanting to leave the flat, I call Clare, an acquaintance with a joiner for a boyfriend. Although his skill is carpentry, I know he'd fit a bolt and change the lock for me. He's a large, strong guy, sporting several tattoos and I figure it doesn't do any harm to have someone, with his appearance, hanging around. I then balance a stool against the door so I will know in the meantime if "someone" tries to use the key to get in.

Clare is the first to phone back and reacts appropriately: "How awful! That's appalling! Of course we'll come over. Are you in shock?"

This is fine from a practical perspective, but really, I needed a close female friend to talk to, not an acquaintance. Really, I needed it to be Josie; someone who knows me well, who knew us, who will understand, having experienced a very similar betrayal. Josie, not an early riser, does not pick up my message for some time yet.

Clare, however, is very responsive: "We're just finishing breakfast– I promise we'll both arrive within the hour to fit a bolt and change the lock – and it is not an inconvenience."

I decide I ought to get up, as you have to, have a wash, and begin the day. I turn on the shower and watch the water cascading down as I wait for it to warm up. My reflection in the mirror doesn't look right. My long, chestnut hair is scraped up on top of my head, secured by a bulldog clip. My deep brown eyes, usually my finest feature, appear lifeless and blank. I am numb. What next? A flutter of panic descends. I tell myself to focus: Just get washed and dressed and keep functioning. I take a deep breath and hanging my dressing-gown on a hook, go to get into the shower cubicle on the far side of the bedroom. I stop. I hear a noise: It's the stool falling.

The flutter of panic transforms to immense proportions. My heart beats wildly and my mouth feels like sandpaper. Instantly, my body jumps forward as adrenaline pumps through my body and fuels my legs. I grope desperately for my dressing gown. Something that would have been so natural only yesterday is now the complete opposite. He has lost the right to see me naked now. I will not be vulnerable. Clutching it round me, I fumble in alarm to tie the gown tightly in place.

Although it seems to me that I have flown down the stairs in an instant, he is in the hallway.

"WHAT?" I demand abruptly.

"We need to talk."

"Do we? What about?" My tone is firm.

"Everything."

"Has anything changed?" I posture angrily.

"No."

"Then we don't…GOODBYE!" I open the door for him.

Now, in a TV Drama it would cut to adverts at this point and the viewers would all be thinking, *"Good for you, girl. You kept your cool, acted strong and decisively. Well done! Show the loser it's his loss."*

Only it's not a film and as my brain is flipping this over, the hesitation obviously reflects on my face and I falter and fail.

The thought of, '*Am I really doing this to myself?'* surfaces, and I pause, only for a second, but it is enough. I see it in his eyes. He does know me, even if I don't know him.

Pushing his advantage, he is back through the door and I will have to go through it all again.

"Do you need anything?" *Did I really just say that?*

As I curse myself for being so accommodating after everything that has happened, he pushes past me into the kitchen and removes a key hanging on the wall. *Her* key. It is there as I took care of her plants whilst she was away last month.

Red-hot anger courses through me. Here I am, being far too obliging, when all he can think about is her.

Without pausing to think, I hear myself exclaim loudly, "Do you really think I'm going to come round and trash her place?"

That is obviously the exact thought behind his action, whether it is his thought or hers, maybe hers. Perhaps this is not the first time she has acted in such a way, and just possibly someone has trashed her place in response. I'm shocked that, given a chance to say or do something in my presence, in the calm light of day, and after everything that has passed between us that he should choose to do this. This being his priority tells me all I need to know. My resolve reinstates and I show him the door.

"GOODBYE, CLIVE!"

Just as he steps through the doorway, I catch a glimpse of movement on the stairs. I cannot believe my eyes. She is here and has been there all this time, waiting for him. I am more than outraged, and having held on so well to my control until this point, can now literally only see a wave of red in front of my eyes. Drawing myself up to my full height, as emotion gathers higher in my chest, I push through the doorway and stand at the top of the stairs and yell, "How dare you come to my home!"

She stops still as I forcefully continue, "You treacherous slut! I treated you as a friend, even helped you when you were unwell, and look how you have repaid me! What sort of woman is capable of such disloyalty?" I am gripping the stair rail so tightly that my fingers have turned white. French Tart Shit Beneath My Shoe turns to look up at me. *Oh yes, I have the advantage in both physical and moral position!*

"What?" she replies in that annoying French accent. "How dare you call me a slut!"

"Well, let's not get caught up in language," I roar at her. "You're currently sleeping with two men! That makes you a slut, or whore, if you prefer…"

"Excuse me," she interrupts, but I don't let her.

"Don't you remember that chat we had about trust?" I ask without giving her a second to reply. "You saying, how important trust is in your relationship? Will you be able to trust Clive now that you know what he is capable of?"

She tries to intercept me with some French phrase as she starts to climb the stairs, passing Clive, who stands frozen to the spot. Without pausing, I continue, "I cannot believe you! I remember you asking my advice about you using a different form of contraception with your boyfriend in Paris, when the pill you'd been taking made you feel sick. Was that a lie to distract me, when all the time, you are in bed with mine? Well, you just keep him. He's a rat; he's too filthy for me now!"

"What we have means more," she propels her words towards me.

My mouth is dry and I am almost speechless at this, but not quite.

"You're a poor little cow if you believe that!" I launch towards her.

Clive is holding onto her sleeve, trying to pull her back, as she resolutely climbs the remaining few stairs. Not wanting to lose my high vantage point or to allow her access into my home, I step forward to block her.

"I am a French woman and know how to keep a man happy in bed – not like you cold English women!" She leers at me and puts her fist forward as if to strike me. Her stick-thin arm is outstretched before me.

My instincts are rapid, as I catch her hand in mid-air and twist. Her squeals puncture the air and echo in the stairwell. She falls backwards into Clive as he cries out, "Stop!"

I am no longer in control of my actions and do not care. He had already pushed me into the abyss last night, so it matters no more to me what he thinks. Here, before me are the perpetrators of a massive crime against me. I will never, after today, be in such proximity to them ever again. Nor will I have this opportunity to vent, so this is my moment to release the hurt and hatred, which might otherwise consume me.

"Are you asking me to stop? Did you not consider stopping? You two who were so consumed with each other that you did not give me a second thought." I thrust my forefinger towards her face, my stream of words spewing forth. "You, who came to me, asking for my help with your eating disorders and anxiety hang-ups. You, who pretended to be my friend and sat in my home gathering my sympathy for your loneliness. How could you? You disgust me! All those gifts you brought me from your trip to Paris – were they just to ease your conscience? My God, I just can't believe I could have been taken in; how stupid I've been. I guess it's my fault for trusting you, believing your stories when you aren't worthy of belief. Were you waiting round the corner until I left so you could sneak in?" I don't let her answer. The look on her face says it all. I shake my head, trying to keep it from exploding.

"You two get out of my sight!" I thunder, letting go of her hand with a push. "Backstabbing, unfaithful pair – you deserve each other!"

Clive just stands motionless. He has never seen me this way – neither have I - nothing before has quite warranted it. He opens his mouth, as if to speak as she reels round and directs a gob of spittle at me. "Bitch!" she cries.

At this degrading act, I've had enough and whirl round on my bare feet, my dressing gown ballooning outwards, and stride forthrightly into the flat. I slam the door so hard behind me that the sound reverberates throughout the flat as it judders on its hinges.

I manage to keep breathing, to stay standing until I reach the lounge. I am shaking all over.

"Enough, Jen," I whisper to myself in the mirror, "It is over…let them go. You are worth more."

Silence descends as the downstairs door closes. I hear only the rapid beating of my own heart as I ascend the stairs and remove my dressing gown and approach the shower again.

After, walking around the flat and completing a rough list of what is mine to take, Lucy, my hypnotherapist friend, phones.

"I'm not in Glasgow, I'm in Wales with a friend. I just picked up your voicemail," she pauses, sucking in her breath. "I cannot believe it. I'm so sorry for you. What a selfish act. What an arsehole! How can I help?"

I don't know the answer to that, but reply, "I need to get out of the flat. I'm collecting my things."

She interrupts me, "Jen, just stop a moment. You can't make decisions right now. You're in shock. Don't do anything too soon, as you might regret it later."

She is level-headed and good in a crisis, so I listen, somewhat detached. "Look, I know you just want to get out of there, but it's your home as well as his. Now is not the time to permanently leave. Just pack up some clothes, get away for a bit. Give yourself time to think this through."

"I'm not sure," I dither, but before I can say anything else, Lucy is giving me instructions, telling me step by step how to proceed.

"Just come away for a few days. Come to me here. You need to be with someone who will care for you. There is a spare bedroom. Pack a bag. Go to the station and buy a ticket to Chester. I'll meet you there."

She speaks with authority. What she says makes sense, so I accept.

As I begin throwing a few things in a bag, Clare and her joiner boyfriend arrive. Clare throws her arms around me. She's obviously got up and dressed hastily, her short, brown hair, normally immaculately styled, is slightly tousled. Her dark eyes are full of empathy, "I'm so sorry this has happened to you. Men can be such bastards!"

She throws a look towards her boyfriend, who shrugs. "How canna help?"

"I'm not sure. The immediate threat has passed. My fears of Clive re-entering have already been realized. I was upstairs about to take a shower when I heard him."

"Were you okay? You must change the locks so that can't happen." Clare's concern is genuine.

"I was okay." I tell her the minimum, trying not to focus on memories of my barrage of abusive diatribe. *Well, they'd asked for it, hadn't they!* I don't know Clare well enough to bare my soul to her, so I rapidly change the subject. "My friend Lucy phoned. She's away and has suggested I go and visit her for a few days to help absorb the shock."

"That seems sensible." Clare quietly nods as her boyfriend smiles at me. "Aye, it does, ye need to be with a pal."

"I thought that, too. I don't want to act on impulse and regret my actions, so I wasn't sure if I should change the locks. The flat's in both our names on the mortgage after all. I don't want to do anything illegal."

Clare looks undecided. "At least fit the bolt, so he can't come in again unannounced," she insists.

"Aye, I'll do that now. Nae bother," joiner boyfriend says, opening his tool bag.

"Come on." Clare takes me by the arm, "I'm making you a drink."

As she leads me through to the kitchen, I realize I'm shaking. She makes me drink a cup of tea with sugar in it and tries to reassure me.

Ten minutes after their departure, I step outside. I have with me just what I need for a couple of days. I'll sort everything else out later. Nevertheless, I feel an overwhelming sense of finality as I walk away. Ever the lyricist, Queen's *"Leaving home ain't easy"* resonates inside me word for word as I depart, red rucksack on my back. The lyrics help me hold onto my sanity. I focus on each word rather than think as I step forward, away from my past.

At the station in the ticket office queue, I am singing in my head about a girl who states *"Destination anywhere"* as she purchases her lone ticket. The song is about the world not having a back door to escape through. Perhaps my back door today is Chester, the destination I buy my ticket for.

Where is Chester anyway?

It does not matter.

I numbly climb onto the train once it arrives, and collapse in the seat. I am only half aware of where I am, let alone where I am travelling to.

Even on the train, as I gaze unseeingly out of the window at unknown places, I experience some positive thoughts. I am the eternal optimist. I am self-employed, so perhaps I have to be. But I think it's just in me, the desire to do better; the underlying thesis that life will work out. So I find a piece of paper and a pen, divide the page in half, and in large capitals, write at the top of each column these headings:

ALL I WANT TO DO AND NEVER COULD
ALL I DON'T HAVE TO DO NOW

ALL I WANT TO DO AND NEVER COULD
Malaysia for Christmas
Horse-riding
A course in the USA
Jive and Latin dancing
Have a garden with pot plants
Live near the beach

Write
Have better orgasms

ALL I DON'T HAVE TO DO NOW
Listen to Disco music
Let football rule everything
Listen to pretentious academic bullshit
Babysit selfish tendencies
Put up with beard trimmings
Fumigate the bathroom and endure someone using the toilet while I'm in the bath
Attend horrendous work "socials" with your emotionally-stunted colleagues.
Listen to TV theme music and popular, classical music.

So where was I?

Um yes, where is Chester…

It's where Lucy, sturdy and motherly, meets me with open arms and where I can, for the first time, truly let go of some of the tension that has been holding me together since last night. Was it really only yesterday?

"Don't ever forget," Lucy reminds me, her blue eyes searching for my understanding, "however secure you are in a great relationship, which seemingly provides for all your needs, how important it is to have true friends."

Luckily I have heeded that advice, and Lucy is that and more.

We travel from Chester through to North Wales where Lucy's friend, Alison owns a cottage.

His text message arrives that Sunday evening: "HOPE U R OK."

DAY 1 is over.

When I jot down my memories of it, I write: *'Impotence, shock, jetlagged from no sleep or food.'*

How do I feel? I feel scared.

Surprisingly, I sleep Sunday evening. It's the last night for a long time.

MONDAY – DAY 2

Despair. So much pain, it is intolerable – strong feelings of being motherless, when I need mothering. The day passes.

I am held within the bosoms of two very strong women. They suggest I withdraw some funds from our joint account, open a new bank account, and buy a pair of sensible rubber-soled shoes (that I only ever wear in North Wales.) I'm with an older, less fashion-conscious, practical pair. The shoes don't cost much but I need them so I can walk over rough terrain and that wasn't meant to be a metaphor for my life at present.

We walk over beach, over wide, open spaces, and over wet sand and rocks. I'm sure it's very scenic, very pleasant, but I haven't a clue really and I don't take a lot in. I could not describe the place or even tell you where we went. Sometimes there is numbness, at other times the sharp pain of a freshly cut wound.

Josie eventually calls. A close friend from my student days, I visualise her sitting in her kitchen, twirling her shoulder-length fair curls around her finger.

"Oh, my God, Jen!" I can hear the anger in her voice. "I just cannot believe what Clive has done." She pauses, raising the volume of her Yorkshire accent, "Especially, after he sat there and listened to everything that happened to me when 'The Toad' shat on me!"

'The Toad' is the term she uses to refer to her ex-fiancé, another 'up-his-own-arse' lecturer, who slept with a girl in his tutorial group for several months before he told Josie he was chucking in his job and going traveling with her around Europe.

"The two-faced, lying bastard! I really thought he was supportive, that he understood my betrayal; that he cared. All that time, he was just playing along. It is totally outrageous!"

"Thanks, for understanding, Josie."

"I am so hurt, so angry with him."

I can almost feel the heat of her words via the phone line. She is taking Clive's act as a personal attack on her, as well as me. It soothes me, as does her conversation, just a little, before the crushing pain envelops my heart again.

She finishes the call with, "I'm going to get some time off work, come and be with you. You won't have to deal with this alone. I'll call you tomorrow. Just keep breathing and let Lucy take charge. She's good at that!"

Surprisingly in the evening, once we are back "home" the pain and numbness subsides to a feeling of normality. Perhaps the mind has to cut off sometimes to protect the body? Perhaps it's a brief interlude that promises that the future will be all right, that somehow some good may materialize. I do not know, but it is reassuring to feel normal and social.

Unfortunately, this does not last past 11 p.m., and when I am alone in the bedroom, I cannot sleep. Into the night my head obsessively plans, over thinking and listing all I should do, remembering things, previously not important, that seem so now.

My mind flits from pieces of friends' advice to wondering which items of furniture I should keep. My brother's partner thinks Clive's left me because he wanted to have kids. We weren't going to have any – we loved our lives without them. Does she even have any handle on the situation? I wonder how he is going to introduce French Tart to his family. If only I knew then, what I discovered later, that Clive posted photos of her for all his friends and family on Facebook that very night - ironic.

TUESDAY – DAY 3

Obsessively I scribble on pieces of paper and plan through the night, letting the monkey mind-chatter prevent anything else from surfacing. I make a list (always a list) of all the previous seemingly innocent events, which now, seen through the light of knowing, were so far from that. The list is two-and-a-half pages long and I entitle it:

NOW I KNOW, I REMEMBER WHEN…

I cry some more and berate myself for being so stupid and not seeing.

"…You told me she was 'like an older sister' – do you shag your sister then?"

I realize how trusting and naïve I have been.

"…She was losing so much weight because she was ill and 'stressed' (guilty) and I took care of her and fed her."

It makes me feel sick.

Despite those feelings, the reality that Clive is not there anymore creeps up on me and I feel fear. I pull out my ear-buds, plug them into my phone, turn up the volume, and try to blast it away. I return to the safety of planning, continuing into the morning. Eluding sleep, I leave the fear to reside in a corner of my brain where I will not go.

The scrawled plans transmute into questions: Why has this happened? We were probably the closest couple I know. Could we have settled, become too comfortable? Was it the lead up to Clive's big promotion, the pinnacle of his career? Had we made it and begun to taking things for granted? Or was that not enough or no longer an adventure? Did he feel that way, and did that feeling catapult?

I can't answer these questions my tormented head throws out. There seems such a large jump between sleeping with someone else (don't forget – for only one month,) to deciding to take them with you to your new life, leaving all you have known. That is a seriously fresh start, especially for someone with Clive's personality, who likes to be surrounded by people he knows who like and respect him, to be at home and grounded in familiarity.

Of course I hope it fails miserably – and I believe it will – but then again, I believe what makes me feel better and happier with myself. I have to, to get through this.

Later that day, I get a phone call from "joiner boyfriend."

"How's it going? Clare asked me tae call. She's away tae Crete on business and thinks ye may want tae go with her."

"I don't think I can but tell her it's a lovely thought."

"Nae problem!"

An unexpected but pleasant chat, it would seem I have support from more than just my inner circle of friends.

I realize I have an appointment in my diary for this evening with my newly acquired computer expert, Andrew. Tall with dark hair, and English, he is a research assistant at the University. We met about six months ago when I had some computer issues and a friend diverted me his way. Tonight he had been going to help me install some new apps and show me how to utilize them to their best, in preparation for setting up a new hypnotherapy clinic once we'd moved.

Rather than just cancelling our meet, I decide to ring him and end up telling him my situation.

"So you've escaped to Wales! Good plan. Only the sheep should bother you there!"

He seems understanding of this bizarre conversation.

"I know this might sound odd, but would you meet my train tomorrow, walk with me to the flat, and ring the doorbell to check whether the Clive is there or not?"

"Um…Ok, I guess I could."

"If he is, you could say we had an appointment; if not, then I can go in."

"And you can't do this yourself because…?"

I'm not sure he understands so I state plainly, "Because, I DO NOT WANT TO SEE CLIVE…Ever again."

"Ok, I'm getting it now. Of course you don't. The guy should be shot for doing that to you!"

After feeling proud of myself for organizing this, I receive a call from my brother with two pieces of news I could have done without. So despite that I am away from it all, somewhere remote in North Wales, I cannot escape that life is moving forward and needs my involvement.

"Clive rang me," he begins hesitantly.

I am angry and nauseous simultaneously.

"He asked if I could pass on a message. A friend of one of your patients, Alice McKenner, rang. Alice has had a brain haemorrhage; she was simply walking down the street! She's dying and her friend is asking if you can go to the hospital."

I reel with disbelief. Alice's reason for initially consulting me had been to gain confidence to have the courage to inform her abusive husband that she wanted a divorce. Having worked with Alice over the last two months, she had left our last session about to inform her two grown-up and moved-away children that she had left the family home and had temporarily moved in with a female colleague from work.

Now it would seem, finally with the new start she had craved for a long time within her grasp, she was to be denied everything she had begun to embrace. Life can be so unpredictable, cruel, and ironic. Ha – but don't I know that. This, of course, puts my own little situation into perspective. When I call to explain that I am away in North Wales, I am informed that she is in a coma and not expected to live out the day.

Lucy takes me for a long walk along the wind-swept coast. We are wearing our rubber-soled shoes, jeans and fleeces. The gusts of salty air play with my long hair, whipping it into my face. We collect driftwood for Alison's cottage fireplace. Despite acknowledging that Alice's situation far outweighs my own, I selfishly ruminate aloud. "I must remember Clive is no longer 'my Clive.' He may still exist on the same planet as me, but he is not the guy I fell in love with."

Lucy just walks companionably beside me, occasionally wiping her eyes, which tear up in the wind, and smoothing her highlighted hair back into place, until I stupidly announce, "I know what I need: A happy new relationship!"

She looks up aghast as I realize what I've said and immediately backtrack. "No, I don't! I don't want to be tied down!"

"Note the negative expression there." Lucy laughs, "You don't want a new relationship yet. It's too soon, and relationships are not worth having if they tie you down!"

"I can't be in a relationship because I will never ever trust anyone again anyway."

Lucy chuckles.

"But I will be, because I know myself, how I function best, and that it is with the support of a good relationship. So actually I'm taking back that last comment. Even if I never completely trust someone again, I will be in a relationship."

My mind is whirring round in circles with confliction. Lucy just listens and after a couple of minutes silence has elapsed, comments, "This piece of wood is lovely. I think I'll keep it."

I hear her but seem unable to stop myself rattling forth, "Josie's been alone a year now. She told me she is ready to settle down with someone new. Do you think after a year I'll feel that? I don't know if I ever will! Think of all those older couples, some having achieved 35 or more years together."

"I wonder if they stay just because it's easier," Lucy says, tucking a loose strand of her hair behind her ear. "I think they do because of the difficulties involved, if one of the pair steps over a boundary. It takes selfishness and cruelty to hurt someone you love, or have loved, or have even just saw as a living companion for so many years. Sometimes it's easier to just accept what you have and not rock the boat"

"But you didn't." I refer to her broken marriage.

"No. I didn't and you didn't. Think positively. You've forced Clive to take a huge risk. You saw him for what he was the other night and you weren't prepared to tolerate a cowardly cheat. Good for you! You'll get through it and you'll find someone else, if that's what you decide you want, when you're ready."

"Okay!" I jest, "I'll just have to make sure I find someone with a good income. It has just been so enjoyable for the first time, this last year, being able to afford things, not to have to worry about spending and to travel."

"Yes," Lucy tosses a shell towards me, "hope you enjoyed that! Although I may seem content with my single life, I worry about things – generally money. I wish I did not have to at age 57. I have to admit a man with a good income sounds tempting!"

As we return to Alison's cottage, armed with our spoils of driftwood and shells, I am ready to tackle the second piece of Clive's phone call. After informing my brother about Alice, Clive has the audacity to tag onto the conversation that I need to call his legal man, to talk about mediation, the mortgage policy, and our finances. I need to sign some papers. After all, it is only just over a week before the flat sale and Clive has to move and, oh dear, he may be homeless if everything does not go according to plan.

Grrr, *he* might be homeless.

"He can wait a few days," Lucy calmly decides, "leave that 'til later."

She keeps me sane. By her side, I absorb some of her strength. I don't know everything that she has been through as it happened long before I came across her, but despite the difference in our ages, when we met, on the first day of our training, we just clicked.

Once I am alone in bed, it is not so easy.

It is no surprise, that Tuesday – Night 4 – is an absolutely horrendous night. I hardly drift off at all, and when I do, I awake abruptly in cold sweats, I'm shaking and drenched through.

The depths of desolation sit with me constantly and I cannot elude them. On paper, I jot, "Never goes away." Distracted by the need to blow my nose yet again, I re-read it as *"never jealous"* by mistake. Interestingly, jealousy never crosses my mind. French Tart is not unattractive. Tall, thin *(too thin!)* with wispy, mousey coloured hair, I guess some men might notice her, but her scowling demeanour and forthrightness could put them off. Have I convinced myself that he has made a big mistake choosing her and that it will not work out? *Get a grip.* Why should I presume that it would not work out? Look what he has done. Even if it looks like things are not working out, he'll have to make them, just to save face.

No. I think there's no jealousy because the person French Tart has, is not the person I thought I had, all those years. Has he had a metamorphosis, or did I really not know him? Whichever, I'm not jealous. As Lucy said, who would want to be in a relationship with a man who has performed so inadequately and cowardly? Yep. No jealousy, and that's one good thing.

I need to get a journal. I always wrote before. I found it helped to make sense of things and to work out what I was feeling. I started it long ago, sitting on my bedroom windowsill, curled up with a cushion. Looking out at the moon, I dreamed of all the possibilities that my life could bring once I had truly begun it, once I'd left home.

I wrote while I was away at University, getting to grips with my loneliness and shock at living in a large city. Then to express how I felt about the course I was taking and whether I would use it in the 'real' world; about the friends that I was making, and boys I thought about getting together with. My journal was my confidante, and then after meeting Clive, I had left her neglected. Now, I need her to help me process it all, to plan, organize and make sense of my life, to decide which move to make next.

Just as I think that thought, my mind takes a jump and dares to tiptoe into that far corner:

I'M JUST SO SCARED TO BE ALONE.

Everyone has been so great, but how long can that last before they all become bored with my tragedy? It is not like me to self-obsess to people. I have not been on my own since I was seventeen years old, and even then I knew how good it was when I wasn't.

"Ok…then I know, I'll find someone else, if that is what I want – but not like him…" I write, and I go no further towards that corner.

My mind ruminates onto Alice McKenner, to whom I said a farewell to earlier today, as I stood by a waterfall, reading the text message that told of her death. I remembered her bubbliness, her love of life. I'm glad she had left her husband, because in that last week, she was happy. In the midst of all her harrowing last year, I know there were good times with her friends, which meant a great deal to her. We talked of positives, and she buried herself in these to escape the stress. The waterfall seemed an appropriate place to say goodbye.

Two hours sleep.

I find being alone almost impossible.

There are hours and hours in the night. I need someone to hold me. So now it's the early hours of Wednesday – Day 4. Is that all? I am so exhausted, so tired of pain. I cannot even cry. I'm too tight, too cramped and desolate.

At seven o'clock, I go through into Lucy's room and gently wake her. She holds out her arms towards me. Her strength gets me to the place just above desolation. I live through another night.

WEDNESDAY – DAY 4

"What seems like courage is really persistence and patience."

I am on the train with Lucy, heading back to Scotland, when Josie calls.

"How are you coping?" There's a pause, as I know she knows I'm not. "My boss has let me take a week off. I'll be with you Friday."

"It will be so good to see you, Josie."

"Right! We'll sort your stuff out together and I think you ought to come back with me and stay awhile. You need to be with someone, Jen." When I don't say anything, she continues, "You need me. I've done this. It is awful, but you'll get through it."

"I'm scared, Josie," I whisper so Lucy doesn't hear. Lucy is so independent and capable, that I feel ashamed to admit this in front of her. Josie is softer and expresses her emotions much more freely.

"I know," she responds empathetically, "I would expect that. You wouldn't be normal if you weren't scared. That's why you need me and that's why all your friends are and will be helping. Are you seeing anyone tonight after you leave Lucy?"

"The computer guy, Andrew, is meeting my train. I already had an appointment with him," I explain to her briefly. "He is going to come back and make sure Clive isn't in the flat."

"Good!" she says, "Is he all right? Will he stand up for you if you need him to? Get him to punch the bastard in the face!" she blurts out. "And do that before you see about legal advice, you know, get a solicitor. Look, ring me tomorrow. Let me know if this Andrew has beaten Clive to a pulp." She laughs. "I'll be there soon! Hold it together!"

I think about what she has said. I do need her and it is good not to have to ask. Should I leave and go back south with her?

Saying goodbye to Lucy when we reach Glasgow is difficult and tearful. I have got through the first few days because of her. I know she is only an hour away, but she has helped me more than she will ever know; I will miss her tonight. I only hope that I could one day be half as helpful to a friend in a similar situation.

On her suggestion, I buy some aromatherapy oils to help keep me sane and nip into the bookshop to pick up a journal. I cannot decide between two so I purchase them both – with the joint credit card. He can start paying.

Ariving at Glasgow Queen Street well on time, I am fortunate to board the earlier, fast train, which is running late. This of course means I will be early, which messes up my meeting-time with Andrew. Perhaps I should have waited, but waiting gives my mind too much thinking time.

Getting off the train shakes me. I linger until the crowds disperse and follow behind the streams of people. Taking the most longwinded route imaginable to avoid meeting anyone, and two certain people in particular, I circumnavigate the town, my eyes constantly scanning the crowd. Does it seem crazy that I am acting so strangely, that I don't want to be seen? I am looking also for any sign of Clive and French cars. I feel it is paramount they do not know I am here. If they knew, would they leave the flat? I need them to leave the flat so I can get back in. *I so should have changed those locks and not just gone with the bolt option!*

Our flat backs onto a restaurant car parking area and is adjacent from a typical Scottish tenement block, which corners the High Street. It is therefore easy to round the corner looking like I'm with a group of people heading for the back entrance of the restaurant. Once at the back of the restaurant, I pause next to a car and spend fifteen minutes looking up, checking the large kitchen and bedroom windows. There is no sign of anyone. I tell myself that I am being ridiculous, draw up some courage, and decide I am going up. What are the chances that he or they are there? I could have been inside ages ago.

I decide that if it turns out he is in and he answers the intercom, I'll just run. Shakily I walk up the steps, bobbing my head down as I pass Kyle's window and buzz on the intercom.

Nothing…

I need to be sure, so after what seems an incredibly long time, I buzz again.

Still nothing, and relief is beginning to flood through me.

Yippee! But as I am just about to put my key into the lock, the intercom buzzes back.

HE IS IN.

Having momentarily let my guard down and almost experienced relief, I am a little shaken.

Nevertheless, I am down those stairs in seconds, flying down the alleyway, round the corner, into the tenement block next door and safety.

Collapsing on the stairs, breathing in the dankness, I know how close I have come to an encounter. I recognize from my reaction that I certainly cannot deal with that. Sitting on the cold concrete, I wait for my legs to morph back to substance, collect myself and realize I have brought myself to the right place. It is damp and cold, but I have a great vantage point. Standing, looking out of the window at the top of the flight of stairs, you can see the steps leading to our flat and the front door. I say, "you" because someone of average height could. At only five feet, two inches tall, I am quite clearly not.

Infuriated, I look around for something to stand on, and then I see it, so appropriately positioned: a plastic rubbish bin and yes, I'm checking, it is full so it will take my weight. I climb to stand on the dustbin, next to some dog pooh, (fortunately old enough to no longer emit a smell), wait and watch. My plan is to do just that until he leaves and then take possession of my home. Simple enough and I don't see why it won't work. I will endure the wait to achieve my entry.

I have to admit that I have never been into this building before. Other than the view, nothing much would inspire me to stay. I think the block is council owned but I have never noticed anyone coming or going. There is a distant bang from downstairs. I freeze, but no one appears. Slipping myself off the bin, I venture upwards. There is one more flight of stairs and then a door leading to the roof. The rooftop, I decide, might be a better option but I return to my bin top when I see, alas, the door is locked with a huge padlock.

Recalling that Clare had said her boyfriend knew someone who lived here and remembering I have his number logged on my phone from his call, I phone him. If I could get someone to open that door for me, my stakeout might be slightly less uncomfortable.

"Hi, Jen," he answers immediately. "What's happening?"

I reply in one rapid breath, "I'm next door to the flat waiting for Clive to leave so I can get back in. Clare told me you had a friend who lives in this block. I was hoping I could give him a knock and ask him to unlock the door to the roof, so I can sit up there and see when Clive goes."

I don't really think before admitting what I'm doing that it might sound the teeniest bit odd. As a result, "joiner boyfriend" probably believes that I have lost the plot somewhat.

"He moved oot a month since, it wasnae a great place. Ah'm going on ma way." Before I can protest, he interjects, "Sounds like ye need a wee bit of help," and hangs up.

I suppose my plan and current location does sound crazy.

Another half an hour passes of watching nothing. I suspect I may be here for the evening, as there is a football match at 7:45 p.m. I'm judging that if Clive is not out by 7:15 p.m., he will be in watching it at home. All things considered, it is very unlikely he will leave, as she does not have a TV. (How backward is that?)

"Joiner boyfriend" arrives, assesses my situation, laughs and decides, "It would be best if I call in, see if the lad looks like leaving."

I provide him with a cover story regarding an item he could be viewing to buy and off he goes. I watch him buzz and get admitted.

I wait for what feels like forever on the rubbish bin, my eyes focused on the door until he reappears on the top of the stairs …

Simultaneously I observe the sleeve of French Tart's black coat at the bottom.

Horrified and spitting bile, I watch as they pass on the stairs, 7:30 p.m., the same time she came round for football before. Nothing much changed there.

"Joiner boyfriend" arrives at my side. "Alreet! Nae good news, ye ken," he grimaces. "He's obviously going nae where. He's just oot of the shower, nae socks, shirt loose, settled for the night." Stooping to look into my eyes, he adds, "Hey, I'm sorry. Was that the lass?"

Acknowledging the look on my face, he comments, "Nae much of a looker, rather po-faced!" Quickly assessing that I want to hear no more about 'French Tart', he follows with, "What, the noo?"

"I'm going to wait," I say firmly. "You go, and thanks for doing that. I really did not want to come face to face with him. I'm going to wait and go in once they leave."

"That'll be an age!" He raises his eyebrows.

"I know it'll be a while, but I'm meeting a friend, so it's fine." I'm not convincing him. He's still evidently reluctant to leave me here, so to confirm that he can go now, I say, "I'll wait outside." Offering me a hand down from the bin, he walks me back into the High Street, just as Andrew appears.

"If yer needin somewhere tae sleep the night, ye have ma number," he calls over his shoulder, glancing at Andrew and turning to finish with, "Call anytime! Cheerio."

Now that "joiner boyfriend" has played Andrew's part by buzzing the intercom and surveying the situation inside, Andrew's planned role is now redundant.

"How about we go for coffee then?" he offers on learning this.

"Ok," I agree, "but it needs to be somewhere where no one will recognize me, as I do not want anyone to know I'm here." As I explain this to Andrew, I feel as if I am caught up in some bizarre movie plot and am the paranoid star.

"How about McDonalds?" Andrew, not batting an eye, suggests. Knowing I am vegetarian, he chooses well.

"Fair enough, good choice, I have never or ever will again be in there!"

We walk silently down the street and enter, choosing an unlit table in the basement but need not have bothered. There are only a couple of teenagers present. Andrew eats some fries while I relate the saga, finishing with, "Is this really my life, doomed to spend my evenings sitting on rubbish bins adjacent to dog pooh with a trip to McDonald's as my only relief?"

He chuckles.

"I apologize for your wasted trip, but thanks for the coffee and your company. I'm going to get back now to my 'delightful' spot!"

Evidently, the bizarre movie plot promises to be more entertaining than an evening watching football, as he refuses to leave me on my own and instead offers to join me on the rubbish bin. *I don't imagine it would hold both our weight!*

On second thoughts, he probably fears for my sanity and is too much of a knight to abandon me.

I return with him to the scene. Observing his horrified look, I shrug, "Well, I know the rooftop would have been preferable, but the door is padlocked." Before I have even lifted my foot to begin my ascent back onto the bin, he takes the stairs, three at a turn, up to the locked door. Luck upon luck: The lock is broken and the door opens. It is a small victory, but such relief for me. I feel comfortable in the knowledge that now I can watch all night, if necessary, without any one disturbing me (or deciding to commit me to an asylum).

On the rooftop there is a broken chair, a clothesline, and some discarded paint pots beginning to rust. There is just a small ledge and a view over the roof of our flat, the same perfect view of the outside steps, also a slim view into the small attic room through the window - fabulous. No one would think to look up.

"Joiner boyfriend's" last words come back to me, and I know that I have to plan for the possibility that they may not leave the flat that night; a thought I am obviously not comfortable with, but have to prepare for.

Tonight, I seem to have developed, without intending to, a posse of tall men; both "joiner boyfriend" and Andrew are over six foot. They are two guys I know hardly at all, but playing such huge roles tonight in this tragic comedy. I know I need to exercise some caution here. Perhaps "the betrayed, loopy woman" is attractive to them. Perhaps it's physical. Tall guys like to take care of petite women. Either way, I am not up to negotiating male egos, so I definitely need to stay with a female tonight. I decide upon Mhairi. It feels a million months ago, since I chatted and stayed over with her only last week.

Pulling my phone out of my back pocket, I realize the battery has died. *Typical!* Mhairi doesn't live far away. Still with the second half of the football match remaining, I have time to call on her. Andrew insists on accompanying me. I am still scared to be seen. What if Kyle and Nancy are walking back? Andrew suggests I go in disguise. He is really enjoying the subterfuge, and after missing his big debut earlier, I allow him to dress me in his huge, long, black coat and hide my hair under his wool hat. He then proudly presents me with a pair of sunglasses. I must look utterly ridiculous but I do not care. This is the part in the movie where the producer introduces the comic relief, designed to relieve the tension of the story and make the audience laugh. I am far more attention-catching now, but as Andrew points out, no one will recognize me.

We make our way down the stairs, myself a little gingerly as it is now dark, there is no lighting, I'm tripping over the coat and…oh my, I have sunglasses on.

We make it through the town to Mhairi's residence but there are no lights on and no one is at home. A boy spots me, points me out to his friends, and they all collapse laughing. Andrew and I make a hasty retreat back to the protection of the rooftop.

Andrew regains his coat, and after ten minutes announces he is off to purchase some supplies.

Left alone on the rooftop I am suddenly aware of some movement below. Instantly crouching down, I watch breathlessly through the slim attic window. It's French tart. Wearing a strappy, yellow dress, revealing her bony shoulders, she sits at Clive's desk looking at the computer. *How long has she been there? Has she noticed us above? Surely not – I'm being paranoid. More to the point – What the hell is she doing upstairs in our home in his study?* Now I'm beginning to fume – she seems so comfortable. I torture myself by ruminating over how often she must have been there without my knowledge.

She is reaching and struggling with something on the notice board on the wall behind and it's that movement which has caught my eye. As I watch, she pulls off a photo pinned to it. She studies it meticulously. It is one taken last summer of Clive and me, his arms entwined around my waist as I smile up at him. It's a good photo. He is looking adoringly back at me. I lower myself onto my stomach to get a clearer view. Slowly and intentionally she rips the photo into two pieces. I stifle a gasp as my hostility rises. *She is in my home destroying my possessions and my history with Clive!*

As I observe her impertinent conduct, she suddenly swings round and leaps up from the chair. Panicking that she's heard me I drop my head and am unable to see anymore. My heart is thumping as I open my mouth and listen intently – I can hear muffled sound but no more.

Unable to resist looking, I cagily raise my head and peer down. I can see the top of Clive's head, where his hair is thinning. He is standing opposite her, holding two wine glasses, one of which he is offering her. She is talking to him, both hands behind her back, concealing the shredded photo. How will he react to her action? *Will he even care?*

He appears to be urging her to take the glass and she's hesitating, while transferring the pieces into her left hand. From a height I can see that she is going to drop a piece as she moves forward to accept the wine. I'm monitoring every move as it flutters to the floor. *Has he noticed? Has she noticed?*

She has. Much to my disgust, she steps backwards onto it, while she puts the glass onto the desk and pulls him towards her into an embrace. Gagging, I am witness to the full force of it and wish I had not been. I wince as she passionately forces her tongue down his throat as he tenderly touches her neck. *Okay, I do not want to ogle. Turn away, Jen!* Yet I don't. *Perhaps I'm sick. Why would I torment myself this way?*

Clive puts down his wine glass and grasps for her other hand. I hold what's left of my breath. *Perhaps he'll find the photo now and even if its destruction doesn't offend him, it might at least shatter their romantic moment.* Oh no – she's too clever for that and easily distracts him by single-handedly caressing his torso, lowering her hand to his jeans as she pushes him towards the doorway and out of my range of vision. *Please, please no.* The images of them, having sex in our bedroom persecute me.

Hearing a noise behind me, I turn to see Andrew returning with vodka, beer, water, and even a pack of cigarettes. He takes in my new position and the strangled look upon my face and politely inquires, "I thought perhaps 'in times like these' you might need to smoke." He doesn't know me well so I guess it's a fair assumption as is the varied choice of drinks. At this point I am extremely tempted to do anything to dull my vivid imagination, but having never smoked, I doubt starting now is going to help. I suspect nothing is, but sit up and take the vodka. *What the hell!*

It is a very kind gesture on Andrew's behalf so I open the bottle and down a couple of long swigs neat. "Wow! Okay, I got that right!" he grins, taken aback. It tastes vile. I never liked vodka but the hot burn on my throat is soothing and I avoid telling him what has just transpired. But I can't escape the memory now etched on my mind and I daren't envision what, this minute, may be taking place below.

Andrew has ascertained that the football match has gone to extra time so we will have to wait even longer through the extended, allotted time and maybe, just maybe she didn't manage to seduce him. Extra time is very important and he wouldn't want to miss it. I shiver from my thoughts and because it's getting really cold now. Andrew, seeing me uncomfortable, reaches for a red fleece-lined jacket, hanging on the washing line and tells me to put it on. After five minutes he goes down to the car park and lingers, talking into his phone, prowling up and down convincingly while distractedly glancing up at the bedroom and kitchen windows. He does a lovely audition, having a one-sided argument with a girlfriend who doesn't exist. In a happier place I would have been entertained. A few customers leaving the restaurant gaze over at him when he raises his voice in mock argument but no one notices that he is watching for signs of movement in the flat above.

I am still feeling the cold evening air so plug in my iPod and move about in rhythm to the music. It is as much a coping strategy as it is to keep warm.

Andrew is watching me. I am watching him.

No one else is aware of either of us.

This is the strangest evening.

After some time, Andrew returns. He delivers his report

reluctantly, watching my face for reaction, "'French Tart' is washing up and putting things away and she obviously knows where to put everything! She is already skivvying for him!" Exclaiming a little too theatrically, he adds, "Perhaps, she's been doing it a while!" He grimaces and then tries to look concerned.

I am just relieved that she is in the kitchen and not in the bedroom. He hastily goes on to say, "Clive is watching the TV – the extra-time and post-match chitchat. He has all the twinkly lights on, it's all very cozy, but the blinds are up. I'll go back."

I can tell by Andrew's hesitation, that he is not sure how much to share with me for fear of damaging me. Although he's enjoying his role, I'm not sure he could cope with me breaking down. My over-suspicious mind wonders if Clive knows that we are watching. *Is he staging this? Could they both be? Did she know I was watching their shenanigans in the study? No, they couldn't, surely, and it's just me who would pull the blinds down, and I'm not there.*

This seems to be taking an eternity and is so surreal. I decide hesitantly that it's time I went down. Taking off the red jacket, and having literally just pegged it back on the line, the door opens and I freeze like a cornered spider. One of the male residents comes out. My head reeling and fearing eviction from this, my new safe place, I launch into a diatribe of my situation and why I am here, conducting my surveillance mission on his rooftop.

"You just stay, love," he retorts with a thick Scottish accent and brings me over the broken chair. "Have a seat, lass!" Then he is gone, along with the red jacket, which he has collected from the line.

His kindness overwhelms me and I do smile at the thought of his wife – the owner of the red jacket? She will never know how it kept me warm through the unfolding of one peculiar night, which took place on her rooftop, while she was completely unaware downstairs.

At quarter to twelve, Andrew signals he is coming up. Packing our bags, I know it's time to move. Walking over to the other side of the roof, Andrew, ill-at-ease, points out the obvious to me, "It's nearly midnight; they've been relaxing, watching football. They aren't going to be leaving now. As much as I know you do not want to hear it, there's a perfectly good bedroom upstairs."

A true gentleman or maybe to avoid any more embarrassment, he agrees to stay on the roof five minutes longer to cover the view of the back stairs, as I go down. I'm heading for the jeweller's entrance, opposite. It is set back off the street with stairs leading up to the door, under cover and now shrouded in darkness.

Exiting the tenement block, the light from the stores on the street appears very bright and fearful of being visible to eyes from above I scuttle across to the jewellers where I crouch down on the top step to get a clear view of the living room window. A man walks past and does not notice me. Good.

It is then that the living room lights go out. My heart is hammering as I wait for some sign of what is happening. Are they going to bed? Should I check round the side? Pain sears through my chest and breathing in feels like swallowing a knife. I am immobile at the thought of them both traversing up the stairs to the bedroom. Time seems to be frozen as I expectantly wait for some sign of them.

Then miracle of miracles, the door to the alleyway opens and they come out. They haven't gone to the bedroom.

I shrink into myself, edging backwards. Do they know I am here? Do they know I am watching them?

They walk a shoulder width apart, a poignant distance, across the road from me, heading down the street. She turns her head only once to look into the pizza takeout, which is still open, but otherwise they look straight ahead, not a word spoken. Andrew arrives at my side as he has witnessed their departure from above. They turn into a small street at the bottom of the road, and with the realization that they may have her car and that the only way to drive out of the street is to pass us, I grab Andrew and we sprint across the road. Almost falling against the alleyway door so recently opened by them, we continue to run down the passageway, up those stairs I have eyeballed all evening, and I finally put my key in the lock and turn.

Yes it still works and I'm up the internal staircase, unlocking our flat door. I collapse on the sofa and stop breathing. Literally, I almost suffer an asthma attack and sit wheezing whilst my eyes accustom to changes in the room.

I am in.

Andrew watches the street from the window, watching them in the stupid French car, drive up and turn round the corner. They've gone and I'm home. I'm safe and my stuff is still here.

THURSDAY – DAY 5

"It is always better to know all of the truth from the outset."

I wake from little sleep, as usual, in a cold sweat.

The next phase begins: The panic of packing up, shipping it out trying not leaving the flat; the bolt permanently down in case someone should come back although I really doubt it.

Part of my victory of the seizing of the flat should have been that they did not know that their last night was their last night here together. No, they had already decided that and Clive has left a note on the table informing me of just that. It mainly outlines our mortgage and financial commitments, informs me he will no longer be buying the house I had chosen near to his new job's location:

"It's a lovely house but it would have been ours." *Uh, yeah, if you didn't cheat and break up with me! Yep, I'm sure neither of you want to live in it now!*

He writes that he has to rent somewhere to live in while he "rebuilds his life." He tells me that he won't be unexpectedly arriving at the flat without warning and finishes with, "I am so sorry that this has happened and the way it has happened. I really do hope you are okay."

Thirteen years of my life reduced to, "I really do hope you are okay." How could I possibly be okay? It is beyond belief; how did I think I knew this person?

My brother is with me (well, on the end of my phone) while I pack up CDs: music, the most important thing right now. We just chat and there are some pauses, just like there would be if he were here. It means a lot to me, it feels like I am not alone. He helps me decide what to leave, some of Clive's more dubious selections, and ensures I keep most of the CDs I have chosen. I'm very fair and leave Clive more than half, quickly copying those of his I do want in iTunes.

Andrew calls round with a filled baguette from the local deli and to check I've survived the night.

"I didn't think you'd have cooked any lunch," he smiles, placing the baguette in my hands. He's right. I'm touched again by his kindness. After the previous night's experience, our acquaintance has expanded to friendship. As he walks with me to the bank so I can discover how much is in our joint account and withdraw some money, I touch his arm. "Thanks for helping me."

"Not a problem, it could have almost been fun if it weren't so awful." He chuckles, but I am nowhere near being able to acknowledge last night as 'fun'. I'm shaking, my eyes constantly darting around, and it's a long wait. I'm nervous being away from the flat and do not want to be noticed, nor engaged in conversation with anyone I meet. Andrew seems to recognise this and stands protectively adjacent to me.

I am aware that his concern for me has the potential to develop into more. Dark-haired, tall and slim, he is not unappealing and his companionship has been more than commendable. He is around the same age as me and I'm aware, from a previous conversation we had, (when I was safely in a permanent – *Ha, permanent!* – relationship) that he is currently single. I think that when you have a platonic relationship with someone of the opposite sex, there always comes a point when the question of sexual attraction has to be addressed. At this stage, I do not have the energy required to even have this conversation with him, so I thank him for escorting me, as we walk back up the road, implying that he should now depart. He takes the hint, leaving me outside the pub, opposite the flat and promises more support, should I need him. I block his attempt to plant a kiss on my cheek by pointing out a woman behind him. "I think it's the owner of the red jacket," I whisper, bringing my hand to cover my mouth and moving backwards as if to hide behind him. As he turns to look, I make my escape. "Oh, no it's not – my mistake!" I call as I cross the road.

Perhaps I was too familiar with Andrew and "joiner boyfriend." I've forgotten how to have male friends as a single woman. *Too many complications!* There's enough on my plate without that kind of pressure.

Which leads me on to my next interaction with a male, via the realization that here I am choosing which CDs to take, when I have nothing to play them on. Clive has taken the stereo system. This leaves me a little panicky, as playing music in Wales and on the rooftop had helped calm me down, and it has now become a crutch. I need more than my iPod, phone and computer, so I visit the Sony store a few doors down, next to the pizzeria.

Undeniably, I cannot yet put things into perspective, my life is way off-kilter and I portray this by telling complete strangers so much more than I should. Take for example, the poor man on the rooftop, out just to fetch his washing in, not to receive a whole soliloquy from some desperate, unhinged female, trespassing on his rooftop.

Well Neil, the manager of the Sony store, also gets the whole, sad story. He should never have begun with, "How are you?"

It's fatal, as I'm going to answer that question, in a lot of detail. It's a Thursday afternoon, he isn't busy, and his colleague is checking stock upstairs, so he becomes a willing counsellor.

"I'm crap. The bastard I used to live with left me for a piece of French Tart that wasn't even tasty."

He looks at me with shock. "Aw, love, that's a sad story."

"Well, no one else thought she was tasty – just him and now she's moving with him to his fancy new job and I'm not!" I blether on rapidly.

He stands, murmuring sympathetically, making all the right noises as I fill in the details and of course is only too ready to solve my musical issue by utilising the balance on our joint credit card.

"Here's a wonderful little HiFi."

He demos it loudly with the track *'If you tolerate this.'* I am lifted by the music (I'm tolerating a lot), the prospect of my problem resolved, a lovely new sound system and his kindness.

"I'll take it," I say, opening my purse. "Here's my credit card, registered in his name, so there's plenty of money available."

"Are you sure you dinnae need anything else then?" he laughs aloud and for the first time, I manage a smile.

He carries it back to the flat with me, installs it, hugs me, and says, "It'll be all right, love."

Everyone is so kind. I'm not sure I can take it all.

Mhairi calls me.

"Jen, I picked up your voicemail. Is it true, Clive has left? I've been away with the boys, but I'm free tonight. Shall I come over?"

It's Thursday evening; she helps me make a list of what I should keep and what prices I should try and sell the remainder at. She acts the non-emotional, organised mother. She sees what is necessary to achieve to meet the goal of packing up. She takes over, her large figure bustling endlessly from room to room.

"You should sell everything and raise some funds. I'll help you make a list tonight and come back tomorrow to help you pack up." She pauses. "I have to tell you something."

I look at her concerned brown eyes expectantly.

"Remember last week, when we were talking and I'd said I'd seen Clive?"

I nod.

"I did not tell you when. It was Tuesday morning. I did not tell you where. Where does she live?"

"That road near the station next to the dance studio - were you there?" I swallow with expectancy.

"Yep! Well, I asked if he wanted a lift. He said he was visiting a friend. It all falls into place now."

"Oh, God, Mhairi!"

"I'm sorry, I just never thought," she says, touching my arm.

"That was the morning he had told me he had to go into work because he was so busy - a different type of busy then."

"Unbelievable!" she thumps her hand on her meaty thigh, "and, to tell you that he was at the office!"

More lies uncovered.

Between Thursday – Day 5 receding, and Friday – Day 6 emerging, I wake again, drenched in a cold sweat, slapped in the face with the memory of Mhairi's realisation, and me having called Clive on his phone Tuesday morning, he being very loving, pretending he was at work, all the time he was there at hers, presumably in her bed.

How could he?

How could she?

Deceitful Treachery.

FRIDAY – DAY 6

I call into see Angus Bell, the solicitor dealing with our flat sale and fortunately catch him between appointments.

"I was very surprised to hear from Clive, as previously all my involvement with the sale has been through you."

I tell him the situation. As we are just common-law partners, he does not see much hope for me.

"You would need an agreement drawn up. You're not in a strong position, as there's no marriage certificate, but you should qualify for legal aid."

Lucy calls round to help me pack and has the same conclusion from her solicitor. She plucks a roll of black plastic bags from her canvas bag. "Right, here's a trash bag, this is going in," she indicates a stack of Clive's discarded paperwork as she gathers it and drops it in the plastic bag. Whilst her decisive action is mainly a good thing, some of the trivia she throws away I have to rescue afterwards, as there are some items that I am not ready to trash so soon. We find a flower card I've kept with *"To the woman of my dreams"*, written on it. Lucy bins it. I cry and retrieve it. I know its rubbish, but I want to believe it was true at the time, that the whole relationship hasn't been a complete lie; that once upon a time, he did feel it.

As Lucy ploughs on, I detect Josie's footfalls on the stairs: My next saviour is here. She hugs me and I cry. She cries, too. It's five o'clock and now I have constant support. Lucy has to organise us both, because Josie is more emotional than I am. She has driven five hours straight from work and is now reliving something very similar to what she has recently suffered through.

Lucy leaves to catch the train back to Glasgow and hugs me Goodbye. "Look after her," she instructs Josie. "Here's a bag of chocolate to help absorb the grief."

Josie cooks spaghetti bolognaise.

"Start from returning from Wales" she says encouragingly, "And don't leave anything out!"

She cooks as we chat and we both get enraged, both cry and both giggle at some bits. She loves "joiner boyfriend" said French Tart was po-faced and that Andrew thinks I'm far more attractive. She hates the episode I had to endure on the rooftop, watching them together in the attic-room, and we guffaw over thoughts of me balancing on a dustbin next to a pile of dog pooh.

I pour the Rioja she has brought, swirling it slowly to inhale the gorgeous aroma. When she throws some spaghetti at the wall to see if it is al dente, we decide just to leave it there.

Andrew calls round to work on the computer and is accepted as an honorary female for the night. It's either that, or he gets spat on. With Josie's recent experience and my open wounds, there is not much space for any kind words to be directed towards the opposite sex. We have eaten the spaghetti by the time he arrives and have nearly finished the wine. Fortunately, he brings a bottle with him. Mostly we just ignore him as he is focused on the computer. We don't mean to, but there is plenty of bitching to do. Andrew learns a lot about scorned women that evening. We talk about plenty that he should not really be party to, but his company is fairly easy and we have so much to discuss, that we forget he is listening. Let's hope, experiencing first-hand how cruelly we have both been treated, and witnessing the hurt, he will never behave that way. As the evening progresses and the wine bottles become lighter, there is plenty of laughter, generally inappropriate, but very therapeutic.

That Friday evening, I think Andrew finds the worst of it on the computer. "Ow!," he interrupts Josie's spiel about Academics being too full of their own self-importance to acknowledge anyone else's feelings.

"Clive has left his sent emails in the sent box."

There's a pause before realization dawns and Josie screams, "Show us!"

"Are you sure? " Andrew asks tentatively, obviously now regretting he had pointed them out. "It's not good. I'm not sure you'll want to see these, Jen."

My stomach turns over on itself as I inhale rather too deeply. "I need to know," I reply cautiously. "I know I won't like it, but I'd prefer to see it all so I can deal with it now. I don't want to find anything later."

"Yes," Josie backs up my decision, "show us now!"

Andrew grabs the laptop and joins us on the sofa-bed. It's rather soft and we sink even lower with the addition of his weight with ours.

"There are two." Andrew points to them. "The one to his mother is the worst. He's explaining her background and mentioning he may need some cash. He has attached these scanned photos of her to show his family."

"Loathsome pig!" Josie declares violently.

"It's worse than that," Andrew clarifies, warming to his dramatic role as narrator. "He's sent photos of himself to her – French Tart!"

"Gross! What arrogance!" Josie is horrified.

We are all leaning in towards the screen immersed, our heads touching as young children's do at Primary School, to try to get a better look.

"I took those photos of him! Right!" This egocentric email and the vomitus act of sending photos of himself to her, boils my blood and I react, before allowing myself to think. Jumping up from the sofa, almost sinking Josie and Andrew as they lurch against the cushions, as I remove my weight, I race upstairs.

"Self-obsessed bastard!" I mutter to myself, feeling fury coursing upwards inside, as I enter his study. Yanking at the filing cabinet drawer, I delve into the files and mess up his beloved articles. He has a whole filing cabinet full of photocopied articles. Soon the pages are all out of sync and swapped around. Not at all obvious, but when he comes to reference something and discovers the pages out of order, it will be a nightmare to fix. It is an automatic response to hurt something precious to him because I am feeling hurt. It is not something I am proud of. I do not want to be the wronged party who vengefully scrapes her key down the side of his car, the ex-girlfriend who puts rotten fish through her letterbox. Oh no, my revenge will be much more subtle and the aim, is not for him to hate me, just for him to realise what a big mistake he has made and how superior I am to her.

This is a good point, which I don't doubt for a minute. Perhaps it is because I knew her so I know I am. Maybe it is just because I could never, ever act in the way she has: Befriending me and then sleeping with my partner behind my back. My self-confidence is intact – and that is a very, very good thing.

SATURDAY – DAY 7

Josie and I spend Saturday morning packing up – female comradeship. There are some of Clive's suitcases half packed in his office. We fill the pockets of his suits with my lingerie and pairs of stockings – yes, he was into dress up and I'm not going to need those again.

"Needless to say," Josie giggles, "I didn't know this about him. Quite funny, if he unpacks this case with her!"

We work on silently for a while, but even I relish in the comic relief.

"Hey, Jos, I've got something else we need to do."

Looking up, she notices my grin. There are two pairs of black boxer shorts, which I bought him recently that he has, no doubt, worn to impress her.

"See these?" I smirk cunningly. "I have read a little tip involving wiping fresh chilli peppers on the crotch, which once warmed up by body heat, activate later in the day."

"Ooh! Do it!" she encourages.

"Guess what I bought?" I laugh, egged on by her. "It's the hottest chilli pepper I could find."

I also leave some inscriptions in his beloved books, just one of the sentences from the *"NOW I KNOW, I REMEMBER WHEN"* list, randomly placed at the top of one page per book.

"…You decided after thirteen years that you needed a secret password for your email account.'"

Josie brings the books over to me.

"This is just so I will not be forgotten. Nor will what he has done, ever leave him. Academics are oh-so proud of their libraries. Let's hope he's still finding these little memory joggers in years to come."

"You're good! This is quite calculated." She watches over my shoulder as I scribe the next sentence:

"...You kept running up your phone bill. Phoning her late at night downstairs?"

"Oh and what will a colleague borrowing a book believe?" I raise my eyebrows to her.

"...You complained about not having a separate bank account and said you needed one so I wouldn't know how much money you'd spent on a gift for me."

"No doubt they will have devised a wonderful little story for their arrival at the new University of how they met and their relationship together," Josie says with disgust. "There is not much likelihood they will be admitting the truth, is there?"

Quite a few friends and acquaintances call round; the grapevine is flourishing. I still jump when the door buzzer sounds. Mhairi calls to collect my plants, which she will babysit; "joiner boyfriend" collects some boxes Clare will store for me. We leave my rocking chair downstairs with Kyle. Always going to be a difficult visit, the tension is heightened by the lack of Nancy's presence, also because Josie loses it.

"Your pal is unbelievably selfish! How he could do this to Jen is inconceivable. How does he think she'll manage? She's just given up her work to leave with him and the flat's sold. What does he expect her to do? Go and sleep rough? I hate him!" She is yelling now.

Everything that she is co-experiencing with me is too reminiscent of her recent betrayal. The valve just gives way and Kyle, as a fellow lecturer, is on the receiving end of a huge outburst.

"Clive knows exactly what I went through and you are just helping him, enabling him! You academics are all the same. You think you live somewhere above the real world – think you can just excrete on us mere mortals and get away with it! Arrgh!" She stops to wipe her eyes, watering with emotion, as she paces Kyle's kitchen. Her face puce, Kyle looks on horrified and speechless. He obviously harbours some guilt so it isn't all undeserving. He extends his arm towards her but she pushes him away, sinking into a chair at the table.

"I'm sorry," she says quietly. "I know it's not your fault, but he's not here is he?"

SUNDAY – DAY 8

I am leaving today with Josie.

Can it really be a week ago? I am so busy securing my stuff that I almost miss the anniversary.

The actual moment of departure is heart-wrenching. It feels like my soul has been destroyed. I'm leaving my home to the man who's desecrated it. *I'm going to do it in style!* Josie and I spread significant items in the flat in various places for Clive to discover, to perhaps jolt him into some awareness of what he has done. I scrawl a *"Bye"* on the mirror in my lipstick and leave a previous Valentine's card on the bed. *Am I supposed to just accept my fate quietly?*

As I try to slam the door on my thirteen years, Clive's shoe gets caught in the way and my resolve wavers. *"Typical! I won't let this happen!"* Holding my breath, I kick at the shoe and try again. The door jolts to.

Pulling out of the car park in Josie's car I lose control and cry violently. I cannot stop myself; the pain searing through me is unbearable. I literally feel my heart shattering, shards of glass ripping into me. Josie reassuringly grasps my hand. She doesn't say anything; there is nothing that will express what she hears, the depth of emotion in my sobs.

We drive to the University, calling at Andrew's en route to say goodbye and thank him for all he's done. He has agreed to hold the computer. I feel guilty about taking it, as it's more Clive's than mine, but I'm not ready to leave it just yet. Andrew greets us at the door. "You look terrible!"

"This is it," Josie explains quietly, "We've just left the flat and Jen is coming to stay with me. We've just a little delivery to make first." She smiles revengefully.

Then we visit French Tart's place of work. Josie and I march triumphantly down the corridor. We are two of Boudica's warriors, our resilience, resolve, and strength, emanating off us. No one dares to stand in our path or question our presence.

In silence, we reach her office door. We cannot of course, gain entry into her room.

I have brought one of a pair of "F-me" boots he enjoyed, with one of her guilty gifts – a pot of honey. I place this inside the boot along with some well-thought-out lines. It's subtle, it's harmless, and yet hopefully repays a little of the hurt she has dealt me. Indeed, it makes me feel better, so it is worth it.

Driving down the country, I expect to bridge the floodgates of feeling. We stop for a drink and some chocolate in transit and arrive at Josie's rented two- bedroom flat Sunday evening.

Did I think this would work?

Did I think I would be ok?

I didn't think at all, did I?

Suddenly I am left floundering, kicking out into nothing. I am without my partner, I am without my home, and I am without my work. I am in the unfamiliar. There is no safety. I am kicking out as if abandoned in space, desperately trying to reach out and touch something solid, and am unable.

I cannot deal with this.

I feel as if I do not exist.

This constitutes my scariest moment so far.

It is the first time I acknowledge to myself that I cannot manage everything, not all of it at the same time anyway.

My mind has to break it down, and the only way for me to surface – to kick out and grab onto reality – is to tell myself that I have not left my home. That I will be going back. I know this isn't logical. Josie and I have just packed everything up and have left. The finality is all too stark. I just cannot handle it, alongside dealing with no Clive, his betrayal and no job. There is nothing anchoring me, and the thought of returning to the flat provides enough gravity for me to find my footing.

MONDAY – DAY 9

"I was wondering if I could find out the limit on my IKEA card?"

"Sorry, but it is not registered in your name so I cannot tell you the amount…but, I can tell you it is a considerable amount. He is responsible for it, and yes, you can use it until he cancels it."

I haven't had time to think until now and suddenly with Josie gone to work, I have all the time in the world. I recall last night and how I could not manage, how I had lost my grasp on reality.

I do not like that. I hate being out of control.

After a week, I am dealing with the fact that Clive has left me and chosen another woman over me. It's very hard: The pain, the shaking, the not sleeping, the sweating, and the not eating. As Josie comments, I have dealt with bereavement before. I just have the betrayal and rejection on top of that. *(Not much then!)*

To add giving up my home to that list is paramount to disaster. That is what has resulted in my huge panic attack. I need to be grounded.

Floating off into the universe with no solid ground underneath is what frightens me. I had to make up the little story of going back last night, just to cling to something, to stop me from dying. I keep it up; I pretend I do not have to leave the flat. I will let Clive go in and clear out his stuff and then I'll return and rebuild my life on a recognisable foundation, a secure footing. (I don't like to use the same word as him: *"rebuild"* but he doesn't need it in the same way I do. He has work and someone to hold his hand and that was his choice.) I will rebuild all of my life but from a safe base, even if I do not stay long.

Can I buy him out of the mortgage? It seems plausible, although realistically I know I am creating a fantasy. But maybe it isn't? Yesterday I made it feel possible, but desperation will fuel any fanciful notion into a belief. I add ideas to this chimera to make it acceptable: I will get back some clients. I could rent out the spare bedroom so I can afford the mortgage.

Do I want to be in Scotland? I have friends, all those wonderful people who have helped me out, but I cannot rely on their support forever. How about being single in a small town? I knock that thought down as soon as it surfaces. I'm not exactly going to be putting myself out there for some time. I'm too injured, so what does that matter?

My conclusion is to weigh up loneliness but coping in a location I know, to floating aimlessly without roots. (Neither seems a great choice.)

My eyes flit for the fiftieth time to where Josie has left her contactable times for the day, and then silence. I cannot get out of bed. I am slipping away. This is not the 'me' I recognise. I wait for realisation to kick me in the stomach, but instead, an odd sense of quiet within resounds. My mind urges me to focus, to go back to making lists to stop pontificating on dangerous subjects. I must focus on the short term rather than give up and die. I need to be doing.

Get up. Take a shower…

Obediently, I begin to function once more.

After my immobility has passed, I plan that Josie and I will go to IKEA after work. In preparation, I follow my list: Tidy her flat, comb my hair, and put on some make-up. As I peer into the mirror, I realise I had forgotten how I look with make-up on. It seems such a long time has elapsed and I remember back to the last Friday before that Sunday night. I looked in the mirror before going out and announced that I was happy with the way I looked. Clive had looked surprised. Now I realise because he no longer saw me as beautiful, but I was confident that night and believed in myself. How long will it be before I feel that way again?

Eventually, I hear Josie's key in the door.

It's time to do some comfort shopping at IKEA.

A good plan, but foiled by Clive calling my brother again, who then phones me to relate the conversation. "I can tell when it's Clive phoning. The ring is sheepish."

Again, it is financial demands delivered completely coldly and formally finished with a goodbye to my brother. "Well I'll probably never speak to you again."

"Well that's your decision, Clive."

"Yes"

"But Clive, was it the right decision?"

"Only time will tell."

I bet "French Tart Shit Beneath My Shoes" wouldn't be very impressed by that comment.

I call Lucy, whose wisdom I follow, "Go ahead. Keep the flat as it will screw up his plans, and yes, go and shop in IKEA as legally half the furniture he is taking is yours, so go and replace it."

By the time Josie and I get into IKEA, we have only fifteen minutes in which to shop. We are like two crazy women doing a supermarket sweep, charging round hysterically. At the checkout I enquire what the maximum amount is that I can spend on vouchers? When the woman replies, I return with, "Yes, please I'll take that."

"Jen," Josie cuts in, "our friends might like a gift rather than just vouchers for their wedding present. Shouldn't we consider a lower value?"

The doubtful expression on the woman's face disappears and I silently thank Josie for her caution. We don't want to draw too much attention and be accused of fraud. Anyone vaguely suspicious enough to watch the CCTV of us in the store would be convinced we were certainly acting strangely.

Instead, we leave with our integrity intact and high on successful revenge.

WEDNESDAY – DAY 11

I woke needing to phone him - desolation.

I wanted to call him and say, *Do you know what you've done?* Of course he doesn't. Why bother? He wouldn't listen.

So I cry. I cry on Josie until she has to leave for work and I'm left alone in her home.

Then I do phone and he's not there in the flat. *Just as well.* My finger hovers over his mobile number, but no – I phone Kyle instead.

"I need the keys."

"It's good to hear your voice." He sounds genuine.

"I need the keys because I have nowhere to go."

"Do you want to live in the flat?"

"I don't know," I answer truthfully. "I can't deal with losing everything at once. He's destroyed everything I have – my home and my work."

"I know. What he's done is awful."

"No, it's worse than awful. I don't think he knows what he's done. No one believes it; it's so horrendous!"

Kyle sighs. "I know. I'm his best mate, but I do care about you. I'm here for you. Did you know he's leaving today? He's taking a lot of stuff. There won't be a bed."

"I could not sleep in that bed. I'm surprised she can, but then I guess she already has!"

Kyle exhales loudly. "What they've done is awful."

"Awful? It's one of the most selfish things in the world that I know of!"

To which I get no reply, just a quiet, "Where are you? Do you have a forwarding address?"

How can I have one, when I have no home? Stupid man.

"Clive says he left the computer in good faith and you took it."

I remind him, "I let that slag into my home in good faith."

There is a pause before he adds more quietly, "Clive has to rebuild his life."

"Yawn. That old tale, when I don't have a life to rebuild." *I've had enough now!* "Kyle," I say with finality, "I don't care about him, but I can't deal with losing everything at once. You know how strong I am, but this is too much." I'm greeted by silence. "I need my home. I need the keys."

"Okay."

Afterwards, I have some bizarre notion that Clive will phone. Do I want him to? I feel better for calling Kyle. Whether it is because I am now safe in the knowledge that I can get back in or whether it is, as I know Kyle will relay every last word of our conversation to Clive, I am not sure. At least he will hear a little of how I am feeling and my response to his silly, insignificant little comments.

Perhaps I should have just asked for the keys and left it at that?

Do I really care how Clive feels?

Kyle calls me back. "Nancy and I have just been up and left you a quilt and a pillow. The sofa bed is still there. If there is anything, you need ask Nancy, as I'm away a couple of days. I'll be thinking of you."

Focusing on my "To Do" list, I call for some legal advice. Angus, the solicitor, confirms that I can delay the flat sale due to an issue with the roof, discovered by the surveyor. The vendor has brought this up, hoping for a deduction. His discovery and greed has perhaps presented me with the opportunity to dissolve the contract. Life appears to be on my side. My fantasy might be possible.

I have a book that I refer to as *"The Oracle."* (It's actually Titania's Oracle by Titania Harding) It has a lovely blue velvet cover and I use it when I am in a quandary and need a useful snippet on my life. Inside is a list of a hundred questions from which I select a relevant one. Then shutting my eyes, I let my finger be guided by my inner self (if she's paying attention) and I get an answer. Usually I smile because deep inside of me, I already knew the answer, and funnily enough, there it is in print for me. I bought this book on a whim, when asking it *"Where should I live?"* while in a bookstore.

It replied *"Anywhere in the Southern Hemisphere."*

I found that so hilariously true. I was living in Scotland, permanently craving sunshine and warmth, so I bought a copy based on the one question.

Now I ask: *"How shall my current problems resolve themselves?"*

The reply: *"Laugh at yourself a little, then start climbing that mountain again. You will have better luck this time."*

It all sounds so simple.

THURSDAY – DAY 12

"Why the bloody hell, are you so upset? You must have seen this coming. We'd been together thirteen years – it's a long time. Don't you agree that our relationship had lost some excitement?" Clive stretches out his arms and locks his hands confidently behind his head, leaning back into the chair. "Good things don't last forever! Admit it, you don't respect me in the same way you did – and look at me – I'm a Professor now, and that deserves some reverence!" He half-smirks behind his glasses and I can't tell if he is joking or actually serious. "You used to put me on a pedestal, you saw me as someone special and you just don't now." He shrugs. "That's why I noticed someone else. She saw me, recognized my strengths and achievements. Of course I was going to respond to that! When a vixen makes a play to seduce me, well…" he rolls his eyes and egotistically thrusts his groin outwards.

Yeuch!

My mouth is open and I'm desperately fighting to formulate a few appropriate sentences in response, but no words are forthcoming. My head is exploding with the effort and I'm suddenly become aware that I'm drenched in sweat.

I wake up with my heart pounding.

Today is his first day at the new University and our Welcome Party tonight. Someone had phoned me way back in that life and asked me questions in preparation to an article they were presenting about Clive's arrival to his new position and my new Hypnotherapy practice. I wonder if he managed to cancel that in time, or whether they are all expecting me?

I will be so glad when I no longer know what is happening in my parallel universe; the life I might still be leading if I had not pushed to unravel everything.

If I hadn't have asked, I think you might just have taken me and let her go back to her boyfriend in France, all for an easy life and seen how things worked out. You arrogant git! Do you really think you could have manipulated me so easily?

I pause and question myself: *Would I have gone if you had asked me? No, I am not that sad cow.*

I truly hope you are suffering, Clive.

Shuddering at the thought of me having moved with him, my impotence raises its head. I'm still at Josie's, in suspension. I feel that I need to get back and get on, although I am ignoring that small corner in my mind where the fear still resides. It occasionally bats out a question such as, *"What if you cannot deal with it? Josie won't be there."*

Ok let's just push that aside. Lucy's advice to be remembered today is: "Bill him for every accrued cost due to his actions."

Then a crafty grin, as I think – French Tart is probably unpacking boxes now, discovering little surprises.

That night, when Josie and I pick up a few things for dinner at the local supermarket, my credit card is declined. He has cancelled it, and rather than embarrassment and shame that I might expect to feel at the checkout, instead, my heart hurts more.

SATURDAY – DAY 14

"There's nothing half so real as the things you've done…inexorably, unalterably done." Sara Teasdale (1884-1933) American Poet

I have to write about yesterday.

We came back and now we are in the flat again. Although it was depressing to be back in Scotland, the flat feels okay. It is empty and filthy (yes, leaving the spaghetti stuck to the wall backfired on us) but it looks like I could live in it.

I went out to get us wine and a pizza and everything seemed normal.

Except when I got back, we realised that we did not have anything to open the wine with.

Another bizarre episode as I bravely visit the "Old Codger's" pub on the corner to ask the barmaid if she could kindly pop the cork. I don't question my actions anymore; people here seem only happy to help me. I guess the gossip about the poor girl, betrayed and left with nothing, has got out. The room in the pub is full of misfits, and it is therefore no surprise that the barmaid, who is cultivating her very own beard, (*truly*) is not equipped to open wine.

I'm not doing badly, I feel safe now. I'm home, but I could close my eyes and hear his key in the lock and expect everything to be normal. So how different can I make this flat to move forward?

I don't even entertain the possibility that the concern with the roof raised initially by the buyer won't be able to break the contract. That is too much for me to consider.

Unfortunately, Josie and I have to go down to Nancy. We only have one quilt, one pillow, and nothing to open the wine with. After her previous outburst in Kyle's kitchen when we delivered the rocking chair, Josie is almost as reluctant as I am. Tender-aged Nancy, never having experienced the hurt and betrayal Josie and I have, just witters on about Clive and then French Tart, whom she believes is in France. Before I can control it, my mind does a U-turn and I feel hope that she has gone back to her boyfriend and that Clive might come back to me. Disturbed by the very thought, I immediately chastise myself, recognising my stupidity. Clive has chosen and he has not gone back on that choice – and why the hell would I want him?

I am dumbfounded that I have even thought it, so, still reeling from my sudden weakness, I only half hear Nancy. She is talking about Kyle helping Clive pack up and how hard he found it because I should have been there.

"It had always been the three of you, and it was just the two guys, and you weren't there."

Obviously French Tart wasn't either then.

"Mind you, you had better not say anything to Kyle, unless you want Clive to know every word!"

Her casual words cut into me like knives, which keep on cutting as she goes on to pontificate about when she guesses they got together. I am bleeding in front of her, but she does not see the gashes.

Josie's vision is better and she pulls me away so the blood can gush more freely upstairs. I hate myself for wanting him. Knowing she is not with him has encouraged this desire and I want, with all of me, not to feel it. Where is the anger in which I need to survive?

The knives twist and turn, grating against bone, just breathing is all I can manage. The duvet smells of Kyle's flat and the smell is safety. I just want my life back and that's not possible. Finally, sleep overtakes me and temporarily, I feel nothing.

SUNDAY – DAY 15: 2 WEEKS

Awakening at seven, due to the lack of darkness and uncomfortable floor, memories kick me in the stomach: Waking, wanting, and wishing.

Failing to reject the need from me, I get up so I can focus again. I need to keep my mind occupied. Tomorrow I am seeking legal representation and I need to present some kind of financial information. I tiptoe upstairs and sit on the floor in the empty study, and here I find a semblance of peace.

Josie surfaces at ten. At breakfast I am calmer, despite the apprehension of her anticipated departure turning my stomach over.

"It's been a roller coaster of a weekend," she sighs. "I hope I've helped and not made things worse?"

A smile escapes as I recall her downpour on Kyle. "Of course not! It's been so wonderful you being here. Thanks for everything."

I don't want to let her go and fail to stem my tears as she gives me a final hug, climbs into her car and leaves. I stand momentarily, still gazing at the corner she has driven off round until I can draw up some strength to continue on my own and focus.

I work methodically round the flat, cleaning and rearranging. I'm doing okay, fuelled by thoughts of the human kindness that I have received, and mulling over my new life. My new stereo creates harmony and homeliness, my new IKEA light creates a calm ambiance and my (sofa) bed looks inviting. I've slept and not sweated for two nights now. No Josie, but I'm me, here in my own place.

...Drip, drip, drip...a leak in the living room. I overreact or realise that I wasn't really okay because just the smallest thing, a leak, has the ability to demoralise me to floods of tears. Is fate telling me I shouldn't be here? Taking a deep breath, I go upstairs, crawl into the attic and find the source of the leak. The light bulb blows. I crawl backwards out of the darkness, find some saucepans (he's taken all the buckets), put the saucepans in place to catch the water, using the light from my phone screen to see and call Lucy.

Lucy tells me: "Call the insurers."

Why didn't I think of that? They'll come out tomorrow but I have to pay initially and then claim it back. I mentally scream at him and am tempted to phone him and cry out: *"You have spent all the money in our joint account and your home has a leak!"* But I don't give in to the desire and instead decide I am going out. I phone Jill, an acquaintance from the University, residing nearby, who said I could go round anytime.

This is when the day flips on its head and starts to get delicious. *Well it's about time.* Not only do Jill and her husband serve up dinner, but along with it the tastiest news, I've received in two weeks: "Great news, Jen. The F.M. Boot with the honey has been found!"

"And?" I'm desperate to know.

"Yep! Discovered by all of 'her' department, who gathered round it, reported it as a suspected bomb, and were present as a crowd to witness it's unveiling."

As if that isn't funny and satisfying enough, it gets better.

"Her colleagues had already heard the gossip concerning her and Clive – bastard – and were already gunning for her as they have covered her workload because she had been absent," Jill relays excitedly.

"So she was 'supposedly' sick but obviously not too ill to be conducting an affair!"

"Yep! So, as a result of finding out, the head of department has announced that she will be staying an extra month to make up and he will find all the work he can for her, so she will not be moving with Clive just yet!"

This is a fantastic result. Who would have thought the boot could achieve so much? I bask in vindication and successful revenge.

MONDAY - DAY 16

It's the first day of the rest of my life.

Predictably, I am awake early, all on my own, no Lucy, no Josie. I manage about an hour sat by the window, making notes of what I have to achieve today, before I am desperate to be doing something. Where can I go? Who is up? What is open?

I never have been very good at dealing with silence, just being. I never could meditate and I like company. Without it I'm not sure what to do. I know this is incongruous considering my occupation, but not everyone manages to practice what she preaches. I'm about to become a person who runs on empty, flitting from one thing to the next, filling my time so there is no space left. It's a good thing that I have plenty of friends willing to socialise, as I'm going to need things planned to keep me hopping from one thing to the next.

It does not take me long to discover an answer to my current predicament: The gym will be open. Having been a member for a couple of years ever since my chiropractor recommended it to me, I regularly attend three times a week. A short walk through town, I am happy with the familiarity and friendly faces. It is an all-ladies gym, not because that was what I specifically wanted, I chose it due to the convenient location.

The solution devised, I fetch my gym bag (to my relief it is still in the cupboard – he didn't take it) and head off to what is soon going to become my new sanctuary.

I am greeted by the staff, questioning my time off. I am only too happy to recount my tale. This is when I really begin to appreciate the fact that I did join an all-women's gym. Staff and fellow users, whom I've previously only known to say, "hi" to, are suddenly so concerned for my welfare and suitably outraged by Clive's behaviour.

"Just get on that treadmill. Run it off. Pound those weighs. We're here for you. We'll be right here supporting you all the way. You'll do better without him!"

So I do. I run faster and for longer. I lift more weights and the adrenaline rush kicks in and I feel good. I never want to stop. I have found something that is to help me get through.

Still buzzing, I talk to Angus, the solicitor, who informs me that the flat sale contract can indeed now be cancelled. I then talk to the bank manager about whether I can take on the mortgage. He provides me with a glimmer of hope: "We don't like our clients to be homeless – we'll do all we can."

I have to provide some accounts.

I have a credit card application declined but am granted a small overdraft facility - tiny steps.

Andrew meets me in town on his way to an appointment to hand back the computer. Josie has called him to explain. He grins as he sees me approaching and greets me with a hug. "I'm glad you're home in Scotland. Give me a call sometime!"

I spend another good night out – this time with Mhairi. Her husband is at home with the children. We eat and get drunk and talk too loudly, laughing about things we shouldn't in public. Life is short, who cares? What would I do without my friends? I discover alcohol-fuelled nights are another rescue.

Returning home, I meet Nancy on the stairs and foolishly agree to a coffee. Kyle arrives back from his travels while we are in the kitchen. (More than likely he was with Clive, as French Tart isn't.) The alcohol has loosened my tongue and rendered my caution to nil.

"So I wonder where you've been, Kyle. No, don't tell me, I don't want to know." I say far too much, mainly about Clive's selfishness and rant on, not letting Kyle or Nancy get a word in. "Do you know, I've always doubted if he'd be able to care for me if I became sick – like my mother did? So it's probably a good thing that he's gone so I can find someone who would!"

"That's a little harsh," Kyle interrupts. "It's not all roses for him right now either but I do appreciate that he's brought this on himself somewhat, and you haven't."

"Thanks. More than somewhat though! Do you know everyone is staggered by his treachery?" I mention the kindness from the traders on the street and the leak and him having taken all the buckets. "What does he want all the buckets for?"

As it is, Kyle agrees with much of my ranting. "I'm glad that you have so much support. You know I'm here for you, too. It's just not easy being in the middle!"

I boast to him, "I have at least four people each day who ask how I'm doing. Who does he have, Kyle? Oh yes that would be you and only you because you are his friend, although you were mine and you have made the wrong choice."

Poor Kyle, I know he is suffering – but I am suffering more.

TUESDAY – DAY 17

I don't do hangovers, so instead I'm out early, training at the gym. Afterwards, returning via the indoor shopping precinct, as it is raining (surprise, surprise – not!) I notice a new outlet – Cinnabon.

Oh wow! I eat these when I'm away in the U.S. and I love cinnamon. I'm not sure what Scotland will make of them. I cannot believe there is a store here. I think I need a treat, so I'm buying one. And no, I don't need the free sample - I know how scrumptious they are. I'm soon laughing with the guy serving. "I'll be back, see you tomorrow."

So, visiting Cinnabon and jesting with "Mr. Cinnabon" completes my daily gym habit.

I return home to a message from Angus, in complicated Scottish legal jargon and the conclusion: "I cannot represent you solely, so you must find another solicitor. He/she should write to Clive explaining that the contract has been breached due to the roofing issue, and that the process of the sale is now not going through. Clive will need to sign a minute of agreement to transfer the deeds into your name. Good luck!"

He has served me well and I am really grateful for his help. I set about calling round prior suggestions.

This takes me through to lunchtime when I meet up with Mhairi again, to do an IKEA run. I still have to replace several of the items he took.

Disappointingly, Clive has stopped the IKEA card. My reaction is better than the stopping of the credit card. I manage to shrug it off and gloat on how well I have done with it and I still have the vouchers, so Mhairi and I chose a set of chairs and huge table to create a new look to my living room. They match the sofa bed and mean I can eat at a table (something I have always found important and preferred) and I can invite all my friends over for meals.

Today, after Mhairi departs, I walk upstairs, without thinking, to the study – his room, his office. It's the spare room now – I gaze at its emptiness and realise he has taken the postcards with little relationship quips on them. How bizarre – why would he take those? At this discovery, a pain sears through my chest and I fall to my knees on the bare, wooden floor. The thud I make echoes throughout the room, reminding me that the Turkish rug has gone… he has gone and I am alone. Deep, racking sobs emanate from within my core and tears splash endlessly onto the bare, wood below me. I curl myself up into a ball and tucking my head to my chest, trying to gain back some control by rocking back and forth. How little it takes for me to dissolve back into desperation; all over some stupid postcards that shouldn't mean anything to him but did to me. I'm on a rollercoaster, up and down, down and up, and all I can do is await the next ascent.

Someone today, and oddly enough I cannot remember whom, (maybe that's because of the whisky I've drunk, which mercifully, I found he also did not take), has said, "Underneath, you are very strong."

I disagree. *"Underneath I'm very cut up and hurt, the strength is on the outside."*

THURSDAY – DAY 19 (EARLY)

Maybe the whisky wasn't the best idea, but maybe it was, because I have ascertained another path for surviving the night. It is a bottle of ten-year-old malt Laphroig, with a spectacular peaty bite, which hits the back of my throat and my raw emotions in just the way I need. I drink it neat from the bottle, dancing round my new living room to the vibrations of my new HiFi. I have collected together all my tracks, which contain appropriate lyrics for the way I feel. Played at high volume, they soothe my spirit.

By 2 a.m., I have experienced the up and am in the grips of hopelessness. I have swung the window in and sit on the ledge, idly watching the street below, my feet precariously dangling in the air. I no longer have that rush of vertigo. I no longer care. It's July, so not too cold, and I have my music cloaking me for companionship.

Wretchedness descending around 2.30 a.m., I start observing the drop down to the street below – what would it feel like? Could I just let go of all this pain? I breathe in sharply and turn away. No, this is not the moment I promised would come; that is still later.

Listening to my music, I pull my phone from my pocket and go and do it. Yep, I've done well to have not succumbed to contacting Clive all this time, as there have been numerous occasions when I have wanted to call him and shout, rant and rave. Also, I'm loathed to admit other moments I've wanted to call just to hear his voice, but comfortingly, less of those times. At this juncture, I'm pleased to admit, it's the former. *You arse! You should know how I feel.*

With the speakers up full, (Neil, at the Sony store, would be proud – it's a gloriously undistorted reverberation), I watch numbly as my finger hits his number. The vocalist, in full throttle, clearly pitches his famous lines about being alone and feeling like a failure, culminating in the lyric referring to screaming in the middle of the night…

At which point, I hear the loudest, longest, banshee-like howl, which, shockingly, I am the source of. Erupting from the very soul of my being, it is pure visceral feeling. It needs no rehearsal and it is interesting how this sound expresses more than words ever could.

The cacophony of noise that spews out obliterates the next few lines of the masterpiece until the last line overtakes the end of my breath, and is quite clearly audible: It's about self-belief and how to ignore open windows. This penetrates just before I hang up.

I am shaking and do not know whether I've reached Clive in person or his voicemail. He might just wake up to that gem.

I feel okay, but I want some reassurance so I phone my brother – I'm so glad he works nights. "It's me! I just called dickhead…" I confess to my actions as I'm sitting on the toilet, peeing. Glancing down, I notice my leg is bleeding. I've apparently cut it stumbling over the toolbox to get to the bathroom. Don't ask me why the toolbox was in my path to the bathroom – it just was, okay? *What am I like? Is this sad? Is this angry?*

This is 43% proof Laphroag…Just keep passing the open window.

LATER THURSDAY – DAY 19

The Aftermath

I wake with an emptiness bordering on slipping into a pit, and need sugar. I can't focus on today's "must do" list. Are my legs wobbly from emotion, or alcohol? They are shaking even as I sit on the bed.

At the top of the list, I see my task is to plan a reaction should I ever see *her* – French Tart Shit Beneath My Shoe.

At this moment, my thought is to knife her. I close my eyes and can clearly see myself brandishing a machete and slicing her diagonally. I don't stop, just becoming more frenzied with each attack.

However, prison is not a good option. I know – I've been working at the local one. Funnily enough, when I started, I had a feeling of "Here by the grace of God go I."

I find a photo of my mother to sustain me. It was taken on a visit to Fort William on a cable cart. My mum is smiling. She looks happy and well, although when I peer in at her a little closer, I can see the brownness under her eyes, enough to know the cancer was there.

"I need you, Mum," I whisper. "Why is it so hard?"

FRIDAY – DAY 20

"That little heart must be mighty empty." - Mr. Cinnabon

On the way back from my daily trip to the gym, Mr. Cinnabon surprises me.

"I'm looking for someone to fill the position of manager. I'm just over from the States to set the store up and I need someone to step in and run it and I thought of you?"

He knows because of course, I've told him everything (yes, I haven't come so far that I've lost the telling of my tale in inappropriate places ability) that I am currently workless. He pauses, shoots me a grin and continues as I gawk back at him. "I've spoken with you enough to know that you would be an enthusiastic, vivacious manager. Are you interested?"

I am flattered and taken aback, so reply, "Thanks, I'll give it some thought!"

Exiting the shopping centre I run into our, (whoops, correction) my postman. I notice he is sweating profusely and wonder if he has a condition, or whether it is from carrying his weighty bag.

"Ah'm sorry to hear ye news," he is softly spoken.

I am flabbergasted that he knows, but forgive him this intrusion.

"Ye are well known and respected in the area," he continues, as a bead of sweat drips down his face. "Ye will get yae business back and it will work out."

Normally a shy, retiring fellow, I can hardly confess to have previously said more than a couple of sentences to the man who stands before me. I think he reads this in my surprised look.

"Postmen," he explains in a confident manner, "ken a lot more aboot others, than most people ken. Ah have been delivering yae mail for a few years and I ken with all the traders in ye street. They all wish ye well."

After I finally muster a reply, thanking him for his kind words, he informs me he has just delivered a legal-looking document, addressed to us both, through the main downstairs door.

"Let me ken if I can help at all." He lifts his bag higher on his shoulder as he walks away.

Astounded, I round the corner, take the steps two at a time and open the main door. No letter.

Having observed that the mail has thinned somewhat recently, this confirms my suspicions that Kyle has been abducting post for Clive. Hasn't Alex (yep, I've noted the postman's name badge) just said, 'Addressed to you both?'

This flips me out somewhat. I am finding it hard enough that Kyle has sided with Clive as it is, but to downright commit this crime against me I find inexcusable. I am overreacting and break my own rule about never responding immediately. Angrily, I fetch pen and paper and tape a sign to his flat door, which reads in loud, forceful capitals:

HOW DARE YOU TAKE POST WITH MY NAME ON IT!

In my experience, it is never good to act hastily without allowing a cooling-down period, and leaving this curt message posted on Kyle's door is not one of my finest moments. As often is the case, these things come back to bite me on the bottom (just like the loo brush will later, but again, I digress).

It is no surprise then, when later, a small brown sheet of paper is pushed through my letterbox, also printed in capitals:

I TRIED TO RING YOU. I AM SORRY YOU FEEL YOU HAVE TO LEAVE UNPLEASANT MESSAGES ON MY DOOR. CLIVE INSTRUCTED ME TO TAKE MAIL WITH HIS NAME ON IT. THE ENCLOSED WAS AN ERROR, IN HASTE (PERHAPS EVEN CONFUSION).

I WILL BE MORE CAREFUL IN FUTURE. I CAN ASSURE YOU NOTHING ELSE IN MY KNOWLEDGE HAD YOUR NAME ON IT.

CLIVE MAY HAVE BEEN DISRESPECTFUL TO YOU, BUT YOU DON'T HAVE TO BE DISRESPECTFUL TO ME. I AM JUST TRYING TO CARE FOR YOU BOTH IN THE

MIDDLE OF A DIFFICULT SITUATION. I MAY NOT ALWAYS GET THAT RIGHT, BUT I AM NONETHELESS TRYING.

YOU KNOW WHERE I AM IF YOU NEED MY HELP.

Ow! I feel bad!

So, firstly, I post an apology through Kyle's letterbox.

Then, I rip the letter open, while my stomach contracts – it doesn't look good. Are they ever when they arrive in brown envelopes? My heart twinges as I see it is a copy of our offer on the house, and with it, a compliments sheet, which reads, *"I have now sent your file to the main office for issue of your offer."*

I think back to viewing that house and how I had imagined our future there, together – the cozy dining room, with potential for an open fire. But, then he was already with her. My feelings of nostalgia quickly morph into rage. Perhaps it would have been better if Alex had said nothing and I hadn't overreacted with Kyle and finally got this.

Open-mouthed and turning on the laptop, I enter 'mortgage' into the search box in the emails. I don't know what I am hoping to find (or not), but this letter implies that Clive is indeed going ahead with the house purchase and I need to know if this is the case.

One result is returned. Horror of horrors; It is an email I have not previously seen. It is dated two days past and is in the sent box, which is why. My eyes dart ahead, speed-reading certain words in my haste to absorb the content.

It is a reply to his brother (scribed two days ago), answering an email dated at the end of June. I'm not sure how this is here. I will have to ask Andrew. If Clive has sent it from another computer, could I still access it here in the sent box? That must be a yes because it's here . . . and it is very distasteful: A posse of questions, posed by his brother concerning the whole event and details about French Tart and how Clive finds her French accent sexy. *Yuck!* Two fingers in my mouth for that one.

There amongst it all, highlighted by my query, is the word

'mortgage.' It's about how financially aware I am and how he knows little about our accounts and mortgage. Then I see, *"I have to try to prepare to move and make plans for my new mortgage."*

Confirmation of what Josie refused to believe, but what my brother and I suspected: Clive is still going ahead with the purchase of the house I chose for us. Sinking to the floor in the hallway, I recap on what Clive has stated:

TUESDAY, DAY 3 – Clive tells my brother he is not going to buy the house.

WEDNESDAY, DAY 4 – Clive writes a note for me. In it: *"I am not buying the house. It is lovely but it would have been ours. I don't want to live there now."*

THURSDAY, DAY 19 – Clive writes to his brother: *"I have to try to prepare to move and make plans for my new mortgage."*

TODAY, DAY 20 – a copy of the house offer arrives here.

MORE LIES UNCOVERED!

It is a bad day, and it's not even lunchtime yet.

I just feel like doing nothing…collapsing, but I can't.

Each time I discover yet more fabrications the knives twist into me more keenly.

That evening is worse, I'm alone crying. Twice I nearly go down to Kyle just to stop myself, giving up. Stupidly, I look at Clive's Facebook page and discover a horoscope compatibility document now posted that he did in March with her and I slide onto the floor and more or less stay there, curled up most of the night. Not even the Laphroiag helps. March to June is a lot longer than one month, and I don't even want to remember about events that had occurred during that time span.

SATURDAY – DAY 21

It's a Saturday.

I hate weekends. They will always be harder.

I suppose it is because traditionally, they are the days when you spend time with your husband, partner, boyfriend or family, and no, I don't have any of those right now. No plans this weekend is suicidal for me. I need to start booking something up each weekend, anything in advance. Only today it's too late and the emptiness is looming. Knowing that this could be catastrophic for me, I start working on possible solutions when I wake.

Half an hour later, still floundering, I reach for my gym bag. I still have nothing planned all weekend, which is way too scary. While running, I decide I will call Lucy and go through to Glasgow. *Dilemma solved!* I walk back with more skip than I had going and bump into Kyle.

"How are you?" he asks, obviously realising that was a stupid question. "We wondered if you were free to play badminton at lunchtime?"

I figure badminton is badminton and there does not need to be any conversing, and it is an acceptable truce after our recent correspondence.

This is a success as I forget everything as I focus on the game and in the changing room, Nancy invites me to the cinema. "I thought you might like to join us, if you've no plans?"

I feel awkward – I'm not sure it is such a sensible idea, as I know it will be difficult. Before, dealing with bereavement, I have sat in the cinema escaping into the film for twelve or fifteen minutes forgetting everything, only for my stomach to then cramp up, remembering with a start, that things are not all right. The alternative, a night in on my own however, doesn't offer much escapism either. "Yes, thanks Nancy – that sounds fun."

I sit in the cinema with tense muscles. The film is not very absorbing and I struggle to get through it. I cannot cry, so sit silently choking up. I feel worse in the car as Nancy plays inappropriate music. *She's obviously not a lyricist!* The soft but clear vocals harp on about a lasting relationship, which endures all. Good for her, the singer. I sit in the back, tears falling off my chin – it's all so hard, and what's the point?

"Jen, come in for a drink. I can make you a hot chocolate. I don't want you going upstairs alone like this." Kyle is persuasive so I meekly follow them in, my nose in a tissue.

"I'm sorry…"

"We know it's not easy." Kyle and Nancy exchange knowing glances.

"What?" I ask defensively.

"Well…" Kyle tentatively begins, "Um, it's just that Clive is coming up to pick up some more of his things."

Oh, my God! "Please don't let him stay here!" The words are out before I could control my tongue. "It's just that… I don't think I could bear it… I don't want to see him. What does he want? I could give it to you for him?"

Nancy tries unsuccessfully to put her arm around my shoulders. I'm on the defensive and she and Kyle feel part of the enemy camp.

"I'll find out," Kyle answers softly. "He can stay with someone else. Don't worry about that."

"Thanks." I manage a weak smile, down the rest of my chocolate in one gulp and excuse myself.

Time to get the lock changed. I will not allow him to enter my new home and desecrate it with his presence. Top of tomorrow's to-do list is: *"Phone J.B. – joiner boyfriend."*

SUNDAY – DAY 22

It's been three weeks, which seems impossible to believe, and yet ironically, I think this Friday and Saturday have been the hardest.

Determined to brighten things up, I head out on a walk out of town and towards friends in the countryside. It is a gloriously warm day and the sunshine lifts my spirits, as does leaving town. I don't phone ahead because if they are not in, I'll have nothing on my agenda, so I stroll forth hopefully. Walking across the fields, I reflect about my new life. I need to start working again. I have turned down Mr. Cinnabon's offer. I've been employed in retail before. There is nothing wrong with my work; I just need some clients. But do I feel as if I could manage? My hands trail in the growing wheat as I decide that I cannot let Clive rob me of this part of my life, too. I will start working again.

Pete and Agnes are unbelievably supportive. No longer in the University circle, they have heard no news at all, and are completely horrified by the turn of events. They are friends Clive and I have known since moving up to Scotland. Pete is English, but stayed after completing his degree and then met Agnes, from Glasgow. Over the years we have spent many evenings eating, drinking, and chatting together.

Pete has a vast collection of vinyl, which we sample and discuss, delving backwards into history. Tonight is the most emotional exchange I have shared with them. After three weeks, and telling my story to so many listeners, I have forgotten the ability it has to shock and create disgust. Pete is absolutely outraged. He paces the room as he declares, "I'm horrified by how he's treated you. It's quite simply unforgivable."

Agnes nods her agreement and mutters, "Aye, shocking!"

"Thanks, you're right, of course, Pete!" I witness his hurt.

"I feel that Clive's betrayed me too." A gentle man on his surface, Pete usually comes across as mild-mannered, only portraying any underlying aggression when riled. "I can't believe he just left. I'm thinking about all the discussions we've had over the years, the books and gifts I've given Clive." He stops pacing and extends his arms upwards, "I wish I hadn't. He deserves nothing. I thought I was a good judge of character, but I had him so seriously wrong!"

Agnes touches his arm, trying to soothe him, but Pete isn't ready to let go of Clive's crimes that easily. "No, he's despicable – an unforgivable sinner. I hope he fails!"

He is a great ally to me.

After some food, which Pete cooks and which we eat outside, we walk over to the nearest pub. Sitting in the sunshine among friends, I momentarily feel content. I suppose it is all about balance and time. I just hope the enjoyable moments and contented spells elongate as the days pass. I am getting ahead of myself. It is far safer to keep myself firmly ensconced in the present.

When it is time to leave, they both walk with me to the bus stop and wait until the bus arrives. Pete kisses me and Agnes holds me tightly.

"Come over anytime! Dinnae stay away – please let us help."

I know that they mean it genuinely, also that I will need to take them up on their offer.

It's been a good day. I am grateful.

MONDAY – DAY 23

You will not believe what I discovered this morning. Getting up and about to shower, I glanced in the mirror. Admittedly, I have not been doing much of that, but today I did a double take.

My bum had fallen off - *"Seriously!"*

I've always had quite a rotund bottom, not really large, as I am petite, but not one you would describe as small. Now, the "c" shape that used to stick out is not there. When did this happen? I had noticed my jeans were loose but hadn't thought any more about it. It would seem that my entire shape has changed.

Yes, I have been training fairly heavily at the gym, and on a really, really bad day, have even been known to go twice. My brother has coined the phrase: *"If all else fails, go to the gym."*

I suppose my diet has changed, but not really in a good way. It is heavily on the liquid side, wine and whisky, which fuel my morning gym trip. Then, because I am drinking every night, I am waking, requiring a stodgy breakfast, which is where the Cinnabons come in. They must be densely calorific. I must be the only person in the whole town eating Cinnabons and shedding weight. *Wait until I inform Mr. Cinnabon – he'll want me for a publicity campaign!*

I am eating daily one meal: Vegetarian chilli and rice or fresh pasta with a ricotta cheese filling, which I douse in parmesan cheese, and then there are the meals out with various friends. In conclusion, it cannot be the diet.

But I am certainly not complaining – I look svelte and that can only be a fantastic side effect.

Uplifted, I begin the day by ringing round some of my old regular clients and arrange a few appointments. Most of them are only too keen to return.

Now I must tidy and clean to prepare for them. I am washing out a waste bin when I realise I am washing out Clive's beard trimmings, and the more I seem to get rid of them, the more the *'little bastards'* cling on. In my desperation to rid my flat of such unwanted memories, I knock over the bottle of cleaning fluid, typically all over the cleaned side of the floor and then the power cuts out. Is the world against me this morning? *Arghh!*

The intercom buzzes, I jump with fear and answer tentatively, "Who is it?"

It is J.B. calling round with some of my boxes he and Clare have been storing. I buzz him in, with relief. The whole 'Clive, back in the area' thing has me wound up. "Would you be able to change the lock for me?"

"Nae problem! Ye shouldna let me do it fur ye the first time," J.B. grins. "We're just back from a braw week in Crete. We've achieved plenty – Clare's beauty studio is getting there."

Another buzz on the intercom and this time I don't jump.

"It's me, Lucy – I've brought you something. I'm glad you're in!"

We hear some sighing in the hallway as Lucy arrives, struggling with a large piece of foam.

"Let me help! Ye cannae manage it!" J.B. goes to grab it and I think for a moment that his actions might result in 'fisty cuffs'. Lucy is very independent and I can see her bristling.

"It's fine – I can do it!" she states tersely. "I've brought it through so you can borrow it, Jen, until you get a proper bed. It's surprisingly comfortable." She twists the foam out of his grasp and starts forcing it through the doorway. J.B. and I look on amused. I know not to interfere with one of Lucy's plans.

"I'm extremely grateful, Lucy. The sofa bed has worked, but this is so much better. I can sleep in a bedroom again!"

J.B. finishes the lock while we install the foam upstairs.

"I brought you some new sheets for a new beginning too." The sheets are a lovely, bright turquoise. I hug Lucy in gratitude. "You're too wonderful! "

"Enough!" She pushes me aside. "We have floors to scrub and a new table and chairs to assemble!"

When we finish, my living room has a boardroom quality to it but it is certainly different, and I love it.

I am up on a high that night. I have replenished the whisky and am dancing hypnotically to loud beats, bottle in hand. At some point I become the beat and this is when I stop feeling and can evade the pain. It doesn't usually last long, but the journey is worth the sensation. My thoughts and emotions are finally still in the menagerie of dynamic movement, and I feel free. Some days I just can't wait for the night to descend so I can get to here. On occasion, I can sleep soon after this point. At other times, the desolation pulls me back under.

TUESDAY – DAY 24

I start working. It's okay. I manage.

My solicitor emails to say Clive is seeing his solicitor tomorrow. Then I really collapse because I cannot deal with the thought of him in town. The fear rushes out of the small corner, where it has hidden dormant, and stages a coup. I cannot think for parallelisation and I have no idea what to do. I don't feel I can put myself through any more.

I have this irrational desire to hide under the bed.

WEDNESDAY – DAY 25

Angus phones, presumably after a visitation from Clive, to ask, "Do you have the new mortgage in place?"

"No," I reply quietly, "the bank has not got back to me."

"Then there are two options: Sell the flat or see what offer his solicitors would accept from you, which might be best, as Clive needs the money for his new mortgage. Can you think about it and let me know this morning, please?"

Can I let him know this morning!

"I'll try,"

Coincidently, Alex (the postman) arrives with a letter from the bank. I pull open the envelope to be informed that I do not qualify for a mortgage. Hum - so much for the bank not wanting to render their client homeless.

Standing in the bedroom at the window, my heart pangs, and half of me wants him back, for all of this to go away, for my life to be back to normal.

Am I effectively squatting then? Just as before, when I arrived at Josie's flat, I am floating in thin air. My home is going to be taken away from me. All the security it has provided for me over the last two weeks is ripped from under me, and I am floundering again.

Here it is: The moment I seriously consider jumping out of the window.

It is as before. I can deal with all of this (if you can call what I'm doing 'dealing') as long as I am grounded in my base. As soon as my home is threatened, I become lost, petrified, and unable to maintain my survival instinct.

If I had known it was going to be this bad, I would have jumped before. I see everything in slow motion as I hesitate before the open window. The pavement below seems grey and distant, but the imagined sensation of aimless flight entices me. I could just leave all this behind and surrender.

Knowing I need help, I call Lucy. I call my brother. Neither of them have any suggestions, but both are there for this most recent crisis. I am not alone. Hyperventilating, a mountain of tissues on the floor, and with swollen eyes, my brother stops me from jumping and pushes me to go back to the gym. "Just get out of the flat, focus on running – don't think at all! I'll try to think of something."

The member of staff on the desk notices my new shape and tells me I am a beautiful woman. Even with swollen eyes?

I am on automatic pilot on the treadmill, focusing on only placing one foot in front of the other so that I do not voice the inevitable cry for help:

"Save me, please!"

THURSDAY – DAY 26

I fail to get out of bed on Thursday.

What's the point?

The landline rings – I ignore it. My mobile vibrates – I push it to the floor. Finally, at midday, I reluctantly answer the banging on the front door. It's Kyle.

"Clive wants to collect his things this Saturday."

"Fine! I'll leave them outside the flat in the hallway then."

"He'll be away by the end of the weekend. Things have not been easy for them."

"Well, that's comforting to know."

"There's no need to be like that! He had to go away and come back again, unexpectedly. He has a lot to do."

"Kyle, do you really expect me to care?"

"Well, yes… no I suppose not. It's not easy for me either."

I shrug. I don't have the energy to massage his ego right now. *Take it to Nancy,* I think, but don't say. *Isn't that what she's there for?*

Have you noticed at those pivotal moments of your life, when you have given up thinking because you have exhausted all the options and there is no answer, how from somewhere deep at your core, a small, clear voice may guide you?

If you believe in God or some kind of afterlife, you might ascribe it as this. Or you may feel it's your deceased loved ones or ancestors guiding you onto the right path, pushing you towards a solution you haven't seen.

You would have thought that now might be the optimal moment for one of these insights to miraculously materialise for me, but no, it is not to be.

SATURDAY – DAY 28 BASTARD LEAVES

I limp through Friday, but have to get up on Saturday.

I'm calm in mind, but my legs shake. I will just focus on today.

I take all his stuff outside and decant it in his two bookcases.

Kyle comes up with a message from Clive. "He wants the remote control for the TV he's taken and his filing cabinet. I'm going to help him pack at the University."

This time I do lose it. "The remote! The bloody remote!"

"I know." Kyle looks apologetic.

"It would only cost, what, about 20 pounds to replace?"

"Hey, I'm just the messenger." Kyle tries to avoid my wrath.

"I may have accidentally misplaced the remote. He is counting pennies then. He has the TV. Cheeky git!"

Kyle leaves, embarrassed.

I decide, after all, that I will leave the remote for Clive, with, perhaps, a little etching of his name on it - his new name, that is.

On the bottom of the coffee table, that he chose, which reminds me of him, which I also leave out for him, I write:

"I really am a complete and utter wanker to destroy the life of the woman who has supported, cared for, and loved me for thirteen years: A woman with such resilience and strength, I can only envy, for I am a selfish, cowardly wimp."

That just about sums it up – yes I do have resilience and strength. Courageously I decide that I won't be tempted by the open window today. It would have been great to leave now. Unfortunately, there is the small matter of the filing cabinet, which I cannot even budge, leave alone carry down a flight of stairs. After my initial panic with this discovery, I breathe in and acknowledge that I need assistance. I'm getting a whole lot better at this asking for help stuff. Racking my brains to decide whom I can ask and who can be here quickly, I decide on the Sony guys.

Neil is in the store, when I rush through the door and kindly agrees to execute the task along with his colleague. "Och! Always available to aid a damsel in distress!" They chuckle together and follow me back.

I think perhaps they regret this decision once they appreciate the weight and awkwardness of the cabinet. I really want to say that it isn't important and let them go, yet it is. My eyes keep flitting to the clock as they discuss how best to tackle the task. What if Clive appears earlier than Kyle has said? I swallow, trying to abate the rising nausea of panic ascending.

"It's ok, we'll have it down these stairs and out in five minutes," Neil sensing my anguish, tries to reassure me. To me the execution of this feels to take a lifetime, but with much grunting and sweating, they complete the project. There is now less than half an hour before Clive's arrival.

"Thank you so much, guys, I owe you big time." I am suitably grateful as I try not to bustle them down the stairs. I grab my bag and lock up. Now, I can leave for the afternoon, safe in the knowledge that Clive can go in, pick up his things but cannot get into the flat and at my belongings, as the locks are now changed.

As I exit the alleyway, not only are the Sony guys outside their store watching on the pavement, but also Mario from the Pizzeria and the adjacent art store owner. They all wave and send their encouragement. It looks like they are waiting to view a procession or carnival. They will watch him come and leave and report back to me. It means a lot to have their support.

I head towards the station, buy myself a bottle of water and catch a train.

In Glasgow, I meet up with Lucy for some retail therapy.

"Let's shop!" she exclaims joyfully. "Shopping always helps. It will take away any thought of what's happening elsewhere."

"Wonderful!"

"You need new clothes," she says, pulling at my waistband, "These are hanging off you!"

I perform a twirl for her to assess my weight loss.

"You cow!" She jests. "I hate you being so slim. I can never lose any weight."

I buy some thick-wedged black sandals that Clive would have hated and a blue-grey cargo dress, size 6, which fits me perfectly and makes my reflection in the mirror look extremely slim. Lucy and I bask in the sunshine listening to the buskers singing. When the weather is this good in Scotland, you must enjoy every second – and we do.

It stays light late in Scotland. These long evenings in the northern hemisphere are fantastic when the weather is fine and it is after 11 p.m. when I say farewell to Lucy and head home.

Stooping low, but not caring, I inspect the rubbish bins on my return. *Ok it doesn't look good that I care but I do!* He has left a toy camel *"Tertullian"* – I brought it back from Tunisia, bartered for it with chewing gum and biros. It was a silly gift, but one of the first things I had bought for Clive. I rescue it. It deserves a better retirement than the trash can.

Despite the seemingly good day, my homelessness hangs over me. When I get to bed, I startle myself awake – only twenty minutes later. I'm reaching out and there's no one there. I am alone on this piece of foam. There is no one to share with, no one to hold onto and no one to talk this latest catastrophe through with. My mind is full of doubts and the questions are continually in my head. What am I going to do? Where am I going to live? Why did he do this to me? What went wrong? Could I have prevented this? Why did he not just tell me sooner? Will I ever trust anyone ever again?

...Despite everything, do I still love him?

Then I remind myself of his lies and then I end it all by visualizing my arm slicing repeatedly through them both with a machete.

After an uneasy night, I force myself to get up. I howl in the shower. It is such an inhuman sound, but it vents the frustration, hurt and anger, and rids some of the internal suffering. *But what am I going to do?*

Desolation is creeping up on me again. Mhairi calls round late afternoon and is reluctant to leave me. "Jen, I'm worried. I've never seen you so low. Let me buy you some food." We call into the Pizzeria and Mario makes us an extra special pizza. We share it together, sitting at my oversized table. She squeezes my hand as she leaves. "Call tonight if you need anything, ok?"

I'm so grateful for my friends but I can't go and live with them. As I try to get off to sleep that night, again I plead for help, for some kind of miracle.

I doubt such things exist.

WEDNESDAY – DAY 32

But I never said a saviour would not appear.

My phone rings with my brother's tone. His comforting words are unexpected, "I've called Aunt Cheryl. She is going to help you."

I do not have any idea how, but wait obediently for her to ring. Aunt Cheryl is our mum's sister.

When she calls, I have to sit down.

"I have 'Big Help.'" She pauses to ascertain that she has my full attention. "I will lend you the money to pay off the mortgage."

My head is spinning. My family members are not wealthy; how can she afford to do this? I have to hear more. "How?"

"Paddy and I have been saving the money to purchase an investment home – something we can use once we've retired. We're both happy for you to borrow this money for two years, interest free."

"I'm gobsmacked! Are you sure?"

"I'm sure, Jennifer. You've had a rough deal from Clive. Your mother would have wanted me to help out."

Here is my miracle. Here are my saviours.

My day has suddenly transformed from black, through to grey, to a brilliant, shining orangey-yellow. Yes, I have been extremely fortunate and this goodwill has materialized out of the blue, but I can't help but assign it to my belief that to be positive is always a better choice. Jumping out of the window, which should never really have been a serious option, was too weak.

I call my brother back to tell him the fantastic news and thank him for his input.

"I didn't know exactly what she had planned," he admits. "I knew she would save the day!"

"She's more than done that! Thank you so much of thinking to call her! I can't believe it – wait 'til I tell Josie!"

"I don't feel I've done much. I'm sorry I've not been able to help you more, but I've arranged some time off work and can come for a visit."

"Even better!" My emotions are soaring. "How much will I enjoy walking casually into the bank and paying off the mortgage? *"You did not want me as a client – so I don't want you. Here's the money I owe."*

"Yep – stick it to them! Look, Jen, I've got to go – I'll call you about coming up."

This feeling is one I haven't felt for the duration – happiness. I have my base for two years at least. I decide that I will work manically and save every penny to take advantage of this interest-free loan. Does my Aunt appreciate how much she has saved me? This will have a major impact on my life.

I impart the glorious news regarding the mortgage to Angus Bell. He is really helpful in suggesting how I move forward, and reminds me, "Don't bend over backwards to help him."

Whatever Clive has said or however he has behaved has not gone down well with Angus.

My own solicitor is noticeably absent. I eventually get an appointment with her on Tuesday, when she opens a letter in front of me that she received from his solicitor, over a week ago. It kills me and I have to have two swigs of whisky when I get back before I can even contemplate working. Tomorrow my brother is arriving. It will be good to have someone staying in the flat with me.

THURSDAY – DAY 33

I just phoned *him.*

I felt I did not have much choice.

Walking through Glasgow, on my way to the airport to meet my brother, I receive his phone call. "We missed the flight."

"How come?"

"The kids struggled on the escalator at Victoria, it was real busy so stupidly I thought we'd be better in a taxi… but it took forever. I should have stuck with the tube. We didn't make it to the airport in time. I'm sorry, Jen."

"Are there seats on the next plane?" I'm frustrated, but try not to sound so as he tells me that the woman at the ticketing office requires considerably more money to put them on the next flight. He doesn't have this, nor do I, but I do have the overdraft facility. "Put her on. Let me pay it!"

I imagine my brother's stress, sat motionless in a taxi in central London, entertaining his three children, watching the minutes tick by on his watch, attempting not to sweat. Another impotent situation leading to arising panic, and then disaster, as his airport arrival is too late – and finally, embarrassment, because he does not have the extra funds required.

I am dealing with Clive hurting me, but now his actions have led to my brother and his three children, innocent bystanders, suffering too. I lose my patience. Before I am aware, I have hit speed dial on his number. I should have erased it, but I kept it so I wouldn't answer it if he rang.

What didn't I say? It all came tumbling out, no thought, no hesitation, but quite coherent and controlled.

"My brother has missed his flight up to me," I spew forth, continuing before he can interject. "He does not have the money to pay any extra to get on the next flight and I do not have it to pay for him. And I wonder why that is, Clive? Could it be, because you have spent all the money in our joint account? Some of the money in it was mine! In fact, the account is overdrawn. Something you have done! If I had not visited the bank manager and pleaded, it would be more overdrawn, because there would be a lot of charges. But no, you did not think about that – just in the same way, that you did not think about anything – just yourself, Clive, you arrogant fuckwit!"

"I…" he tries to reply, but I'm too quick.

"I'm talking!" I shout forcefully. "You will be paying the extra money my brother needs, because he is only visiting because I need him, because of what you've done, Clive." I emphasise each 'because' with a turbulent tone.

"I'll pay it!" he quickly talks over me.

"You will!" I confirm resolutely. "You and your cowardly actions have completely screwed up my life." I go on to elaborate with detail.

I am standing outside Borders bookstore in Glasgow. There are four or five guys digging up the pedestrian precinct, which is cordoned off. I am leaning against the temporary barrier, hollering down my phone. I am not generally pugnacious, but this is my moment.

"Don't interrupt until I say you can!" I thunder. "You need to hear what consequences your actions have caused."

When I finally pause and let him speak, he does sound a little ashamed *(or maybe I presume he should be, so I hear it that way?)*

"I did not tell you about her sooner, because you said that guy shouldn't have told his girlfriend about his affair, on EastEnders."

Not believing what I'm hearing, I have to confirm: "You did not tell me you were shagging someone else, behind my back, due to some throwaway comment I had made about an 'EastEnder's' TV show plot?"

"Yes."

"As if that translates to life! What an excuse!" This time I'm speechless, which gives him the opportunity to intercede, which he grabs.

"I agree, I didn't do this the best way I could have." *You think? You sad ignoramus!*

I had not made my decision that Sunday, between you and her," he declares. There it is in black and white. I don't go there, trying just to listen.

"You don't have to worry about the flat and the debts and the extra money for your brother; I will sort it and pay it." *As if!*

"Despite the fact that I'm now five thousand in debt." *Oh, poor him!*

Foolishly, I try to describe the physical torment: the knives, the emptiness, and nausea. "Oh yes, I nearly look as anorexic as her!"

"I knew you'd make this about weight," he immediately replies vindictively, "That's not why I chose her."

Astounded by his rudeness, I interrupt with "I know I am one hundred percent better than her and have no self-esteem issues."

He does not disagree, but goes on to admit, "I know that I have made numerous mistakes…"

"Yes," I butt in, "and you'll realise the biggest, if you haven't already, in a few months!" (I am such a better choice than her!)

As I throw these truths out so confrontationally, I am aware that my solar plexus and the area all around my heart are aching. I am rubbing it as I speak. He really had not decided between us. If I hadn't pushed, would I still be with him?

"I'm not buying the house and I cannot understand why you don't believe me." He sounds anguished.

"Because, you have lied and lied!" I scream. "How can I possibly believe a word you say?"

I tell of the open window, but admit that I am too strong to jump through it, although that would be so much easier. One of the workmen is ear-wigging and stares at me, forgetting to hide that he is listening in.

I tell Clive (and the workman), "I need to get on with my life! You need to work with the solicitor so I can and I certainly should not owe you anything."

"The money is not important," he forcefully states, before reiterating, "I hadn't decided that weekend – I had wanted to talk to you for ages."

"Would that be 'ages', much longer than a month?"

He has no answer. The line is silent for a few seconds and then he admits, "I was pathetic." *Yep and the yellowest of cowards!*

"Let me remind you, Clive, of how I did everything those last weeks, because I believed you was working so hard, only to discover you were not even at work but at her house shagging! " my voice accelerates at the completion of my line. He says nothing until I pause for breath. Then, he says quietly, "I haven't stopped loving you."

"Bollocks!" I respond, the workman is gawking now. "You liar! You could not treat someone you loved, like you have me!"

Am I calmer, because I've heard him, because he still loves me, or because, I feel I have portrayed (and he may have absorbed a little of) what I have been going through?

He is continuing, although I'm not really listening.

"I'm aware that I cannot call you, but you can call me whenever you need to, Jen."

What!

I remind him, "This situation is far past a point when I will ever need you." *There I've said it!* "This is the last conversation we will ever have…"

He doesn't fill my pause so I finish with a reminder: "Due to *your* behaviour, I will never completely trust anyone again – thanks for that."

Here I should hang up, but I can't. I have said all I need to, but am totally aware that this is finally the end. I will never speak with him again, and I linger. He does the same. It is an old game we used to play. Who will hang up first? *"Love you,"*

"Love you, too,"

"I'm going to hang up now," until finally one of us would say, *"I'm going now… I am really."*

I go ahead and end it: "It's not fair, you can't do this anymore.

You made your choice!"

I finally hit the 'end' button, but it does not feel as good as it would have five minutes ago. It feels final. It feels very sad. *Please don't make me think there's still a possibility, please; please not! And yet some of his comments implied that.*

I need some whisky and I need someone to hold me.

The time is 13:02, and as much as I want to return home, to a safe place and whisky, but no arms to hold me, I have to get to the airport. This is probably a good thing and at least my brother is there to help me absorb the shock.

When we do get back to the flat, there is a domestic crisis. The freezer won't close after I remove some food to cook for the kids due to an ice build-up. My brother takes control and unpacks all the stored food, in preparation for an overnight defrost. "We'll need to take this somewhere – Kyle's?" he suggests.

I am reluctant, but agree and then I wish I hadn't because Kyle says plenty he should not. He knows about my call with Clive already and as we try to find space in his freezer he tells me, "Clive said that he misses you and acknowledges that he has been selfish."

My brother snorts in disgust and Kyle remarks that Clive and French Tart are too alike and that it will not work.

I do not want to hear any of this, and fortunately we cannot linger as my nephew needs the toilet and is uncomfortable using Kyle's bathroom.

It feels like I am back to square one. Once my brother and the children are asleep, the desolation consumes me. I am going through the conversation continually in my head. I don't feel like getting up in the morning, and I cry when my brother enters my bedroom asking, "What's up, sis?" The tone he uses is the way he talks to the children, and I feel strangely comforted.

Mhairi calls. Because my brother and family are there, when she hears yesterday's tale, she suggests a therapeutic daytrip to the zoo. She drives us all: Her two boys, my brother's two daughters and son, plus us adults in her camper van. It's an adventure for the children, and their excitement rubs off on us. Some sunshine filters through the clouds. The children get on well together and my spirits are lifted, ready for the next onslaught of events, which explode when my brother and I go down the next morning, to collect the frozen food.

SATURDAY – DAY 35

Sometimes justice is swifter than ever imagined. I'd call it 'karma' for his previous actions, but not even I expected anything so soon or so severe.

Kyle opens the door, his hair in tufts, looking as if he is just up, which indeed transpires to be the case.

"Come in," he utters quietly, acknowledging my brother behind me. "Clive was admitted to hospital last night with severe angina, and has had a heart attack."

My legs are shaking as I reach out for my brother's arm, with a startled gasp.

"Sit down!" Kyle pulls back a kitchen chair at the table as my brother directs me to it.

"What happened?" he looks at Kyle.

"Clive told me he'd been getting some pains for about a day and a half. Last night it got a lot worse, so as he doesn't drive, he resorted to calling for an ambulance."

Yes, do the sums – that takes us back to Thursday afternoon – just after I had phoned him. As I later tell my friends, it isn't guilt I feel. My call has done what I intended it to. Dealt him a dose of truth and finally he realises some of the consequences of his actions. I believe that this heart attack is a direct correlation from messing with matters of the heart.

"What about the girlfriend?" my brother immediately questions. "Where was she?"

"She got back just as the ambulance was arriving," Kyle states, looking at me, watching for reaction, "but she is leaving this morning to attend a conference in Canada."

I don't think, I just react: "Tell him I'm here if he needs me."

Of course, I should not have said that, but it's true. Whatever has transpired, I have been with this man thirteen years and I am not heartless (there's an adjective!) I cannot (unlike her) leave him alone in his hour of need.

Both men react. Kyle says kindly, "I will."

My brother makes our excuses and removes me to the safety of upstairs.

"What are you thinking?" he queries angrily. "Don't react so quickly, think this through first."

He is right. I call my friends, gathering opinions on what I should do. I am so glad that my brother is here and I am not absorbing this new situation and facing making these decisions alone. He and the children sadly have to return home Monday morning.

Lucy says I should go, but is concerned that I might not have enough self-protection. *"Remember, he has shut you out once, and he may do that again."*

Mhairi feels I should do whatever I can live with. She reminds me how they are both extremely shallow to have been so disloyal to me, and that Clive does not deserve my assistance.

Neil and his colleague at the Sony Store exclaim that it must have been carrying the filing cabinet that initiated his ill health.

Josie provides the answer I resonate best with: "Don't go. His pain is less than yours is; it is physical, more minor than what you are dealing with. Doesn't it say it all, that he is in hospital, having had a heart attack and there is no one there with him? Put yourself first. It would be worse than anything you've been through if you went. He'd just use you while she was away."

I interview myself, to ascertain my motives:

Why do I feel I should go? *He has no one.*

What happens if I go? *It will kill me.*

Do you honestly see yourself back with him? *No*

What good will it do? It won't.

What bad will it do? *Bucket loads.*

So, acknowledging that Josie is spot-on, I decide I will not go, but instead will call the hospital for an update, after the weekend. (I won't learn any more until the consultant is there.) It is killing me.

MONDAY – DAY 37

After seeing my brother and family safely to the airport, I am ready to make the call. At 1:05 p.m. I speak to the ward nurse and learn that the Cardiologist is waiting on blood results.

"He's just here, I'll put him on," the nurse hardly hesitates.

I hastily decline.

He does not ring back although the friendly nurse insists she will tell him I've rung. A fact, I'm sure, he is fully aware of.

Later that afternoon, the situation intensifies.

Clive's dad has a heart attack at his local railway station. He has driven there to drop off Clive's mum so she can travel by train to visit Clive in hospital. Kyle has come up to tell me this, and together we process our shock. At this point, Clive's dad is still unconscious.

Kyle is travelling down this evening to see Clive in hospital, picking up fresh clothes from wherever it is he is living, on route.

Recalling the 'prepared' boxer shorts, I feel it is only right to avoid this punishment during his hospital stay, so without confessing to my crime, I give Kyle a clear description of the offending items and forbid him to pack this set of underwear.

Kyle just accepts this. Too much has happened to even provoke a query. He probably presumes they were a gift from me or have some associated memory to me.

There is so much overriding everything, that Kyle and I are the most relaxed we have been in each other's company since the beginning. We are propping each other up. This is a good thing, as Tuesday afternoon, Kyle reluctantly calls me from the hospital. He doesn't say what my heart wants to hear: Clive does not want my help.

THURSDAY - DAY 40

Thursday evening, when Kyle returns, he rings me on the landline, letting it ring just the once, indicating he wants to come up. This is something we always used to do before. With my heart feeling like it is scraping along the bottom of my stomach, I call him back, with just the one ring, meaning sure, fine come up. Only, of course, it's not fine.

He hovers in the doorway, waiting for me to invite him in, and when I do, he perches unevenly on the edge of the sofa-bed, looking uncomfortable both physically and emotionally. I might have laughed had the situation not have felt so grim.

"I've seen him," he pauses, having stated the obvious. "He's okay, well not okay, but not in any danger, so don't worry."

I wait as I watch Kyle choose his words with care. He seems almost embarrassed as he says, "I know this seems unbelievable, but Clive still has no realization of what he has done to you."

"Really?" The word, expressed with shock and surprise, is out before I can try to withhold it. *Perhaps if he had realised more, the heart attack would have been worse!*

"He is a little worried about her response to the situation."

"I bet he is!" I growl.

"Jen, you are not even in the picture. I thought he might want you there, especially as you'd offered to drop everything and just go, but no." It feels as if Kyle is expressing genuine feeling and is actually on my side. *At last!*

"He admitted that you would be the most caring person to be there in the situation! You would be."

I interrupt with, "Is that all I am?"

"Yes, he doesn't deserve you, Jen. You need to forget the last thirteen years and move on. He isn't worth your love."

With that, I need to sit down. Coming from his best friend, that is a strong statement. Even Kyle sees it. Thank God I had the sense not to journey down to the hospital. The experience would have crucified me.

Having delivered what he came to say, Kyle stands and awkwardly tries to hug me. "I am truly sorry," he says with feeling. "Can I do anything?"

I bravely decline his assistance, in an attempt to make him leave more quickly, which succeeds. I need to be on my own to process this.

I feel like I'm back at the beginning. I have stupidly set myself up for this rejection and wish, yet again, that this had never occurred. He has chosen her over me again, and the knife slashes feel just as fresh as the first time. She is not even physically present and still he picks her. *What did I do that was so terribly wrong?*

I must not think that way. I will not give him any more opportunities to hurt me again. I can feel his latest rejection like a slap in the face, stinging inside and out.

This is it: The End.

My anger for everything he has instigated resurfaces. I can't believe his behaviour – that he can get away with it all – but he hasn't, has he? This is real karma, I truly believe that his heart attack has occurred, due to his own actions and now he has the health of his father is on his hands, too. *What a complex web you've woven, Clive…* and French Tart Shit Beneath my Shoe, has chosen to absence herself. What an apt title and what a wonderful choice she is turning out to be.

For me, another bottle of wine down, another good evening with friends, another painful night.

FRIDAY – DAY 41

Another little visit to her office, which I feel she deserves, but my brother thinks may well come back to haunt me. How right he is.

I leave the toilet brush and a little memo:

"His shit – learn to deal with it.

Leaving for a conference the morning after he has a heart attack.

Still not returning after his father then has a heart attack.

Redefining selfishness."

SUNDAY – DAY 43

Clare and JB call round. Clare re-invites me to Crete, and this time, I say yes. I'm ready. It's very scary to leave the flat, but I need to. I must take this opportunity while I can. These are genuine people, holding out helping hands and offering me some restful healing somewhere neutral.

That evening I walk to Agnes and Pete's, across the fields. Another good evening and I bite the bullet and stay over. It's my first night away from the flat since I've regained it and everything is fine, nothing has changed when I return the next morning.

In my journal I scribble,

"I am young and you are old

Because I have no guilt.

Your heart is not my problem

I am slim, fit and healthy

And am going to Crete

With my pierced belly button

And low-rise jeans because my stomach is flat

Screw you!"

Kyle asks a favour. His brother is driving up to drop a car off and returning on the train. "As you're free, would you let him in?" he asks. In my confident mood, I open my mouth too quickly and register the shock and hurt in Kyle's face, as I reply without thinking. It has been a standing joke since I met him once, that I fancy Adam, Kyle's younger brother.

"No problem, I'll just take him upstairs and shag him then!" Yep my conversation is evidently still inappropriate.

TUESDAY – DAY 45

During my training, we touched on numerous, worldwide healing Traditions. Chinese Five Element theory was one, which resonated. Within this, there are five personality types. Someone who has a 'Fire Causative Factor', as part of their makeup, is a person to whom relationships, love, and happiness are of utmost importance. These personalities can be the life and soul of the party when they feel fine and all is going well in their lives. Alternatively, when all is not one hundred percent, they can feel vulnerable, retreating into themselves, portraying shyness and lack of confidence.

It won't surprise you, I have been diagnosed with this and Clive hasn't. Today isn't about Clive. It's about Adam, and I suppose it's my first experience since, of a meeting with someone whom I'm physically attracted to. Fortunately, it is no more than a meeting, because I am not ready for anything else at this stage and so, it is a slightly awkward half hour only.

As I hear his knock at the door, my stomach does a little backflip. I slowly open it up and my breath catches a little as I take in this sight of him. He is tall, but not too tall, with the same brown eyes as Kyle but much better hair and a more masculine build. He appears slightly nervous and we both start to talk at the same time. I shake my head and smile. "You first. What did you say?"

"Just that I'm sorry about, you know, everything…"

I lead him through to the squashy sofa, making sure I perch at the opposite end to him. I'm not really ready, despite what I've said, to lurch unexpectedly into his arms.

"So how are you? Are you ok?"

"Yes, fine, "I lie unconvincingly, so I say abruptly, "I might be going to Crete."

"To live?" He looks surprised.

"No, as an escape from being here on my own, and to stop me from hurling myself out of that window one night, when I'm drunk and desperate." *Oh God! Did I just say that! Inappropriate, again!* I turn away. I daren't even look at him.

“I get it.” That’s all he says.

I don’t currently do small talk, so there’s a difficult pause before I make it worse by saying, “My heart’s sore, I’ve closed it down. I don’t think I’ll ever trust anyone again.” *The guy must think I’m nuts.* I jump up, embarrassed, “I’ll make you a coffee!”

Why such deep issues? Where is my common, brash, could-not-care-less portrayal of myself? My vulnerability is showing through and I’m feeling self-conscious. *Did Kyle tell him what I’d said?*

After a couple of minutes he follows me into the kitchen. I’m aware of his warmth and musky aroma as he brushes passed me to reach the milk in the fridge. “Have you been to Greece before?” he asks. “The sea has this clear, turquoise quality to it. There are wonderful sunsets and little fishing boats lined up on the shores. It would be a great place to go… and recover.”

“Sorry I said that.” I wince at him.

A half-smile plays on his lips as he replies, “Sure. You’ve been hurt. I understand. Kyle told me.”

As we drink our coffee, the conversation improves but I’m relieved when he leaves. I don’t know how to behave with men anymore.

I have my own little theory on relationships, which I have espoused and nurtured since my adolescence, which fits wonderfully into Five Element Theory. I named it *“The Tube Theory.”*

“All of us have tubes situated within the solar plexus area. When we develop a relationship with someone, they touch the outside of our tube. Generally then, we have many people on the exterior of our tubes, but it is rare we let someone in completely. When we do, we put ourselves under great risk because that person is truly inside our tube, with potential to really hurt us.”

I have discussed this on numerous occasions with Clive and Kyle and they coined the phrase *“Tubist”* for me.

Currently my tube has a huge, gaping tear in it and is suffering beyond what I ever believed possible. Yet today, I feel there were two people with Fire personalities, talking about the heart but hiding most of their vulnerabilities in their tubes. Whether Adam really understood the hole in my heart and was tiptoeing round it, or whether he has one too, I did not ascertain.

He reminds me of my brother though, which I find comforting. Yes, there's still a chemistry, which I'm not ready to address, but primarily I am aware that I feel small, lost, and confused.

FRIDAY – DAY 48

So isolated at night, I feel so abandoned.

What am I longing for? Close company? Any company?

At 2 a.m., I open the flat door and descend the stairs into the hall. I sniff in Kyle's aroma and that makes me cry because he is so integral to all of it. I am struggling with everything, and nothing appears to make sense. Should I be withdrawing from Kyle? Our relationship has become a lot stronger since Clive's hospital admittance. I need comforting, and Kyle understands. It almost feels as if Clive has died and left both of us, and this pain has drawn us together. Kyle sat on my sofa today, asking me questions about my thoughts for my future; what I deemed necessary in an intended partner. I'm not sure of his motives. Was he trying to push me forward, away from Clive? Was it due to Adam's visit, or the two of us getting closer?

I'm still nowhere near a position to read anything clearly. What is unmistakable is that I need a retreat. I need to get away somewhere neutral and escape all of this. Could the sunshine in Greece heal me and put all of this into some kind of perspective?

I am failing to deal with it tonight.

I'm on the ledge, drowning my heart in Laphroig.

My vision has blurred, yet I do not feel drunk and I cannot reach that place of escape, so sought after. None of my late night saviours are answering their phones. It's cold tonight and the night air is penetrating. I'm in my nightly routine, dancing with whisky and desolation, trying to reach that ecstatic high of forgetfulness, where I become the music, but it is extremely evasive.

What is the point?

Will the desolation in my soul ever disperse?

More whisky to deaden it: The room is spinning, yet red-hot swords penetrate and I feel their serrated edges, jaggedly moving up from my stomach through my chest.

"I remember when you loved me, Clive, when I was happy. How could you

betray me in such a devastatingly, cowardly manner?"

Josie is right; the pain I feel tonight is so much greater than that of a heart attack. *"Did you feel anywhere near like this?"*

I crave so much for death in this state. It would be such a welcome release, such an easy escape, but I have to keep dealing. There is no let up, no caring nurses holding my hand.

I'm freezing, alone, standing at the window.

SATURDAY – DAY 49

Today is a day trip with Lucy, to the coast. We take the train out of Glasgow and we walk along the beach, the August wind whipping at our hair. She tells me I'm looking fantastic, that she knows a single guy from California who is in her Tai Chi group. "Are you interested?" she asks and then, knowingly laughs. *Am I interested? Am I anywhere closer to considering a question like that?*

"You will be, at some point over the next few months," she concludes. "You know, Clive wasn't perfect. What man is?" She tells me a story from her past about her ex-husband. How her next-door neighbour made a pass at her and how her husband was so angry, he went straight round and threatened to beat him up. Now, would Clive have ever acted that way? I don't think so.

I need to live each minute, live each tear, and time will pass. Then I will be ready to give it a go. What I had, although enjoyable, was clearly not flawless and it would be better to be in a relationship with someone who respected, loved, and cared for me that much.

Returning home on the train, automatically I start to text Clive to let him know I'm on my way back. I stop myself. *"How long will it take?"*

Clare and J.B. come round in the evening. Clare thrusts a piece of paper at me.

"The itinerary," her mouth breaks into a broad smile. "Tickets bought. We fly Monday!" She clasps my hands and her intoxicated state of excitement washes over me. "It'll be great to have you along. I can't wait to show you everything I've done so far and I think I'll be opening properly next week!"

I feel apprehensive, yet excited for her and thrilled to be part of something. Unselfishly, I beam back at her. "I can't wait. Sunshine, here I come! Would you like a drink to celebrate?" I extend the invitation to J.B. who is standing to one side, looking a bit left out.

"A wee dram?" he looks up encouraged.

Clare rolls her eyes. "You would! Look count me out I have to sort out some stock to take. I'll see you back home." She hurriedly hugs us both and gives J.B. a peck on the cheek. "Pack the sun cream!" she cries joyfully as she descends the stairs.

I hold up the bottle of Laphroig.

"Aye, now yer talking!"

Seated in my kitchen, glass in hand, chatting to me about his work, I examine his features. He's good-looking in a rugged way but I don't feel any magnetism to him as I had with Adam. There are no uncomfortable sensations flooding my stomach tonight. Self-absorbed, I'm only half listening to his conversation as startled, I realise he is now confiding in me that his relationship with Clare is floundering.

I'm not in a position to hear this, and I'm about to spend fourteen nights away with her. "Don't say any more!" I stop him. "You need to talk to Clare about this, not me!"

I dispatch him fairly soon afterwards.

SUNDAY – DAY 50

It's raining on the ledge and my feet get wet. It is my last night of loud music and whisky for a while – my last vigil. When the craving for company becomes unbearable, I visit Mario in the pizzeria.

"Ciao!" he greets me. "What is happening in your world?"

He listens sympathetically and makes my eyes well up with tears because of his kindness. He gifts me chips because I haven't eaten all day and because I can't afford to pay.

"Life is about relationships," he muses. "I think you still love him and you'll take him back."

I'm shaking my head aghast. "No, Mario, I don't want to hear it! Because I don't love him and he isn't going to be asking," I state emphatically. "I'm off to Crete to enjoy and forget!"

He is so kind. I'm engulfed by the human kindness I've witnessed on this street. I'm eating free chips at 11:30 p.m. and they are the best I've ever tasted.

Back in the living room, there is euphoria in my drunkenness tonight. It's not just the whisky, it's friendship and kind, selfless acts. Yes, I admit, I probably do still love Clive. It takes an immense duration for that intensity of love to fade, but it is fading and it will. He isn't enough. I deserve someone far better than he'll ever be.

That, I think, is a good conclusion to end on before my adventure in Crete begins.

MONDAY – DAY 51 TO MONDAY – DAY 65 IN CRETE

I'm humming a song about a heart being lost and wishing it would realise its owner was better off on her own. If only I could accept that.

I'm in Crete and it is as confusing as I thought it would be. Right now, and ever since we were halfway here on the plane, I have wanted my life back, which includes Clive. I was okay at the Airport, trying not to watch Clare and J.B. saying their goodbyes, and initially on the plane. Clare and I did not have seats together, yet I just could not focus on reading.

I am struggling, trying to not be sad, and it's not working. I need to go to the gym and I need my window ledge. *How long will I feel this way?* A hundred times I question *"Why?"* I want him to be feeling the same but he won't be, he has French Tart. *How can I even visualise a future when I feel this way? How will I feel on DAY 101?*

"Just the same," answers my heart.

What am I supposed to do here?

Greece is so idyllic if you are happy, and so lonely if you are not. I am certainly not ready to leave my flat to start a new life yet. It's too soon to even think about it, so I will focus on just getting through these two weeks away.

Now, begins the adventure in the southernmost Greek Island. Clare rents a car to get us from the airport to her studio apartment, which is high up a dirt track, one of four, and very Greek. Have you seen those picture-perfect Greek postcards? The small homes painted in white and turquoise blue, with wide steps leading upwards to the front entrance, some old pots placed on the side of the steps, and sometimes an idyll cat sat in the sunshine. The paintwork on the wood is often faded and presents a serene, rustic setting. Well, it is like this. There is a wide step at the front, which we sit on acclimatising the first night and relaxing last night, drinking local wine and appreciating the warm, balmy evenings.

I am sleeping on the sofa (if you can call it that, as it is tiny. *Just as well, I'm little!),* which acts as the barrier between the bedroom and the kitchen area. This effectively means I am in the same room as Clare, which is going to be difficult; no screaming, dancing, or roaming in the small hours. I'm opposite her, so let's hope I don't rant in my sleep.

The first morning, Clare shows me to her salon. "Well what do you think?"

"I love it!" I am honest. It is a small shop on the high street, which she is decorating in the same blue and white. She has a huge cabinet that J.B. has attractively crafted, full of products. "This is perfect," I say, admiring it, "and what I love most is that you've brought elements of your shop at home with you and yet here they have a nautical twist."

"All my own idea," she admits, beaming at me. "Now, we have an appointment at the Tax Office. That'll be an experience for you. I hope you've brought a book to read as we will probably be sitting waiting for the rest of the day!"

It's only 10 a.m. but Clare is right. The Tax Office involves an immense amount of patience and I applaud her on dealing so well with Greek bureaucracy. As the day progresses she gets pushed from one clerk to another. I forget how many men I am introduced to and shake hands with, but I become embroiled in her story, her dream. It is 5 o'clock by the time a sweaty little man provides her paperwork with her tax number and a till. She thanks him and turns to me. "The till means effectively permission to open! I've done it! I was really bricking it there for a moment and I was convinced we'd have to come back for another day's wait. Jen, I'm a bona fide shop proprietor in Crete." She rushes towards me and we are hugging each other, a large old-fashioned looking till sandwiched between us. It is good to be part of someone else's life, to share her exuberance.

We drive back to her shop and install the till. "I have to give back the car now," she tells me. "We can rent mopeds."

"Okay," I answer, taking this in my stride, still euphoric from the tax office victory. "I've never rode a moped before so that's good – another first." However, I'm not accounting for my poor sense of balance, but surely my enthusiasm will counter this. *How hard can it be?*

Clare knows the owner of the rentals well and she picks an attractive and very sexy-looking number, which she will rent at a fine discount. “My friend,” she explains, “hasn’t driven a moped before.”

An assistant takes me over to a much smaller, old donkey of a moped and explains that he will teach me how to drive it. I obediently get on behind him, place my arms around his waist, and we are off. I don’t get a chance to be frightened. *Probably a good thing!* He demonstrates all that I will need to know, as we traverse the main streets and head back to the rental lot. Then we swap seats and it is my turn. *Panic!*

‘I’m a little nervous,” I admit to him.

“Fine. All good.” He waves his hand demonstratively in the air. “No scared!”

With that he signals that I should go.

He is very patient, which is good, as is Clare later on. It is not as easy as it looks. I’m not a natural driver, but I gradually begin to master it, and I finally pay for my rental and hit the road following Clare. A few times up and down the main road and I am beginning to taste some of the exhilaration of my achievement. Okay, so it isn’t a throbbing motorbike between my thighs, but I’m in Greece, the sun is shining, and I’ve found a freedom. I can now go wherever I fancy on the Island without Clare’s leadership.

Fear is still here – it is not something I ever leave behind, but rather I take it along for the ride. Being in Greece initially felt like the first night at Josie’s flat, but I have fought the panic, the emptiness, and kept the terror down. This time I know I have my base at home, and although I am without my props, which get me through, I’m doing it by just focusing on one day at a time. These two weeks are a diversion – but isn’t that what most of life is anyway?

I just have to continue on, one minute at a time and not think ahead because it is too scary, too overwhelming. So I spend my mornings in the salon with Clare. I’m reluctant to say, “helping”, as I’m probably more of a hindrance. I even manage to drip the blue paint, as I put it on too thick. Clare must despair of me and must be questioning why she ever offered to bring me along. I’m usually an organised, practical person, so I can tell the emotional stress is affecting me physically.

In the afternoons, I drive out to the beach, rent my solitary sunbed, and listen to my music, absorbing sunlight and warmth. Occasionally Clare joins me. She is ready to open, and as I deliver flyers to the local bars and cafes, she takes her first few clients.

Wandering down the streets in the early twilight, I become aware of my age for the first time. Here, in party town, everyone is in their early twenties and younger. I, admittedly, lean and bronzed and looking good in my shorts and strappy tops, do not warrant a single glance, because I am older and therefore utterly past it in the eyes of this crowd. I'm nowhere near old, but I begin to feel it. I have transgressed passed the staying out partying all night phase, although maybe not the drinking bit. This is the first time I fail to catch anyone's eye and do not even receive one wolf-whistle. Perhaps that does not bode too well for my romantic future.

Some days, I see Greece in a different light. Sometimes I'm thinking whether I could work here next season. Why the hell not? Spend a summer here, get an apartment, have various friends visit. My mind does the arithmetic. What I would need to earn, it might be possible? Then my mind says, "Clive could visit," and I backtrack, *"What did I just say?"* I was doing so well trying not to think of him.

Then I go through two sleepless nights and crave my ledge in opposition to the cold sweat and memories in my head. I think about driving over a cliff on my moped and what Clive's reaction would be. I want to go home.

Whatever that is?

Home is where the heart is.

Where it was destroyed then?

My home has always been with people not places, so I don't have a home right now. There is a huge vacuum engulfing me. At times like these, it is how to get through the minutes, let alone the days. Then the rest of my life looms. I am so tired.

There's a steep slope up to the apartment. It is strewn with pieces of rock and small ditches, and it's where I fell over on my moped the first night. I could not lift it off my leg. As if this isn't hard enough to negotiate, three-quarters of the way up, there are two fierce-looking dogs, which run out barking and baring their teeth, straining on their chains. The noise they make is enough on its own, to knock you off your bike.

Each night this climb to the apartment seems insurmountable and I start dreading it at the beginning of my journey back, and yet I always make it back eventually. Sometimes it seems easy and I don't know why I worried about it, yet other days, it is so hard, that my arms are still shaking, whether I fall or not, for some while after I've reached home.

I see it as a metaphor for what I'm going through right now. I can never predict which days I'll be okay and which days I'll wobble and end up with the bike still throbbing on top of me, with new bruises. This morning I would not even have contemplated it. I couldn't have even got on the bike. I hope that means tomorrow will be a good day.

Life is not that easy.

When it gets nearly unbearable, I call my brother. I know the roaming charge isn't cheap, but I need to hear someone I recognise. "Hi you in a hot place, it's raining here!" We talk about nothing in particular, but it makes me feel better. I'm back on track. Sometimes I just need a familiar voice.

The song of these two weeks – "My adventure in Crete" is one in which the singer speaks about wrestling with her shadow, with the dark clouds looming, while she waits for release from her loneliness.

I am still waiting.

Finally our time in Crete ends. Clare and I are on a night flight back to Glasgow, which J.B .meets. They drop me outside my flat at 4:30 a.m. Opening the door with great relief, I notice a small, white card, which has been pushed underneath it. Probably it would have been better to ignore this until morning, but foolishly, I don't.

It is a message left by Central Scotland Police informing me to contact them…

TUESDAY – DAY 66

There are not many people I can call at 4:30 a.m., but I'm guessing the police station is open, so I make the call immediately. Having no idea what this can be regarding, my fear rises, waiting for the appropriate sergeant to be sought. After what seems eternity, he is deemed unavailable. No one can tell me what the card is concerning. A message is left for him to contact me when he is next at work.

That doesn't sound too urgent, but then they haven't discovered what it is in reference to, so I'm not going to sleep tonight. I could call my brother to check that all the family are okay, but he'll be up soon enough if I wait a couple of hours. Surely he would have texted me if anything were amiss.

I sit it out, imagining all the possibilities. There aren't many that would involve the police, and it crosses my mind that it could be Clive, on his own, having another heart attack. If he were unconscious and she, likely absent, might they call me? Would he still have my contact details in his wallet?

By the time I can call my brother, I am in quite an agitated state.

"Everyone's fine!" he declares, still yawning. "You only went to Greece. I'd have texted if anything was wrong!"

"I'm really relieved to hear that. That leaves Clive perhaps."

"Who cares about him? You shouldn't. In fact you should be rejoicing. Maybe he's keeled over again!"

So I call Kyle and wake him.

"Come downstairs," he instantly replies, which infers he knows what this is all about.

"Why? What's happened?"

"Just come down now!"

His reaction heightens my anxiety, so by the time I am in his kitchen, I am convinced something terrible has occurred.

Kyle sees my agitation as I enter and probably realises I haven't slept yet. Immediately wanting to put my mind at ease, he rushes towards me and says, "It's nothing important. Do not worry!"

"How do you know?" I demand. I'm shaky and I'm feeling very cold. *Well, I am back in Scotland after two weeks in the sunshine!*

"You know, how I know," he now looks embarrassed as I grimace. "Jen, it's the toilet brush!"

"What?" I stammer, my face showing bemusement.

Kyle is still squirming under my scrutiny. "Um, she reported the toilet brush to the police and is trying to claim harassment. That's why they came to see you."

"I cannot believe it!" *Could anyone?*

"Yes, it's rather extreme," Kyle is still talking.

But I don't hear any more, as my legs give out on me and I am vaguely aware of my back sliding down the cold wall, before I hit the ground with a bump. The next thing I'm aware of is Kyle, crouching over me as I sit knocking my head against the wall. I know I'm doing this and I know it's bad, as does Kyle.

I force myself to stop and mutter, "It's the shock, I'm okay." Coming round a bit more, I dramatize a little to make my behaviour seem more acceptable. "I thought it might be my Nan – that she had died." I don't mention that I thought it could have been Clive having another attack. I'm not going to give him the satisfaction of that. (Because, even though Kyle has been nicer to me lately, I'm not stupid enough to think he isn't still reporting back to Clive).

"Look, I need some sleep. I'm sorry about my reaction. I just expected the worst as you do when you find a card from the police at 4 in the morning. Thanks for putting my mind at rest." I smile weakly and make for the door. I've completely embarrassed myself and I've only been back a few hours.

As I ascend the stairs to the flat, I see the funny side and begin sniggering to myself. French Tart Shit Beneath My Shoe has reported the toilet brush to the police and is trying to claim harassment.

Once more, my brother was right. I recall his words of wisdom – that little act has definitely 'come back to haunt me', biting me right on the butt.

Honestly though, French Tart's reaction is so extreme, that it proves I achieved my aim. It must have so pissed her off. Can you imagine reporting to the police that someone was harassing you, by leaving you a toilet brush? It must have been the laugh of the week at the police station and she must have been forced to admit, to some degree, her part in the story, Now that the anxiety has dissolved, the whole thing is somewhat hysterical. I am shattered both mentally and physically – time for some sleep. I doubt I'll be hearing from the police station any time soon.

They never contact me about it. Would she be pleased or annoyed at that? Ironic that what the whole toilet brush episode achieved, was more concern from me for Clive. I cannot believe that was her goal.

When I surface, I am back on track. Off to the gym, where I'm greeted like the prodigal daughter, and then home via Mr. Cinnabon, who puts extra topping in my bag. Stopping for a word with Alex, the dripping postman, I wave across the road to the Sony guys. Neil calls me over for an update.

"How was Greece?"

I am back amongst people who care; it is reassuring. This is home.

After the upsetting arrival, I am now engulfed by a positive energy. I am alive and chatty with my clients and agree to a trip to the local bistro for afternoon tea with Kyle, who has phoned to check that I am feeling better. This begins well, as we stroll through town and bump into one of his colleagues, Paul. I know him vaguely through University events that I have attended. I have thought well of him, but cannot profess to know much about him. After enquiring of Kyle, he turns to me, his eyes penetrating through my several layers of protection, as he empathises with the tragic turn of events that I have undergone. I am pleasantly surprised that he, an academic, can convey emotion so immediately and genuinely. I've mixed within this circle for some time, and the cliché about academics in their ivory towers, in my opinion, is often quite apt. Paul has a beard and his hair is grey and balding, but he is physically fit, a stocky, muscular man. I have seen him cycling to work.

He pulls out a notepad and jots down his phone number and address, which is not far from mine.

"I understand how you must be feeling," he says warmly. "Please call me and come round for coffee, I know how important it is to have company at these times."

Thanking him, I inform him that I may take him up on his offer and that Kyle and I are off for tea if he wishes to accompany us. He refuses, but reminds me to call, so it is just Kyle and me.

Mistake - of course, he has an ulterior motive.

Entering the bistro, we order a drink at the counter and Kyle orders a muffin. I decline. We grab a table at the window and I am gazing out as Kyle starts talking. "This morning was fairly horrendous for you. Are you feeling okay now?"

I nod. "Yes, thanks."

"I have to tell you something else." He momentarily looks away.

"Is there more? Do I really need to know, Kyle? You were the one who told me to move on, get on with my life!"

"Yes, I know. It's also that I need to tell you. I need some support too."

So, Kyle wants me as a shoulder to rest his concerns and anxieties on. I'm not sure that I am ready to play this part, at least not when it involves Clive, which I really feel isn't fair.

He ploughs on, "I want to tell you that Clive's dad died while you have been in Crete. The funeral was yesterday."

"Oh no!" I'm aghast. "How horrible! How's his mum?" I wonder if she blames Clive, or does she see it as a tragic coincidence? *(I find out later – she blames me! Well, of course!)*

"I have no idea. Clive has not talked to me about this – he hasn't talked."

I wonder how guilty he must feel. His dad had died!

"She is away, teaching in Paris, so not much support there." Kyle speaks of her in a derogatory tone.

"Why doesn't that surprise me!" Perhaps I shouldn't say it, but I can't help myself.

"Apparently, that is how she does relationships," Kyle mutters disparagingly. It is not how Clive did.

"Well he made his choice, so he'll have to deal with that!"

"He's not managing well. He also has financial worries and cannot afford to pay anything towards the mortgage for the flat this month."

Poor Clive! Kyle is talking to the wrong person if he is expecting sympathetic noises.

'He has a final demand for his phone bill, which threatens court action, so that is his priority. He does not seem to know how to cope!" Kyle takes a bite of his muffin as I point out, "You know that his new salary is immense. He could surely get a loan to tide him over! Is his phone bill really more important than the mortgage?"

"I don't think he's being malicious. I think it's more a lack of financial awareness." Is Kyle trying to convince himself?

"I'm not so won over." I am glad that I have managed to keep the news concerning Aunt Cheryl to myself. Neither Clive nor Kyle need to know about this until all the paperwork is completed with the solicitors. And that, as always, when solicitors are involved, is some way off.

"I could almost feel sorry for Clive. Don't worry, I said '*almost*,'" I say, grinning at Kyle. 'I'm sure he would appreciate someone close with an experience of bereavement. Why isn't he talking to you? He knows you've lost both parents."

Inwardly, I wonder if he could just be playing me via Kyle. I am certainly not ready to send a bereavement card just yet.

I notice that Kyle is slipping back into old ways and treating me much more as a friend and confidant. He is probably far more loyal to me than I am to him. I have not forgotten all of his transgressions, and am rightly cautious of this.

On Thursday, Day 68, I am to understand this more. I have become his only confidant of recent days. He and Nancy are breaking up.

I am the supportive friend, but Kyle is so concerned about how much he has upset Nancy and how she must be feeling, I cannot help comparing. If only Clive had felt this way and behaved accordingly. Why could he not talk to me? Where was his integrity? Why such great betrayal?

I need to be cautious, to hold myself back. Kyle is all that is familiar and he has slipped back into that role too easily. We are both hurting as a result of Clive. Added to that, is Kyle's vulnerability over splitting with Nancy.

"I think Nancy is very young. I admit that an older woman, someone around my own age would be better."

"Would you prefer it, if she was veggie, like you?"

"It would be easier. You know how it is! I'm sure a vegetarian is on your checklist, right?"

We spend another evening philosophising about relationships. Again, when he asks what I would require in a partner, I am aware that he fits most of it. I manage to refrain from informing him that I'm now beginning to feel as randy as hell. *Well it has been a long time!* Even I can see that mentioning this to Kyle would not be a good idea.

"I'm off to a conference next week. Who knows who I may meet?" He laughs.

I decide this is fortunate, as living just below, he has become an easily available crutch. I conclude, as I did prior to Crete, that some time away from each other is a good thing. It would never work for our lives to become more entangled than they already are. At some point soon, I decide that I must let go of his support by finding it elsewhere, or by surviving alone. Kyle is too embroiled in everything, and being constantly fed snippets regarding Clive is not helping me move forward.

When the next mini crisis occurs, Kyle is, therefore, not present. I return from the gym to a voicemail from my solicitor, informing me that she is taking some emergency leave and am I happy to await her return, or would I prefer her junior colleague to step in?

I have to face the fact that she has been letting me down for some time now. She has never been there when I've called and does not keep up with the requests from Clive's solicitor. Sympathising with her personal problem is fair enough, but I need this to all be over so I can try to move forward. Instead it is drawing out. I don't have confidence in a junior colleague and do not know whom to turn to for advice.

Fortunately, practical-thinking Lucy is over for lunch. "I don't know anyone myself, but why don't you ask that 'Paul' guy from the University?"

"Do you think?"

"Yes, Jen. Accept help! You need a solicitor in town whose office you can easily call into to assist with a 'kick up the arse', if deemed necessary."

I laugh.

"Paul, having lived in this town for years would probably be able to recommend someone, and has already offered his assistance so gallantly."

I call him while Lucy sits beside me and arrange to have coffee with him after work, the next day.

"Good!" she concludes, "I'm sure he'll have a suggestion."

Ironically, returning from escorting Lucy to the station, I am greeted by Mario, closing up the pizzeria after lunch.

"You're looking well!" He stops for a chat.

"You too! I am but my latest predicament is lack of legal representation."

"Are you not sorted yet? Have you tried Terry? I'd recommend him and he works from an office on our road." He points to just further along. "What's more," Mario informs me, "is that he has been in a similar situation romantically, so should understand your plight."

"Brilliant! Thanks! I'm going to see if he's there now."

Armed with this information, I feel there is no time like the present and head up the staircase to his office. He has two rooms, his own and his secretary's. I am delighted as I recognise her from the gym and feel that perhaps, I am in the right place. I sit and chat with her while her boss completes his phone call.

Terry Maxwell, a short, sturdily built man, with a full head of red hair, invites me in. "Now, firstly what are you currently earning?" he asks, having heard the brief details of my story. He establishes that I qualify for legal aid and starts collecting all the information. "Yes, I would be happy to assist you in this matter. It is at this point, all about who has spent what from which account, how much the insurance policies are worth and who owes who what. Then we settle, and you find out how much you need to buy him out of the mortgage. Hey presto! – not that hard!"

"I don't believe my solicitor has done anything then!" I tell him unhappily.

"It would seem that way. Negotiations should have been further on by this stage. I don't imagine Clive – is it? – will put up too much of a fight, considering his emotional and financial state. If he is concerned about a phone bill, he will not want a hefty solicitor's bill. So hopefully it won't take long."

I just hope Terry is right.

TUESDAY – DAY 73

Because each night I spend with a friend is one when I don't contemplate killing myself… escaping the pain.

I walk through town, heading out towards the park. It's a beautiful street; the houses are Edwardian, with large sash windows and long gardens with driveways, which are elevated above the road. Paul lives at number 81, as I am soon to discover, with only his son, as his daughter has recently completed her degree and is now in London on an internship.

"Ah, Jen, - wonderful to see you! Come on in!" Paul greets me at the door, oozing gratitude that I have called, while escorting me to the living room. Here, two sofas and a TV overlook a restful garden via French doors.

"A drink perhaps?"

"Coffee is fine," I reply, perching on the sofa nearest the door so I can talk with Paul as he makes it in the kitchen.

I am on my best behaviour so absent of late, because Paul and his home demand it. I can tell from the art and literary journals scattered on the coffee table, that Paul's world is far more cultured than mine. Ten years with Clive, attending University events and dinner parties, have prepared me for such. I can bluff with the best of them and possess a little genuine knowledge of my own.

We chat superficially until Paul presents me with coffee.

"Now, tell me your story, if you can bear it, please." He wants me to recount all of it, so I oblige.

He listens assimilating proficiently, and then relays his own story. "My wife left me with two young children to raise on my own."

Yes, I have found someone who truly understands, having gone through something far worse than me.

We switch to the drawing room at some point for a stronger drink. This is the apt title, which instantly jumps into my head when I enter. There is an open fireplace – unlit, two armchairs, a chaise-lounge, and not a lot else. It is simple, but elegant. I sit in an armchair, my back facing the window, savouring the burn of the Talisker on my throat. This single malt whisky is distilled in the Isle of Skye, off the West coast of Scotland. It has a rich, peaty taste, which I adore. I have visited the distillery in now what feels like a former incarnation. *Happy days!*

It is refreshing to be somewhere new; discussing life with a person I feel could become a good friend. With the support of my favoured liquor, I am unaware of elapsing time as Paul is easy company. It is late when he walks me the five minutes back to my flat. A true gentleman, he leaves me at the top of the outside stairs. "Thank you for a delightful evening. I've found a new friend. Call me and please come round again."

"I will. Thanks, Paul."

DAY 74

…is a "No point day – wish I could die."

Yes, I'm still getting them but I guess they are not so frequent – or is that just wishful thinking?

The desolation comes flooding back in immediately as I stop focusing on the mundane after I've woken. I get so deep so quickly, that I don't even remember the trigger. I have run out of whisky, so with puffed red eyes I exit the flat to purchase more, encountering Alex on the stairs.

"What time does the off-licence open? " I ask him rhetorically but recognise the concern and pity in his eyes as I announce my destination.

"A bit early!" he declares but this does not deter me. How few of us know that whatever assists in the evasion of emotional anguish, is well worth enduring these glances from outsiders. The day does, at some stage, improve, but it's a bad day and I mentally slash two images into pieces for causing me all this pain.

In the evening of DAY 75, J.B. calls round unannounced. The pretext is to invite me to an art showing with Clare and himself on Sunday, but he is in a talking mood and is only too happy to accept a 'dram' of whisky… and then another.

"I grew up on the poorer side of town. You ken, the estate behind the castle." He looks to me for acknowledgement.

"I know it. I've done community workshops there, paid for by the council."

He nods, playing with the Celtic ring on his little finger, "Aye, it was tough. I have six siblings. Am the wee 'un. There was never enough money, ye ken, so we got free school dinners. I wasnae very happy at school. I comfort ate and put weight on. I was the class fat boy in primary school!"

"Really?" I exclaim. I can hardly believe it, as J.B. carries no excess weight now.

"Aye, I was a right 'lardy.' I got teased a lot and I guess I got used to being unpopular. I spent a lot of time on my own. It wasnae much better until I got tae aboot age 16. I wasn't an early developer," he laughs. "In fact, I was a wee bit behind most of the lads. None of the lasses were interested in me, ye ken, so I kept myself to myself. It was safer." He stops talking to take a drink.

"I can't believe that. You seem so confident now."

"Aye. I finally grew up. I just kept growing taller so of course, my weight evened oot. As I got slimmer, some of the lasses started tae pay attention, ye ken," he nods at me. "I wasnae really sure what tae do!"

"Oh sure!" I tease. "I'm betting they helped you out with that!"

He chuckles, "Aye, it was about the time I became an apprentice, training in woodwork and carpentry, and honestly, I hid behind that to a wee extent. But actually a man with a trade appealed tae them more. But ye ken, after a time, I wasnae happy with the lasses on the estate. They'd all knocked around a bit and I did nae want someone else's castoffs. I wanted someone with more intelligence and her own charisma. And that was when I met Clare."

"She's certainly bright and very motivated. I was amazed at her determination, while we were in Crete. She worked really hard." I pour him another drink, as he continues with his story.

"'Twas good. We saw each other fur a long time before she asked me tae move in with her. I've done a lot of work on her flat. It's been fun and sometimes challenging. She's quality, very precise and kens exactly what she wants, and that was fine."

"Was?" I query, wondering what's coming next and hoping it's not what I'm guessing.

"Och. I was happy initially. I'd transformed from this gawky, fat bairn, tae a confident, attractive…" he looks slightly questioningly at me, until I nod.

Yes, he isn't unattractive, but I don't want to overplay this, as I already acknowledge that this conversation is tracking slightly off-line for me. I need to be careful.

He continues unfalteringly, "…Aye, and am with this great lass, who was obviously going places. I was happy to let her lead, but of late, we're having a few fights. She can get very dour – moody, ya ken! I've still been growing up, while we've been together. I ken it's taken a wee while," he smirks, "but am beginning to feel that my life is headed a different way from Clare's." With this, he stops and turns to face me. "Am noo sure what tae do. Any ideas?"

Ah! I so, did not want to hear that and I so, do not want to answer. What can I possibly say that isn't going to be hurtful to either him or Clare? I pause to think before replying, *because I have to say something!*

Finally, I say, "That's really sad news. I thought you two were doing really well together. Do you think you could talk about it and tell Clare how you feel? It isn't easy to find a good relationship. It's worth trying to accommodate each other, before losing what you have." I pause. "Selfishly, both you and Clare have provided me with unconditional support and I would not wish to choose to side with either of you and not the other." *Did that sound safe enough?*

After he leaves I am left, again, thinking about my developing relationships with all these male friends. It has been a good evening and I have enjoyed his company and his honesty. I have a big issue regarding honesty now.

Later, when I report back to my brother, he comments, "I could see that coming!"

"What do you mean?" I reply, surprised. "J.B. is in a relationship, admittedly rocky, with Clare, and I especially will not climb over those boundaries."

"He might. I thought he liked you."

"Really? I don't think so. I think he just wanted to confide in someone and I'm easy to talk to. It's my job. I'm not physically drawn to him." *But I acknowledge that I need to be wary of my hormones kicking in and my need to be held, now so immense that I am craving touch.* I refrain from adding this. *My brother doesn't need to know everything!*

At least, I am not missing Kyle. It is time I sought solace more with my girlfriends. They are a much safer bet.

Time is elapsing. While I have been wrestling with myself, a stronger identity emerging from the bitter remains of the last thirteen years, the whole summer has passed me by unnoticed. It is September now, and although there is still warmth in the sun, I have failed to notice the onset of late summer. People are beginning to exchange sandals for shoes and adorn fleeces. There is a cool wind. Remember, I am living in Scotland, and despite the long evenings, there is a nip in the air; it is no longer summery (well, perhaps that was a wistful description anyway) on the window ledge. I have not noticed this change, and it is only when Neil calls over to me one morning, "Why are you still just wearing vest tops?" he enquires, that, I realise time is moving on. That can only be good. I am surviving in this new life of mine and days passing must eventually numb the ache.

Still running on empty, I am literally sprinting from one distraction to the next: the gym, the odd client, or the next meal out with friends. I have not stood still long enough to feel the cold, and I should have noticed it even more, now that I no longer have a bum, stomach, or thick thighs.

"You'll need tae put some weight on for winter!"

The vest top accentuates the outline of my now-muscular triceps. He's right. There is not an inch of fat on me. I have developed a totally new shape without even conscientiously trying. Now that's worth smiling about. But it comes at what cost? Sighing, I reflect that I'd rather have all the fat and soft muscle back, in return for this not to have ever happened.

One year ago I was happy. One year ago Clive loved me. One year ago I had no doubts that we'd still both be together. It all felt so real and I wish with all of me that it was one year ago.

DAY 76

Today I am testing myself.

I am trying to turn the page, to move things forward and stop drowning in the past. I turn to my reflection in the mirror and peer at it. My strength and brightness has to fill the absence. Memories have to become erased, just like chalk on a blackboard. Am I really as confident and brave as the woman I have been portraying to the world?

I intend to rent a car and drive down to see Josie for the weekend. This might not seem huge to some, but I only passed my driving licence four years ago. I've never owned a car and have only rented one on a few occasions. To say I am a confident driver would be a lie, so my premeditations on today have not all been positive.

As I walk towards the car hire office, I am mentally working over the foot pedals to reassure myself that I can cool-headedly drive out of the garage, round the corner, and get out of eyeshot. Then after a brief pause of self-congratulation, over having fooled the car rental staff, I will drive the two hundred and seventy-five miles, to my destination.

Oh yes, I have set myself a proper challenge, an utter distraction from all thoughts of Clive and basking in desolation. Having Josie's company as my reward spurs me on. It will be good to languish in female camaraderie. I have chosen this weekend to participate in Josie's home move into a swish new apartment with fellow worker, Victoria.

The Citroen car rental office smells of artificial car freshener, but I guess it would.

"Good morning!" Louise, the attractive saleswoman, puts me at my ease with her smile, as we fill out the forms together and I sign all rights away. Her overall-clad colleague takes me out to my gold hire car and runs through all the instruments. He gives me a smile as he leaves me adjusting the car seat and wonderfully, does not stand to watch me pull off. Desperately praying I will not stall, I start the engine, put her into first gear, and tentatively put my foot on the gas. Fine, it'll be fine. A deep breath and I am off.

Amazingly, I complete this initial task without a hitch and pull over a few minutes later to open the window, put my music on, and organise myself before I leave for Josie's. Wow, I'm really doing this and I am proud of me. Clive would not recognise this poised, unperturbed female, whom I am fast becoming, and that is the best revenge I can think of.

Two hundred and seventy-five miles later, after only one rapidly executed pee stop, I triumphantly arrive outside Josie's. I am truly on a high at my accomplishment.

"Jos," I cry, knocking furiously at her door, "I survived, I made it!"

"Jen! I'm so glad you're here!" She hugs me.

Paired with her enthusiasm and excitement regarding her move, we are flying above the clouds together. I have missed her so much.

"Right, some quick lunch – I made a vegetable flan for you and then we pack up your car."

We drive two loads in our separate cars to the new abode. Another colleague of Josie and Victoria lives on the ground floor, so this home will be social. This is the beginning of Josie's next stage, as she is exiting the flat in which her relationship betrayal occurred. It feels fitting for me that I am present to witness and share, as I know that I will emulate when I finally feel ready to leave my own flat.

Six strong arms carry the boxes in and before long, the move completed, we sit in the kitchen, wine glasses in hand, toasting a new start for Josie and Victoria.

At a distance, I am able to regale all my tales regarding my male friends back home with great humour and disregard. If only it were really so easy. Here with the girls, the situation is illuminated.

"Just let life happen," Victoria tells me as if it's really that simple. "If something occurs and you get off with one of these guys, no big deal – just enjoy it!"

"Really?" I'm shocked. "I'm not sure I could!"

"I'm not convinced that's wise," pipes in Josie.

"What's all the fuss?" questions Victoria, who grew up in London.

Perhaps people are more forward there! "It is all experience and each social episode takes you further away from Clive."

"Well, yes, that's true," Josie concurs. "You definitely need to dump Kyle as any sort of friend." She's reiterates my own knowledge.

"I know you're right. I'm trying to, but it's not always easy because he lives downstairs! With a decent solicitor now acting for me, I should soon be rid of any dealings with Clive soon, and if I continue any connection with Kyle, it is as if I am allowing Clive to piss in my yard, because Kyle will relay snippets of information."

"Yeah, exactly," Josie chimes in. "Give up Kyle. He chose the wrong person; don't waste your time on him!"

"What about the joiner?" Victoria asks. She really seems to want to pair me off.

"He's got a girlfriend," Josie states dogmatically.

"And?" raises Victoria. "Their relationship sounds like it's on the rocks. What's he like? Do you fancy him?"

"He's been really nice and helpful, but no, I don't think so and I wouldn't do that to Clare."

Josie firmly agrees with me.

"What about Andrew then? Is he single?" Victoria is nothing but persistent.

Laughing, I reply, "What do you think, Jos? He's not really for me. Again, he's been really supportive and helped me out, but I only see him as a friend."

"Yes," Josie says. "I agree. Not quite mature enough for me. Not really geeky, but,… well, I don't fancy him either!"

We all giggle.

The girls' conclusions at the end of the weekend are:

1) Conclude with the solicitor.
2) Leave Kyle behind.
3) Advertise my treatment room for let to other therapists.
4) Look for a lodger (once my nightly vigils are under control).

It all seems so straightforward when I am removed from the situation, and I wish my life was there, and that I could move in with these two vibrant and spirited women. Perhaps one day I will and it will be.

I do know, as before when I was here with Josie, not enough time has elapsed yet. I still need the familiarity of my home for some time longer. It grounds me. Who knows what my future holds? Participating in this weekend has been a positive experience and shown me that there are possibilities for my future.

DAY 79

It is with reluctance early on Monday morning that I leave Josie, but with renewed vigour and new concrete plans for my on-going present.

My journey home is thankfully uneventful. I sing at the top of my voice and drive too fast, but enjoy this newfound freedom that a car has allowed me. It is a sunny September morning, and England seems much more accessible and I intend to go away for weekends to visit my friends far more often. For the first time since, I feel as if I am living and as if I can plan for my future; and I like those feelings.

My emotions on passing the Scottish border and circumventing around Glasgow are not negative. I have the car until the following, morning and when I reach the outskirts of town, I park on a side street, a little further up from Paul's, to avoid town centre parking fees. Coming home is okay and I am so proud of what I have achieved. I have competently driven there and back on my own. This is the nearest I have come to feeling happiness since.

Reflecting on this, as I stride purposely forth, a car horn toots, penetrating my exhilaration. Stopping to ascertain its origin, I see the driver beckoning me over. Lost as I am in assertiveness, pride and contentment, I do not stop to consider fear or stupidity as I cross into the road, to see if I can be of assistance.

"I just had to stop the car!" the male driver utters.

As I obviously look bewildered, he continues exclaiming,

"You are the most beautiful woman I have ever seen!"

Well, it takes me a little while to absorb what he has said and when I do, I respond by laughing. It's a happy, delighted laugh because after all, I'm very flattered, if not a little taken aback. Here I am in the middle of the road, stopping traffic. Fortunately there is nothing else approaching, so I'm unlikely to be hit.

Drawing his card from his pocket, he offers it to me as he spontaneously invites me out for a drink that evening. I accept the card, not wanting to appear rude, and thank him politely for his comments as I sensibly return to the pavement. Another car is now coming up behind him so he mouths, *"Call me,"* and grins broadly as he drives away.

Oozing confidence, I walk on and turn to catch my reflection in a store window, as I pass. *"Am I really looking that good?"* Perhaps it's the sandals I bought with Lucy that give me height, lengthening my legs or the pale baby-blue fitted dress I'm wearing, which accentuates my slim proportions, clearly defining my waist.

A little boy stops to gaze in at the window too, obviously perturbed when he sees nothing of interest in the window that I could be looking at, so I leave him with a smile and head home.

Before five o'clock, I call in to see Terry Maxwell. It is so much easier having a solicitor just up the street. He too comments on my appearance and tells me that my case is progressing well. Clive has not put up any resistance so far.

That evening, Lucy and I drive to HMS Cornton Vale, the prison where we are to work, one evening a week. We have been offered another short contract, following up on one we completed in the spring. Our time is funded by a lottery grant, and is a pilot scheme to see whether our interactions with the prisoners, produce any positive results. On arrival, and having passed all security checks, we are escorted to different blocks. Lucy is working in the middle block, whereas I, more fortunately, am posted with the long-term, better-behaved, inmates.

That evening, I see three prisoners. My last, although I obviously do not profess it, is my favourite, as we share a good rapport. She is a convicted murderer serving a life sentence. She murdered her husband, although she still claims her innocence, declaring that she remembers nothing, only blood everywhere. I am not judgemental, and after hearing her story, can quite easily understand why she may have wished him dead.

After our session, waiting for the guard to appear and sign my worksheet, I tell her about the traffic-stopping event earlier.

"Go and call him!" she immediately urges me.

I dismiss this with a *'As if'* expression, but she persists with,

"Och! What have yae got tae lose?"

I shrug in return.

"Look," she replies forcefully, "see it from ma view, Ah'm stuck in this minging place and cannae go anywhere. Ye are free. A guy stops his car fur ye and invites ye fur a bevvie. Why nae go – just because ye can and he thinks ya look brill? Ya ken, - how often does stuff like that happen?" She looks at me and still not seeing a nod, sighs. "Would ye consider doing it fur me then ee-jit, because that cannae happen fur me stuck in here?"

She wins me over with this line of argument, so I promise her I'll give it serious consideration.

I discuss it in the car with Lucy, driving back.

"Why not?" she queries. "I doubt much will come of it, but it's just a drink."

"Do you not think that I might appear 'slutty' if I agree to go out with a guy I've only spoken with for a minute?"

"No. It's fine. He might well be a lonely salesman looking for some company, but you are only agreeing to a drink. Just make sure you pay your way and aren't obligated. You're confident and come across as independent, I don't think he'd misread you, and, Jen, I know you can handle yourself if he comes on too strong."

"Thanks for the vote of confidence. I've just forgotten how this all works, Lucy."

"You sound like an old lady!"

"Thanks, friend! It's just been, what? Probably about 17 years since anyone asked me out for a drink. Time has moved on. Language has changed. Words sometimes mean other things and I just want to make sure I don't get it wrong! Perhaps I'm an anachronism. It's a long, long time since I dated."

"You weren't with Clive that long."

"But, I practically finished the last relationship I had, just as we met so I wasn't really single and I definitely didn't date!"

"Okay, I see. Well, I don't think it really changes that much. I've been out with a couple of men in this century and they've not been that desperate to drag me into bed on the first meeting." She turns to look at me as she adds, "It might be me though!"

"You're not old or ugly!" I laugh with her as she jabs me in the arm. "Just strong-willed and assertive, like me! So, yes, we're both women who can be in control. You're right. I can handle myself. What am I scared of?"

I figure, *"What the hell!"*

Back at the flat, fingers shaking, I tap his number into the phone, and half an hour later, I am heading out to the top of the town to meet, as the card tells me, Oren, who owns a jewellery company.

Looking back on this moment, I am amazed that I did not stop to research him. I should have looked him up on Facebook, but after my weekend away and my driving accolade, I am still jubilant and full of bravado. I have previously dabbled within the jewellery world, and although I am certain my teenage designs would not anywhere near aspire to Oren's company, it gives us a commonality on which to begin a conversation.

The pub Oren has picked is strangely not one I have frequented often, but it is offers a warm atmosphere, with historic artefacts adorning its walls. As it is Monday and now nearing quarter to ten, it is fairly sparse of custom, so there is no one to overhear our conversation.

Oddly, I do not recall much of significance about our evening. It passes time in a comfortable manner and is pleasant distraction. I am glad I phoned but at the end of the evening, we can both maturely acknowledge that our paths will probably not cross again. Oren is in Scotland only once every four months, checking on his Israeli jewellery stocks, which one shop sells here. When I leave him, he thanks me for calling and urges me to check his jewellery out. I do, at some stage go to look in the shop window, but never venture any further.

The whole event is one to remember, his card to assign to my treasure box, to smile fondly on later in life.

What I will remember, more than the man, is the thrill of being traffic-stopping.

DAY 80-82

I feel that I've turned some corner. The positive experiences of the last few days have helped, and time is moving onward. I am allowing myself to think about more than just the current day, and that is new.

I could also be convincing myself that our relationship wasn't as wonderful as I'd always presumed. I remember Clive's reactions in certain situations. Before what I accepted, now I question. Looking back, I debate, was it really so good?

I am not ready to tear holes in our thirteen years, but even if doubting elements of our shared past is a tactical decision, does it matter if it makes me feel better? Yet, I am still unsure if I could ever trust a man enough to have more than just friendship.

Will I ever open myself up again? Instantly as I ponder, I know that my answer is no, not ever will I give myself a hundred percent as I had. There will always be a part of myself that I will keep back, a part of me ready to run, if I have to. Thanks, Clive, what a lovely legacy to offer the next important man in my life. Most people are scarred in some way, so the likelihood of me meeting a single guy, unblemished by a previous relationship, is nigh on impossible anyway. I guess we would just need to work through our past issues together, if we weren't so crippled, we were unable.

It all seems so immense right now, to even consider a new relationship, but I know that I am not happy alone. I am currently healing, just surviving really. As my strength grows and the desolate days diminish, I am thinking more about my future and I do not envision it as lonely. I know I am lucky to have such an embracing circle of friends, who have held and lifted me up, but I crave a living companion and I yearn for physical contact. How long before I will be emotionally ready for this?

Kyle and Nancy are back together again. She is buying her own flat though, which makes me think, *"good for her!"* As Kyle is now preoccupied, it is easier to extract myself from him, so sticking to the decision made with Josie and Victoria, I slowly withdraw. I have more than enough friends to fill the void.

I meet J.B. for lunch at the local bistro, at his request. I agree as I am remembering what Lucy said – 'I'm in control.' Clare is working, but he is with his friend Max who lives in Edinburgh. *That's okay, right? We're just friends!*

"Jen, Max. Max, Jen!"

His eyes sparkle as he takes my hand in his. *Electricity or what!* Here's a man I instantly fancy. Dark-haired, tanned skin, glittering eyes, he's not too tall and in fantastic shape. *Yum!*

"The man here's told me all aboot thee! – Nice to meet, at last."

"Likewise," I reply, wondering what exactly J.B. has given up.

He must catch my expression as he laughs, with a rich caramel tone, "It was nothing bad, I heard you were a top lass and I'm sorry for what has happened, but look here, you're making some braw new pals and being single can be fun!" He flashes a genuine smile.

"Ha, I guess so, you're right. I have made some lovely friends and their boyfriends are not bad either!" I nod towards J.B. who says,

"The best!"

Max laughs again and hands me the menu, his fingers brushing deliciously against mine.

I find his company compelling. He's a good conversationalist. Too bad then, that he is married, and strangely enough it transpires that his mother-in-law was previously one of my clients.

"She is a lovely woman, so I'm sure her daughter must be too."

"Aye, she is that. I'm a happy man!"

It is an enjoyable lunch, we enjoy a harmless flirtation and I do not think about Clive once. This does prove to me that I am alive, as I do find some men instantly appealing, so my answer to Victoria now would be: "No, I don't fancy Andrew or J.B." *I'm learning!*

On my return, along with the unimportant mail, Alex has left me a gilded-edged envelope containing a wedding invitation and a hen party request and is for my best friend from school, taking place in two weeks. She has, as wedding formality requires, included a plus one on my invite, but has pointed out that this was not supposed to offend and she is quite happy if I come alone. This will take some planning.

For all the positive feelings during the day, I suffer an evening of "lack of point." Am I just treading water, because this evening I don't feel like I'm moving forward? Straddling the ledge, I watch the movements in the street. Everything seems unanswerable. What to do? Where to go? I am running out of things to focus on, and my life of survival is focusing on one event each day, never important prior. I am not really living, but then, how many of us can say we truly are?

If I asked you right now how happy you were, how worthwhile you felt your life was, could you give me a score, a number out of ten, ten being the ultimate, the most wonderful?

So what is your score? Did you make it past a five?

DAY 82 sees two more invitations.

One is for a drink with Paul on the following Tuesday, and the other is from an old colleague of Clive's, up in the area this weekend and wishing to catch up with me. It's a Saturday night and that's a night I need socially filled, so it's a yes and I've always had a soft spot for Mark. Now bald, approaching sixty, a philosophical man, who enjoys talking about his emotions, I always enjoy his company. A long time ago, while I was studying for my degree, I took one of his classes, but our history, even if at the time we were unaware of it, dates back to before I have even left the parental home.

As a seventeen year old, I was confident and outgoing and more interested in my extracurricular events than my studies. I had put my fifth year exams at the forefront of my life. I pursued good results at a cost to any kind of developing social life, so entering the sixth form at school was my right of passage – time to socialize, explore life, and meet boys. Cosseted in an all-girls' school, I finally found freedom. I had a different social event, club, meeting every night of the week, so it was no surprise when it was recommended that I just take two "A" levels rather than three, which was the norm.

The downside of this decision reared its head, during my

University applications. Unbeknownst to me, the stern Head had the audacity to write a negative letter of recommendation, questioning my academic ability to succeed at degree level, which was mailed out with my applications.

Fortunately for me it was Mark, in his role of admissions officer, who received one such letter and in reaction to such a cruel offering (God only knows what I had done to upset the Head), he turned a somersault and offered me a place regardless of my achieved grades, just to place a fist in the eye of such an embittered Head.

Due to the stream of other rejections (*now I know why)* I did attend his University. Only after I left, did we rediscover each other, as our lives again entangled in Clive's academic circles. By then, Mark had completely forgotten about the place he had awarded to the maltreated sixth former and whom, I'd like to add, had gone on to vindicate his belief in her, and prove his decision as wise.

Mark is up on departmental funds and staying in a University residence. He offers to take me out for a meal, most of the cost, which the University will reimburse him for, so we make the best of it and pick a fairly upscale restaurant. It gives me an opportunity to dress up, which is always a pleasure.

Mark arrives in a taxi and greets me cordially as we enter the restaurant. Swiftly seated at our reserved table, he takes my hand,

"I am so sorry to hear of events over the last few months." His paths have crossed with both Clive and Kyle, so he knows the most of it, although not from my perspective.

"I understand how difficult it is to lose a life partner, but I have not experienced such betrayal," he continues stony-faced. "I know it is ten years since I lost my wife to cancer, but it seems like yesterday. I still find living without her so hard." His wound is still raw and his eyes water when he talks of her. I sympathetically nod.

"I understand how it is to miss your companion and how loneliness seeps into every pore, but not how you can simultaneously hate that person for their duplicity. How difficult that must be, Jennifer." He takes my hand from the table and grasps it. "I do hope you have friends who are taking good care of you, helping you to overcome the sadness."

I was feeling fairly buoyant about dressing up and coming out tonight, but already my mood is in decline and I feel I must steer the conversation along a new route, before we are both sit here in tears.

"I'm getting there, Mark, and yes, I have plenty of good friends."

"Good," at last he cracks a smile, before adding more seriously, "I have helped various other friends through treacherous breakups, and I profess that self-confidence the key to recovery."

"Indeed," I agree. "Fortunately, that I possess. He did not take that from me, because I knew her, and cannot understand what he saw in her. I have not lost my self-confidence; I've even lost some weight, so I know I'm looking better."

"You have always been an attractive woman," he beams at me. "I'm glad you recognise that."

Mournfulness dismissed, we manage the bulk of the meal without any further depression ascending. As we deliberate over whether to have a dessert or a shot of spirit with coffee, he asks about my work and how it's picking up.

"I'm doing okay," I put him in the picture. "When you work with people with problems, there are only so many you want to see in a day, especially when you have your own issues to deal with! However, their problems help take my mind off mine, although sometimes as I'm listening to someone chitchat on, I can't help think, 'What are you so worried about – your life is so easy compared with mine!' Sorry, that's really bad, isn't it?"

"Not at all!" Mark laughs, "I'm sure it is, and let me tell you, the students' little problems, which I deal with, are even less significant, even when they think they are enormous. I find focussing on something creative helps me." He tells me about his recreational diversion as a budding artist.

" I and my female friend, Pat, often take weekend courses to improve our skills. We are working on life drawing. Perhaps it is something you could consider?"

Frowning as I recall my grades in art, I admit to my lack of ability, confessing, "Mark, I can't draw, I failed my Art exam!"

"Jennifer, you have misunderstood. I'm suggesting that you fulfil the role of model. You have, as you say, lost weight and have obviously been working out."

"Right!" I say, thinking about how to answer politely and not cause offence. This provides Mark with the opportunity to expand on his request. "If it should be something you would consider doing, it would seriously help rebuild your self-esteem. If you are as confident as you say, I think you would enjoy it. Please think about it."

I am troubled as I do not feel I have issue with my self-esteem and having spent an entire evening with me, I am perturbed that Mark thinks I may. What have I portrayed?

As I have not responded, he bounds on, stating, "I am aware that you are not totally on your feet financially and you do have time on your hands."

I can't deny this.

"We can teach you various poses which would enable you to advertise yourself as an artist's model, should you ever need any kind of extra income; the hourly rate is apparently quite high."

I'm about to decline and shut down this conversation, when he finishes with, "It really would help build your self-esteem."

Unflinching, in a moment of 'I'll show you,' I respond that I would not indeed have any issues with it and that I am truly confident and comfortable with whom I am.

Without a hesitation, he gives me no chance to recant my position and informs me that he and Pat are looking for a model for their life drawing practise this week. He would pay for the cost of my transport and the experience could only enhance my feelings of self-worth. I can hardly back down now.

Somewhat flabbergasted, I hear myself acquiesce and times and places are arranged and exchanged. Am I paying an unfair price for trying to exhibit my confidence and dignity – isn't that exactly what I may have to lose? As he hails a taxi, I wonder what the hell I have let myself in for now. It's another first, another new experience and certainly something Clive would not expect, so it scores points and I'll do it. *What the hell; life is for living.*

TUESDAY – DAY 87

I meet Mhari in town on my way home from the gym.

"I hear you're looking for therapists to rent your treatment room." She puts her shopping down. "I was surprised not to see an advert up in the health food store!" She looks at me facetiously. "Want some help?"

"Sure." I smile. She knows I could be organised, but that she is so much more so. "I'd appreciate any help I can get, Mhairi. When are you free?"

She glances downwards at her watch, "I have half an hour now," she proposes. "Any good? What are you thinking of charging – hourly rate, percentage of takings?" She pauses, assessing my blank gaze. "Okay, so we need to think about that, too," she jests. "Onwards!"

She comes back to the flat and together we design some quick flyers. Although I am now working, I am only seeing a few clients and could easily share use of the room with others, rather than have it lay empty. We set aside three days, in which I have time to allow other therapists use of the room. I don't expect to make a fortune from this, but even if it brought in some income, it would be extra to what I am earning. This is currently a better option than taking a lodger, as any therapist using the room would have left before my nocturnal sojourns. We print some flyers and posters off and when she leaves, she takes a few to distribute. She will do so more proficiently than me.

Tonight, I am meeting Paul at a pub of his choice - ironically the same one Oren chose. It has, apparently, a stock of over fifty different single malt whiskies, so he has chosen it with me in mind. When I arrive, he is at the bar, so I join him.

"What will it be?" he inquires in an uplifting tone.

I survey the bottles, lined up behind the barman and chose a single malt distilled on the Isle of Islay, "A Lagavulin, please," I politely answer. "I'm toasting my proposed new venture as a landlady."

"Let me join you then."

He pays for the drinks and we make our way over to an empty table. He pulls back a chair for me, as I tell him about my idea to rent my treatment room out to therapists.

"I know a Sports Masseur who is looking for somewhere in town to practice from," he says, stroking his beard. "I'll find you his number."

"Excellent! Thank you, and here's a toast to it working out then."

We clink our glasses together and I take a sip of the whisky. It has an intense, smoky taste and I savour it lovingly. We are still learning about each other's lives and his company is relaxed and easy. Two hours fly by and I know he has enjoyed laughing and regaling tales with me.

"Now, I must switch to alcohol-free drinks," he chortles. "As you could seriously drink me under the table and I have work in the morning."

My tolerance for alcohol must have increased, as I hardly know that I've had a drink.

"I was hoping you would like to come and share a meal with me at my home next week."

I smile enthusiastically, as he adds, "I would love for you to meet my son. He is studying Musical Theatre in Glasgow."

"You must be extremely proud of him," I comment, remembering that Paul has brought him and his sister up on his own.

"I am. It hasn't always been easy. My mother and father have helped, but being a lone parent and having to make all the decisions about how to teach them about life, where to educate them, which friendships and hobbies to encourage, which to not. Ah," he sighs. "I'm nearly there now. The worst thing was tights!" Seeing my puzzled expression, he goes on to clarify, "Tights, stockings, or even pantyhose, as I believe they say in the U.S.A. That's what I found the hardest – little girl's tights, getting them on my daughter for school. It took forever!"

"I see!" I say, understanding now and grinning. "Yes, they can be difficult and I guess you'd need them in Scotland!"

He continues to talk about his children as we walk down the hill, back towards the flat.

"Thank goodness Clive and I never had a child. How much more that would complicate everything. See, that's a positive observation about my situation!"

"Yes, definitely!"

Calling in for a bag of chips at Mario's, we chat and joke together with him, while we share them. I make a slightly rude gesture while referring to Clive. Paul jovially taps me on the shoulder as if to tell me off.

"Be careful!" Mario jests.

Paul and I walk back down the street, arm in arm. I stupidly do not notice that this obviously means more to Paul than it does me. I have not considered any romantic motif in his intentions. I am, therefore, taken completely unaware when he pauses at the end of the alleyway, saying, "I've had a lovely time," and attempts to kiss me. Our lips have brushed before I can extrapolate myself.

"Paul, I'm so sorry," I splutter. "I wasn't expecting that, and honestly, I don't feel I'm ready for it!"

"No, I'm sorry," he declares, still caressing my arm. "Of course you aren't. I hope you can forgive a man a mistake and that we can continue to be friends."

I nod, now understanding Mario's comment more as the warning it was intended as. I may not have seen this coming, but he did. (When I next see him, he warns me that I should not saddle myself with an 'old man.')

"I do hope you will still come round next week." Paul comments.

"Yes, I will," I reply hurriedly, trying to create some physical distance between us, "Sure I have no problem with that…"

…But I do have a problem with what has just occurred, and after enjoying an evening, which would have left me in a good mood; I am now left dealing with a searing disappointment, as reality hits me in the face.

For the first time, I look into my face in the mirror and ask, *"Is this it now? All I can manage, guys in their fifties and sixties?"*

I don't mean to be rude or dismiss Paul, because I genuinely like him and enjoy being with him, but I have never dated anyone much older than myself. Okay, so I danced with a twenty-four-year-old when I was seventeen and found that shocking enough, but I don't think I would ever consider a relationship someone that much my senior. *He is nearly at retirement age!*

This evening with Paul has been a stark contrast to the night with Oren, far more memorable and fun, but I do not see him as a potential boyfriend, and value a friendship with him too much to destroy that with leading him on. I hope that I have not squashed his ego too much and that I'm allowed the little white lie about not being ready. To be completely truthful, if it had been Max on the steps, I would not have hesitated and would still be pressed up against him, frantically snogging him now. (Not true, as I wouldn't snog a married man, but you get my gist.)

It does not take many more swigs from my bottle of whisky for things to spiral downwards. I just pray this won't damage my self-belief too much, as I have enough to deal with without a new problem. I hope tomorrow I will jest at my emotions and at the thought that my only potential relationships will be with guys pushing sixty. Tonight, however, it has floored me, and as I slide my back down the radiator and my knees collapse under me, the tears are cascading down my face and I am unable to contain the sobs.

The tissues pile up on the floor beside me. Tomorrow I am due to become the artist's model. At this moment, I couldn't care less; I'm just doing a favour for a friend. Being naked is just that and nothing more. I have no issue with it, and as for finding it exhilarating or freeing and confidence building, Mark, that is where you are wrong, because I doubt it'll touch me at all. What you'll get is a swollen-eyed model with a blotchy, red face on the day after the night before. Is that what you envisioned?

DAY 88

The train journey takes me about three hours, which gives me ample time to effectively sober up from the night before. The drink still in my veins, my head still floaty, I sit aimlessly gazing out of the window.

Do I regret last night? No.

Do I feel I said too much? No.

Did I put out the wrong signals? No, I don't think so.

Admittedly, I am used to male company solely as friendship. Now, that I am, indeed, single (*and admittedly pretty hot! – Ah, my self-belief is still intact then!*), I suppose it's an ulterior motif for any man I agree to drink or eat with. Do I need to exhibit more caution?

Sighing, because I don't know the answer to this, a smile crosses my face. It is fairly amusing then, that here I am, about to take my clothes of in front of yet another single man. Caution does not seem part of my vocabulary. Shrugging, I conclude that the completion of the topic is that I don't really care. Of course, I do not want to be upsetting people but the whole question seems so miniscule compared to the big picture. What really matters?

I scour the faces of the passengers opposite. What do their lives hold? Are they wondering about the girl sitting across from them? If they knew what I was about to do, would they be shocked, or is it fairly commonplace? Never having been prudish, it does not seem so bad to me, but Josie is surprised at my lack of inhibition and vigilance.

"Jen," she exclaims warningly, "take a step back and look at what you're doing, this really might not turn out well."

I dismiss this thought, as she, having a history of being a lot more body-conscious than I, would react this way.

I do not spent long pondering on it, and have no reticence greeting Mark at the station entrance.

"I made it! Are we all set?"

"Wonderful, Jennifer, but it's just me. Pat was a little under the weather."

No, not even Pat's cancellation has a lot of bearing on me. Reflecting afterwards, perhaps this was naive. I suppose I could have been placing myself in unnecessary danger, and I omit to tell Josie that Pat never ever materialised. Does this show that, in retrospect, I do think I put myself at a slight risk? Was Pat just an invention of Mark's to get me to agree or am I reading too much into the situation?

Whatever the answer, it was all fine. I disrobed, did various poses, and did not feel uncomfortable at any point. I enjoyed the peacefulness. It's very rare I let myself experience quiet.

"All ok?"

"Yes, fine."

Mark was the artist and nothing seemed inappropriate. I did not have to deal with any unwanted advances. Nor did I experience any exhilaration, or any of the associated highs that Mark was so sure I would. He did treat me to a meal at his local pub, and importantly for me, another day passed without thinking of Clive or contemplating giving it all up. So the day ends on a positive note.

With each new experience I am growing into a different woman from the one dumped after thirteen years and robbed of her life. I decide on the return journey that I will hire a car again next weekend. I'll drive down to England, just to remind myself I can, and perhaps to escape another episode huddled on the floor, my pores exuding alcohol. I also plan to visit my friend in Germany for a weekend, and perhaps a week away to visit an old friend in the States. I need to look at my finances and see what is achievable. *Amazing what you can accomplish in your head, on a train journey!*

I arrive home to a message on my answer machine, heralding forward movement:

"Terry Maxwell, here. Just to let you know that your ex has agreed to the division of funds I suggested, and appears we have reached a conclusion. You can take over the mortgage and pay him the difference of the flat's worth now, as opposed to before, minus the negative balances of the bank accounts. You just need to arrange a valuation of the flat. I recommend the estate agents further down our road. Call in once you have this. Thank you."

SATURDAY – DAY 91

Yesterday, I called into Clare's salon and tentatively invited her and J.B. over for a meal. They appear to still be a couple, so I presume J.B. has not made any decisions yet, nor voiced any concern. I'm hoping all is well and I can show my appreciation for all their help and support. They have accepted, so I plan to make the evening a success and intend to put some effort into cooking. Having hardly seen Clare since returning from Crete, I am looking forward to spending some time with her.

I pull out all the stops creating a three-course meal from scratch and am suitably rewarded by my efforts. I used to cook often, but the time spent of late, in the kitchen has been minimal. Lately, I exist on my two menu plans of either chilli or pre-prepared fresh pasta. It does not appear to be doing me any harm.

Clare bustles through the door, with J.B. trailing behind her.

"Wow! I've had a long, hard day and I'm hyperactive. I'm so looking forward to this. I feel as if I've not seen you properly for ages," she gushes. "I've been so busy. Don't you just wish we were back at Demetrius's Taverna?"

"Eating bread and olives and drinking Ouzo!" we exclaim in unison.

"I can offer you some Merlot or Cabernet Sauvignon, which is far nicer than Ouzo!" She chooses the Cabernet Sauvignon, which J.B. opens while I continue cooking. Due to my diligence preparing the meal, this is my first glass of wine for the day, but I catch her manic behaviour and soon mirror it back. J.B. monitors the food while Clare and I are laughing and spontaneously crying and hugging each other, while reminiscing some shared episodes in Crete. This is an entirely different interaction to those I have previously shared with J.B. Sitting observing two exuberant females, he is probably astonished to witness me in this new light. Ironically, I suspect he thinks us drunk, when unusually my alcohol intake this evening is near to minimal.

As we eat, I tell my 'Oren, Paul, and Mark' stories, embellishing a little, to captivate my audience. Not that I have to exaggerate much, as in retelling my recent escapades, I realise my life is far from boring. After finishing with what occurred (or actually did not) with Mark, I touch a little on my anxiety. "Do you think a younger man will ever make any advances towards me?"

"Of course! You're not old. There will be plenty of younger men interested in you," Clare responds encouragingly.

"Ah! We younger guys just arenae always so up front." J.B. raises his eyebrows.

"Especially you!" Clare looks to me. "If I'd have left it to him to ask me out, I'd still be waiting. Maybe you'll have to find someone and be assertive." We all joke a little about it.

"There will be someone when you're ready," Clare reassures me.

"And ye willnae need tae resort tae men far older," J.B. confidently announces.

"Although, sometimes they have more money and treat you better," Clare states, giving J.B. a friendly shove. "Is it only older men you've seen? Aren't there any younger ones you've liked the look of? What type of guy would you fall for?"

I am not so stupid to mention Max, so I say, "Someone confident in himself, who isn't too cocky but who has friends, who isn't too tall and who isn't fanatical about football."

"Ooh, that last one's a bit harder!" jokes Clare.

"Couldnae give up Celtic for a lass," confirms J.B.

"Well, my list may have just got shorter, but there are some things I'm not going to put up with a second time. I'm happy for him to have his own interests. In fact I'd insist he did, but not hobbies that are too encompassing." I top up their glasses. "I've always had a bit of a thing for Kyle's brother." I pause because I'm not sure they know who Kyle is and Clare asks, "Kyle, who lives downstairs?"

"Aye, I've seen him, small, blonde, skinny guy?"

"Yes, but his brother looks and is very different," I say, thinking of the vast polarity. "I like a man with some muscle and Adam – that's his name – is a lot more handsome."

"There's some lust there, alreet!" J.B. jibes.

"Um, I may have messed up as I made a casual remark to Kyle about shagging Adam and I think perhaps Kyle said something to him because he was awfully shy when I saw him!"

"No, you're kidding – tell me you didn't say that!"

"I did!"

Clare shrieks with disbelief.

"He also lives quite a distance away."

"We'll find you someone local then," she says, regaining her composure. The mood is positive as I concentrate on serving the main course.

Clare enthusiastically outlines her career plans in Crete and tries to entice me along. "You could join me in the salon, use the back room. Couldn't you just see yourself, working there in the sunshine? We could get a two-bed flat closer to town."

It all sounds wonderful. J.B. does not seem to be included, but I don't draw attention to that now. It could all be so idyllic, leaving all this far behind and working somewhere warmer.

"Am I courageous enough, though?" I ask, my eyes flicking upwards to the left. "I remember how lonely I was sometimes in Crete." And then add hastily, "Not, when I was with you. But it was very reassuring to see all my friends and acquaintances on my return. I'm not quite sure I'm ready to give them all up just yet. Maybe in another year, tho'."

The evening is a success. Clare and J.B. leave very much together and I hope they will remain that way. As I tidy up in the kitchen, I think back over the evening's conversation. It all illustrates that I do have possibilities, and I must remember this when I feel I am being sucked down into the quagmire. Life is full of potential, and I am journeying nearer to experiencing this. Perhaps it won't be much longer before I can let go of the familiar and I am ready to fly away.

DAY 92 – THREE MONTHS

Can I believe it? In some ways, yes, it feels like three months, but in other ways, not at all. I am still not used to living alone, but also still not ready to allow anyone else to live with me. Why is everything so complex?

Tomorrow is my first day of someone else working in the spare room in the flat. Odd that it should be the person I had the least expectations of, but still it's good. Murray is a homeopath and is hoping to cultivate a business here as a sister practice to his primary workplace in Glasgow. Lucy has kindly directed him my way. He is seeing two people tomorrow and paying me twenty-five percent of his takings. Unfortunately, he does not see his clients in person that frequently, but still, it is a start. If this will help pay the bills, I'll accept the slight intrusion into my private dwelling space.

Mhairi arrives, excited to tell me about her weekend. "Guess what?" she nudges me, "I'm just graduating from a weekend course on Feng Shui and I'm about to transform your life!"

I nod sarcastically. "Bring it on!"

"Oh, I plan to!" She reaches into a recycled cloth shopping bag she is carrying and fishes out a selection of crystals, mirrors, and tassels. "I'm going to hang these," she informs me in a self-assured manner, "in all the correct places. Upstairs first."

"Ok! - Anything to help. I'm up for it." I encourage her as she leads me into my bedroom. "I've found a course I fancy in New York and I'm seriously thinking of attending, if I can find the funds. It is scheduled for November, so I should be able to secure a relatively cheap flight at that time of year. What do you think of that?"

"I think magnificent – do it!" She smiles. "Now, I'm going to build a small shrine thingy. It needs to be in the right-hand corner of your bedroom." She makes for the far window.

"I love planning trips," I explain to her as she pulls out a stash of small red items. "The more time I spend searching for flights on the Internet, the more excited I become and I might even extend the trip, to visit my friend based further south in Georgia."

"Great, Jen, how brave of you. Are you going on your own?"

"When I told Lucy, there was no way she'd let me go without her! She simply cannot pass up on a shopping expedition and one in Manhattan promises to be is among the best. She hung up the phone so quickly to consult with her computer!"

"Well, I'm not surprised! I would too if it wasn't for the boys – another twelve years or so to go and then I might be able to go too!" She sighs. "I won't need to change anything in your travel corner then!"

I laugh. "So what's this one here in my bedroom then?"

"This, my dear girl, is your relationship corner and here is a pressie, I bought you for it." She passes me a sparkly, glass heart with red swirls inside it.

"I love it. Thank you." I'm touched.

TUESDAY – DAY 94

Today is the date of the promised meal at Paul's home. It is a mild September evening, and despite a slight awkwardness after our last interaction, I am looking forward to a pleasant evening. I'm positively confident that Paul can recover from my rebuttal and maintain the friendship, which was flowering prior. I hope that is how he sees it anyway, as he has insisted that all is well and I must attend this evening. Clutching a bottle of wine, I arrive at his doorstep. I am wearing the same corn blue dress that enchanted Oren, with a silk crocheted lilac bolero.

Paul, as anticipated, is the perfect host. As the meal completes its cooking period, we adjourn to the garden and sit in quiet conversation.

"I'm planning a trip to Indonesia," he tells me excitedly. "Have you ever been?"

"No," I respond, "I'm planning trips to New York and Munich, somewhat less exotic but still exciting!" Together, we talk about our proposed travels. I've booked my flight to Germany for next February and tell Paul, "For me to plan something that far in advance is amazing. Who knows what I'll be doing then, but the security of having a weekend planned is immense and it gives me something to look forward to."

"Well done! Your life may be in limbo now, but you're anticipating forward movement – that's wonderful!"

The sun, low in the sky, still contains some warmth, but we retreat inside when Paul notices the goose bumps on my legs. *Yes, he is clearly still looking.* Generally, the evening is a success. I meet his son, who interestingly, does not bat an eyelash about his father entertaining younger women.

"Dad's last relationship was with someone half his age. It doesn't bother me so you don't have to worry."

"Oh no! Ours is a platonic friendship. We've experienced a lot of similar issues and he's helping me chat through them." I attempt to correct his opinion of me as another potential partner for his dad, but I am not sure he is convinced. A charming young man, I wish he were fifteen years older. He is an absolute credit to his father, confident, well-mannered, and very good looking, but excuses himself to his bedroom after we have eaten.

As the wine flows, Paul tells me more of his forthcoming trip to Indonesia. He is visiting various family members there and his plans sound enchanting and exotic. “I’d love to take you.You would love it there.”

I can see during the evening, that although thwarted, he has not entirely given up on me as more than a friend. Just look at the benefits it would accrue. *Shame I don’t fancy him!*

THURSDAY – DAY 96

I have no whisky left, but it's raining, that continual rain that Scotland does so well, and I refuse to get wet to go to the off licence. That must be a good sign. I did not drink at all last night and I won't tonight as I met a member of my old jive class, who cajoled me into returning to class tonight. *Why not?*

Since the weekend, J.B. has called twice. Despite him not appearing to feature in Clare's ambitious plans for Crete the other evening, they seem to have slipped back into a comfortable relationship together. For this I am glad.

"We're flying oot ta Crete together this weekend. I cannae wait! Wanna join us?"

There is no room for me in their rented studio and playing gooseberry is not my forte. "I have other plans. This weekend I'm going to my school friend's hen party."

"Ooh! Braw!"

"And… After considerable debate, I have decided to invite my brother to her wedding, next month, as my plus one." After receiving his agreement, I have dispatched him the train fare and booked us a hotel room. He, of course, knows Aisling as we all grew up together, whereas none of my friends would. (Deciding whom to invite amongst the many possible male candidates, might also have been a little tricky.) "We are booked into the hotel where the reception is being held the night of the ceremony."

"Och – very nice!"

"So this weekend I'll be in Manchester."

"At a hen party!" J.B. bursts out laughing, "I dinnae see you prancing around with a plastic penis on ya heed!"

"It will not be that uncouth!" I set him right.

The old me probably would have not surpassed the difficulties required for me to attend this prestigious event and would have sadly declined. Aisling, possibly expecting that, was surprised but delighted when I informed her that I would be there.

"I'm meeting an old friend, Michael, from University, before." I try to erase the hilarious but degrading images J.B. is imagining.

"I'm off fur a bevvie, wait until I tell Clare!" He is still laughing as I show him the door. I shake my head in disbelief and ponder about the weekend. Aisling's party will not be anywhere near as raunchy as J.B. imagines. It'll be fun though, as will meeting Michael be.

Two years my senior, Michael now works and lives in Dorset with his wife and two daughters. He travels up north to visit his parents and is happy to meet up with me on Saturday. I am looking forward to seeing him and this coincides nicely with my intentions to rent a car again. This will require me staying overnight somewhere. Josie is at her parents' in London, so staying with her is not an option. She and Victoria have invited me to a flat warming party the weekend after, so I am scribbling plans onto paper, endeavouring to arrange two road trips in short succession.

This is where Kyle finds me when he knocks on the door. I rarely get an evening without someone turning up. *No complaints, I love it!*

"I was concerned because I've not laid eyes on you for some time."

"Just busy. Would you like a drink?" I offer as I invite him in. "How is everything? How is Nancy?"

"Good – all is going well," he answers, sitting down at the table.

"You appear happier and less anxious." I verbalise my observations and he admits, "I'm feeling more settled." He does not mention Clive, so neither do I, instead he asks, "How is your work going?"

"So-so I'm getting there," I reply honestly.

"Have you received the valuation on the flat yet?" Perhaps he does have another reason for calling upstairs.

"I will be discussing it with Terry tomorrow."

That seems to satisfy him and seeing his eyes falling on my open computer page, I explain, "I'm trying to organise a couple of proposed trips to England." This seems a safe conversation to have with him.

"I've been invited to a hen party in Manchester and I'm going to be picked up at the station in a limousine – should be fun!"

"Where's the venue?" Kyle enquires with interest. Having been an undergraduate in the same city, he knows it. Also, having known me for many years, he is also aware of my old friend Michael. I invite him into this external aspect of my life to avoid talking about anything more personal. I have made my decisions regarding Kyle and feel I am implementing them successfully.

"Should be a good night out!" he smiles knowlingly.

"Any ideas where I could stay on the Saturday night? Josie's away and having looked at the price of B and B's, I don't feel this is an option I can afford. The hire car and petrol will cost me enough."

Neither of us, however, can initially think of any contacts we have who could accommodate me for the night but halfway through his drink, he provides an answer.

"I know! You can stay with Adam."

Before I have a minute to contend against this, he has drawn out his phone and is making the call. "Yes, that's the solution, I should have thought of it earlier," he says, not letting me interrupt him to disagree. "Hi," he greets Adam warmly.

I gesticulate widely with my hands, but he waves me aside. Five minutes later the deal is struck and I will be staying over with Adam, who lives a forty-five minute train ride away from Aisling. I have conflicting emotions regarding this, but do not intend to examine these with Kyle. Later, I'll deal with my apprehensions once he's departed.

"Right, excellent, I'm glad you are doing okay and that I could help you out. When you get back, call in and let me know how it went." He obviously feels he has made a major contribution to the situation and leaves pleased with his efforts.

Remembering the last meeting with Adam, after which, Kyle swore he had not revealed my earlier remark, I am not so sure. Ah well, it all adds adventure to my life and at least it enables me to see both my old friends at relatively low cost.

SUNDAY – DAY 99

What I remember most about this weekend is walking around Manchester with Michael. Arms around each other, closeness and warmth with Michael, whom I've known longer than Clive, is comforting. We've maintained our friendship over the years despite distance, and slip easily back into each other's company. Michael, a family man, is tactile and gregarious and knowingly bestows what I need the most: touch. I appreciate this so much and Michael happily provides it. He reminds me how I was there for him when he was going through a serious relationship breakup and wishes he lived closer to help me out. We talk about what's been happening in each other's lives since our last meeting and too soon, the day is ending. Just as I cried getting off the train when he flung his arms around me, now I cry again as he waves from the train window.

"Goodbye, and thank you," I mouth. I am alone again and I miss him instantly. I am very glad I have the hen party to focus on and not a night in on my own.

The evening's event passes more slowly. I catch the train out to Aisling and am greeted at the station by the limousine driver. Well, that is an event in itself and I make the most of it, luxuriating in the back. On arrival at Aisling's, I am thrown into the final preparations for a fun evening.

"Hello my dear, it's wonderful you're here!" Aisling grabs my hand. Her strawberry blonde hair is twisted up and held in place by a diamante clip. "You remember Ally?"

Her best friend Ally is shouting orders up the stairs, stuffing her handbag full of props, and generally organising all the girls and cajoling them into the limo. "Hi, Jen, glad you could join us. Do you need to get changed?" High heels and skimpy, thin-strapped dresses dominate and I just have time to quickly transform myself in the bedroom before I reclaim my comfortable seat in the limo. My company of late has predominantly been male, so this balances the scales somewhat.

We share a meal with plenty of laughter, wine, and typical hen party shenanigans (minus any ostentatious and vulgar head gear) and then move next door to a club. Aisling, as has always been her style, has an insecure little cry about whether her intended husband really does love her. "What if he changes his mind and doesn't want me?" She sniffs into a tissue.

"Highly unlikely!" replies Ally, silently mouthing to the rest of us, "Too much wine!"

Nothing calms Aisling until Ally finally lets her phone her intended for reassurance.

Returning back in the limousine is the highlight of the evening for me. Our numbers reducing as we drop various girls off on route, we spread out, stick our legs out of the sunroof, and sing along to ABBA tracks while waving flamboyantly to people as we pass. Yep it's been a fun evening and a full day for me.

The limo driver drops me at the station, and with a final hug and a "Good Luck!" to Aisling, I catch the train to Adam.

The day has been so joyful, that I refuse to play host to expectations and apprehensions. I do change back into my daytime clothes in the train toilet. The short dress accentuating my slim figure leaves little to the imagination, and as full as my bravado once was, after our last meeting I am treading carefully around insecurities.

It's not quite a Max situation then, but I'm only feeling what I do about Max because he is unattainable. Really, despite the swagger, I'm a sissy and regardless of thinking I might be ready for an evening of lust, I know deep down I'm not. *All mouth, no action, that's me!*

My shyness is counteracted by the convivial evening I have just enjoyed so I hope I do not come over in either extreme. I have little time to worry regarding this, as Adam is waiting for me on the platform.

"Hi," he greets me, enthusiastically grabbing my bag and ignoring my half-hearted protests. "I'm just round the corner. How was the hen party?"

We walk a short distance to where his car is parked as I answer questions about my evening.

When we reach his flat, he immediately fetches me a drink and sits opposite me. *Why not next to me?* Perhaps it's safer, but I feel I would have preferred it if he had sat next to me. Maybe, that's what he felt in my flat?

"So how have you been?" It's not a casual question. He leans back in his chair comfortably, his dark eyes probing my defences.

"It's getting easier, but it's still hard. Sometimes I feel normal and excited about beginning a new life, and yet I don't feel ready to leave Scotland and all my friends yet." I sound like I'm talking in riddles, and yet he looks as if he understands me.

I tell him about my current situation and wonderful friends, including the episode with Paul. "I agree with Mario," he says while topping up my wine glass. "That Paul is far too old for you and he should know better than to try to rush things after everything you've been through."

Not wanting to linger on the topic of potential relationships, I ask him questions about his family and about losing his parents at such a young age.

"I had to grow up fast. While I was at catering college, I lived with my mum. I think it helped us both after my dad's car accident. It was such a huge shock and she was lonely and I wasn't quite ready to go it alone. Kyle was away lecturing by then and I was lucky enough to get some work experience in a successful restaurant and they took me on. I was just arranging to buy my own place when my mum got ill."

We swap some experiences about caring for mothers with cancer and then to lighten the topic, he tells me tales about his boss, the restaurant owner, who apparently had some rather dubious connections. I watch his quiet confidence, as he talks. He seems to manage perfectly well on his own. I'm still very self-aware in his presence but the atmosphere is a lot more relaxed than our last meeting. Perhaps it's the alcohol. I hate to think how my tolerance has grown, but there is a lot of emotional depth, to our conversations. It is late, (well, early) when I release the yawn, which has been threatening to escape for the last hour.

"Time for some sleep and I better let the dog out for five minutes." He glances towards the beanbag in the corner where she is sleeping, one leg occasionally twitching. "She's chasing rabbits in her sleep again." He smiles tenderly at her as he stands up and adjusts his T-shirt.

"It's this way to the bedroom."

No, I'm not that easy! Things have not progressed anywhere near that stage. It is a one-bedroom flat and he has elected to sleep on the couch to accommodate me. Such a nice person, but I don't know if I am attracted to him. How are you supposed to tell? Why am I even thinking that way? Lying awake in the dim light of the bedroom, running through our conversation in my mind, I question what I said, what he said. *Did he really say I was beautiful at one point?* I push it aside, I probably misheard, it's been a long day and I've had a lot to drink. As I am falling asleep, I wish so much that he was beside me in this bed so I could feel his warmth. Whether it's him or anybody I crave, I can't be sure.

The next morning, I wake late and have to remind myself where I am. Although I can hear the coffee machine in the kitchen, I don't hear any other sound, so I put my arms back under the covers and close my eyes for a little longer.

I must have drifted back to sleep because the next thing I am aware of is the aroma of coffee and pancakes. There is a slight pushing at the bedroom door and as I hastily sit up. The dog noses her way in and sits panting by my side. I am a little unsure of dogs having been bitten as a child, so I remain fairly immobile for what seems like half an hour, until her presence is obviously missed and she responds to a summoning whistle.

I take this as my cue to get out of bed and hastily throw on my jeans. In the kitchen, I find that coffee and pancakes are indeed being served. "I thought you'd appreciate something sweet and stodgy after last night." Adam glances towards the two empty wine bottles on the side.

"Did we drink that much?" Accepting the pancakes, not expecting this fine treat, I pour the maple syrup on liberally. "Thank you this is wonderful!" There is not much conversation over breakfast and I find myself a little hesitant and unusually for me of late, slightly tongue-tied. Adam does have some effect on me then. I watch the muscles in his arms contracting as he moves around the kitchen and assess his stature. He's average height, his hair much darker than

Kyle's, and he has a much more defined physique. His jeans are good quality and I sneak a peek at his bum as he washes out the bowl he used – *very sexy!*

For all my previous rules about not talking about the mundane, I find I am thinking more carefully about what to say. *Is this good, bad, or what?*

"I wondered if you'd like to come with me to walk her?" he bends to stroke the dog.

"Sure! That sounds like a good plan after all this eating and drinking." I pat my stomach gently. The slight awkwardness lifts. Having a dog is a little like having a child in the room, something to take away the focus from us.

We walk around Roundhay Park, alone yet together, circumnavigating a huge lake. This is one of the largest urban parks in Europe, so it's a lengthy stroll. "It's our favourite place to walk and they hold fantastic concerts here." It's a sunny morning and Adam greets a couple of other dog walkers as they pass us.

Our communication becomes easier as we drop back into the casual conversation of last night. This guy is much nearer my own age, appropriately single and yet, I seem unable to be tactile with him. Typical, as with all these others, (whom I consider unfitting), I have no problem. Perhaps that means I do feel something and I am scared to reach out in case I get rejected. *Or even worse in case, accepted!* Whichever – we walk round with what feels like a great space between us. Several times I think of grabbing his arm but I don't.

Too soon, we are returning and I have to grab my bag in order to catch the train back to Scotland. At the last minute, I remember Josie's party next weekend and bravely extend an invitation.

"I think I'm working." He glances towards the calendar, hung on the kitchen wall, picturing yachts. "I'll see if I can swap shifts. I'll let you know later in the week."

I haven't quite been rebuffed, but again, a little of that un-comfortableness returns. Our journey to the station is fairly quiet.

As I glance back at his retreating form exiting the station, I note that the absence of any touching as we said farewell seemed more out of place than if we had. *Or at least I think so.* I'm obviously not very good at this. Maybe he isn't either. Next weekend could be interesting if he can make the party.

MONDAY – DAY 100

"To live, is so startling, it leaves little time for anything else."

Emily Dickinson (1830-1886)

One hundred days has gone. I congratulate myself on still being here – having got through the worst – and for being able to envisage some kind of future.

Mhairi phones to question, "How are you? I haven't seen you in a while."

"I'm good. Guess what! Today is Day 100!"

"Fantastic! You've done well. Jen, it's time you started dating again. Put a picture of a couple in your relationship corner. You might meet someone!"

"I'm not sure I'm ready yet."

"Just put a picture there, what harm can it do?"

"Okay, I'll do it for you, Mhairi! We must go out soon, when are you next free?"

After she hangs up, I behave and find a small picture of a boy and girl holding hands and walking into the sunset and place it in position, figuring that'll keep her happy.

Lucy calls. "I've booked my flight to New York! I'm so excited!" she exclaims, almost squeaking. "I found that route you told me about, via Iceland. It was much more reasonable. Thanks for forwarding the details. I told Alison about it. Remember Alison?"

"Of course I do. I can't thank her enough for putting up with me in Wales."

"She was wondering if it would be all right if she comes, too? It will make the accommodation even cheaper and the hotel we've picked advertises a pull-out bed. What do you say?"

"Yes, tell her to join us. It'll be great!" I enthuse. After everything Lucy has helped me with, I can hardly refuse, and anyway it will be lovely to catch up with Alison again. Being in her home in Wales seems a complete lifetime ago. I really do feel like I have progressed.

Putting the phone down, I can't help but reflect how my life seems to have become a little travel crazy. It is midweek already, I feel as if I have only just returned from Manchester and I am travelling down to Josie's on Friday and here I am planning a trip to the U.S. Is all the travelling beginning to feel a bit much? I am running so hard, but I think it is working. With my adrenaline pumping on continuous, I am getting through and avoiding desolation. It might not be perfect, but I'm keeping my head up. I will worry about burning out later.

The most dominant need not being met is the one I have for close contact. Being with my old friend, Michael, at the weekend provided so much, but has brought this craving to the forefront. I suppose I have had touch on demand, whenever I've wanted it, for so many years, that it is an addiction to which I am suffering withdrawal. This huge desire within me is reminiscent of my teenage years. Then, I was just learning how wonderful it could be to be held, kissed and pressed up against someone else's body. This all came without the complications of commitment and responsibility. Do I wish to be there again? I think I am too old and experienced to be so. I suspect things would move a lot faster this time around and that's what I am not sure I am ready for.

DAY 108

It's Tuesday and I'm just back from Josie's.

I should have and could have kissed Dan at the party, and I wish I'd done it, but I did not quite have the nerve. My confidence wasn't quite there, so I surmised right, I wasn't ready, but I'm impatient with myself. *Next time, I'll just do it!*

That aside, it has been a great weekend. I drove confidently and this time, the next size of car up, and surpassed myself. I succeeded in reverse parking it, so I feel that I can proudly say I am a driver. Seeing Josie was, as usual, therapeutic. It was a decent party and I shared two great nights with friends, red wine, and strong single woman talk. It was a very enjoyable visit.

Tonight on my return, I await responses from two brothers; neither of whom I feel will play a major part in my future. *(But I'm not always right, so who knows.)* They are very different. Kyle recently seems to fall at every hurdle. I had arranged to share a meal with him tonight, as knowing how I am on my return from being away, I had thought it wise not to spend the entire evening alone. Kyle, obviously, does not understand and has not materialised. With no left message, he has let me down badly. Pulling away from him is proving far easier than I thought. I feel disappointed and I'm angry.

To avoid a downward spiral tonight, I need someone to chat with, but who is there? J.B. and Clare are in Crete and Lucy is in London and I act on impulse and call Adam, but he is also unavailable. I don't leave a message when I reach his voicemail.

Maybe I call him just because he's one of the last people I had a meaningful conversation with. Adam is caring and understanding but … I'm not sure what? He did text to say he could not make Josie's party, which was a pity. It would have meant more if he had phoned. Now, however, not having even left a message, why am I thinking he might call back? He did suggest he would phone me this week to see how the party went, but guess what – no call yet. I suppose the week isn't over yet, *but what am I thinking?*

I'll just subsist on my own tonight then.

Back to Dan, whom I'll probably never see again – a single friend of Victoria's, up from London for the party – he would have been the opportunity I needed to get back on the horse. (That's *so* the wrong metaphor, bringing all sorts of connotations to mind) but I'm sure I'm illustrating my point. He was available, so was I. I'm sure Victoria thought something would happen. It was a party, but I couldn't quite bring myself to make the move, and the very instant he leaned towards me, I shot into the kitchen on the pretence of securing another drink; utterly hopeless.

Even the fact that I'm entertaining such thoughts is good, surely? It hasn't been very long, so I'm not going to expect more of myself.

I must try not to lose the plot tonight, so I call Mhairi and yes she has time to come round. With her, life is always entertaining and she lifts me up by placing my limbo position in the relationship field into parody.

"So," she begins, after hearing my latest adventures. "What we have are five options: The first, an old man, friend of a friend, who is tripping over himself to get to you, to whom you say you are not ready and yet, still he waits. That equals a problem!" She raises her wine glass and takes a sip.

"The second, another old man, who wants to look at you naked. That equals another problem!" This time as I laugh, we chink our glasses together.

"The third is in a relationship with a friend of yours, but often calling round to see you. That would cause even bigger problems!" She gives me a 'head mistress look' before continuing,

"The fourth, having an on and off relationship with his girlfriend, but is best friends with your ex. That equals huge problems!" She shakes her head.

"The fifth is the fourth's brother and is probably the best bet out of an extremely poor bunch, but he does not live in Scotland! I would say wipe the slate clean and look elsewhere!"

When it's put like that, it seems refreshingly simple, so heeding her advice I decide to focus on my girlfriends and let life just happen.

WEDNESDAY DAY 109

An incident after my jive class upsets me. The class is generally going well and I find it a useful distraction on a Wednesday evening. We are a dedicated bunch of six to ten regular attendees, having presented ourselves for three to four years. We are all fairly experienced, yet enthusiasm outweighs our grace. This evening, we boast two teachers, a computer programmer, a manager of a travel agency, a retiree, a scientist, the dance teacher, and me.

I can dance if I don't think. I'm like this with most practical things. If the teacher tells me to think about a certain step, I can't do it. It is almost as if my feet need to learn the steps without any sort of involvement from my head. I'm not sure if that makes sense, but I can remember it being this way, even as a child. Dancing has always been a passion for me. In a similar way to music, it touches part of my soul. I sadly dismissed it as a career option at University. I always enjoyed Latin American and Ballroom dancing and having passed exams in these when I was younger, auditioned for and joined the University dance team. Unfortunately being short, it was difficult to secure a partner (he could not be much taller than me) and this proved to be my stumbling block. After a couple of competitions with mediocre results, I disappointingly accepted that dancing was just to be a hobby.

Tonight, it is the retiree who upsets me. The class knows all about my summer and how I am getting through my betrayal. They have been kind and supportive and kept me dancing. Ray, who sometimes gives me a lift, is fairly opinionated and I suppose I should have expected some kind of rebuff.

"I hope you have a good evening," he says as he stops his car at the traffic lights.

"I'll probably share it with my bottle of Tallisker," I foolishly indicate.

This triggers a lecture on the dangers of alcohol. "I really don't think whisky in quantity is safe for a girl of your stature and drinking alone could indicate a much bigger problem. Do you find yourself drinking alcohol every day?"

Being imprisoned in the passenger seat of his car, I cannot walk away or ignore him. "Look, Ray – I know where you are going with this and no, I'm not in danger of becoming an alcoholic. Thanks for your concern but I was just making a joke – you don't need to be anxious for me." I do not bother to try to explain, because it would get me nowhere. If he does not understand that recovering from such deep treachery requires whatever crutch works, then I am not even going to attempt an explaination. You have either been there or you haven't. Fortunately, we have now reached my street and I can hop out of the car fairly pronto.

Nevertheless, it knocks my evening somewhat and leaves me self-doubting whether I should have progressed further by this point.

I think I am advancing, and to me, any measure of headway is favourable, *so please keep your opinions to yourself, Ray.*

Of course it never does me good to get ahead of myself. Just when I think my life has been fairly settled for a phase, and there is some kind of stability, the universe will throw me something else to deal with. *Let's just give the girl another test and see how she is really bearing up..*

FRIDAY – DAY 111

The test comes in the form of J.B. He arrives, a little dishevelled at my door a little after lunch hour.

"Am needing a pal. Clare's thrown me oot of her flat. The lass has lost it! Can I talk to ye?"

"Of course," I say, grimacing within. "Come in and tell me what's happened." I will be there for the two of them, as they have for me.

"I have naewhere tae go," he tells me somewhat pathetically, but I'm already ahead of him, as I'll be offering J.B. a drink, not permanent shelter. I'm not sure I'm up to sharing the flat with anyone yet, let alone a man wanting a shoulder to cry on.

"Where does your family live? Can you not stay with one of them?"

"Most of them stay on the estate. Aye I could bed down at my sister's I suppose, because there's nae hope in hell Clare will allow me back!"

"Really? What have you said? Is she really upset?" I am presuming he has said something similar to what he had told me the other week – his path was headed away from Clare's. I'm not surprised if she's taken that badly.

But, no, this is not what has transpired. Looking decidedly uncomfortable he delivers the whammy, "Clare has accused me of sleeping with ye!"

This completely takes my breath away.

Perhaps you aren't shocked to read about this accusation, as he has been spending a fair amount of time with me, leading up to this last trip to Crete.

"Oh no! So, after being blamed of having this affair, you have come immediately to me. I don't think that was a good idea, despite it being a ridiculous claim." *Does that remind you of anyone? It does not look good to an outsider.*

"Aye, I didnae think." I can see that. His actions have been in desperation, and I suppose he's come to me, as I would understand some of how he's feeling.

But I am shocked. Not because I naively don't see when this supposed liaison could have been conducted, but because Clare has spent two weeks living with me. If she believes, that after the breach of trust I have endured, that I could deceive a friend of mine in this way, then she does not know me at all. I am hurt and angry, at the same time as wanting to provide comfort.

It is a big, horrible mess and I suspect that it will take some time to work through. I should have heeded Mhairi's advice sooner.

"I'm sorry, but I don't think it's a good idea for you to be here, despite my – our innocence. Naturally, I will try to help you both, but I think you better leave now."

He nods. I despatch J.B. more rapidly than perhaps I should a grieving friend in need of help, but I feel seeing Clare is the more dominant concern. J.B. being with me in my flat, reads as an admission of guilt and I don't wish this situation to appear any more sordid than it already does.

"Aye, I ken," he says quietly. "It's ok, you're right, I shouldnae be here. Sorry! Will ye go and see her? I'm feart for her."

I nod.

J.B. heads off somewhere, (I feel it best not to know). A big man, muscular and over six foot, he appears much smaller, and I am struck how much stronger women seem in these matters. No doubt Clare will be like a hornet, defending her nest. I grab my jacket, and sighing, head off to a destination and interaction I really do not relish. Did I say how much I try to avoid confrontation? Today, that won't happen.

On reaching Clare's salon, I recognise the hatred and devastation in her eyes. She cannot spit the bile she wants at me, as her client is still present. However, her tone is very icy.

"I have no free appointments," she states brusquely. "You would be better leaving."

Because her client is taking out her money to pay, I say, "That's fine. I'll wait."

She casts me a gaze that would render me a position lower than that of a cockroach, but says nothing. Her client, unaware, debates about which hour to book an appointment for in a month's time. The atmosphere in the room has heightened by the time she finally decides, and bids Clare a fond farewell.

Once the salon is empty, the full force of Clare's wrath hails down on me. "Why have you come to my salon? You are no longer welcome here. After all I have done for you, how could you take my boyfriend?"

"I did not, I have not…" I try to speak.

She does not stop to listen to anything I am trying to tell her.

"I knew something was up. He hasn't been himself for a while, but for him to be with you. I'm flabbergasted, after all the crap you've been spouting."

"Clare, there is nothing going on!" I manage to interpose.

"Don't lie to me!" she bellows, turning puce.

"Really, I'm telling the truth, I am not seeing him, honestly. Who's said this?"

"No one has said this, but I know," she states coldly. "I am not stupid."

"I have done nothing," I try to declare my innocence for the third time, trying desperately to appeal to her. "I would not and could not do that. You are my friend."

"Was!" she cries as the door opens behind me. Two women enter and we can say no more.

"I'll come back later," I say, pulling the door towards me.

I have to leave, promising myself that I will return, soon, when I hope she is calmer. With the situation far from resolved, I do not feel any relief. It is out of my control, which I hate, but I have clients booked in this afternoon, so I unhappily have to withdraw and return to focussing on work, presumably as Clare must too. In retrospect, it was unfair of me to take this to her workplace.

TUESDAY - DAY 115

I feel proud that my own work is slowly picking up and I am amassing funds towards the payment that will be due to Clive. I'm happy to be surviving independently and not racking up debt. *You can do it girl!* My costs are mainly car hire, petrol and off-licence requirements. The latter is reducing but is still a major percentage. Ten-year-old malt whisky does not come cheap. Food-wise, I buy little and I have not shopped for myself since the trip to Glasgow with Lucy. The flights to New York and Germany, I am paying off monthly.

On my way to the gym today, I briskly walk past Clare's salon, promising myself that I will call on her tonight after work.

Pounding on the treadmill releases my tension, but with this comes another new problem. *Sure, bring it on. I can cope. Just chuck something else at me!*

I am running on the first treadmill in front of the window, so I can overlook the street and watch the shoppers below. It helps to be able to stare outwards, instead of letting my eyes constantly flicker towards the illuminated figures, counting my time and distance completed. I am aware of someone joining me on the adjacent treadmill and casting an eye left, acknowledge Terry Maxwell's secretary. She smiles, but as we are both listening to music with headphones on, the conversation begins later. She completes her workout and signals that she wishes to speak with me. Removing my earplugs and slowing the machine to a halt, I wait, questioning her with my eyes.

"Have you heard the news?"

Taking my lack of a nod as a no, she continues, "Terry has gone under!"

She acknowledges the shock in my eyes, as she groans, "So typical, just as I thought I'd got a permanent job. "

"I'm so sorry," I say, registering this shocking news.

"He has not even got the money to pay my wages, so I haven't gone in today. I feel sorry for him, but I cannot afford to work for nothing."

I shake my head, agreeing with her.

"You will need to find out how far he has got with your case and take the notes to someone else. I think he'll be there now, moving his files out. You might catch him."

This is all I need. Will this lengthy, drawn-out process ever end? My gym session halted, I head for the changing rooms where I rapidly shower and pull my clothes on expediently, before exiting out into town. This I could do without. *Will Terry still be in his office? Will I ever see him again?* Not knowing any personal information about him, I have no idea how I would track him down if he is not there.

Taking the stairs two at a time up to his office, I am relieved to discover his office door still ajar and Terry, himself sat at his desk.

"So you've heard," he sighs. "News travels fast on this street! I'm sorry I won't be able to complete your case."

I know I'm being selfish, because in front of me sits a very defeated-looking man, but I need this paperwork completed yesterday, so ignoring his horrible predicament, I ask, "What should I do next?"

"I suggest you return to Angus Bell. As Angus no longer represents either of you, as the flat was not sold, he can act for you now. He knows your situation and should be able to complete fairly fast, as there is little more to do."

"Thanks, Terry, for all your work." I smile and add some comforting words before vacating. Feeling guilty, and yet unable to take on another problem, I stick my head into Mario's.

"I'm just letting you know that Terry Maxwell's business has collapsed. I've just come from there. I think he could do with some support."

"That's bad." He shakes his head and gesticulates in Italian. "I'll call up straight away." Un-tucking his tea towel from his waistband, he flips his sign to "closed", and ascends the neighbouring stairs immediately.

That's about all I have to give to Terry. Perhaps going bankrupt is his form of karma. Yes, during our conversations I have indeed found out that his '*similar situation to mine'* differs in that he is the transgressor. He is the one who had the affair, and the woman he betrayed works down the very same road, in the Estate Agents. Perhaps having seen some of what I've suffered through, he might have regretted his actions – but then again, maybe not. Without a second glance, I traverse across the road and round the corner towards Angus Bell's workplace.

Here, I wait some time for an audience, but finally get to see Angus.

"Yes, I'd be happy to conclude issues for you. I do not do legal aid work."

"Perhaps Terry shouldn't have!" I say in jest.

He smiles.

"I doubt that I would now qualify. My work is picking up."

"Well, that's happy news. It sounds like the little I will have to do to complete will not cost much."

"Great and thank you," I say rising. That achieved, I head back home.

That evening I finally manage to have a calmer conversation with Clare, in which I do get my point across. I push my defence saying, "Clare, you have to believe me please, I would never ever betray a friend in such a manner, and surely you can see why."

"Well…" she wavers, but I can see that I am not yet in the clear. She is very insecure under her tough outer coat and I acknowledge that she is clearly hurting as much, as she is suspicious.

"If it's not you, who is it?" She says this more to herself than me.

I don't want to admit J.B. has spoken to me about their relationship so I don't answer.

"I know he's seeing someone!"

"I'm not the person to ask," I confess. "Look how blind I was!"

This just seems to fuel her fire. "He admitted he's been round your flat," she jabs a finger at me.

"Just as a friend," I reiterate, "that's all, Clare, I promise. You have both been so kind and helpful and if I can return the favour, just ask."

She is silent so I make excuses to leave. To profess my innocence too insistently will only make her question more, so feeling there is little more I can achieve I head home. That's enough for one day.

WEDNESDAY – DAY 123

Only eight days later, returning from the gym, I meet Alex on the outside stairs with a possible conclusion.

"Important-looking letter fur ye," he grins, drips of sweat beading on his face.

I smile in return, but my stomach turns, as we know important-looking letters aren't my favourites. Hurriedly entering the flat, I retrieve the recently deposited envelope. It has Angus Bell's firm's' postmark on it so I'm hopeful it's good news.

Tearing it open and removing the contents, I read that the finances are complete. Clive has agreed to Terry Maxwell's demands, and after taking into consideration our two insurance policies and the accounts Clive has withdrawn from and left in deficit, what I am due is only a small amount. Enclosed is the bank form I have already signed for changing the mortgage into my name only, along with something short of miraculous: Clive's signature on it. Although I flinch at seeing the all-too familiar scrawl, this is it: the finale. All that remains for me is to take a cheque for this amount to Angus Bell and to visit the bank with this form and funds to dissolve the mortgage, for which a due date is given.

I am so grateful to Aunt Cheryl, because without her help, this letter, with its deadline, would have been for me completing the sale of the flat to meet the bank's requirements. As it is, any alcohol consumed today will be of the celebratory type.

There is no time like the present. I have had everything in place for this joyous occurrence for some time, so it is only one hour later, armed with joie de vivre, that I drop the cheque with Angus' P.A., as he is absent. A brisk walk across town finds me pushing open the glass door to the bank and approaching a teller to arrange to pay off the mortgage. Despite the dropping of his jaw, the whole incident is complete in less than fifteen minutes and I am no longer indebted. How much easier these things become when you are blessed with funds. Triumphantly with an edge of *"stick it to them!"* I hold my head up high and walk back out through that door. My account is closed –

I never need to return to this bank.

So many things in my life are completing.

Walking back through town I am surprised that I don't feel any different. That is it. No more ties to Clive. Mortgage dissolved, relationship dissolved, but instead of what should have been happiness, I feel a pang of loss. Can I really feel this way after everything that man has put me through?

It is the ending to thirteen years and I cannot just cast that aside. Positively, I must see this as the creation of the next episode of my life. I had some good years. I will ignore the manner in which it ended for now so that I can allow myself to grieve without feeling any malice. Life is change, consisting of both endings and beginnings. I have been in limbo for what feels like a long time, but is only four months. Today I won't beat myself up for feeling sadness, as some tears to conclude that phase of my past, are appropriate. Shedding them just signifies the momentous completion of my life with Clive.

As I wander round the flat, savouring the feeling that it is now mine and not ours, my emotions lift. My tenuous movements evolve into quicker steps and I perform a kind of celebratory dance.

"I have got through it! The flat is all mine."

Sure I know there will still be bad nights, but no more contact with Clive is ever necessary and that produces a wave of good feeling. *I am so glad we did not have children.*

Do you know? I do need to celebrate, and maybe I'll do that quietly on my own. I will buy some paint and make the flat feel like mine, some bright colours to erase the last few pieces of Clive being there. Then perhaps I can refer to it as "my flat," rather than "the flat."

I will also go and order myself a bed. I need a treat. Lucy's foam has been comfortable, and a lifesaver, but it is time for something more permanent now.

SATURDAY – DAY 126

It is Aisling's wedding weekend.

I drive down to Josie's on Friday morning and pick my brother up from the station Friday afternoon. It is nice to see him on his own and we find a city coffee shop in which to sit and chat.

"How are things with J.B.?" he smirks.

"Don't," I reply unhappily, "I'm still not convincing Clare, I'm sort of avoiding them both."

"Are you sure he doesn't fancy you? I had a feeling he might."

I shrug. "What would I know? I'm not very good at reading the signals!"

In the evening Josie, Victoria, my brother, and I go out to a club.

"Here's to the end of your financial ties to Clive." Josie clutches an ice bucket with a bottle of champagne in it. "To acquiring your flat." She emphasises the 'your.'

"Thanks, I love you all!" I acknowledge Josie, Victoria and my brother.

It is a fun night, although the club is jam-packed with university and college students and a bit too sweaty. It is years since I have frequented such a place; my brother too. *What it is to live in the city!* A kid, just about old enough to be my son, asks me to dance; I rapidly decline.

Saturday morning, I don my purple party dress, throw a thick cardi on top for travelling in, and chuck my heels on the backseat. I'll drive in my boots. Checking my reflection in the mirror, I notice that my dress gapes open a little over my boobs as I lean forward. After frantically searching for a safety pin with Josie –

"I'm so hopeless at domesticity!" she laughs. We desperately thread a needle through both sides of the dress, holding the material closer together. Checking that this holds as I move, I chuckle, "At least I have a secret weapon, if I need to fend anyone off."

It has rained heavily overnight and it is quite misty as we leave. Having checked our route on a map and got rough time estimations from Josie and Victoria, I am overconfident about our time schedule. I did not account for the mist transforming to thick fog as we ascend into the Peak District. I am unable to drive quickly due to the bends and tight corners, and it proves extremely easy to take the wrong turn.

"We're lost!" my brother states the obvious.

"Ok, we'll stop for help."

When we eventually find a roadside shop, clad in my strange attire – completely inappropriate for the weather – I sprint in to ask for new directions.

"We are surprisingly, or perhaps not, well off-course," I inform him sarcastically, on my return to the car. With new oral amendments, we head back onto the correct road.

After two or three further smaller mistakes, he turns to me with a look of 'I told you so.'

"We have to accept the fact that we probably will not make it to the church on time." I admit, grimacing.

"The reception is the important part, as far as we are concerned," figures my brother.

"Aisling is unlikely to miss us at the church as it'll be so full. Hopefully if we just turn up at the reception, she will never know we weren't at the church." (These are our foolish hopes, but Aisling proves to be a lot more observant.)

As we enter the hotel where the reception is to be held, in a stunning dress, she is posing for a group photograph on the mezzanine level below the door we try to sneak unnoticed through. It did honestly look like a quiet back entrance from outside. Immediately on cue, she looks up, and halting the photographer's progress, steps forward as she exclaims her greeting to me, "Hello, my dear, I wondered where you'd got to!" so loudly, that every one of the many faces look up in my direction. Completely caught out, all I can do is laugh and throw back my own greeting with the same enthusiasm. It is her wedding and portraying joy is the order of the day, after all. Our friendship is strong enough to endure my bad timekeeping and I am confident of her forgiveness.

The day settles down as we move from drinks reception to dining tables to speeches, in true wedding fashion. I know the girls from the hen night and Aisling's immediate family. My brother, only really knowing Aisling and her brother Craig, (and being generally less social than I am) is more isolated. While I am grateful for his role as my plus one, I do not feel I have to spend the entire evening keeping him company, and intend to enjoy the evening. I am therefore up and dancing with the girls whenever possible and Aisling does join us on occasion, and more so as the evening progresses as she has less formal social interactions to complete.

My brother catches me on a rest break. "Requesting permission to find our room and retire for the night?"

"Really?"

"Yep, last night at the club was always going to be the better night for me," he explains. "No offence, but it's already 9.30 and I'd prefer to experience the delights of a five-star hotel room – something I've yet to encounter – than to socialise with a group of people I won't meet again."

I smile. "Fair enough."

So we head off, first collecting our bags and key, to find our room. The hotel has so many small twisting and turning corridors that negotiating the labyrinth is not as straightforward as we imagined, and this takes a fair amount of time.

"Wow!" he exhales, "I'm fine here, mini bar, satellite TV all to myself, no kids – I'm happy! "

Leaving my brother comfortably ensconced inside with the orders not to wait up, I trying to commit the corridor turns to memory, while returning to the party. Aisling has noticed my absence and comes over to check that everything is okay.

"Of course, everything has been lovely! You should not be concerned about me. It's your day – are you enjoying it?"

"Absolutely," she assures me, "I've finally secured my 'F.H.'" This is a synonym from our school days. An 'F.H.' being a guy, worthy of the potential to be a 'Future Husband.'

"He's wonderful," she comments gleefully. "I'm sure your life will work out too. I can't imagine you will be single for long"

"Ha!" I reply tutting, "I hope you're right!"

"You're very good looking and a nice person," she assures me. "I'm sure plenty of men find you attractive."

"Well, thanks for the reassurance. I'm not so sure!"

One moment, we are standing together laughing, and in the next, the music has slowed down (as it tends to at wedding receptions) and a man is asking me to dance. I had not seen that coming, but with Aisling's encouraging permission, (he is a good friend of the groom) I allow him to take my hand and lead me to the dance floor.

SATURDAY – DAY 126 – TWO MINUTES LATER

Before I am aware of it, he has whisked me forwards and we are entwined, one of his arms, supporting mine, and the other on the small of my back. I do not know anything about this man who is holding me. Although he is not embracing me closely, the proximity between us makes it difficult for me to examine his features or to have a conversation. I've managed a "hi" and that's about all. I am dancing with a complete stranger, his arms cradling me to him. He's not that much taller than me.

What is more surprising is that I did not really hesitate. I had not even noticed him, and yet I did not even pause before agreeing to dance. Have I turned full circle? I suppose I am trusting Aisling's knowledge of this man, despite not even having spoken to him. Mhairi had previously said, on noticing my invitation, that weddings are always good places to meet men. Her reason being, that every man there is a friend of a friend, which seems somehow safer. I'm sure if I examined that rationale more closely, I may not agree, but it's the thought I have now. Although I can't deny having been open to this possibility, the reality of it thrust upon me, is a little daunting. I am quite shocked at myself for agreeing so easily. It is just a dance and I'm enjoying the musky, masculine scent he is exuding, as well as being supported in his arms.

"Thanks for saying yes," he whispers to my head. "I'd have looked a real plonker, in front of everyone, if you hadn't."

"No problem. Thanks for asking." I laugh back.

I guess it was brave of him to come over to me.

As we dance slowly around the floor, I see Aisling has grabbed her husband and has danced up to us to give me the thumbs-up signal. Time falls away and dissolves before my eyes. It suddenly feels like we are seventeen again, when we used to attend discos located in village halls and sports clubs together. We had a whole sequence of signs to navigate us around the pitfalls of accepting a dance with the wrong guy. So, she would be watching to see if all was well, or whether it was quite the opposite and I needed to be speedily extracted from the situation. The sign for this was to scratch the top of your head. Well, I've not scratched yet and this unplanned activity is beginning to satisfy a small part of my need for touch. I grin at Aisling.

Just as I am beginning to relax and melt into memories of my past, the music changes tempo and he removes one of his arms and enquires, "Can I buy you a drink?"

I agree, and not letting go of my hand, he leads me to the bar. After purchasing me a whisky, (single malt, of course) we sit at a small table, adjacent to the bar, opposite each other. My head starts taking over and my body, formerly content just to absorb the physical contact, reluctantly now, plays second place.

"So, how do you know Aisling?" he typically begins. He's fair, of medium build and suits his full wedding attire.

Our conversation quickly supersedes the initial enquiries regarding where we live, what we do and how we know the bride and groom. I interview him as I would a client, with questions such as, "If you had to describe yourself in two sentences, what would you say?" and "What is the most important thing, to you, in life?" Honestly, some of those questions I use in diagnosing come in very useful. They are designed to delve beneath the surface and reveal a person's characteristics, which can only benefit me in this situation. This is a skill I did not have when dating, prior to Clive, and possessing it now can only aid my decisions on whether I spend more time with this unknown man. Already, I know my initial feelings are good. I'm not scared as I was at Josie's party and I feel safe sat here with him now at the bar.

Sid is one of Aisling's husband's University friends. Working in IT and sales, he spends many hours on the road, lives about an hour and a half from here, and is obviously keen to discover who I am. He has apparently been watching me all evening, which I get a slight thrill from, as opposed to creepiness. He has discovered it was my brother accompanying me, by quizzing Aisling, who has already divulged some of my history.

"Wait until I get another moment with her!" I tell him. "I might have guessed, after her comments that she's helped set this up."

"No, I'm not giving her all that credit," he replies readily. "She just answered some questions I had. I needed to know that you weren't with a boyfriend, before I made a fool of myself."

Our conversation flows fairly easily and I am unaware of time passing. A small, scrunched-up piece of paper napkin lands on the table in front of me, and then another. This interruption breaks our focusing solely on each other as we search for the source. A group of men are sitting on the other side of the bar, hiding behind menus, flicking over the torn shards of paper napkins.

"My friends" he murmurs apologetically. It would appear that it is not only me regressing back to teenage years.

"Okay," he says decisively, "do you think I'll get this on target?" He plucks up the last piece of napkin fired at us and launches it back, in the direction of the bar. "Spot on!" he confirms, before turning his focus back to me and quizzing, "Is it just the one brother you have?"

As I give him a little of my family background, we are interrupted again. After initially joking along, Sid finally has to speak to some of the guys involved, as he fetches more drinks from the bar. There are a few suggestive remarks, which I smile at, yet refrain from interacting with. *What is it with guys?* They are probably drunk, the alcohol producing more bravado than restraint. I am not too bothered, but then it is not my performance they are evaluating. I marvel at Sid's tenaciousness. Not only has he plucked up the courage to ask me to dance, he is now having to impress his audience, who are examining his interaction skills with a member of the opposite sex. I am reminded of a peacock and check whether he is ruffling his feathers as he returns.

"I've sorted it," he says reappearing at our table. "The guys have paid for this round of drinks as an apology and promise to leave us alone."

I'm fairly impressed that he has dealt with this so effectively, so I see no reasons to extract myself from his company. I must admit, I am enjoying talking with this seemingly competent man. "So what about you?" I question. "What are your plans for life?"

"Another huge topic," he makes fun of me. "Well, I'm happy with my job. It's going well. I'm due my next promotion in January and I can't complain about the salary. The driving becomes a chore when I get stuck in traffic for hours, but that isn't every week. I have my own place, a nice flat I bought about two years ago. It's in a good location and I've got to know some local people. There are some good bars, pleasant places to go out to, and I'm not that far away from my friends. I see them reasonably often and we all get together at least three times a year." He smiles at me. "Was that the right answer?"

"What about girlfriends?" I dare to venture, figuring I've nothing to lose.

He laughs. "Not for a while. The last one was slightly crazy so I thought I'd take a break. But I miss seeing someone, you know, having someone to go out with at the weekend."

"Yes, I do! After my last relationship – thirteen years of living with someone, being on my own is hard and really strange."

Two hours later, we are still sat in the same place, oblivious to the thinning out of the bar population. Although Sid does not have as much past relationship experience as I do, he has passed my initial evaluation. He is very much aware of my recent history and is tiptoeing around certain subjects. As the barman closes up, he tentatively enquires, "Can I walk you back to your room or perhaps you'd prefer a coffee in my room?"

Whether it's the whisky or whether I've evolved into a complete slut, I don't pause to question. If I decline this invitation I think I'll regret it. I reflect back to Josie's party. I have spent longer with Sid than I did with Dan and know far more about him. (Yes, Lucy) I feel in control of the situation, so trusting my own judgement and what I have so far picked up from Sid, I accept his request, "A coffee would be great."

"Really? Fantastic!"

Not even hesitating as I witness his surprised reaction, I decide that I will set the agenda and announce, "I will not be having sex with you."

He bursts out laughing. "I would never have presumed or expected you to, but I'm happy to have your company."

I can hear voices inside me questioning my acceptance as he leads me by the hand through the maze of corridors. I push the voices aside as I focus on the warmth of his skin touching mine and notice how I am tingling with anticipation. Lucy, Mhairi, and Victoria (certainly) would be behind me here, Josie? - Probably not so.

Unfortunately for Sid, and I suppose me, he has chosen the single room option. "Sorry about the room," he says, "I reckon it's the smallest one in the hotel, I didn't expect to be entertaining."

I'm betting, as he boils the kettle, that he won't make that mistake again. His impeccable manners ensure that I receive the only cup and saucer. There is just one armchair, so I remove my high heels and sit on the bed.

"Please, please sit with me," my body screams while I remain mute.

Here in his room, Sid is quite shy and a lot less confident to the man in the bar, but then there was a table between us. After what seems an incredible length of time – he is messing about boiling the kettle, opening the small packet of provided biscuits, I hear the words, "Come and sit here with me. I only bite if provoked."

Oh, my God, I've verbalised it!

He sits on the bed with me, our backs against the headboard. Due to the narrowness of a single bed, there is no option for us not to be touching, so despite his apprehension (I hope not reluctance), we gradually lean towards each other more.

The feeling of this proximity to someone else, my head resting on his accommodating shoulder, the warmth of his person infusing into me, is almost more than I can bear. It feels like an entire era since I have experienced this. I have cut myself off from contact and just to sit here with him now is satisfying my craving to its core. I do not desire any more. I am heady on touch. For me, this sensation is absolute and I can see that at some level, Sid can understand and is respecting this.

I do not ever want to move and make the small cup of coffee endure. Finally he pulls away. "I need some sleep," he says, getting off the bed. "You are welcome to stay." He ferrets in his neat overnight bag to produce a new toothbrush for me. I vaguely wonder about a man who carries a spare toothbrush – perhaps he is prepared to some degree then. A quick flash of my brother waiting up for me and then even worse, awakening the next morning to find me still absent, flashes through my mind, but I push it aside. Sid is offering me his warmth and shelter for the night. "That would be fine, thank you," I smile at him, reach for the toothbrush and take it into the bathroom with me.

I am already hooked and nothing is going to make me refuse, not even the fact that I have nothing with me, that under my short, tight dress, held in place by a needle, is only my thong. *I'll just keep my dress and that on then!*

When I return from the bathroom, Sid is lying on his back in bed with shorty pyjamas on. He moves over, welcoming me into the crook of his arm and I comfortably settle into place on my side, my head nuzzling into his chest. He does not question the dress and I feel under no pressure, instead feeling ultimate bliss at being held so close. This supersedes any experience I could have anticipated. There is no sexual tension, for which I am grateful. It is not that I am not attracted to his lean muscular frame, but more that I am so emotionally content and blissful, that I feel I have rendered myself incapable of any more in one night.

Perhaps, I am not the slut imagined and I am sure not one onlooker, hearing I have spent the night in Sid's room, will ever believe what has transpired or what hasn't, but I do not care. I am content and I cannot remove the smile from my face. Sid brushes his lips tenderly against my forehead, whispers, "Sleep well," and strokes my hair. Minutes later he is asleep. I am just so happy, that I do not want to lose one second of this experience, so I don't sleep, but indulge myself in sinking into the safety of his arms and chest, inhaling his aroma and masculinity. I know I will never forget this glorious sensation and how precious this tactility felt, after such a famine of physical connection.

I will the night to last longer, the complete opposite to what I have been wishing, knowing that only the passing of time could heal me. This night has gone a long way towards my restoration, and I marvel at what human touch can provide. I do not let my usually overactive mind question my actions. I have never done anything like this before. Instead I just lay almost purring, despite the un-comfortableness of the single bed.

At some point, I must have dropped off or at least dozed slightly, because Sid moving his arm beneath me stirs my repose and suddenly it is morning.

"So you're still here, mermaid?" he studies my eyes. I guess he's alluding to my chestnut mane. He begins to apologise for falling asleep, but I stop him and turning my face upwards, plant a quiet kiss on his cheek, more out of gratitude than anything else. He smiles but then gently pulls away.

"We need to get up, because I'm guessing you have to get back to your room before checkout and it's fairly late."

Glancing at the clock, I reluctantly have to admit that he is right and begin to sit up.

"Do you have to leave this morning?" he asks, and before I can reply, he continues, "I don't, and there is a pool and a spa we could enjoy before we go. How about it?"

"I have to take my brother to catch a train, but if there is any way I can, I will," I reply hastily, turning and hugging him. "I really do have to run."

As I climb into my shoes and straighten my dress he laughs, "You don't have much underneath that, do you?"

I just grin back, remembering the secret weapon that I didn't need.

"Sid," I say, "you just restored my faith in men, thank you."

I am gone, threading my way through the corridors and praying that I don't bump into too many wedding guests. Luck is with me and I see no one I recognise or anyone who looks at me strangely. I arrive at our hotel room just in time.

"The lost sister! Had a good night? I was just deciding what to do as we have to check out." My brother picks up his bag.

"I met someone, whom I spent the night with, but I did not remove my dress for." Why I feel the need to justify myself, I don't know. He is not my mother. He rolls his eyes. Whether he believes me or not, I also don't know and really, does it matter?

"I'll just get changed, will you wait for me please?" I hurriedly pull on my jeans, and grabbing my favourite top, head for the bathroom. "He's invited me to stay and use the spa facilities and perhaps get lunch together. I'd like to. Is it possible, do you think?"

As we make our way to reception, we hatch a plan, involving Aisling's brother. "I can ask Craig if he could drop me at the station. That was all you were going to do anyway. Then you can go see luvver boy!"

I swat him on the arm playfully. Despite my infraction in abandoning him overnight, my brother seems to be in favour of me spending a little longer with Sid. I think he is just pleased that I finally seem to be moving past Clive.

As we walk past the breakfast hall, Aisling hails us both in.

"Have some breakfast, my dears!" her voice carries above the hubbub. "There's a long queue at reception and we have a special relationship with the manager … come and divulge everything."

When we have both, fetched a plate, filled it and sat down, she immediately pumps me for information. I start by telling her that I spent the night in Sid's room. *Not the way to do it!* Her eyebrows rise dramatically,

"I am shocked!" She is so loud her words entice the whole room full of hotel guests to look in my direction.

"I didn't sleep with him," I whisper too audibly.

Now, they really are staring. They think I am a complete slut, whatever I say now, because they read my quick denial, as the opposite: guilt. Aisling pulls on my arm and we both leave the room, just before she breaks down in laughter. I grip her hand and catch her infectious giggles, as we both fall against the wall outside, tears streaming down our faces. Typically, this is when the group of guys from the bar last night pass by, one of them daring to make some comment, which just fuels our guffawing even more.

By the time we have recovered and I've told my tale, the breakfast is cold and I feel guilty having abandoned my brother yet again. He has secured a lift with Craig, so I vow to myself that I will make it up to him another time. Thanking Aisling for a very eventful evening and wishing her well, I promise to call her when she returns from her honeymoon.

Reaching reception and settling up, I feel an arm on my shoulder and turn, experiencing a pang in my stomach, as I see Sid grinning at me. "Hey, mermaid!"

"Hey yourself! Meet my brother." I introduce the pair, just as Craig and his girlfriend arrive. "Right, I'll be back shortly," I promise Sid.

I accompany the three of them outside and wait as they pack up the car. I hug my brother. "Bye, send my love to the kids and thank you so much for coming this weekend – I really appreciate it."

"No problem," he returns, "I've not experienced so much excitement in one weekend for some time. Enjoy this morning!"

Turning after waving them off, I glimpse Sid inside with the guys. For a second only, I ask, *Am I really doing this?*

Yes I am. I have absolutely nothing to lose and all to gain. There is no hesitation as I submit to this new addiction.

DAY 127 – SUNDAY

As I approach, the guys stop talking, so I know I have been the topic of conversation. I guess my actions last night merit it. They hastily make their goodbyes making it all too obvious, with friendly pats on Sid's back, that he has just won man of the match and elevated his position in their team. What has he told them – or is it just presumption?

Sid turns to me. "Are you staying?"

"I am."

"Okay. I just need to put this bag in my car first and collect my swimming gear."

"Right," I say calmly, "I'll meet you in the spa then."

Again, he is prepared when I am completely lacking. Perhaps it's because he spends a lot of time away from home. Once he is gone, I hastily enquire if the hotel sells swimming costumes. Fortunately, I'm in luck, although the price tag makes me splutter.

I have to return to my car for a hairclip, and see Sid in the car park. Wow, he has a seriously sexy car. I'm guessing it's a perk of the job, but it doesn't do my estimation of him any damage. I've never been out with a guy who's had a decent car, (well, only one, but it was his dad's) and this car scores well above decent. I don't generally rate material possessions as important, but hey, they can be a favourable feature, and no don't ask me what make and model it is: I'm a girly.

Sid sees me and waits. "I thought we could swim, use the sauna and Jacuzzi, and get a light lunch. Does that sound like a plan?"

"Wonderful," I reply, as we head towards different changing rooms. "See you in there."

Surprisingly, no one else from our party has thought to do this and the pool and spa area are fairly devoid of guests; our gain then. My prepared plan tonight is to stay with Mark (and keep my clothes on). His home is only a couple of hours drive north, so I am in no rush.

Sid is already, changed and by the pool by the time I exit from the changing room. Now it's my turn to be the less confident one as, although I swim, it's not my favourite sport.

"Come on," he calls, wading in and pushing off. When I finally reach him, he admits to belonging to a gym and obviously swims better than I do, but he isn't competing with me or showing off his prowess. I can't help but notice his chest, which I haven't seen before. It meets with my approval.

After a few lengths, we test the sauna and the Jacuzzi, head back to the pool, and go round all three again. There are only a couple of other hotel guests in the spa area and we lavish in the facilities.

"I'm really enjoying this," I tell him as we climb out of the pool. "It's so relaxing. It's a long time since I relaxed!"

"Me too," he agrees, pulling me into the Jacuzzi. "This bit's the best!"

I love the way he puts his arm around me in the Jacuzzi as we joke about, luxuriating in the bubbles. I welcome his quiet advances and enjoy the wonderful sensation of skin meeting skin as our bodies converge under the water.

It is all fairly innocent and yet, I feel the heavily charged electricity passing between us. Again I am wishing I could slow down time, and so it would seem does he, as we decide to forget lunch and stay in the spa for the extra time. Too soon, our departure is overdue and we have to leave. Standing in the car park in front of my car in the pouring rain, the warmth from the spa still tingling through my veins, I know before I've even got in the car that I will miss him. We have exchanged phone numbers but made no plans to meet. Holding both my hands, he pulls me close. "Goodbye, mermaid, drive safely." There is no more, but he waits for me to start the ignition and watches, getting saturated as he stands waving, as I drive away. *I'm glad I'm practiced and don't stall!*

I am giddy with the excitement of all that has transpired and I find myself smiling as I drive, while simultaneously running through the events of the last 24 hours in my head. When I reach Mark's, I arrive with my shoulders held high and my solar plexus singing. I won't allow anything to dent my mood tonight.

"You look well! I've booked a restaurant for our evening meal. I presume that meets with your approval."

"Wonderful!" I don't want to tell him about Sid, although I'm sure Josie and Mhairi would advise I did. I just feel that I want to keep my memories of Sid all to myself and drown in them selfishly.

I succeed with this until we are eating our second course. Mark has brought me to a very up-market establishment.

"What do you think the other diners will think of the older man with the younger woman on his arm? I'm sure they think we're a couple," he jokes with me.

I know it boosts his ego and I see no harm in this, so this isn't the reason I tell him about Sid. It is because he asks.

"I've noticed that you're glowing, Jennifer, you appear different. Are you seeing someone?"

A smile escapes. I frantically try to suppress it but I can't so I just tell him a little. "Maybe, I've met someone that I might like to see. That's all, Mark, nothing more but I'm hopeful."

I don't say that I have spent the previous night with a man I had just met. He's a man and from an older generation and would certainly presume wrongly.

"How exciting! Will you tell me about him?"

This means I can talk about it, just a 'teensy weensy' bit and I really, really want to, because I find my mind is totally centred on one person.

"He's a friend of the groom, so I just met him yesterday. He asked me to dance." I grin broadly. "We've exchanged phone numbers but you know, he lives about an hour south and I live right the way up there, so it won't be easy. He seems nice tho'."

"You never know," Mark surmises optimistically.

"Now, tell me about you." I try hard to talk with Mark about his work and his health concerns, but my mind keeps wandering back to the memories of last night, and I have to almost grimace to stop myself from grinning outwardly.

Finally, arriving back at Mark's after a few more drinks, I excuse myself early. I cannot wait to be on my own so I can wallow in my sense of fulfilment and serenity. I desperately need to scribble down my feelings, so, armed with pen and paper, I sit on the floor of the en suite, leaning against the bath. Before I know it I am crying. *Are these happy tears?* I think they just signify a release. Something has shifted. I have taken a huge leap away from my past, and Clive, and I feel so grateful.

I know that I need to see Sid again. I love the excitement I feel when I think about him. I miss him already and I experience a wave of fear: *What if he doesn't want to see me?* I so want to phone him, but I recognise that would be too pushy. My mind is already working at possible scenarios of how I could meet up with him. *I could call him tomorrow? I do think he'd want me to phone, but what should I do?* Having not been in this circumstance for years, I feel like a novice. *Have the boundaries changed?* I don't know what's expected.

Then follows an episode of self-analysis - *Am I really missing Sid or being held? Is it all lust? Why didn't he kiss me? Did he not want to or was he respecting my need for a reduced pace? Why didn't I initiate something? Was it because it was too perfect and I didn't want to ruin it?* I shouldn't be missing him, but I was so content and I haven't felt that way in so long and I am reluctant to let go of it. It could not have felt any better. *Wow, that's saying a lot! Maybe it was too perfect?* My mind has an expertise for rattling on and I have to stop it. I am seriously sleep-deprived and need to rest. *What the hell – I'll phone him tomorrow! Life is too short!*

Decision made, I prepare for bed and just as my head hits the pillow, I falter, reach out for my phone and because life is indeed too short, send a text, which reads:

"Hey, Slapper, want to hold and inhale you. Mermaid x"

Immediately, I receive his reply: *"Slapper I to Slapper II, me too x"*

I'm still revelling in the glow that he replied straight back and am resisting the urge to call him, when he phones me.

WEDNESDAY – DAY 130

I'm back in Scotland, but have an invitation to visit Sid next weekend. I am suffering with withdrawal symptoms and am already scared of losing something that I don't have. I'm so excited and feeling like a teenager, I consult 'the oracle', asking: "Will I soon be involved in a relationship?" Despite advising my need for flexibility and patience, the response is affirmative. I am seventeen again because this just encourages the fluttering butterflies already lodged in my stomach.

It's Mhairi I choose to confide in, as I'm not so sure of Josie's or Lucy's reactions and I want to hear only positivisms, as I'm bricking it enough without anyone else's doubts. She is sitting in the flat (*no – my flat!*) with me, making appropriate noises in all the right places, as I captivate her with my story. When I've finished, I look at her, "When do you think I should call him again?"

She laughs.

"I'm concerned about initiating contact."

"Jen, most men like that!"

"He did say he dislikes that it is always the man that has to phone, but I'm not sure."

"If he's said that, do it!"

"My common sense advises me to wait."

"What have you got to lose, Jen?"

"Hope," I answer, a little embarrassed, "I know that sounds stupid, but I'm enjoying feeling hopeful. Excitement, too, I don't want that to end yet."

"It doesn't sound to me as if it will yet," she says matter-of-factly. "He seems just as interested as you are. Stop worrying!"

"There's just one thing. Unfortunately, Sid lives fairly near where Clive is and there is a slim possibility we could be out this weekend and bump into *them*."

"So?" she challenges me.

"I'm not sure I could do that." The knife analogy rears upwards and I conclude, "I couldn't, not even on a new man's arm, someone completely unknown to Clive, I would still have problems."

"Jen, I think it would be great if Clive saw you with someone else. I think he'd be jealous."

"Well, maybe," I reply hesitantly. "I'm moving on, but I'm not quite there yet. I still think it best to stick to Sid's immediate locality and not stray too far."

"Okay, well whatever you think best. So tell me what you like about him?"

I grin and I'm sure she can see the sparkle back in my eyes. "I'm not sure." I pause. "He has a long back. My very first boyfriend had a long back so I always find that sexy. In fact the whole thing feels reminiscent in a way because it almost feels as innocent as that first boyfriend."

"Perhaps that's what you need right now," she suggests, "someone to ease you back in gently."

"Mhairi, do you know, I'm still unsure whether it is actually him I want, or if this temporary diversion is just a solution to my loneliness. Maybe it could be anyone?"

"No," she says immediately. "You haven't felt this way about any of those others…" she pulls a face, "the rejects!"

"Okay, you're right. It's all a bit crazy because I hardly know him, and yet, when I close my eyes at night, it is his face I see, and thinking about his body next to mine produces shivers."

"Ha," she shares my excitement, "that's exactly because you don't know him. Enjoy that, because it might fade once you do get to know him!"

"Okay, I am living in the present and that is much better than existing in the past, and long may it last, because I just can't think about the future at all. I am unable."

"Then don't go there, Jen!"

"This 'whatever it is with Sid' may expire this coming weekend and already, that seems way too scary to contemplate."

She reaches for my hand, "So, be brave, just spend your 'emergency live life fund' and drive down to him and see where it goes. Do you know what – I'm almost jealous!"

DAY 134 – SUNDAY AT SID'S

I took Mhairi's advice and here I am, having spent the weekend here, living in the immediate, at Sid's. Only now, do I have a half hour in which to scribble and examine my feelings.

Do you know what I just realised?

I've been sitting – just being. I mean, just sitting and not doing anything and I haven't been able to do that all this time. I've actually stopped moving. The unfortunate result of this immobility is that I've caught a head cold. I relaxed, my adrenaline stopped pumping, and my immune system crashed. Did you hear that? I relaxed. That's amazing. *Is it just perceptions?* I feel completely different and I'm wondering if I could be this way in my flat, or is it because I'm in his flat? *What if he were at mine?*

There is electricity between us. I was almost too shy to look completely into his eyes when I arrived here, because that is not how most of our contact had been. I'm already dreading leaving. Perhaps I just need to know when and if there is going to be a next time. If there isn't, then yes, I might be upset, but even if we never meet again, and I think that's unlikely, I'll still be grateful. This liaison has given me confidence in my ability to meet men, to eventually have another relationship. I'm jumping ahead.

Driving down from Scotland, with anticipation flooding through my veins, I break the speed limits because I want to get there sooner. I'm like a child looking forward to a birthday party, I can't wait, and yet I'm a little afraid of who will be there. Sid obviously sees me pull into the car park, drive through the archway to his block of flats, and comes out to greet me. This is good, as it takes away the apprehension of locating the correct front door, and waiting to see his expression as he opens it.

He opens my car door and puts his hand on my shoulder. I tingle in response. "Great to see you, did you have a good drive down?"

"Yes, fine," I say, getting out and stretching.

He hugs me and offers politely to take my bag in. He masculine scent is divine.

Inside the stairway up into his flat is open, the light descending downwards through glass panels, which reach up to the ceiling. Everything smells new and probably is. All the kitchen appliances and gadgets are designer makes. His flat is all I'd love to own, but know I never will, because whatever my first thoughts, I am always eventually drawn to something far older with character (and all the maintenance work that comes with it.)

"Does my flat meet with your approval then?" he asks proudly.

"It's lovely, you've furnished it well." It's fairly sterile, everything in place, but then he's probably made an effort, as I'm visiting.

"I've just finished this room," he says indicating the lounge. My mother chose the throw. Do you think it matches?" It's soft and chenille, very attractive but perhaps not long wearing.

Sid is very different from Clive, which is a good thing – very different from all my recent interactions. In fact, probably not someone I would have imagined myself with. I'm enjoying the contrast, and I feel so utterly transformed to the girl who was with Clive, that I view this with unabridged positivism. We have been out to the cinema. He has taken me to his local haunts. We have driven out in his car and *yes, it is sexy* and can accelerate very quickly – something else, I have discovered that gives me a thrill. It's great to enjoy some fine things. Sid does not skimp. After I had insisting on paying for drinks at the first pub, he refused to allow me to pay for anything else, because he said I had paid to get here, so therefore, he would treat me.

So, as I sit here just relaxing while he finishes some paperwork in his office, I am smiling to myself and luxuriating in the present. Physically, we are taking everything slowly, which suits me. Now that my sinuses are blocked, I may as well forget it anyway. However, I now know I'm fine. I am capable of being with someone else, someone around my age. Someone else around my age (not an old man) has found me attractive. Relationships are possible.

This weekend is about us, but also the fact that I am finally looking to a future. Whether Sid will figure in it, I am unsure. I am not so awestruck to ignore the negatives. We live such a distance and our lives are very different, but that does not mean it's impossible. I will travel, if I need to. Love and even potential love would always come before career for me. I'm not saying it should – just that with me, it does.

So, pulling out some paper and a pen, I've tried to sum up the weekend. Thank you, Sid. Whatever happens, I won't forget you.

He wears Armani jeans
Smells of Hugo Boss and Jean Paul Gaultier Cologne
Drives a fast car, I can't remember the make of
Keeps asking me if I'm okay
Has a wonderful body, that I crave touching
Texts me silly messages
Is great at holding me
Irons his shirts and has more ties than anyone I know
Is a candle man
Is a bit OCD about tidying his flat
Won't let me put my gym shoes on his bed
Won't let me sit with wet hair against his sofa
Likes eating Cinnabons with me in bed
Winks at me reassuringly
Never wants to get out of bed and keeps pulling me back in
Likes Coldplay and Radiohead, yet sings along to Taylor Swift
Made me soup
Loves lying in the crook of my arm and having his hair played with

I love the way it feels when he kisses me
Feel safe when I'm with him
Like it when I'm in his car and he drives fast
Like the way he held me walking to the cinema
Liked snuggling up in the back row – never done that before!
Love that he thinks I'm beautiful
Admire his long back and tight bum
Laugh when he says my skin is perfect and my legs look great
Am happy, just being with him

I have decided when I get back to Scotland to start writing in my other journal. It's aptly called, 'Turning Points.' I am going to fill it with the good stuff, which starts with Sid. The first journal is nearly full now, and yet, I'm not so naive that I think I will no longer need it. I imagine there will still be times of bleakness, desolation, whisky, and mountains of used tissues, so I'll use it then and hope against hope, that I won't use all the pages up. I hope that I am finally exiting the period of limbo and my *"Waiting to fly"* phase is over.

PART TWO – TURNING POINTS

In the moment of change, visibility is not always clear. Sometimes it is only later, looking back that you really see the moment it occurred.

CHAPTER ONE

It's Tuesday.

I'm back in Scotland and have completed a full day of work, which has left me with a severe buzz. I am highly social and seriously good at my profession. My confidence is resounding off the ceiling, bouncing around the walls, and as I catch up with it, I say to myself, *"I love my life!"* Then, I exclaim, *"What did I think?"*

Dare I let that emotion in? Record this day because that thought is amazing. *Where did it come from?* I don't believe it possible but my mind is playing with it, making acquaintance with the feeling and exploiting it. *Could I be on the brink of feeling happy?*

As I contemplate this, J.B. phones and knocks my mood down a notch. He is almost tearful, as he narrates to me the last episode in his Clare saga. "Can ah come around this evening? I'm a wee bit doon."

My gregarious nature still flourishing, I assent to this and we arrange to cook together.

I have an hour and a half to myself in which to begin packing. On Friday, I fly to New York. I am spending a week in Manhattan with Lucy and Alison before flying to visit my friend, Christine, in Georgia for a week. In all, I'll be absent fifteen days. Despite the excitement of the trip, I am regretting the timing, as I will not see Sid all this time and we are very much in the early stages of 'something I'm not even sure is an anything.'

I'm still pondering on this when J.B. arrives so as we cook some pasta together, I decide I will confide in him and see if I can't get a male perspective on my situation. However, before I can, he launches into a conversation regarding Clare. He is seriously hurting and finding it difficult to understand her rejections.

"Nae one's seen Clare. The lass is still working but she is noo going out. I'm feart for her. She's blethering aboot me and it's all crap. She's aff her heed!"

"What has she said?" I ask curiously.

"Och, I'm noo tae keen tae say, but it's mainly aboot me and other lasses! Stuff I dinnae do!" He looks a little embarrassed.

"Is she still mentioning me?" I selfishly probe.

"Naw,"

I'm extremely relieved that I appear to be off the hook.

"But a lot of other lassies and she's imagining it all. She's pure no reet!" He pulls a face. "She won't let me in the hoose so I havenae been able tae defend meeself. Aye, I do miss her but it's getting a wee beyond that point. I'm getting angry, really radged!"

As we sit waiting for the food to cook, he does tell me some more details. J.B. is unsure what could have provoked this response.

"I'm aboot to give up with the lass," he desperately states. "I dinnae ken what else to do. The more I ask her gonnae tae no dae that, the worse it seems tae get."

I am worried for her as well as for him, but don't feel in a position to help Clare.

"Are you still staying with your sister?" I question.

"Aye, but I wanted to talk to ye aboot that."

I shouldn't have mentioned it but try not to look concerned, as he asks, "Could ah flat-sit for ye while you're away?" Having had a bottle of wine by this point, I agree more readily than I should, without thoroughly thinking the consequences through.

"Braw! It'll give me some thinking space – ye ken. I'm gonae take good care of yer flat, Ah promise."

After all this, asking naive questions about how to behave in Sid's company would appear inappropriate, so I let go of my minor concerns and we go on to talk about the practicalities of him flat-sitting.

It's only once he has left that I question my decision. Will allowing him to stay reignite Clare's initial belief regarding a relationship between J.B. and myself? In helping one friend am I pushing another aside? At 11 p.m. when I finally climb the stairs to my bedroom alone, everything feels too confusing to contemplate. I'll nudge it aside until tomorrow.

My phone is vibrating and it is a late night call from Sid. Who better to take my mind off today? I pick up the phone as I put the flat to bed.

"Hey, you!" I say. A glance out of the window reassures me that all is well with my tiny corner of the world. The road is quiet; Mario's light the only one still shining forth, only a few pedestrians on the pathway. Pulling the curtains closed, I nestle down under the duvet for a chat with Sid.

"I'm working in Birmingham on Thursday, the most northern part of my region," he tells me enthusiastically. "I wondered if you would care to share my hotel room Thursday night. I could drop you at the station so you can get a train to the airport the next morning, if that would help?" He delivers this quite rapidly so I am unable to interrupt.

"Sure, that sounds like fun!" I don't hesitate in answering, despite the extra travelling it will result in for me. Staying in a hotel is always enjoyable for me. It isn't something I do unless I'm away relaxing, so the decadence of it appeals, but, of course, it is the evening and night in Sid's arms prior to fifteen days away that creates my enthusiasm. I'm not going to refuse.

"Okay, that'll be good then. Are you looking forward to going to New York?"

"Yes, I am," I decide to be more honest, "but I live in the present, I'm looking forward to seeing you on Thursday." *Was that too forward?*

"We can get a drink in the bar."

Honestly, do you really think so? I don't. Wine in bed is a maybe, but I keep this thought to myself because I don't wish to ruin the moment and I want to feel good about Thursday. "Maybe," I say instead.

"I'll email you the address," he says as I hear him already tapping away. "It'll be good to see you before you go away. Goodnight then."

"Goodnight."

I'm smiling to myself as I descend into sleep, and that hasn't happened for a long time.

The next evening I spend with Paul. His home is fast becoming one of my safe havens. I have even stayed over a couple of nights in his daughter's bedroom when it's got really late. Peeling posters of last decades' boy bands are stuck on the wall by the bedside. I always whisper a *"Thank you"* to her for letting me use her bed.

Tonight, I don't intend to stay. We share a bottle of wine and Paul cooks salmon. "So tell me about this Sid?" he asks me as I sip.

"I don't know. He's everything I wouldn't normally fall for!" I am at ease as always in his company, sat at his kitchen table as he opens and closes the fridge, collecting ingredients.

"It's good to experience something different, even if you return to the familiar."

I share a little of the weekend with him, but do not elaborate, preferring to focus and rave about my recent feelings of euphoria. He smiles, congratulating me on having achieved such in just over four months. His sincerity reflects his own experience and I am grateful for his friendship. How hard it must have been for him left to raise his children alone and how proud he must be to have achieved such excellent results.

"Hi, Jen!" His son pops his head in before leaving for a friend's house. He seems to have accepted me as one of his dad's friends rather than conquests, although Paul admits openly that he hasn't completely dismissed the idea.

"So if you're not available yet," he jokes, "I was thinking about joining this Edinburgh singles club. What do you think?" He passes me his iPad open on the site. Surprisingly we can talk at length about this with plenty of commonality, despite our age difference.

We share supper, and as usual, I linger at the table and eat far too much cheese. It just tastes so fine with his Italian red wine. When I finally take my leave, I am pondering on my time away, reluctant to leave what has become my safe world, but I am able to dismiss this with the anticipation of Thursday evening.

It all passes in a blur and it is not until Friday on the plane to New York, that I find time to myself to reflect. It is the afternoon after the night I spent with Sid.

The hotel was mediocre. I suppose it would be when work had paid for it, and obviously they weren't to know Sid would be entertaining someone in it and they probably shouldn't. Me, being myself, took a candle in case the ambiance wasn't great and attempted to make it a little more relaxed, which Sid approved of. He, obviously, spending plenty of time on the road, was used to staying in rooms devoid of any personality and cared that I'd tried. We ate together which was nice enough, but that was about it, not much time left. Sid, exhausted from his day and the prospect of a few hundred more miles to drive the next, relaxed his head resting next to mine, only to fall asleep once he had found comfort. Yes, I was a little disappointed and bemused that nothing else happened. Did he even notice the care that had gone into my choice of nightwear, not too obviously skimpy, but surely suggestive enough? I did consider waking him. Would it be too forward of me to initiate something more the eve before I leave for two weeks, or would the anticipation of sexual contact between us heighten during my absence?

Unsure of the answers, and observing Sid's deep slumber, I chose to simply enjoy the experience of sleeping next to him, absorbing his warmth and the ripple of his muscles under my hands when he moved. I dozed on and off, rather than slept. Friday morning came far too quickly and waking to the sensation of fingers caressing my back, I only wish there had been more time.

Driving me to the station despite his schedule, Sid promised to pick me up at the airport on my return. I lingered, watching his retreating car as I stood on the pavement outside the station, wondering. He did lean over to the passenger seat to kiss me on the cheek. Having to drop me as we were in the height of rush hour and there was nowhere to park, that was all that passed between us. With a wink and a wave he was gone and I am left, still not knowing much more about whether anything is developing or not. It is a little frustrating, but maybe a quandary is a better way to leave things. Who knows where either of us will be in two weeks' time? It leaves me with the opportunity to indulge myself in the fantasy of what could be, and sometimes that's better than the reality.

My brother writes songs to express life's twists and turns. I just find pen and paper and write when I need to clarify events and pontificate. Usually, it's prose, but today, high in the sky, while Lucy and Alison are occupied with in-flight movies, I sit with my face towards the window and compose poetry:

SID, I'M ANCHORED IN YOU
Need to write about you
'Cos I'm slightly drunk, 1000's of miles from you
What is this I'm feeling?
I can smell you on my wrist
Why is it we never have enough time?
Why is it so hard to get out of your bed?
Why haven't we really kissed?
Something about your touch
The way our bodies feel, wrapped up together
Want to drown in your eyes
And yet still a little afraid
Of what you'll find in mine
And now I'm crying
Because I'm not as strong
As I appear, am I?
I am emotion
Stuck on a plane going in the opposite direction
From you.

AND THAT'S SCARY TOO
The longer I don't see you
The more I doubt what I'll find in your arms
It seems I spend my time with you
Exploring your body under my fingers
And yet I don't know your face
Maybe I'm just scared
What I'll find reflected there
Something scary about meeting yourself in someone else
Escaping the pain by caressing your body
And listening to you sleep
Sometimes I think I could just lie there
Awake for days

Being in your space feels too easy
So comfortable and obvious
But I don't know what you're thinking
What you're feeling or whether
It should really matter
But I think it might
And that's scary too

SUNSHINE IN YOUR ARMS

It's almost like we're too scared to talk about it
Because it's good the way it is, you bring
Sunshine in your arms
I live in the present and yet, maybe I need
To know the next future with you
Craving the feel of your muscles under my lips
The feel of your hand on my stomach
Nuzzled up against my back
Everyone sees us in me
Lots of presumptions, lots of relief
And yet the turmoil in me melts into
Sunshine in your arms
Content and cat-like, curling and purring
Warm, sleepy and lost with you
It's almost like we're too scared to talk about it
Because it's good the way it is. I am
Sunshine in your arms

Lucy laughs aloud over something in the movie she is absorbed in; the stewardess offers me a drink, which I decline because:

I'm writing poetry on a plane to New York
I am not a romantic
I'm not asking for too much
I don't know what lies ahead
Perhaps I don't want to!
I like living for today
But is today two weeks?
I know I may lose myself
And carry only vague memories of you

Because that's what I do
Lose reality, because it's distant
Question what I thought I knew
Because perhaps I didn't
Withdraw from the obsession, because
I need to breathe and I always feel too much
And perhaps it really is too much
Or, maybe not enough?
Both at the same time
It's overwhelming if I think
Then don't.

CHAPTER TWO – MONDAY LUNCHTIME ON A COURSE IN NEW YORK

"One belongs to New York instantly, one belongs to it as much in five minutes as in five years." Thomas Wolfe, American Writer 1900-1938

So I just phoned Sid and we chatted about nothing for ages (for us) and it was okay. It took me most of the day before I build up the courage to call. My excuse being, that I had to work out the international dialing code and time difference but honestly – I was just scared. The sensations in my stomach as I waited for him to answer were reminiscent of school gym sessions, lots of jumping and turning upside down and yet, that extreme fear of standing in the line to vault over that box in case I caught my foot and fell head first over it.

Ridiculous how this could reduce me to a prepubescent schoolgirl and yet now, phone call over and a resounding success, I just want to come back into the room and smile and giggle because…

…I think I'm happy. I'm effervescent, bubbles are popping inside of me and I feel all shiny, just from a phone call.

Already though, as those translucent bubbles pop, I start doubting. *Should I have said this, should I have said that? What am I like? Is this how it should be? Grow up, girl! How stressful this is!*

I'm sweating and laughing inappropriately while questioning myself.

I just have to let it go and conclude that whatever this is between us, it makes me feel good – yes there's a stress, but it's a good stress and I need to not worry and just believe in the now.

This current week, Lucy, Alison and I live on 94th Street, by the Hudson River. We travel downtown on an express train, via the subway to 14th Street daily, where Lucy and I attend the course. I even bought a gym pass so I can go to the gym every afternoon on my way home. It all feels so right, so real, this illusion. Home is two inexpensive rooms, divided by a bathroom on the Upper West Side. Alison spends the day wandering and triumphantly scouring out the restaurants for our evening meal. Her criteria are those with the best-looking desserts, of which we order three and share, taking turns to take a spoonful from each. We have discovered some great stores. My favourite is a health store, which supplies me with a ginger and beetroot concoction for my breakfast each morning. I love it here. It is fun, and a great release and diversion from my life in Scotland.

The rest of the course passes fast. I am satisfied that I have learnt enough to warrant my coming and certainly enjoyed my time with my roommates. My only regret is that I did not join a couple of newly founded course friends on a clubbing night out. "No thanks," I'd said, "I'm staying here with some older friends and I'd feel bad about abandoning them."

As much as I might have gone on my home turf, I wasn't brave enough to join two relative strangers for a night out in Manhattan. That was a minus on my imagined score pad as I failed to achieve a first there, however, I did get asked out by the attractive guy who works at the juice bar. "Sorry I'm leaving tomorrow," I explained, but it was a confidence booster, which scores a points.

On Wednesday morning, Lucy, Alison, and I reluctantly leave our rooms, calling into the health store for one last juice cocktail, before catching buses to different airports. "I love you guys!" I call after them as they board their bus. They wave from the window and pull faces – they are both approaching 60. *Who'd believe it!* They are headed home to the UK; I am journeying onwards to Atlanta.

I panic slightly when my bus driver enquires of the girl in front of me, "Your flight time?" He scowls at her reply. "You'll never make it!" *Her flight leaves fifteen minutes after mine!* I decide to keep quiet and watch the clock, as we traverse through the city. My hands are sweaty as I grip the rail and my heart sinks each time we meet a red light. "Mine leaves before yours!" I quietly confide to her. I'm sure this helps her feel better, as does her whispered reply to me: "The roads are quiet today."

We make good time and his fears are unfounded: I am soon sky-bound, headed south.

Arriving in Atlanta is not such an easy story. As always, this airport is bustling. It is a major hub, with many travellers changing planes who often have to sprint between gates to catch their connecting flights. I have been here on many occasions so know the layout; however, I haven't rented a car here before, as I haven't driven in the U.S. before.

The new me, always up for a "first time experience" went ahead and booked myself a car rental with Avis and it is only when I find myself seated in the hire car, with the key in the ignition, that I realise American cars are different. First off they are automatic. That surely should be easier. It takes me a while to work out that I need to put the car into the 'Drive' position before it will move and then even longer to ascertain that this particular model needs my foot on the clutch to start the ignition. It then requires considerable 'oomph' on the gas pedal to get it going and the brakes are ultra-sensitive. As a result, I crawl slowly around the car lot, lurching, as I test the brakes. Finally, I limp towards the exit only to be presented with two different airport exit options. Do I want the I-75 or the I-85? Not remembering, I guess. Cars are passing me on both sides and I have little time for indecision. Fifteen minutes later I discover going north was the wrong choice and I am headed in the opposite direction to my destination, and am approaching the downtown area. Worse still, so are several hundred other cars, so it is not long before I find myself gridlocked in six lanes of traffic going (or actually not going) the wrong way.

Eek! Dusk is falling. Trying to reassure myself that it will be okay as the traffic picks up momentum, I gingerly try to reach the nearside lane so I can exit, turn and re-enter on the opposite lanes. It pays to be pushy, but I am far from an experienced driver so some time and distance elapse before hands shaking, legs quivering, I make it off.

Foolishly deciding to turn down towards a lit-up storefront to get a bottle of water and enquire about directions, I observe that I am not in the best of neighbourhoods and feel fear creeping up my spine. I do get out of the car and speak with the female assistant behind the bars while purchasing a drink. Receiving confirmation of my mistake, I sprint hurriedly back to the safety of the car. My heart pounding and no longer caring, I perform an illegal U-turn, completely back to front, but get away with it to get myself back on track. I only relax thirty minutes later, when I recognise familiar names on the road signs.

I reach Christine's address an hour and forty-five minutes later. She lives in a residential area located only five minutes from her workplace. We have been friends since University and this will be the first time I have visited her without Clive. She or her partner Julian usually picks us up from the airport and it would have made so much sense for me to not deviate from that successful practice. Having stayed with her once a year for the last six years, I know the immediate vicinity fairly well and fortunately the neighbours also, as when I triumphantly pull into her driveway, I realise that Chris has not yet returned from work. *Yep, that and the fact that Julian is away, was the reason that I rented a car – now I remember!* As I exit the car, the neighbours come over to greet me, and a few minutes later I am sat relaxing in front of their garage in an arondyke chair, drinking an icy Mike's Hard Lemonade and entertaining them with my driving escapade. *I really feel I earned that drink!*

This is where Christine finds me on her return and throws her arms around me. "Jen, honey, it feels too long! How was your flight?"

We go into her home and chat into the night. I feel safe in familiar surroundings and at some points of the evening, forget that everything is not the same; that I will not be returning home to Clive. Chris must be feeling his absence, as I have only once stayed with her alone, without him, but she listens and dissects all the past occurrences happily with me. "It sounds like you're slowly getting there, hon. These things don't resolve themselves overnight."

The next morning I receive an early transatlantic call. My heart leaps as I imagine it might be Sid, but it is Aisling.

"Sorry I couldn't call before – what's happening? This is so exciting!

We're just back from our honeymoon. It was wonderful, but I couldn't wait to hear what has happened between you and Sid. Tell, tell!"

I hesitate before I reply, "*Precious little*", because despite the tortoise-pace of our liaison, (note I will not say relationship) plenty has happened. "I'm very fond of Sid," I start, choosing my words carefully, "and I can confirm that from the acrobats somersaulting in my stomach because you are just asking me about him."

"Then it's going well," she rushes in. "What's happened? Have you seen a lot of each other?"

"No, not really. He works all the time and keeps falling asleep on me, so there's not a lot going on if you get my drift!"

"Oh, rubbish! That's no good." She hesitates, "let me tell you what I know about him, because that makes sense to me. I first met him on a ski holiday with a group of friends. I think he is a nice, genuine guy, the loyal pivot who keeps his friends together. He fancied a girl on the trip, you could tell by the way he kept looking at her, but he took too long approaching her. She'd lost interest. Apparently he was timid because his last relationship ended badly with a woman obsessing about him and practically becoming a stalker!"

"That makes sense," I say, thinking it over, "you'd imagine I'd be the timid one after everything that's happened, but yes it's him. He seems content to just be holding my hand and sleeping next to me!"

"Hasn't he even kissed you?" she asks, raising her voice in disgust.

"Yes, of course, but no passionate snogging and I've seen him a few times now. I am beginning to wonder…"

"Just a bit slow?" Aisling queries. "Perhaps you need to give him a push. He's a high earner with a good career, extremely sporty, and I like him, so I think it's worth hanging in there for a bit! I love his car!" she adds. Back to feeling seventeen again, we gossip and giggle. "It's all very exciting!" she repeats.

I'm grinning internally and trying not to externally, but I don't maintain my restrain for long and Chris, passing by the kitchen where I'm perched on a barstool, shoots me a look before she laughs at me.

Aisling then admits, "I'd asked my husband – God, that sounds weird!" She laughs spontaneously, "to find a single man to ask you for a dance. He replied that Sid was already waiting for an opportunity! So it wasn't set up, he liked the look of you. Did you fancy him? Had you noticed him?"

I tell her truthfully, "I guess I do now, but honestly I'd not been looking, I was talking to you! But thanks, because whether or not we go anywhere, it's been a boost to my confidence."

Pleased, she sums up encouragingly, "Give him a push. He must be interested, just slow. Don't forget that this proves you're an attractive woman with good relationship prospects."

"You're a lovely, loyal friend. Go and enjoy being newly married. I'll phone you when I get back."

I finish the call with a grin and because I'm fired up, I attempt to call Sid before I start to panic about doing so. Unfortunately, the line's engaged, and when I do get through, we get cut off. When I call again it's awkward. We both talk at once, I stumble over my words. I confess, "Aisling has just spoken with me," then instantly regret it.

"Has she? What's she gossiping about?"

Too hurriedly, I say, "I should probably let you get back to work before we get cut off again."

I hang up, am inundated by doubts and I wish I'd never called, because before I called, I felt so happy and secure. *Why didn't he ask for the number and call me back? Why didn't he mention meeting me at the airport? But then I didn't!* I hate this, but as Chris says as I babble on about it, "This is better than a mountain of tissues and a bottle of whisky."

I guess I just go on believing until I know different.

I enjoy talking with Chris.

"Tell me everything, hon!" She is willingly interested.

"I don't want to bore you!"

"This is friendship, Jen and I feel guilty that I haven't been over to visit you."

"Thanks." I touch her arm.

Chris is interested in the same supportive way that Mhairi is. I think this is perhaps because they have the same need in their lives for a close relationship. This is different, perhaps to Lucy and even

Josie, who may want that, but have got used to not having it. They choose to live on their own, or at least profess to having made that choice.

"Jen, initiate a little!"

"I don't want to spoil the perfection!"

"Is it perfection tho'?" she disputes. "It certainly won't be if it doesn't move forward. Look, honey, you'll develop hang-ups about having bad breath or facial warts or some other reason why he isn't glued to your lips for at least three minutes without breathing!"

"Okay, okay. I do not have warts or bad breath, at least I don't think so," I say, breathing into my hand and then sniffing to check. "Perhaps we need to talk about some things, if we had some time to be together and could have a conversation."

"Less talk, more action!" Chris laughs at me and noticing my expression, cries, "Now what?"

"Do you think I'll have been away too long?"

"Oh, God, Jen, stop behaving like a lost teenager. We've already established the guy's backward so he's hardly going to have moved on to another woman if you're absent for two weeks! I think it's more likely you'll still be together at Christmas but as to how much further forward you've got, well it sounds like that's up to you!"

"It would be nice if I'm still with him at Christmas because otherwise I've no idea what I'll do or who I'll share it with and that's hard." I'm already painting a nostalgic, possible Christmas for me in my mind and getting hopeful about it.

"Even if it isn't this guy – and Jen, honey, it sounds like it won't be, at least not long-term," Chris says, shattering my daydream. "You will find someone, and to be honest, Clive wasn't that terrific. I did have some reservations about Clive's integrity even before this bombshell."

"I don't want to discuss Clive," I reply sharply, "so whatever former opinion you had of him is irrelevant. That is, as long as you now view him as a total bastard after his actions!"

"Absolutely!" she agrees. "Call that Sid tomorrow and let him know how lucky he is even to get a chance with you!"

"Thanks."

"Confirm he's picking you up at the airport and sort out when you're seeing him. Guys like to be pushed and find it flattering, hon. You need to know he's going to be there."

"Okay," I reply but I'm not so sure. *Yes, I do know one thing – Sid, you lose big time if you don't want me. Thanks, Chris, for kicking me up the butt!*

There is something comforting about being five hours behind. I know Sid will be settled and sleeping, also that his next day will be halfway through by the time I wake and that'll make it closer to our next rendezvous. As I said to Chris, he'll ask, *"How was your trip?"*

I'll respond, *"It was really great, but I missed not seeing you."* I'll think I'll have said too much, but I will have said it anyway.

Chris sighs. "Just go home and take him to bed."

On Saturday, I experience a scary feeling growing within my solar plexus area, because Chris is pushing me to make a call and I don't want to admit that I'm putting it off.

"You need to find out what's happening," she declares,

I wait, watching the hands on the clock move round, mentally adding on five and telling myself that I'm waiting for some space, some privacy to phone. It's rubbish and it's only because I'm dreading that I might feel worse afterwards.

Horrendously dismayed with myself, I suggest to Chris that we go for a walk, anything really, as I am becoming too obsessed and I don't like myself for it.

This is a good idea and we spend some time talking about her life and how she would never in a million years return to the UK.

"I've an excellent job, great salary, lovely home and Julian. Why would I want to go back to a cramped house, narrow roads, and shite weather?" Obviously, I can see why not.

She is one of my constants in life. Whatever I do in the next five years, one of the only things I'm sure of is my visiting her here in Georgia. Just saying this lets the realisation that I don't want to leave surface. I try to hold back my tears as a feeling of loneliness swells within my chest, and I confess to it. "Sorry," I snivel. "Just when I think life is okay, something has to remind me that it might not be. I think my tears are concerning security and safety. I don't want to return to my flat and be alone. This feels reminiscent of when my brother and his kids left." *Can I go back to surviving on my own?* I blow my nose. "Whereas here, I have been living, there, I just exist."

"You are such a drama queen!" Chris sighs.

I attempt to see it as she does. "Ok I suppose so! You have to laugh, as two weeks ago I was questioning leaving that little world of mine behind."

Chris gives me a hug. "Jen, honey, don't be silly, you're doing really well on your own."

Somewhere inside me is an urge to argue and say, *I'm not alone, Sid is there*, yet in my heart of hearts, I know he isn't and he pales into insignificance when desolation beckons. On the edge of the isolated whisky state, I recognise that I need stability. Sid is not that. He throws everything up in the air in a precarious manner and leaves me panicking. Do I fight it or do I accept it? I've been so proud of myself, felt that I was moving forward, but this wave of insecurity hits me in the stomach. I am grappling with all that came before and craving my music to provide escape. Inside I feel defeated as if something is laughing at me and saying, *"I've been waiting, and you haven't seen the back of me yet. You thought you could just toss me aside: Ha, I don't think so."*

Chris silently witnesses my inner turmoil, takes my arm and tucks it into hers, "Here, have another tissue," she offers as we head back.

When we reach home, I innocently request to use her landline. I'm not scared anymore. I've surrendered to bigger issues. Forthrightly, I dial Sid's number. All is well – he is enthusiastic when he hears my voice and immediately launches into plans for meeting me.

"I'm working in London Thursday and Friday, so I thought I could get a hotel, pick you up, and you could come back with me and stay over the weekend, as I'm working from home on Monday and you could get a train back."

I just have to say, "Yes, fine!" and all that worry dissolves.

He knew what time it was here, so I even suspect he had been waiting for me to call. At last, he's done some initiating and worked that all out.

Chris is as excited as I am. "See? You enjoy being a silly teenager too at times!" We giggle together.

CHAPTER THREE – THE FLIGHT HOME

I leave the U.S. full of hope and anticipation after all. Yesterday's downer was just that, and as I've said, they are going to happen and to have only one in the whole time I've been away is fairly good.

Checking in at the airport, I bravely ask the check-in counter assistant, "Can you sit me in a seat next to a single man please?" (*Why not? I have nothing to lose and all to gain!*) Yes, that catches her attention and angling for an upgrade, I'm not going to get, I add, "Preferably an attractive one with money!"

We both laugh as she assigns me a number and I head off to Passport Control.

I get Sid some of the cologne he lavishly sprays on – the one in the bottle shaped as a man's torso. I spray some of the tester on my wrist and let the aromatic fragrance transport me back to his bedroom. I also pick up a gift for J.B. He is effectively flat-sitting, even though I suspect he'll have come out the winner in that arrangement.

I sleep fitfully on the plane. The girl at the desk has done well and I am indeed sitting with a lone male. Whether he's single or not, I'm guessing neither she nor I know. Whichever, he is better company than large, sweaty woman in the opposite row or the fidgety child, separated from its siblings two rows ahead. We chat amicably for some time before I decide to get my head down in preparation for tomorrow morning. I doze on and off, but this is much harder travelling alone when you are sat in close proximity to a complete stranger, as I certainly don't want my head to lop onto his shoulder, or God forbid, drool on his sweater. As a result of my concerns, I keep waking myself up, just as my head slips into a comfortable place and just to check that it's not in the dribble zone.

I panic after "the hour to landing announcement," as I stare at my reflection in the bathroom mirror. Yes, I know airline toilets are prone to be poorly lit and hence show you the worse image of yourself, but honestly, is there much hope? Already apprehensive about our rendezvous at the airport, this does not help build my confidence. There is little I can do to unravel the kinks in my hair, but at least I can apply some makeup.

Of course, when Sid greets me with a kiss and a hug, I don't even remember the slept on look.

THE TRAIN TRIP BACK TO SCOTLAND ON MONDAY

I'm sitting on an intercity train, hurtling through the English countryside. It's time to analyse and take stock.

This morning, waking to croissants and fresh coffee in bed, frightened of my future insecurities, once I'd left, we had 'the conversation.' As always, it was me who swayed the equilibrium and opened my mouth.

"I'm beginning to feel more like a friend than a potential girlfriend. Yes, I've had a good weekend. It was fun, meeting your friends Saturday night, but I feel as if you've been avoiding spending any time alone with me."

A pregnant pause before the caught-in-the-headlights-like-a-lost-rabbit look, I witnessed Sid becoming defensive and I was party to a speech worthy of a defence lawyer. *Was I really asking too much?*

Sid, apparently prepared for this question, sucked in some air and rapidly announced, "I'm completely happy with my life as it is. I do not need responsibility, the 'big C' – commitment. What we have –"

What is that, I wondered?

"…is good as it is – going out as a couple at weekends, holding hands, hugging, kissing and being close in bed."

Had he transported from another age? As I sat, dumbstruck, he followed with, "I may move to London anyway and would hate to get tied down. My last relationship held me back, and I am not prepared to let that occur again. I'm going to be very busy the next two weeks."

That just about said it all!

I was a little taken aback. I had wanted honesty and I certainly got it, but to me that was clearly a *'nothing much going on here'* answer, bordering on a *'piss off'* answer. *What happened while I was away?* I wonder why he wanted to see me? I sat silently numb, in reaction, as he then conjectured, "I suppose that's a bit selfish."

"Do you think just a bit?" I finally answered quietly. "My translation is that, you want someone on your arm at the weekend to parade around town." There was a pause.

"I admit I'm a little scared of you," he said, looking away.

And I presume, of 'this' developing any further.

"You're very self-assured and have a lot more experience than me, and I have never been in love." He shook his head. "I've only said, *'I love you'* once, and that was a lie."

How old is he - nineteen? Now I knew why he was a 'Mr No Snog.'

"You'll be fine you know, Jen. You're a great girl. I'm going to make some more coffee, do you want some?"

That was it. I'd left shortly afterwards.

As the train lurches to one side and I clutch at the bottle of water in front of me to stop it falling, I'm thinking that something slow-moving had initially been good for me, but that I'm ready for more. I don't need the full-on commitment of being with someone continually, but I do need someone reliable, whom I am confident is there for me, whom I will see every two or three weeks.

Sid, espousing these criteria is not for me, but I do not have too much to fall back on. "*Just a little longer, please,*" a part of me pleads, especially as it is now December and that heralds Christmastime and with it, all sorts of insecurities about being alone over the festive period. Talking with Chris and on the plane back, I had begun to fantasize about being with Sid at Christmas – very stupid.

So, is this over now or do I get the chance to play along, be the girl on his arm and accept his limitations and constraints? Do I want that?

I'm tired and not in the best moods, as I alight onto the platform and make my way through town. A delicious aroma greets me as I put my key in the latch and open the door. J.B. has cooked a meal for me.

"I thought I'd cook but ahm at ma Mam's tanight."

I'm ready to collapse on my own, but the meal is for us both and he starts by saying, "These tae weeks have been pure, dead awful. Clare hasnae stopped her havering!"

It won't be an early night for me, however much I crave sleep and oblivion. J.B. needs a friend, and, boy, I understand that one.

"The lass called the polis!"

"How come?"

"Harassment! Things Ah dinnae do!"

I'm sure it's not a toilet brush this time!

As companionable as I am, selfishly, I'm scared and do not want to get drawn in. I also wonder if I should be glad that I've got someone to take me out and hold me. I am worried for Clare and wonder whether, as J.B. suggests, "The lass shouldnae be on her oon. She's aff her heed and talking oot her fanny flaps."

Is she lying with a persecution complex? Does she need help or is she just hurting? Remembering back to the time she gave me in Crete, I feel guilty that it is J.B. here, with me now seeking support and not her. *Would it be wise to visit her? Could I ever get her to believe that I am not the enemy?*

I'll try tomorrow.

J.B. has "a wee dram" and declares, "Ahm aff fur a bevvie with Max. Wanna come?"

It's very tempting but I decline and he leaves. I'm shattered and decide to have an early night, only to wake a couple of hours later – jetlag. I sit up and write a letter to Clare including details of Aisling's wedding, meeting Sid, and my trip to New York. I express how much I have missed her company and that I would love to see her. Well, it's a start and even if she rips the letter up, at least I have tried. I pop it into the salon on my way back from the gym the next morning.

My brother phones me the next day. "Sid is like our father – he just throws money at situations instead of expressing his emotions. How can you not see that?" *Maybe he's right – I picked a guy like my father!*

"Did I really screw up so quickly!"

"Sid's the one screwing up. Leave it to him, wait and see when he phones and wants to see you. Talk with Aisling - see if she can sort him out."

I don't get a chance as Sid calls the instant I press end on my phone. I'm cautious, as I answer, but he launches immediately into an apology. "I'm so sorry for earlier, I was an obnoxious git and after I'd had a great weekend."

"Well, yes you were," I'm honest.

"I hope you'll forgive me. I let my past take over sometimes. Sorry, I was awful."

I don't reply, because I'm not going to say it's okay because what he said wasn't. He fills my pause by chatting about what he's done today, his work and asking about my day. "I'll be in London next Friday and not back until Saturday, as I'm training a new employee, so it's probably best if you come down the weekend after."

I'm gobsmacked! He is taking it for granted that I will and want to continue seeing him. I don't interrupt because, of course, he's right. *Am I that shallow?* - Apparently so.

"So why haven't you invited me to the office party to impress all your mates?" *If I'm to be eye candy then I'll play up to it!* But he doesn't pick up on my jibe, instead replying immediately, "It would be beneath you. Most people just get drunk and I only attend because I have to. It's no pleasure."

"I'm too superior then?"

"Yes, obviously. I wouldn't want to waste my time with you by taking you there. I am so sorry about what I said this morning. I've felt bad about it all day! I couldn't focus on work. No doubt you'll keep reminding me how awful I've been."

I don't deny it. I'm not going to let him off the hook that easily, even if he has admitted to thinking about me all day and I've acquiesced, far too easily, to his request of a visit, in a two weeks' time. *Note that he hasn't suggested driving to me!* I am only choosing for the present. I may not be proud of myself, but a near future without him, is still too huge to contemplate just yet, so I don't forgive him, but say nothing to rock the boat either. It's only a week since I was in the States, believing I'd found the next man of my dreams. How did it all go so terribly wrong, so quickly?

Pushing this aside, I catch up with my emails and get absorbed in a Chinese quiz my friend in Germany has forwarded to me. The instructions are:

Besides numbers 1 and 2, write down 2 people you know of the opposite sex. I write *Sid and Kyle.*

Besides numbers 3 and 4, write a family member and a friend. I write *My Nan and Mhairi.*

Besides 5, 6, 7, and 8, write down 4 song titles. I choose:

"I'm in.", "Shut up and drive", "She's not the girl for you", "Wanna make something of it?"

The results make me smile:

Number 1, Sid is supposedly the one I love, who matches the song title "I'm in" *(But is he?)*

Number 2, Kyle is someone I like, but with whom there are too many difficulties, who matches the song *"Shut up and drive"* (*Sounds about right.*)

Number 3, my Nan, is the person I care most about, and number 4, Mhairi, is my lucky star.

The song at number 7 tells me what's on my mind and poignantly, I've chosen *"She's not the girl for you"* (I take it that's a he)

Finally, the song at number 8 is how I feel about my life. Having chosen, *"Wanna make something of it."* I'm happy.

Then, screwing up my eyes and crossing my fingers, I make my wish.

Four hours later, Sid phones and invites me for Christmas. The moral – never dismiss Chinese quizzes, because wishes can come true.

CHAPTER FOUR

"A friend is someone who knows the song in your heart, and can sing it back to you when you have forgotten the words." *Unknown*

The buzzer sounds and Andrew is at the door. "Hi, Jen!" He holds out a bottle of red wine. I have arranged a dinner party to show appreciation for all the help and support my friends have shown me, also to utilize the large IKEA table, which symbolizes my moving forward past betrayal and bitterness.

"Who's here?" he asks.

"Josie unfortunately couldn't join us, as it is midweek, but I have Lucy, Mhairi, Paul and possibly Clare. Come in and I'll introduce you."

"So is medium Margaret here?" he whispers disdainfully.

"Yes, she's in there with Mhairi. Now, be quiet, until we're in the living room and she can't hear you!"

Margaret has rented my room on occasion. She lives in Edinburgh and performs readings. Once cosseted within, a glass of wine in his hand, Andrew makes sure everyone is aware of his view.

"I'm far too practical and straightforward to entertain any belief of psychic prowess," he scoffs, "but Jen, I'm glad to be here. It's been a while and you look hundred times better. Shame Josie couldn't make it."

"How does Margaret do this?" Paul asks, turning to me to explain.

"She asks you to choose three coloured crayons. Once these are picked, she melts their ends on an iron and creates a swirl of colour on some paper, which you keep. Then she reads the different patterns. I've heard she's very accurate."

"I wasn't sure," Paul confesses, "but I met Margaret, a very attractive lady, coming in and I'm keen to get to know her on a one to one so yes I'll give it a go!"

"You're unbelievable" Lucy snorts

"Well, you can't blame a man for trying." Paul winks back at her.

Lucy bristles. I can't see her taking that. Fortunately, Andrew witnesses the same expression on Lucy's face as I do and shoots me a glance before we both burst out in laughing – the possible altercation diffuses.

We take it in turns to visit Margaret in the adjacent room. Despite me wanting to provide all the food, various delicious dishes have been brought and we chat noisily while sampling them all. It is lovely to have my flat filled with laughter and happy interactions. I am lucky and honoured to have such fantastic friends and raise a toast.

"Thanking you all, my fantastic friends for getting me through – you have all been magnificent!"

'Here, here!" Paul is the first to clink my glass. "It's been a pleasure."

"Talk for yourself," Lucy grumbles, "I got the scrubbing the floor bit!"

When I go through to take my turn with Margaret, I bring a pen and paper to jot down her thoughts. *I had not expected such revelations!*

"There is a lot of frustration and a lack of patience, because you have been let down badly," she surmises. "Your roots are in trauma and your heart stopped emotionally and almost physically."

Yep, I recognise this!

"This was a thunderbolt. You were thrown into imbalance and total emptiness," she utters sympathetically. "Positively," she proceeds, "this has brought wisdom and understanding of yourself, which is pushing you forward. The intuitiveness with which you work will heighten." She requests I pick two to represent my past. I pull out 'ACCEPTANCE' and 'RESERVE' from the pack.

"'ACCEPTANCE' indicates that your gentle energy has taken a long time to accept matters and move on, but you have had help from three people especially. 'RESERVE' illustrates that you are still holding back and protecting yourself, waiting for your confidence to completely return."

She then asks me to pull out another two, to represent my future. I pick 'SACRIFICE' and 'ABUNDANCE'. "'SACRIFICE' demonstrates how much your heart has bled and how there is still an element of sadness. You must keep moving through it and find ways for it to exit."

'ABUNDANCE' I hope is more promising, and she explains, "This heralds freedom from chains and also financial gain. Inspiration will always materialise from within and you must trust your inner voice and meditate with music."

(I wonder if the decibel level can remain high!)

"You will travel more next year," she finishes before asking, "Have I covered all the questions you want answered?"

I hesitate, so she offers me the pack from which I withdraw one card: 'RELATIONSHIP'. We both laugh.

"There is a man with extreme gentleness, and supportiveness, who is non-dominant and who does not take the initiative," she interprets. "He is represented on the card as a deer. You are at the forefront of the card and the manner in which you communicate, will win or lose the situation: The deer will vanish if you come on too powerfully, as he is easily scared, despite having almost a puppy love for you. His previous relationship has resulted in fear and cowardice." I'm finding this all rather disturbingly accurate.

"He's obsessed by looking good and possessing quality items, but not as status symbols, but more because he enjoys them. He has a desire to be on television: a small acting part or maybe as a designer, underwear model."

I laugh at this and then am almost open-mouthed, as she physically describes him correctly and says, "Although he would want to hear what I'm saying now, he would be very wary of it and uncomfortable. I can see his hands and I'm counting because something is missing." She frowns as she comments more to herself than me, "The fingers are all there," but then inspiration hits, as she explains that something else must be missing.

She asks me, "Is it his appendix?"

This is not information I have so I shrug just as she exclaims, "I know what it is: It's a testicle; he has had an op because it was twisted."

Well, what a revelation! I wonder whether this explains some of his reticence and if it might affect his future chances of a contract with a designer undergarment company.

Thanking her, I return to my friends. "You'll never guess," I shriek, "Margaret says Sid only has one ball!"

"And you wondered why I didn't want to see this woman," Andrew jibes, then blushing says, "I'm not saying I've anything missing!"

"I'm next in." Paul rises from his chair, "I'm also fairly intact, but maybe you ladies can devise ways in which Jen should gain confirmation of this disturbing fact!"

Our laughter heightens, Mhairi is slapping her thighs and tears are running down her cheeks. "Jen, we should have evenings like this more often!"

It's a good evening and after they finally leave, I collapse into bed smiling, with thoughts of Sid strutting down the catwalk in tight boxer shorts. *That's so funny!*

CHAPTER FIVE

"Even if you are on the right path, you'll get hit if you just sit there."

I see Sid only once before Christmas. He is meeting targets with his work and very busy, so I arrange to stay over a Thursday night with him before spending the weekend with Josie. Otherwise, I won't see him until Christmas Eve and that is too long a wait for me, in my uncertainty.

My friends have met his Christmas invitation with mixed opinion. Josie thinks it is weird he would introduce me to his parents over a Christmas meal when our liaison does not appear very stable. Paul feels that it does not bode well, but admits he is overprotective of me. My brother points out that what we have is not normal, and yet Mario, in his typically Italian way, comments, "What have you got to lose? You cannot be alone at Christmas."

This is so basic and I recognise the obviousness so, despite a prophecy of doom overhanging my head, I plan to go, with little expectation. I realise that I must buy him a present which must convey the right message, so clearly nothing too personal and yet something to show I care. I daren't even wonder what he will produce for me. I'm not a fan of receiving gifts. Perhaps I'm ungrateful, but buying for someone else, I feel, says a lot about how you feel for a person. In the past, I've often felt an overwhelming disappointment and disbelief that someone, whom I've felt should know me well, would have purchased something so completely inappropriate for me.

Sid and I are too different. The caution I hold, because of Clive's actions, is far less than Sid seemingly feels. I know he is never going to meet that openness and that will not be enough for me. Yet, even as I pontificate on this, I know that I am not prepared to go back to that place I was in prior to our meeting. My life needs to shift. I need some replacement for Sid to get through and I'm not sure if that is a person, a something, or a lifestyle change. I guess I need time to fathom out what, so I will not juggle with his emotions just yet, as I know something would get dropped if I did - *probably me!*

I play Thursday night on Sid's terms and Margaret's rules, walking with my hand curled round his arm to the local pub for a drink, when I'd much prefer to have stayed in and chatted. When we return, I accept his intimacy contentedly, without pushing for any more. He has to leave early the next morning, so I don't keep him awake. He will leave me to get up and vacate his flat in my own time. I have borrowed his gym card and plan to use the gym equipment and swim before returning it via his letterbox, and then journey onwards to Josie's.

So I stick to the limitations until my emotions suffocating, ascending to the surface once Sid has left and I am alone. As I quietly navigate his flat, collecting my stuff, I know I need to put pen to paper. So sitting on his sofa, I let my experience of our time together flow from me.

EARLY MORNINGS WITH YOU

The Alarm rings; you swear
And stretch over to turn it off
We get comfy again and
I shut my eyes and nuzzle into you

The Alarm rings; you swear
And pull me closer, entwining feet
Arms encircling me
Five more minutes
Reminiscent of the first time

The Alarm rings; you swear
"I have to get up now
Give me a squeeze"
Footsteps to the bathroom
Deciding whether I should get up and
Make you coffee or to turn over and sleep

You're back in the room, showered
I must have slept

Rolling over to watch you dress
All sinewy, your muscles contracting
As you put in your contact lenses

Do you realise how much I want
To pull you back into bed?
But instead I have to be content
Just ogling, desire betrayed in my eyes
You make toast, perch on the side of the bed
"I have to go now." You kiss me and leave

The flat is empty without you
The solitude enormous, engulfing me
I listen for the sound of your car
How does it feel to leave a woman
Here in your single flat?
Do you resent me being here?

I'll try not to disturb your environment
To leave alien objects in your bathroom,
I'll try to sneak out of your life,
Like I wasn't really there, like I wasn't really in it
Was I?

I just close my eyes for five more minutes,
Snuggle down under the warm blue quilt,
Inhale your smell and get back to
That sleepy blissfulness
Before the Alarm rings and you swear.

My mistake is not to gather up the paper and pack it up with my possessions. Instead, I leave it. *What do you know?* I figure it's fairly gentle and I'm only exhibiting part of my nature I've failed to kerb, but I know, even as I leave this small account of my emotions behind, that I've overstepped and I will pay for this later.

I do, of course.

I know Sid is not ready for anything I want to express, but I am compelled to leave it and have a strong feeling of déjà vu when he calls me that night and begins with, "What's all this writing stuff?"

I could have tried to rescue myself; I could have even hung up. I am still aware of him being defensive, as my mind wanders elsewhere, maybe to what could have been. Before I know it, I realise he is talking about what we'll be doing over Christmas, which I already know. He pauses, "I have to go now, I'll call you Saturday. I'm with friends. It's not that I don't want you." *But of course, it is exactly that – he doesn't want me – just the 'me' whom he wants me to be. Do I want you, Sid?* You are a little on the simple side when it comes to relationships. Do I have the energy for that? If you want me, you cannot choose the bits that you want and discard the rest. You get all of me and that, I reckon, is why I left the piece of paper.

Sid and I have reached the end of our liaison and I should have the guts to call things off.

This is confirmed over Christmas, when I experience more of the same with him. I arrive on Christmas Eve.

"Lots to do," he begins and whisks me off in his car to buy a gift for his mother.

"You've left it a little late, Sid."

He snorts defensively. "Not really."

We pull up outside a shop into which I have to accompany him to buy his mother the most expensive bottle of champagne he can find. He pays for the store assistant to gift-wrap it. I watch as if detached from the situation, remembering all the personalised gifts I have hand-picked for my own mother in the past. Does he not recognise how lucky he is to have her? Is this the way to show he cares?

"Now, we have to deliver a gift, by hand, to a girl, with learning disabilities, Marie."

"How do you know her?" I ask interested. This is a little different.

"She's a sister of a friend who's abroad at the moment."

I am touched by his gentleness with her and recall the sensitivity with which he treated me the very first night we spent together. This exhibits his good side.

On Christmas Day, it transpires that he has bought for me a citrus juice extractor as a gift. I'm not too disappointed. He has thought about this, as he has seen me squeeze lemons by hand, but it is not something I will treasure; it is not personal. "It's a great gift isn't it?" He is very proud of himself for choosing this, but then after his gift for his mother, I'm not surprised. I should be honoured that he's found the time to shop for it. Of course, it is high-end and matches all the designer items in his kitchen: not that I'll be there again.

I get on well with his family, whom I meet for lunch on Christmas Day, but really, it is all too late. I wonder how he has explained my presence. Am I some poor, lonely friend he is saving from a suicidal day alone? I'm certainly not a girlfriend, although he does allow me to curl up next to him on the sofa in his parents' presence after we have eaten. But he is gently pushing me away, waiting for me to gain the confidence to let him go. He doesn't seem able to just tell me goodbye. I wonder if he'll regret losing me later?

It happens in the local pub and the barman picks some of it up. I actually have to ask, "When I drive away tomorrow, will I ever see you again?"

"You're too far away,"

I always have been - that's just an excuse!

"Are you hungry?"

The conversation is over then.

As I leave his flat for the last time, I'm not too bothered. Life is too short, Sid. I could have been good for you, but you never coming to visit me and not wanting anything more physical than a kiss, isn't good enough. I deserve so much more. It is your loss, Sid, and I will find someone else. I don't even think you could count as a friend, because friends care, and you didn't. I don't really think you were interested in my life, beyond me visiting you, and that is simply too poor. Nevertheless, I'm listening to your music, Sid. I miss what I thought you might be, but of course you weren't. You probably aren't even aware which lyrics I found important, relevant to you and us because, as my brother comments, you wouldn't be the kind of guy that listened to lyrics. *What a mismatch!*

Still I'm grateful. Although in my head, and to my friends I now refer to him as 'Mr. No Snog' (*Come on! It's better than Mr One Ball!*) Sid has moved me on.

Goodbye, Sid.

In the depths of my core is
The black tar that swells and bubbles,
Spitting out occasionally.
You'll never ever come close
To touching those undercurrents
So don't think you can really damage me.
There has already been so much.
I squash it all down; try to believe it never was
But at the desolate times
I can't suppress it.
There is such a BLACK VOID
With all those names of things like
HATRED, BITTERNESS, LOSS, AMBIVILENCE
Climbing out of the viscous sludge,
Dripping venom, trying to drown me.
The desire to flee grows, such urgency to just drive
But swamped and dragged down,
I no longer care, I find myself
Just slipping down into the darkness:
Just to let go of everything and
Escape feeling.

And that's it, Sid, there isn't a great more to write. You were just a turning point, a catalyst after the desolation. Onwards, upwards, I'm moving on with the flow of the future.

CHAPTER SIX

"Don't be too timid and squeamish about your actions. All life is an experiment." Ralph Waldo Emerson, American Poet 1803 –1882

"Wondered if ur free to come up 4 Hogmany. Ur welcome to crash at mine. J." I reread the text I've just written. *Dare I send it?* I insert the word 'party' after Hogmany. That looks better – more as if it wouldn't be just the two of us. My finger hovers skittishly over the send key.

J.B. has told me about this event at the local Bistro on New Year's Eve. Josie and Lucy are with their families. I want to go, but not alone. My eyes flit back to the text, I've still not sent. *Why the hesitation? I've nothing to lose!* I press send and then spend an apprehensive 30 minutes awaiting a response.

Ping! My stomach jumps as I see Adam's name on the screen. "Soz J - working. Have fun!"

Huh – always working. I'm disappointed. *(I'm sure he wouldn't be a Mr. No Snog and New Year's Eve would have been a great opportunity to find out!)*

I give Mhairi a call. "I'm a bit desperate and I don't want to go on my own. Please could you just come out for an hour or two?"

She sighs. "It's not really my thing, but for you, ok. You're buying the drinks tho'!"

It's bitterly cold as Mhairi and I walk arm in arm to the Bistro. "It's not so bad, Jen. There will be plenty of single people who don't dash to find someone to hold and kiss at midnight." She reads me so well.

So, I start the New Year alone, but in a positive place. Finishing the year, in which this betrayal took place feels good. It is not something I want to dwell on and a fresh year makes the whole episode seem further away.

New Year's Day I find harder, because I am alone and the gym is closed. I had not quite prepared enough. My mind wanders to Sid and I miss him, because he was escapism. I know he's not enough, but I still crave the feeling of leaving in a car to cross the border, believing in the possibilities. I'm glad he hasn't called since Christmas, even though I really want him to; to hear him say, "I miss you, I was wrong."

Paul and Mhairi are my best friends during January and February; the weather is too treacherously icy to be journeying through the borders to reach Josie, and even a trip through to Glasgow doesn't appeal. Paul takes me out places, so that I needn't be alone. Most of his friends are academics, so I have, again, found myself submerged in their worlds. Sometimes I drown, swamped down by all the cerebral conversations after perhaps, a trip to the theatre. I'm sure they all believe I'm in a relationship with Paul, but I no longer care. Clive is talked of as an outcast, and that suits me just fine.

Mhairi helps me decorate my flat. I have finally purchased a new bed. When she sees my relationship corner, she glances disapprovingly at me. It is the picture of the girl and boy, sweetly holding hands.

"How can you hope to have a relationship with that in your corner?" she cackles. "You honestly don't see it?"

"What?"

"This is a picture of two children holding hands and there is definitely no snogging going on there. You have only yourself to blame! Go and find a picture with more passion and sex!"

She won't let this go until I have produced something more suitable: A postcard of man and woman, naked, entwined around one another. *Who knows?*

"It's little wonder your romantic life is static. That should push things on." She places the card next to the glass heart.

"I know there have been some mornings recently when I haven't wanted to get up, but January can be like that. I thought I was just suffering from Seasonal Affective Disorder." (S.A.D.)

"Possibly," she reluctantly admits, "Scotland is one of the darkest, dampest places you could be, and I don't think staying here is doing you any favours. Would you leave?"

"I would." (*Especially for the right relationship, but I don't say that, because it is far too shallow!)* I'm not good on my own and I know all it would take to shake off this regression is to focus on someone new. "Perhaps focusing on something new would also work." I say instead.

"Think about it… Discuss it with your other friends, too, but I reckon you should."

It's Mark I see next - up for a departmental visit so we dissect the idea of me leaving, even delving into the 'nitty gritties' of finances and how I might achieve it.

"Jennifer, I agree that it is time you left the area where all the negativity occurred," he states matter-of-factly. "Have you considered taking a course somewhere far flung?"

We are sitting in a quaint tearoom in town, with a roaring log fire, sharing some Earl Grey.

"Although that appeals, I don't know whether I possess enough courage to leave for a completely new destination, where I know no one at all, Mark."

"Maybe that's a little daunting! What about in this country?" he suggests, reaching for some jam to spread on his scone.

J.B. has already mentioned renting a room off me and could probably find a friend to rent the other, so I admit, "Leaving is a possibility, but what would I do about my work? Despite a course sounding interesting, and I've found one in Hawaii, I need to be earning rather than spending, because of my deal with Aunt Cheryl concerning the flat."

"Yes," he agrees, "I forgot about that, but Hawaii sounds wonderful!"

"I know, but it's a hell of a long way from my friends! I was excited when I saw the course, but I also have a real opportunity to place myself firmly on the housing ladder with my aunt's interest-free loan. I want to take full advantage of that and earn all I can, to achieve some financial security. After this loan ends in two years, I have to have enough equity to get a mortgage in my own right on a self-employed income, which is never easy. The more equity I have, the easier it will be, so financially, taking a course rather than working is not wise, however nice it may sound."

Mark, licking his lips, is now contemplating the other half of his scone, laden with jam and fresh cream. "Okay, how about finding more work in different locations?"

"Yes, I'm open to that idea," I confess, taking a sip of tea. "One of my patients has suggested I rent a room in Glasgow, at a chiropractic practice where she works, and is offering me some referrals."

"Well, Jennifer, that makes sense to me as more work will secure your financial future and occupies your time." He finally bites into the scone.

"Especially, as I'm no longer spending hours driving up and down the country. My work at home is flourishing, and I know I could build on that, by adding clinics in different places."

"That's the way forward," he declares, adding, "delicious scones here. You can spend your free time socialising with friends!"

"Who don't fall short of my expectations!" I throw in with a laugh.

Inspired, I search the Internet for any job prospects or clinic space available, researching the fees and potential earnings. I find an eight-week contract for one day's work a week in Dundee, which I immediately shoot off an application for and a locum position in the North of England. This needs more investigation, but the location looks possible. It is about a four-hour drive away, but comes with free board and use of a car. It is time to sit and do some timetabling and sums. My adrenaline is spiking with the potential excitement. This way I could half leave Scotland, which is appealing. I could spend half the week here, in my own safe little locale, and the rest exploring somewhere new and different, with actual financial gain and time occupancy thrown in. It sounds like a perfect plan. Perhaps I've finally waded through enough of the black emotional tar to be able to get my head into gear and think sensibly. This new adventure could propel me forward, both economically and emotionally. I'm immersed one hundred percent as I reach forward for the phone to inquire about the locum position. "Hi, I'm phoning about the locum position you have advertised…"

Ten minutes later, I have an interview and an on-site visit arranged for the following weekend. There is only one other applicant, and my confidence soars. I have presented myself well and am feeling extremely positive. I'm sure the job could be mine, if I like what I see on Saturday. The position is for six months, covering the practice owner, who wants time off to travel. She has approximately twenty clients a week and wants just twenty percent of my takings. With accommodation and car rental thrown in, this opportunity seems ideal for my current circumstances.

My future is calling. After a sluggish start to the year, my joie de vivre re-emerges and I become reacquainted with hopefulness and all sorts of unknown possibilities. Who knows where this could take me and whom I could meet? It also places me nearer to Josie, Aisling, and even Adam. *So who can guess?*

CHAPTER SEVEN

"The race is not always won by the swift but to those who keep on running."

It's Tuesday after the Thursday of Mhairi's visit when I've placed the erotic picture in my corner and I have a man in my bed. *Yes, that's a shocker!* This is just when I have made a conscious effort to focus on work, too. That just goes to show how people appear, when you are least expecting them to.

I could say I picked him up at the bus stop.

Despite recognising that I could just fulfil my physical needs, I couldn't, when it came down to it. *Think positive' – at last, someone is passionately snogging me. That can't be bad!*

I've known him about five years. An authentic guy, to whom relationships and honesty are important, he, naturally, knew Clive and had heard last summer's news on the grapevine. Stopping me as I walked past the bus stop, where he was stood, he greeted me with smiling blue eyes. "How are you stranger? I havenae seen you in ages,"

"I'm doing okay. How about you, Phil?"

"Aye, good," he paused before continuing, "It must have been terrible for you." He runs his long fingers through his fair hair.

"Yes, they were. It's been very hard," I could see the sympathy in his eyes so said, "but I'm surviving well."

"Good for you!" he said with meaning. "My bus is about due, but I'd love to catch up with you. Are you free to meet up later?"

"Yes, that would be great."

"How about that café, up there," he had suggested, turning to indicate the one around the corner from the bus-stop.

"Sure, perfect, how about 6.30?"

"Aye. That suits me, I'll meet you there!"

I did not read anything into this, nor consider it to be any more than a friendly drink.

When I met with him later, we talked about relationships.

"I split with my long-term girlfriend six months ago, so I guess we are both healing from betrayal and both have open wounds."

Phil, unlike Sid, is competent in expressing his emotions. I remember this about him from before. Time just elapses, and becoming aware that he had missed the last train back to his home in Edinburgh, suddenly we're back at my flat. A coffee leads to a hug and then, we were in bed. It was much more normal, but I have none of the tingling anticipation that I experienced with Sid. Phil's not what I would have classed as my type, as he is slight, bordering on skinny and not especially muscular. Not that I did not enjoy being with him, but it was all happened so quickly. *There's no pleasing me, is there?*

The next morning, lying in bed with a coffee, we talk.

"We're two adults with no ties. Och, I'd like to see you again, Jen."

"Ok," I suck in my breath, "but you should know that being with you feels comfortable, so I'm not sure." *I should feel more of a buzz – shouldn't I?*

"Bravely put! So I'm like an old shoe? I ken – I'm still not sure either, but what the hell!" He grabs my hand.

"Yes, and I'm loving being held, hugged and kissed, but you fell asleep last night so I'm judging that neither of us is ready for this to progress to sex."

"Again, a wee bit candid, but I like that and yep I if I'm honest you're right. I'd like to avoid the fear of more hurt by not becoming too involved. Do you fancy a night in Edinburgh this week? We could see a movie? You could stay over?"

"That sounds nice."

He confidently gets out of bed and struts naked towards the shower.

I stay Friday night in Phil's top-floor flat in the heart of Edinburgh but have to leave early Saturday morning, picking up a hire car to drive to meet my prospective new boss. "Will you call in on your way back?" Phil asks with a grin as I start the car.

"Can do!" I blow him a kiss. "Wish me luck!"

As I drive down country I examine our time together. It may not be passionate but it provides a new focus, and this time, we are both mature adults and it really matters to no one whether we are together. It is nice to have his company, I've enjoyed being out on a Friday night in Edinburgh. I'm not blown away in his presence, but when he kisses my neck lightly, I could imagine losing myself, so given time, maybe I might?

Exiting off the M62, I have to concentrate on the directions the Sat Nav is giving me. Arriving a little early, I meet Lesley, the woman I am replacing, in her front garden. She leads me inside to her clinic, which is in her home. I'm in a small village, just outside the peak district.

"Phil, guess what – I got the job!" It's an hour later and I have secured the six-month locum position. This begins mid-March and has effortlessly fallen into place. Margaret, I'm sure, would feel it destined.

"Congrats. I'll cook a special meal if you stop here on your return."

"I'd love to. I'll see you tomorrow when I get back from Josie's."

It's not a laborious run over The Peaks to reach Josie and I view it as a dry run for the next few months. I arrive earlier than anticipated. She answers the door with her hair still up in a towel, wispy blonde curls escaping from all directions. "So?"

"So – I got the job!"

She hugs me.

Over a cup of tea, I tell her about Phil. "I'm kind of seeing someone."

"Kind of?"

"I think we both recognise that we are temporary props for each other. His name is Phil and he lives in Edinburgh. He's extremely caring, consistent, and close to hand, but I don't find him all that sexy."

She screws up her nose.

"Sex isn't everything!"

"Hum! You don't think? I'll give it a couple of months then!"

"Ok – you could be right. I'm just entering this relationship with more realism and less excitement, Jos. His ex treated him terribly towards the end of their three-year relationship and he still hasn't completely recovered from her, so we're both a bit injured."

She nods, "If that's working for you, then fine. It's more than I have just now but I'm holding out for a good one this time."

"And," I say, "I think J.B. will rent my flat while I'm gone."

"What will Clare say? Have you seen her recently?"

"No, she never responded to my letter and I haven't seen her since. She is back in Crete for a time, so I am less concerned."

"Even so, Jen, are you sure?" She has pulled the towel of her head and is rubbing her hair dry.

"I feel less guilty that J.B. and I will be roommates for only half the week. It will be more sensible for someone to be in the flat while I'm away, paying me rent, and more agreeable for me not returning to an empty flat."

"True. You realise you'll have to learn to live with someone else. No more loud music and whisky-filled nights."

"I suppose so. I'm growing up, Josie. Are you proud?"

She thwacks me with the wet towel.

Sunday morning I travel up country back to Scotland. Phil greets me in Edinburgh in an apron.

"Dinner should be approximately thirty minutes. You drive fast, don't you?" Living in the city, he does not own a car and travel is where we differ enormously. Phil just isn't interested. His life and friends are in Edinburgh and when he has time off work, he is content to spend this with them. He plays the violin and seems to be constantly involved in performances around the city.

Due to this and our numerous commitments with friends, what we started settles into a twice-weekly assignation. We spend the weekend in Edinburgh, often out at gigs and Tuesday evenings at mine; the flames maybe lacking in volume, but I am content. Sunday mornings become bagels with cream cheese and salmon and fresh coffee brought to me in bed. We idle the morning away, reading Sunday newspapers and taking turns to bathe, as his bath too small for two, but we quite happily keep the bathroom door ajar and discuss his music collection as we work our way through it. It may not be a red-hot romance, but it is a close companionship, *(with enjoyable snogging!)* which both of us are benefiting from. It grounds me.

This short idyllic interlude continues only until I am due to begin my locum position, although in my memory it stretches out longer. Once I've got settled in the job and established a routine, I still plan to spend two nights a week staying over with Phil, one night prior to working from my flat and the next prior to journeying up to Dundee as I also got the eight-week contract there. It's working in a factory, treating the employees to help them give up smoking. Not fascinating work for me, but financially rewarding. So seeing Phil two nights a week doesn't feel as if much may change. There is none of the longing, excitement, or nervousness over waiting for phone calls that I experienced with Sid but none of the frustrations either.

"I'm happy to hire a car and drive you down to England the Sunday before you start the locum job if you'd like?" Phil suggests as I leave the previous weekend. He is so thoughtful.

I leave my flat with J.B. and calmly prepare for my next adventure. I have called Lesley, whom I'm to replace, to say that a friend will be driving me down and she offers Phil accommodation for the night, as we'll arrive fairly late.

We drive down together, sharing the driving. It's enjoyable and

I'm not apprehensive, so I am surprised the next morning how hard it is to let Phil leave. "It'll be fine" He attempts to put my mind at rest. "I bought you some gifts, and look a teddy bear, so you won't be lonely." He produces a traditional-looking brown bear.

I'm not really a teddy bear person, so no one has bought me one previously, so I am touched, if not a little bemused.

"How sweet! Thanks. I'll see you at the weekend." We have arranged that I will stay over in Edinburgh, when I drive back up the country to work in Scotland. He hugs me tenderly and sets off.

CHAPTER EIGHT

"I think your first day has been fine". Lesley has insisted that I shadow her so I can see how she works.

"I believe I've got a feel of your approach," I reply enthusiastically. She is more ordered than me and gives less of herself, but on the whole, our styles are similar. "The clients I met were interesting. I thought some of them were initially a bit suspicious of me. Do you think I'll win most of them over?"

"Yes, I don't foresee any problems. I think you'll be a suitable replacement." She smiles encouragingly.

"I'll do my best. If it's ok with you I'm going to head off for an evening stroll round the village up into the hills behind."

She nods.

I'm fatigued; I always find it tiring when someone is constantly observing my every move. Lesley is leaving tomorrow, but I need some time to myself sooner.

As I walk, I am full of anticipation of what these six months might hold. I am planning to spend more time with Josie and Aisling, both being an hour's drive away in opposite directions. Therefore, it won't always be the entire weekend I spend in Scotland, before my work there. I am not going to make the same mistake with Phil that I did with Sid, running to him every weekend. I don't feel the same level of neediness. Just knowing that he is there is reassuring enough. I suppose he is reliable, which Sid wasn't and already I have a far greater trust in his ability to ground me. Yes, at last everything seems to be panning out.

Ha, but life is never that easy! Returning, I turn my key in the latch and literally walk into Lesley's boyfriend and co-traveller.

"Hi, I'm Jen, I'm covering Lesley's practice," I say, offering him my hand.

He shakes my hand and says, "Jeff. Good to meet you."

"It's cold," I rub my arms. "I bet you are looking forward to getting away."

He nods. He's definitely not a conversationalist.

"Well, I've had a long day, so if you'll excuse me, I'm going to make a hot drink and a hot water bottle, before going upstairs for the night."

"Sure, help yourself," he indicates the kitchen. "Lesley has gone to bed early, with a headache. We will be leaving first thing, tomorrow morning."

"Have a nice time."

I take my time in the kitchen, unpacking my small box of foodstuffs and when I finally make my way up the stairs, the house is quiet and in darkness, so I turn off the downstairs light on my way up. I'm anticipating eight hours of quality sleep and a slow start tomorrow. Pushing open my bedroom door, I am aghast to witness my quilt moving. Not someone easily frightened, I look again to confirm movement. In the half-light are my eyes deceiving me? No, the quilt is definitely moving.

I am correct, and I stare open-mouthed, as Jeff emerges from beneath my quilt.

"I'm here to be your hot water bottle," he announces joyfully.

I don't quite take in what is occurring and stand, paralyzed in the doorway, my hand still gripping the door handle, my knuckles white. My chest feels constricted and my breath comes in gasps.

"Come on," he continues a little more sharply, "I hear you've had one relationship breakup and then you bring another man with you. I'm good for some!"

Shit! I hear no more, as my motionlessness passes. I tear down the stairs and sit, my legs shaking on a chair in the kitchen, against the closed door. I reach for my phone, still in my back pocket, and call Phil. *Please be there, please pick up!*

He answers immediately and listens patiently to my shocked account of what has befallen.

Instead of reacting with exclamation, disbelief and horror, he competently diffuses the situation, "Just ignore what's happened for the minute and tell me all about the rest of your day."

"But, Phil…" I try to say.

He talks over me quite firmly, "Just tell me, Jen. How were the clients? How many did you see? Do you have Leslie's approval?"

He knows there is nowhere else I can go. I do not yet have Lesley's car, I know no one in the village so I am effectively trapped in this house and cannot go to anyone for help. Therefore, he quickly assesses that the right approach is to disseminate the situation and enable me to cope with it.

I can't tell you how long I sit there in the chair in the kitchen, letting Phil's calm voice wash over me and erase the disturbing memory of the room above. *What kind of grave error have I made coming here?* My life does not seem to be getting any simpler. Jeff is in his mid-sixties and has not an ounce of handsomeness. *What wanton behaviour, with Lesley asleep in the adjacent bedroom!* I do wonder what she sees in him. What arrogance and opinion he must have of himself to even consider I might have accepted his offer. *Does he think I'm desperate? No, obviously that I'm just a slut with no taste!*

When Phil has listened carefully enough to assess my state of mind as no longer in panic, he tells me quietly, "I'm going to hang up and you need to go back upstairs to your room."

Before I can interrupt with a 'What if', he continues by saying, "He will not be there, just go in and lock the door. They are leaving first thing tomorrow. You do not need to see this weasel tomorrow. Call me again if you need to."

He does not let me question his assertion and just repeats the same statement when I try to insert a 'but.'

He is right. Nervously, I tiptoe up the stairs. My room is empty. Locking the door and pushing a chair against it, I climb under my quilt, hugging the now-lukewarm hot water bottle. Instead of lying with anxiety pummelling my stomach, I calmly sigh, shut my eyes, and sleep. It's been a long, first day. *Surely it can only get better!*

Phil is right – I don't see Jeff the next morning, but I do see

Lesley.

"I just need to run through some house trivia with you. Friday is trash day, Monday recycle." It is only at the end of these instructions that she turns to me and apologises for Jeff's behaviour last night.

"He was stoned," she flippantly comments. *As if that excuses him!* She says no more and I wonder what she believes transpired. *What must she make of his behaviour?* It's hardly an auspicious start to their six months living in the small space of a camper van together. She told me that this trip around Europe was to test their relationship, which from where I'm standing does not look very promising. I wonder again, what she can see in such a conceited jerk? How many other women will he try that rouse with on their journey?

I decide my best action is to get out until they've safely left. She hands me her car keys and I go to sign on at the local gym.

Back on a treadmill I settle down. I ponder more about relationships and how much some people (myself included) are prepared to endure, just to experience some closeness with another human being.

I feel that my relationship with Phil is at least honest. Neither one of us is really expecting it to blossom into much more than it is. I don't really think there is enough physical attraction present on either side and yet, we respect and care for each other. I probably would not refer to him as boyfriend; he would introduce me as his close friend. In that regard, we do not talk about a shared future, or make any stipulations about exclusivity. We decide to just keep living this way until it no longer works or until one of us meets someone else.

This is just as well, although, it does not make me feel any less guilty, two months later.

CHAPTER NINE

"If you're going to walk on thin ice, you might as well dance."

Still half-asleep, I try to jolt myself awake. I'm sprawled facedown with my left arm curled above my head. My eyes feel too heavy to open and I can feel myself being pulled back into a delicious sleep.

"Jenny, Jenny…" A soft voice penetrates my slumber.

I try to block it out but I can feel someone stroking my arm. *Go away! Let me sleep.* The sensation of someone touching me does not ease and finally I force my eyelids up. I see a flash of white light as I try to focus and then nothing. My befuddled brain attempts to make conclusions. *Where am?* Lifting my head slowly and focusing in the semi-darkness, my mind settles.

"You're in Lesley's bedroom, it's Sunday night." I squint to look at the clock, *"It's 4.25 a.m."* I groan. *Why am I awake?* Then I remember, only too clearly, the voice I heard and the sensation of someone stroking my arm and I shiver as a pang of fear shoots through me.

Jumping up and out of bed, I run round the house, checking there are no signs of intruders. My heart is thumping rapidly in my chest. *Nothing!* Lesley's home is large and I rattle around in it. It is dark and gloomy, so I spend as little time in it as I can. I am still not good being alone and now I'm completely spooked out.

Getting back into bed, dry-mouthed, I pull the quilt right up to my eyes and bury myself in it, not daring to move. I don't get back to sleep, instead straining to listen to the creaks and groans of the wind and other strange noises, which I'd prefer not to dwell upon.

Finally, the light of sunrise penetrates through the shadows and my heartbeat returns to its normal speed. I vow to spend as few nights here, as possible. I'll need to stay more nights with friends; I'll share myself around so I don't burden anyone. I'm hoping Lesley won't notice the additional mileage on her car. It's a clapped-out Ford Fiesta, so I'm not worrying much. I did tell her I would be driving up and down to Scotland, so I don't figure I should be too concerned.

As I sit, eating some breakfast a couple of hours later, I text round. My eyes are aching from lack of sleep.

Josie phones me back immediately. "Jen, why so early? - you woke me!"

"I'm sorry, I got a bit spooked in this huge house on my own."

"You need a roommate. But the locuming is going ok?"

"Yes, it's great. Lesley's clients are generally accepting of me and I don't find the work difficult." Already my memory of my experience in the night is fading. It's amazing how talking to another human being can make that happen. "There are a couple of people who present me with challenges – the woman too depressed to speak, and the girl with a speech impediment, whom I'm struggling to interpret."

"That really sounds like fun – not! Have you time to come over? You're working so hard."

"I know but that was the idea and I'm earning well, so that I can put some money away towards Aunt Cheryl's loan. The experience I'm getting by seeing so many people a week, here and in Scotland, is the equivalent to what it would take a normal person a couple of years to amass. But you know I'll always make time to come and see you."

"That all sounds good." She pauses and I hear her excitement as she tells me, "I have news!"

"What?"

"I've started seeing someone - A journalist I met in a local pub. It's all happened so fast. Really, since I saw you last."

"So tell me!"

"I'm really falling for this guy. He's always busy, but when we're together, it's consuming. He sometimes pops in when he knows I'm having my lunch hour here, to see me when Victoria's not around, and it makes my day."

"Great, it's about time! Does he treat you well? Is he a keeper?"

"He showers me with gifts as well as attention. It's lovely! I keep telling him not to buy me things but it's really nice!" she oozes. "So much better than the last tight, unmentionable toad."

"And?" I prod her for more information.

"I'm enjoying being in a relationship. It's great to have somebody I'm looking forward to seeing, and the sex is great!" She giggles.

"Good for you, you deserve it! Better than mine then," I joke.

One of Lesley's clients, admittedly one of the least mentally stabilized, is convinced that the house is haunted when I stupidly tell her of last night's experience and offers to perform an exorcism. I'm really not convinced it's that bad.

"Rubbish!" says Phil, who has not returned to visit, dismissing everything when I call him.

This is probably the most sensible approach. I spend about half of the week away, but have to sleep here the other half, so I'll try to quash any feelings I have that surface in the middle of the night and not dwell on night visitations from the supernatural.

"But apart from that all is well?" He asks

"Yep, not much happening, apart from driving, clients and gym – five sessions a week now. I don't have an ounce of fat on me. I've got rid of all my old trousers. They're all too baggy. Oh – how was the ceilidh gig Sunday night?

"Aye, great, loads of people up and dancing. My neighbour, Annie, was there. She stayed until the end and we had to share a taxi back because we got rather drunk. She fell over and into my arms." He pauses. "I stayed the night at hers."

He doesn't go into specifics and I don't question. *Perhaps I'd prefer not to know?* I'm angry and hurt.

Conveniently, the doorbell rings, announcing my next client so I just lodge the information at the back of my mind. *Should I make more of this?* We are just each other's props and we aren't in a relationship after all, but it stings a little and perhaps this is partly why I accept the next invitation I'm offered.

It arrives from someone I meet at the gym, which is no surprise really, as I have precious little time to meet anyone anywhere else. I have finished my time on the treadmill, stepper, and exercise mat and have pumped the free weights. I am heading in, after showering, to spend ten minutes in the Jacuzzi, luxuriating before heading back to work. He is already in the Jacuzzi with a mate, and apparently, getting an eyeful of me in a bikini is all that is needed to precipitate conversation. I see his eyes glance at my fingers, checking for a ring, before he begins chatting me up.

"You obviously train often, but I don't think we've met."

"No, can't say I've noticed you before," I reply confidently, "but I've only been at this gym a couple of months."

"I would have remembered had I seen you before," he grins at me, flirting.

"I'm not often here this late in the day, but I took a break from work. This Jacuzzi's the best bit!" I stretch out. I like the glint in his eyes.

"Sure is! It's necessary to ease those taut muscles. We come on our lunch hour," he says, indicating his friend. "Where do you work? We work in town."

"In the next village. I'm a self-employed hypnotherapist, currently locuming there."

"Wow! That's different!" he remarks, interested.

"Can you hypnotise people and make them do stupid things?" His friend leans forwards and interrupts.

"Why is it I always get the same questions, whenever I tell someone my occupation?" I sigh. "Yes, I reckon I could but that's rather frivolous. What I practice is serious hypnotherapy to help people overcome emotional issues they are struggling with. And yes, before you ask, 'does it really work?' of course it does. As if I'd still be doing it, and earning money from it if it didn't!" I pre-empt them both.

"Ooh, a little touchy, aren't you!" he laughs, lightly punching me on the arm and scowling at his companion.

"Just sick of the same typical comments!" I punch him back as his workmate apologises for his query.

We enjoy a witty flirtation together, as I answer all the same questions I've fielded for years regarding my work, until I turn the tables round and ask them their occupation.

"We don't tell people, it puts them off," friend says, "but we work in uniform."

"A lot of people like that," I joke with them.

"Especially my wife!" says friend.

"I'm currently single, so how do you fancy going out for a drink? Without the uniform!"

Having enjoyed his company and bravado, I say, "A naked date? It's a little cold." I pause and grin. "I think I could be persuaded, provided you have some clothes on."

"Righty oh! A fully-clothed drink at a pub – give me your number. "He climbs out the Jacuzzi. It is only at this point, as he is retrieving his phone, that I realise he stands at well over six foot tall, something that doesn't really work with a just-over-five-footer like myself.

"Tell me your number and I'll text you a time and a place for later this evening?"

I feel I can't really say I've changed my mind, because he's too tall. It's just a drink and I really haven't been out in the local area at all, so it's a good opportunity, so I provide my name and number.

"Call you later, gorgeous!" he flashes those eyes at me as he leaves.

"Bye, gorgeous!" mimics friend.

Once they've gone, I too get out, shower and dress, and as I'm coming through the foyer, I catch a glimpse of them both outside – Policemen. *That explains a lot!* This doesn't deter me, and when he texts later, I tell him to call for me at nine and suggest we go for a drink at a pub in the village. I am working until then, so have little time to reflect.

I later answer the door to his hesitant knock and walk with him to the nearest pub. Unfortunately it is a bit of a 'Slaughtered Lamb.' "(Think: American Werewolf in London)" It's the same in that, when we enter, the hubbub of noise immediately stops and all faces turn to stare at us. Well, this doesn't unnerve Plod, as I expect he is used to provoking this reaction, although more commonly, when he's in uniform. He proceeds to the bar and orders himself a drink and invites me to do likewise. As we settle at a small table with our drinks, most of the eyes have turned back to engage with their drinking companions and a low level background noise has been restored.

We banter with each other, as we had previously, and he tells me a little about himself. "I've been on the force since I was 18 and I've lived here all my life. I'm divorced. Have been three years. It's often a side effect of the profession, but I got married too young. We grew apart. How about you?"

"I'm just out of a long-term relationship," I tell him, while examining his sparkly brown eyes. "I'm not going to say much more about that!" I figure he doesn't need to know and right now, I don't want to think about it. "Tell me what there is to do out and about in the area?"

I am fairly relaxed in his conversation, and at the end of the evening am happy to agree to meeting with him again. We do not set a date and later, when I dissect the evening alone in bed, I wonder whether he meant it. He does not stoop to kiss me as he leaves me on the doorstep, nor do I take his hand or touch him. I'm not, *not* interested, just unsure, and Phil is also on my mind. I talk only to my brother about him, as I know Josie has a dislike of policemen – obviously it is a stopping point for some.

That weekend, at the end of March, I take my previously booked trip to Germany. Fortunately, as I'm now earning a decent amount, I am able to accompany my friend, Georgia and her husband Trent to a lovely restaurant, where we have truffles. Having not eaten these mushrooms before, Trent explains, "They are a delicacy in France and Italy but are now being found here, in Southern Germany. They think it's because of the climate change."

"Yes, supposedly it's getting warmer. Not that I feel that!" Georgia smiles.

We enjoy a cinema trip out and it isn't until the next day that Georgia and I have some time alone. We walk together into town along a long wide avenue. "Jen," she confides to me, "I never really liked Clive. He was very self-obsessed." She looks slightly uncomfortable as she waits for my reply.

"It's not a problem. Perhaps he was?" I beam at her. "It doesn't matter now. I've moved on, and I don't even want to talk about him anymore!" As I say this, I realise it's true and smile to Georgia and myself triumphantly.

In town, I especially enjoy browsing the markets and bring back some quality food items to share with Josie and Victoria. Again, on my journey home, I reflect and am truly grateful for my many friends. Some I may not see often, but when I do, I find it easy to fall back to where we left off.

As usual, I am back at Phil's the Monday afterwards and by then, I've almost conveniently forgotten about my drink with Plod and he hasn't been in touch since, so I don't mention it. He doesn't mention Annie.

Back at the flat, J.B. has installed a new handcrafted kitchen cupboard and has news that a friend of his would like to rent the other room. We therefore, spend most of my time there, discussing the necessities needed and the probability of this being a success. I catch up with Paul and go to the theatre with him on the Tuesday night. We sit up late, evaluating whether Match.com is a good way of attracting a partner. Paul is not convinced about online dating, but is thinking about it. I encourage him to do so and it is not until the drive back down the country, that I hear from Plod again.

My phone vibrates just as I reach the outskirts of Preston, I glance at the text message from him, inviting me over for the night. *Oh, my God!* I almost slam into the back of the car in front of me as I read it twice, to make sure I've registered it correctly. Fortunately, I've left a large enough stopping distance between my car and the nearest vehicle, but this does illustrate why using a phone while driving is not incredibly bright. *Just as well, he's not in the next lane in a police car then!* When I reach Lesley's, fortunately just prior to the first evening client, I call my brother and read him the text. He just concludes, "What have you got to lose? Just text back: 'See you later.'"

I do it.

With trepidation and undoubting daring, later that evening, I dress somewhat provocatively and make my way to his address.

"Hi," he says. "Nice dress!"

"Hi," I say. "Nice house!"

His home is modern and masculine, sporting expensive-looking gadgets and LED lighting. He fixes me a drink while I examine his CD collection.

"Interesting choice of music."

"See anything you like?" he shouts through from the kitchen. I pull out a couple of CDs. "There's a few. It's mainly dance music. Do you go out clubbing often?"

"Most weekends if I'm not working, actually to the club next to the gym. I'll burn you a MP3 compilation for the car," he offers.

As I pick a few tracks and he assembles them on the computer, he shows me a photo of his son and tells me a little about his ex-wife. We resume the flirtatious comments, as he offers me another drink. Agreeing, he goes through to the kitchen and I follow him through. The work surface is a spotless, shiny marble, onto which he lifts me up with one hand, *(these big guys!)* and starts snogging me. *Well he's not a Sid!* So I let it happen and I do stay the night and although there isn't electricity, there is passion, and it's about time I had a dose of that. He is consumed by my body and runs his fingers expertly down my spine, creating all manner of shivery reactions. The sex is indulgent and I finally switch off my head and let my body take over.

Next morning, he laughs as he presumes that I did not bring a change of clothes and that I'll be sneaking out of his house, in its residential area, in last night's outfit. However, I'm not that stupid, so I guess I was prepared. I thank him as I leave, but as I drive away, watching to see if the neighbourhood curtains are twitching, I don't feel too much. Maybe this was a rite of passage, something else to propel me forward. It's been fun and I so needed to lose myself in someone else. I feel a real fondness for him, as I pop the CD into the car player, but somehow, I don't think either of us will be phoning each other soon. Some things are what they are and I'm guessing I've just participated in my first ever one-night stand, (although technically this is the second time I've seen him), so I'm not sure this fits the definition. It's not something I've ever done before, so I presume it's another tick on my list of firsts. I can't help but smile as I drive back.

When I get back to Lesley's, there's a message on the landline from Phil and I see I also have a two, missed calls on my phone. "I know you must be there, because where else would you be?" he says with a laugh. "Och! Can you call me when you get this?"

Now I do feel guilty and know we will have to discuss our friendship and decide if it has boundaries.

CHAPTER TEN

"Don't let yesterday use up too much of today." Native American Cherokee Proverb

"I think we need to talk." Phil looks slightly embarrassed so I nod in agreement to encourage him.

I have also saved my confession until we are face-to-face. I don't really feel guilty. Plod hasn't called, so I convince myself there's not a lot to talk to Phil about. Physically, things haven't progressed at all between Phil and me. We are close friends who sleep in the same bed twice a week more for convenience and companionship. It is not the definition of a romantic relationship.

"I love our friendship, but that's all it is. I dinnae think either of us wants any more – am I right? I've kind of cooled off with the physical stuff. Have you not noticed?"

Again, I nod to allow him to carry on speaking despite that I've only thought about it a minute ago. *Too busy with other things!*

"While I am quite happy with our friendship the way it is," he pauses, touching his hair, "I've been aware of someone at work who I'm interested in knowing better." He glances away a little awkwardly, before adding, "Aye, although I'm quite content for you to continue staying over with me here, if all went well with her, then obviously you couldn't." He looks into my eyes.

Now is when I should say something, but I falter and just reply, "That's fine. I understand." Either, I feel guilty or I feel embarrassed. *Perhaps both – or am I just a horrible person?* By anticipating something with her before anything has occurred, his behaviour is morally superior to mine. I try to justify my actions to myself, by imagining what might have or not, occurred with Annie. I ponder if perhaps it's about the same, so I don't confess to my night with Plod. *Am I ashamed or do I just want to keep it to myself? Or is it not important?* As he has broached the subject, it would have been easier for me to continue the discussion. I miss my opportunity.

"Och, what if we keep things as they are, as neither of us is seeing someone else yet, then you can continue to stay over in the short term?"

"I'd like that. It's more practical than anything else and I'd miss you otherwise." I smile at him and he moves forward to hug me.

"It'll help us both avoid loneliness. We can remain friends, can't we?" He's asking because he knows my history. I don't keep in touch with previous boyfriends, preferring to cut off and move on. As I never really classed Phil as a boyfriend, this isn't an issue. "Of course and I'd like to still see you. I think you've helped me a lot, Phil. Thank you."

"Aye, I could say the same of you."

My contract at Dundee completes at the end of April, meaning I no longer have to stay in Scotland that extra night anyway. Normally my choice would have been to, rather than stay an additional night in the house from an episode of Scooby Doo, but I'm sure I can find another solution. Journeying back to England, I am deciding how I could fill that extra time, a Wednesday evening and Thursday morning.

I don't have to cogitate on this long, as waiting on Lesley's doormat, in a work publication, is my solution. In the situation's vacant column, is an advert for a new start position, working in a podiatrist clinic across the Peak District, on the other side of the M62. Taking this position would justify a once a week trip east, when I could spend some time with Josie. My mind flits back to when I had the longing to be moving into the flat with her and Victoria and living with them. That was not so long ago and here I am contemplating working in the same city and planning to stay over one night a week. *How life twists and turns!*

On Friday evening, I drive over and visit Josie. Victoria is away in London for the weekend, which is probably easier. I can confess to my out-of-character, yet salubrious night with Plod, reflect on my relationship-now-friendship with Phil, and ask Josie's advice regarding the new start position. However, she has news of her own to impart, which renders my news and dilemmas much further down the discussion list.

She opens the door to me in tears. "Jen," she cries, falling into my arms. "The bastard is married!"

"What!"

"My guy, my journalist. That's why he was always so busy and couldn't always see me. He told me he refereed football matches at the weekends but really, he was just with his family." She pulls me inside.

"Family?" I'm bewildered.

"Yes," she raises her voice. "He has a family; a wife and a daughter – and a pregnant wife at that!"

"Josie, I'm so sorry," I reply. What is it we do to attract men that behave this way? "Let me put the kettle on and tell me how you found out." We walk into the kitchen, Josie snivelling.

"A friend of a friend at work knows his wife, and when my friend mentioned me, put two and two together."

"What did he say when you told him that you knew?"

Josie stands forlornly leaning against the kitchen door, wringing her hands, "That he was sorry, but still wanted to see me! I told him there was no way I could entertain continuing to do so, despite how much I might want to. He didn't see why not and said he wasn't close to his wife. She's a marketing manager, very busy. There is no way I can see him now. Jen, he has a daughter and his wife is pregnant. How could he do that?"

I have no answer for her and can only try to soothe her hurting heart.

"I feel sick to the stomach about deceiving his wife and child, despite not knowing," she continues, clearly anguished. "I drove round to his address last night. I sat in my car down the road and waited, and I saw them. His daughter is only little, about three. She was with her mother and I watched them get out of their car and go inside. It was awful. They looked really lovely. How could he treat them like that?"

"And you!" I say indignantly. "He's treated you just as badly, Jos."

"But she's pregnant. I could see. I didn't sleep and I've not eaten. I feel too sick."

I guide her to the table and place the mug of steaming hot tea in her hand. "Try to drink."

She takes a sip. "I really liked him, Jen. See what happens when I relax my guard and give into how I feel?"

I spend the weekend mopping up her tears and supporting her in her decision to end the relationship. She has really fallen for this guy, so it won't be unchallenging.

On Saturday, I find time to locate the podiatrist clinic on a map and arrange an informal meeting with the owner. Josie agrees to drive me over, despite it being an area she does not know. It'll take her out of herself, she states. It is a short, but fraught journey. I'm not the most able navigator and Josie is not in the best frame of mind. We have to turn around twice on the ring road, before we finally recognise the right turning off. All goes well when I arrive at the podiatrist's and I agree to return later that week, to meet with the remainder of the staff, anticipating a start date later in the month. I am enthusiastic and am standing on top of yet another precipice, before leaping into a further new venture. Exciting times are ahead.

It's hard leaving Josie that weekend as I feel her misery. I promise to return midweek and stay over with her. This is the first guy she has let in, since being betrayed previously, and look what has happened. *Why do we bother?*

Returning to Lesley's, I suffer a 'I told you so' the following weekend. Josie is going home to stay with her mum for the weekend and I was due to meet Mark for a meal. When the plans fall through last minute, as he is unwell, I foolishly do not make new ones. I find myself alone at the 'Scooby Doo' house on a Saturday night. The dark dankness of the house envelops my mood and desolation floods in. I grab the whisky bottle and turn the stereo up, and in my desperation at 2 a.m., I text Plod. His reply, "Who is this?", says it all. He has already deleted me as a contact. I'm not really surprised and I don't stoop so low as to reply. However, in my current state of mind, I exaggerate the situation in my head and drink far too much whisky.

The next morning, I open the door to the neighbour.

"I am here to complain about the volume of your music last night," he begins, "It was unacceptable, and when I called round to speak with you about it, you did not even hear me knocking!"

Big whoops!

I apologise emphatically.

His anger diminishes somewhat, when he sees how swollen my face is from the multitude of tears cried.

"I was really upset, but I know that is no excuse. I promise it won't happen again." I grovel as I watch him leave.

Indeed it shouldn't! That was a real backward step and I admonish myself for it severely. It is time I stopped that habit.

Finally, I have reached that point and I resolve to cut my drinking down. It's time I evolved past using whisky as my support. I need to function without a prop. I also promise myself to avoid any nights alone at Lesley's. Her house is clearly not hospitable, and while I recognise I should be able to spend a Saturday night without company, perhaps this is not the ideal location, in which to do so.

It has now been nine months since the night Clive left. In some ways, I feel I have journeyed so far, and look back on that time, as such a distant past. Yet, other times I can reach out and feel those waves of emotion, wrapping around my heart and squeezing. There is still rawness under the newly grown layer of skin and it is still too easy to penetrate, but I'm shrugging off the past and the hurt. Congratulations are in order. I'm still here – alive on the planet. I haven't jumped or slipped off the ledge and I am slowly building a new life for myself. It was never going to be easy, and still won't be, but by hanging on to some of my past, I am learning to embrace a 'new present.' And my 'new present' overall is good. My work is going extremely well, as are my finances and friendships. I am now able to wake up each morning anticipating a new day and can get up with enthusiasm for forthcoming events.

Looking further ahead to my future is harder, but I am beginning to take steps towards that direction. I cannot possibly predict what will happen, the positive experiences, which I will grow from, the mistakes I will make, (and hopefully learn from), the paths I will take, but at least I can envision some sort of moving forward. My wonderful friends are there, by my side when I require support and I only hope that I can offer them the same consistently loyal friendships they have shown me.

A month later, I start two days a week working near Josie's, staying only one night a week with Phil. I still share his bed (he only has one bedroom, so it's easier) but we are just friends. He has a wonderful knack of putting things into perspective and I find him a useful sounding board for any new ideas I come up with. He enjoys my company and I'd like to think I've helped him move forward from his last relationship. Last weekend we both signed up to an online dating site. It was great fun writing each other's profiles, joking, and taking photos to put up. When I return I try to persuade Josie to do it as well, but she isn't interested.

"I'm not ready yet," she sighs emphatically. "I'm still grieving for all that could have been and I'm too scared of being hurt another time."

I totally understand this, of course. We are sitting in the park, near the children's playground. Watching everyone else play 'happy family' isn't something I'm fond of doing often, but Josie has a compulsive addiction to this, despite my view of it as unnecessary torture.

"One day that'll be me." Her voice is full of longing.

"I know." I grasp her hand. "I can't imagine you not having a family, but me, I'm not sure I want kids."

"Have to find Mr. Right first. Need a guy with healthy morals and no wife!"

"Yes, and fully equipped, no missing bits!" I add, laughing.

"Jen, do you know what? If I don't find anyone, I'm going to do it on my own. My desire for a child is greater than my desire for a man."

"Really? Could you?"

"Yes, I've been researching it just in case. I think it's something I could do," she continues seriously. "Don't look at me like that. I know it wouldn't be easy, and it's obviously not my first choice. Not finding the right man will not deny me motherhood. If it has to be a sperm bank, so be it!"

I take a deep breath. "Okay I'm listening. You're serious, aren't you?"

She nods.

"Well, I'm happy to be an auntie, to be by your side through it, but I've no experience. I don't think I'll have any children. That's not an issue for me. I wouldn't be brave enough to have a child on my own and any desire I might harbour to have one isn't that great."

"Do you think I'm mad?"

"No, I think you're Josie. Something'll work out. You never know who you'll meet around the next corner!"

She grins and gets up, linking her arm in mine. "Come on! Let's go find out!"

I have learnt to recognise the fear residing quietly in that hidden area of my mind *(remember that?)* I'm surrendering to it. I am beginning to believe that 'it will be ok' and that things do fall into place, if I allow them to. I believe they will for Josie, too. Perhaps, there are reasons that certain events occur, some people graze in and out of our lives, relationships don't work out, and opportunities appear. I could just be making connections and over-philosophising about patterns in life, when there are none. *Who am I to know? Is there such a thing as destiny?* I think, maybe, there could be. I know this is a minor consideration with which to put forward the argument that fate might exist. But, I have been driving way over the speed limit, up and down the country (even in a clapped-out Ford Fiesta). Yet, despite passing numerous speed cameras, I haven't once got a fine or had an accident. *Now, does that seem likely?* Luck, (maybe fate) has certainly been with me. To me, it feels a little like karma, just as I believe Clive received his, this is a little reward for all I have endured – I shouldn't push it too far. Of course, now that I have recognised it and admitted it, I should endeavour to kerb the tendency to put my foot down too heavily while driving. *Who knows – literally – what is just around the corner?*

CHAPTER ELEVEN

"We become what we contemplate." Plato, Greek Philosopher 428-348 B.C.

It's a warm June evening and I'm sitting on the step to Lesley's home, laptop on my knees, answering emails. I'm about halfway through when *ding!* – a new one appears in my inbox. It's from the online dating site. I'm no longer expectant when I recognise this as I've learnt that there are many desperately sad, single men out there. Who only knows why they chose the photos they did to sit alongside their drab list of hobbies and requirements. You would think someone would pick an attractive-looking photo of himself to set up in front of a potential partner, but no, this doesn't appear to be obvious to most of these men. As a result I've got used to declining most of the invitations I've received. Phil and I have been keeping a tally. He's doing far better than I am, and has met up with a few women. The first reply I opened was from George, age 57, balding with a huge belly, whose main interest in life was growing potatoes. I rest my case.

Therefore, I'm a little surprised when the email I've received turns out to be from somebody who appears half decent. He's a pharmacist, living about forty minutes' drive from here. He's dark-haired, brown-eyed with a cocky grin, looks fairly sporty and he's not too tall. After finishing with my remaining correspondence, I shoot back a reply. *Well, it doesn't look to appear too keen!*

We exchange a few emails to and fro, before arranging to meet for dinner the following Saturday. I still have few expectations but have resolved not to hide myself away. Having finished with the computer for the night I shut it down and head upstairs. *Brr!* Why is it that old houses are always colder inside than out? It's a pleasant balmy June evening and yet, re-entering the house, I'm chilly. Electing to have a hot shower before bed, it's only as I close up the house for the night that I realise I've missed a call from Adam. "Coincidence or what?" I whisper to myself, because Mr. Pharmacist has arranged to meet me at a restaurant literally a few streets away from where Adam lives.

The message is an invitation for a drink with a few of his friends for his birthday. I have seen him only once since Aisling's hen party weekend. Again he seemed very accommodating and competent and, yet still there was a slight shyness. His birthday celebration is at a local pub on Friday. *Well, that sorts out my weekend then!*

Strangely enough on my return to Scotland, I meet Kyle coming out of the alleyway just as I'm entering. He takes a step backwards as he greets me enthusiastically, "Hey, stranger, how are you?"

"Good," I reply genuinely. "How about you?"

"Fine, I'm just off to the cinema in Edinburgh with Nancy. She'll be sorry she's missed you. Are you staying long?"

"Just today and tonight then I hit the road again." I grin. "I have a busy life," I joke, and add, "I'm going to see your brother at the weekend."

"For his birthday?" he asks, yet continues without an answer. "We've all got together and paid for him and his girlfriend to go to a concert at The Apollo in Manchester on Saturday so I think he's out with friends on the Friday." He is talking about the band and their support but I don't hear. *Girlfriend? Since when was there a girlfriend?* I'm trying not to appear shocked and having an internal debate with myself as to why I felt a pang of disappointment and why this matters to me. Kyle is waffling on and doesn't see my glazed-over eyes. I only hear when he says, "She's only 17, a neighbour I think, I don't know how he manages it!"

I endeavour to draw the conversation to an end and succeeding, extract myself from his gaze. Hurriedly, I sprint up the stairs to the doorway. My stomach is turning just a little as I recognise I must have had some feelings for this guy.

Another surprise meets me inside. Joiner boyfriend too has a new companion. He is kissing her goodbye as I appear. He pulls away from her to introduce me. "Och! This is Jen, ma landlady, Jen, this is Stefani." A student from Cyprus studying at the University, she too is a lot younger than him. Small-framed and petite, she smiles adoringly up at him. *What is it with men and younger women?*

That Friday I decide it must be a physical thing, as in my opinion, Tracey, the girl Adam introduces me to, has nothing else going for her.

"Hi," she mutters quietly. She is tall, slim and defensive and keeps tossing her long brown hair over her shoulders with a scowl on her face. She is everything I'm not, and when I speak to her directly, she has little conversation or knowledge and she seems quite hostile towards me. "Huh! Maybe," seems to be her main line of dialogue.

Having met some of Adam's male friends previously, I spend the evening joking with them. When the pub closes, we all walk back to his flat for coffee. I casually arrange to stay at one of his friends' on a sofa bed, but Adam interjects, "No, you can sleep over in my bedroom, I'll sleep in the living room, as on previous occasions."

I give in to his insistence. Tracey is going home. It's late so I don't argue. My mind is befuddled by alcohol.

The next morning the dog awakens me as usual. Getting more confident, I push past her, shower, and go through to the kitchen. I help myself to some coffee percolating on the side as Adam enters. He prepares us omelettes while we chat about the previous evening and the concert tonight.

"Thanks for coming over for my birthday," he begins tentatively. "I'm sorry I've not been in contact for a while. It's been busy at work."

"And things have changed a bit," I reply, alluding to Miss 17.

He feigns misunderstanding.

"Your girlfriend!" I finally have to announce.

"Tracey? She's just a neighbour, us getting together was a mistake." He stoops to fuss over the dog. I decide not to delve into that reply. As far as I know they are still attending the concert together tonight, so instead I tell him, "I have a blind date tonight. We're eating at the Italian round the corner."

"Really?" He turns from the sink, where he is washing his hands.

I can tell I've surprised him.

"I joined an online dating agency. It's been hilarious. You would not believe some of the emails I've received or some of the ugliest-looking men who've sent them." As I warm to my story, the conversation becomes easier and equilibrium is re-established.

"Tell me more!"

"I've been hounded by some very dubious characters, men who want only to take me to weird venues, like cemeteries to watch for U.F.O.s or others that just want to talk about growing potatoes, but it's been a laugh! It's fairly easy to weed out the crazies!"

"Potatoes?"

"Yes, you'd be amazed by some people's pastimes!"

"This guy tonight – is he obsessed by vegetables too?" The oil sizzles in the pan.

"He seems fairly sane actually, which is why I thought I'd meet him. We've chatted over email and I don't have anything to lose so I thought I'd just try it."

"What if he's as boring as hell and you have to sit through a whole meal with him?"

"The food there is supposed to be excellent, so I'll manage," I counter, grinning as he passes me the first omelette.

"It is. We'll have to eat there sometime. Tonight, just be safe," he says, "I know one of the waiters who works there, Antonio. Look out for him and say hello. I'll tell him the score and get him to keep an eye out." Seeing my face, he adds jokingly, "It doesn't hurt to have someone as back up. You never know if this guy is a serial killer!"

"Okay, go ahead," I concede gracefully.

"You're welcome to crash here if you don't want to drive afterwards. I won't be back till late but I'll give you a key."

"If you're sure?" I query and receiving his nod, say, "Cheers! I'd really appreciate that if you don't mind."

The omelette is delicious, but then so it should be, cooked by a professional chef. After a leisurely breakfast, we take the dog out for a long walk and chat amicably about life, Kyle, and his family. Tracey appears on our return, still scowling, and I excuse myself and go into the city to amble through the shopping centre. When I return later, armed with several purchases, they have left and I let myself in with the key.

As it is now summer and a pleasant evening, I choose to wear a sleeveless mid-calf length dress and take a wrap this evening. The restaurant is well within walking distance and I enjoy a nice stroll to it. The area is one of the upcoming, fashionable ones with plenty of restaurants, emitting gorgeous stomach-stimulating aromas as I walk past. I have planned to arrive five minutes later than the allotted time, hopefully so I will not find myself sat alone at the table waiting. I acknowledge Antonio as I enter and his colleague takes me through to Mr. Pharmacist's booked table. He is there, already seated, perusing the menu and stands up to greet me. Yes, he's attractive.

"So your photo wasn't adjusted!" I smile.

"Nor yours!" he retorts, shaking my hand. "What can I order for you to drink?" He swiftly summons the waiter over and places an order. He appears mature and experienced as he tells me about his last couple of days and his life story. "I have two children, one boy and one girl. I have them every other weekend. I was divorced three years ago and now I'm looking for someone to share my life with."

"I'm not there quite yet," I state honestly. "I'm only eleven months out of a long-term relationship and I'm not at the settling down stage just yet. I'm re-living my youth a little, catching up on some of the things I missed the first time, but I suppose if I met the right person I could be persuaded." He smiles and I witness the cocky grin, which drew me to his photo on the site, as he announces, "Too early to be talking about that yet, seeing as you've only just laid eyes on me. Tell me, what you enjoy doing?"

We spend a pleasant evening and the reviews were right, the food is delectable. As we pay the bill – I insist on paying half – he invites me back to his home. I acquiesce and only realise that maybe I'm being foolish, as I'm sat in the passenger seat of his car headed to 'I do not have a clue' where. I have my phone, right? But, who is there to call should I require assistance?

When we arrive at his suburban home, he ushers me through to the garden. Lighting the outside patio heater and a candle at the small mosaic table on his outside deck, he delves back into the kitchen to fetch me a drink. His garden overlooks parkland and we enjoy the view over more conversation. I do not observe time passing, as his company is comfortable. Although not instantly drawn to him, I admit to myself that I could quite like him and that tonight could have been a lot worse. He seems happy with me and I notice he keeps touching my arm as we talk. It isn't much longer before he leans over and kisses me. Again, I wouldn't describe my response as hesitant, but neither is it exuberant. Finally pausing to glance at the time, he acknowledges, "It might be easier if you stay the night."

I'm shocked to see that it is past one.

I've now had several drinks so I shouldn't drive," he says, stroking my arm.

I concede it would be easier and send a text message to Adam saying that I won't be back until the morning.

"This is not normally something I'd do on a first date," Mr. Pharmacist admits. He seems keen to accelerate things, despite telling me that, but I stop him, admitting, "I'm tired and would prefer to sleep."

"Not a problem!"

I share a bed with him and fall asleep next to him only – it's a good experience.

In the morning we wake late, me wondering where the hell I am. *I really have become a slapper!* He has to go to watch his son's football match, so we both have to rush to get up so that he'll be there on time.

"I don't introduce my children to anyone I've met unless I know it's going to be long-term. I wouldn't want them to invest in someone who wasn't going to stick around."

"I can understand that."

"I'll drop you near the restaurant if that's okay," he says happily, "and I'd like very much to see you again. It was a good evening!"

"Phone me midweek, when I'm back from Scotland," I reply with a smile. "I'll know more what I'm doing then."

He drops me as promised and I stroll back to Adam's flat, undergoing internal debate: *What do I think of Mr Pharmacist? Do I like him? Do I want to see him again? I'm not sure! I don't seem to have been sure of anyone since Sid. I think Sid was just the end of a famine, which was why I wanted him so much. So I don't know what I feel. What about Adam?* But I dismiss that – he has a girlfriend, despite his portrayed reluctance.

Not knowing what I'll find inside, I knock rather than use the flat key. I don't fancy walking in on him and Tracey in the bedroom. There is no reply and after a long wait to ensure no one is in fact inside, I let myself in. There is coffee in the pot and a note, held to the fridge with a magnet depicting the Cheers bar in Boston.

It reads: "Out with the dog, help yourself to coffee."

I help myself to a shower and throw on my jeans. I'm just pouring a coffee when they return. It is just Adam and the dog, no Tracey.

"Good night?" he grins, possibly smirking slightly. I'm not sure.

"Ah, yes," I reply hesitantly. I'm a little ashamed of my late night text, which implicates me in a far steamier or even squalid night, than was actually the case. "I wasn't conscious that it had got so late. By then it was easier to just stay over." I'm aware that having said this, I'm digging myself in deeper. I can feel my face getting warmer so I turn away, putting my coffee cup on the workbench, as I quickly question, "How was the concert?"

"It was brilliant," he enthuses, "I thoroughly enjoyed it. It was a great birthday present." As he rhapsodizes over the music and extols the virtues of the lighting and atmosphere at the Apollo, I watch him. I like his genuineness and the excitement I see reflected in his eyes.

CHAPTER TWELVE

"One chance is all you need."

It's midweek and I'm in Scotland. Phil has been only too keen to hear about my date with Mr. Pharmacist. "So will you see him again?" he asks teasingly.

"I want to say yes, but I'm not sure," I reply frankly. "The evening was…" I pause, searching for the right adjective…"nice, agreeable?"

"Och! That doesnae sound good enough, Jen."

"Okay, well better than agreeable, but I'm not sure," I say, shaking my head. "He's texted me every day since, and I think that's putting me off."

Phil laughs. "I think you like your freedom too much!"

"Nothing wrong with that! He's a little too keen and I think ultimately he's looking for a new wife and stepmother. I'm finding that a little daunting… actually a lot daunting!"

Again, talking with Phil is illuminating and via his probing, I acknowledge that I'm not comfortable with the barrage of attentiveness from Mr. Pharmacist. *Another one bites the dust!* I'm thinking.

Driving back to Lesley's house, as if to prove me right, my phone vibrates in my back pocket. Stopping at the services I listen to an exuberant voicemail from Mr. Pharmacist. "I'm having a special barbecue on Saturday and I'm phoning to invite you," his voice is warm and ebullient. "I'd love to introduce you to all my friends. I'm sure you'd get on really well with them." My heart is thudding as straining to listen against the roar of motorway traffic, I pick up his words very clearly. "I thought maybe you'd like to stay the night and we could do something together on Sunday. Perhaps we could walk in the countryside or take a trip into Harrogate? You can decide. Just call me tonight and let me know what you think." His buoyancy scares me, as does his parting comment, "I didn't believe I'd meet someone like you over the Internet. I can't wait to see you again!"

Now I am sure. My stomach is definitely somersaulting, but it's not with excitement – it's with dread. I know I have to make the call now. I don't share his elated feelings and I cannot hurt him by letting him think I might. With a sigh and a deep breath I make "the call."

When I'm leaving Josie's later in the week, she praises me for letting him down so immediately. "It's not good to string people on," she comments, catching my eye. "I don't think you were quite in the same place as him, were you?" she giggles. "How about you, Victoria, and me go out on Friday – a girly night? I need some cheering up." She nudges me, "Let's forget men for a while!"

"Sure, Jos, let's do that!"

The same day, I receive a text from Adam.

"Wondered if you want to go into the city Saturday night with whole gang?"

A Saturday, and another gathering with his friends? I have no plans yet. I'm going to say yes.

It's a hard week. Driving over to Josie's on Friday, I allow myself some time to reflect. I would probably benefit from a quiet night in, but am I ready for that? Perhaps my running around up and down the country is finally tiring me out. I'm aware how wrong it is from a therapist's point of view. Living on my adrenaline for so long will deplete my adrenal glands, raise my cortisol levels, and long-term that could affect my sugar absorption. Shrugging to myself, I figure I'll have time to deal with this later. I am still allowing myself time to move on with my life and I can run for a little longer and hopefully be okay. I'm happy where I am. *How unbelievable to hear myself acknowledge that! Life is so full of wondrous possibilities!* It is coming up for a year now and while I'm aware of the anniversary date lodged quietly at the back of my mind, I don't want to make too big a thing of it. I am moving forward with a quiet determination and healthy confidence. *He* did not take that much from me and *he* would not recognise the person I now am, and that's both physically and emotionally. I feel like a completely different individual. In the mirror I see a strong, defiant, and confident woman whom others find attractive and like to be in the company of. For that, I will be forever grateful and resolutely proud. I have worked hard to achieve this. I'll just enjoy what I have and leave myself free to encounter whatever comes my way. A fully-jammed weekend stretches out before me. I lean over and turn up the stereo volume and smile.

I enjoy the Friday evening. Victoria and Josie greet me warmly. Their flat is my home away from home. We chat avidly while getting ready to go out. Josie is still not her old self but is attempting to be, which is good enough for us. We go into town for a Chinese meal before visiting a couple of bars and then grab a taxi home. We remain chatting together at the kitchen table until past midnight, at which point we retire for the night.

On Saturday, Josie and I drive to the other side of town to a store she wants to show me. I'm surprised when she pulls off down a side street and parks the car.

"What are we doing?" I ask, already half afraid of the answer.

She looks at me pensively and states, "That's his house."

"Who – 'journalist wife-cheater?'"

"Yes," she whispers, and I can see she is close to tears. "I know I shouldn't come here and I know I'm just torturing myself but …" she trails off.

"But, what?" I quietly encourage her.

"But it could have all been so good." She pulls absent-mindedly at one of her curls.

"But it wasn't, Jos!" I take her hand. "He wasn't who you thought he was."

"I know," she says, whimpering. "I really thought… well, you know."

She cries on me and there isn't much I can say or do except sit quietly with her. After she has cried it out, she leans her head on my shoulder. She looks straight ahead through the car windscreen as she says, "I've made an appointment at a Fertility Clinic. I wondered if you'd come with me? It's in two weeks' time."

I squeeze her hand. "You know I will."

She smiles.

"Come on, let's get out of here!" I say, giving her a nudge. "I'll treat you to a big slice of carrot cake at the deli."

I'm late arriving at Adam's, as to be honest I'm not sure about leaving Josie. Victoria has left to spend the weekend in London, and although Josie swears she'll be fine, I'm not so sure. This whole episode has hit her hard and she refuses to accompany me. As I pull up in front of his flat, I can see his friends coming out. "Hey, wait for me!" I shout over.

"We'd given up on you," someone cries.

I quickly grab my purse and keys and leap out of the car. Adam is locking up. There are four guys and me.

"What, no Tracey?" I enquire of them.

"Who's Tracey?" questions one of the guys, laughing. "Tracey is…" and he makes a throat slitting action and whispers, "…that was never going to last!"

"What are you two gossiping about?" asks Adam, walking over to where we are stood.

"Nothing!" replies his friend. "Are we going or what?" He heads off up the street and we follow. Turning he cries, "There's a taxi, run!"

All squashed in together, we are soon on our way. "Any more Internet dates then, Jen?" asks another of his friends.

"Who told you about that?" I'm glad it's dark in the car and they can't see my face. The redundant question goes unanswered, so I add, "That last guy was a little too serious, but the restaurant was great and the food was good."

"Did you make him pay for it?" one of them asks.

"No," I reply, insulted. "As a guy, wouldn't you have thought I owed you something if I'd done that?"

My comment starts a whole debate, which continues until we reach the first bar. The noise of the music pumping forth, disables any more conversation.

After purchasing pricey drinks, we grab a table and a couple of sofas expediently, as their previous occupants get up to go. I am enjoying being the only female in the group. The guys seem to have accepted me – I am, however, slightly self-conscious as I get up to buy the next round of drinks as I figure someone's eyes will definitely be on my arse, clad tightly in stretchy material. *Well, they're men out on the pull, and although I may be part of their group, I'm presumably still fodder!* Trying to forget that as I return, I wonder what the plan is. I really don't think I can tolerate this bar too much longer as my throat is already feeling raw from having to shout a conversation. I settle back onto the sofa, squashing myself in comfortably between its arm and Adam. He is talking to his friend on the other side so I lean backwards and take a sip of my drink. The bar is heaving, mainly with people much younger than me, but I'm in the centre of the city and it's a Saturday night. I allow myself to people-watch. I'm feeling surreal, as if I am within the eye of a hurricane, when Adam turns and leans towards my ear. "Are you okay?"

"Sure!" I shout back. "It's just so loud in here."

"We'll move on somewhere else after this round," he yells, picking up his beer. I just nod and watch as he downs the bottle. I'm slightly surprised at this, but guess that he either wants to leave quickly or aims to get drunk. I know that the intention is to go to a club and that some men have to imbibe fairly large volumes of alcohol to even contemplate dancing. Perhaps he's one of those. As I'm pondering this, I realise he is trying to say something to me. *Obviously, something that required alcohol first!* It really is hopeless – I don't hear a word. I imagine it'll be the same in the club. I shrug at him and mouth, "What?"

He leans towards my ear and starts shouting into it. Even then I can only just hear him so I bend in closer. I am aware of his breath tickling my ear and neck as I hear him bellow, "I wanted to talk to you."

You sure picked an inappropriate location, I think to myself. However, our positioning does not allow me to reply, so I just listen as he begins, "I want to know what's going on with you and me? You come over to see me and I like that, but then you start dating all these other men."

I'm gobsmacked, as I hadn't anticipated this was to be a heart-to-heart and it takes me completely unaware. I just sit completely motionless, as his words tumble forth, "I'm not really happy about it, because I thought perhaps there was something between you and me. I can't believe you haven't felt it. We get on well together and I think a lot of you. I've always liked you even since we first met years ago, but obviously you were with someone else then..."

As he pauses to collect himself, I'm aware only of the warm feel of his breath and the widening of my eyes. Why wasn't I aware of this and why hasn't he said anything before? I'm wondering if I should reply and then what I would say? And then how I'd even speak to him as the logistics of my current position make it fairly much impossible.

"...Then you were suddenly single but I thought you needed some time, and I've waited, and now you are dating other men and I want to be with you."

He stops and ironically I'm aware only of silence.

My mouth is gaping.

My mind is telling me that this man has just made an emotional speech, not quite worthy of an Oscar, but one that I must respond to. How can I not? What should I say? What do I want to say? *Hurry up, Jen! He needs a reply! You're keeping him waiting!*

I'm panicking, so I switch off my mind and turn my head, where of course I meet his face in close up. Completely unplanned, I lean in and kiss him passionately and he kisses me back and it's so good we keep doing it. The hubbub of the bar has completely disintegrated. The only thing I'm aware of is the sensation of his lips on mine – so unexpected and yet, producing a mind-blowing tingling coursing through me. I absorb myself totally in this minute and it keeps on going. And yet, in an instant, that bliss is destroyed as I dare let a thought interrupt me. *What are you doing?* It nags at me. *You better mean this because you're being unfair if you don't!* I pull myself free, which isn't easy in more than one way. I catapult myself into standing position, and extract myself swiftly. Accelerating as I push myself through the throngs, I reach the door to the ladies' bathroom. For once there's no wait. I shut myself in a stall and let go of the breath I wasn't aware I was holding. Pulling out my phone, I hit my brother's name – I need reassurance. I wait impatiently as it rings and then launch into, "I've just snogged him and I really don't know if I should have."

"Back up," he orders, "Who? When? Where? Why?"

"Arghh! – Adam, Kyle's brother. He just yelled in my ear that he liked me and that he wanted me, and I didn't know what to say so I turned and snogged him… for ages!"

"And?"

"And what?" I'm shrieking down the phone.

"So what's wrong? I take it you like him, Jen?"

"I think I might," I confess.

"And that the snogging was good?"

"Yes," I mutter, which is a complete and utter understatement as it topped anything I've experienced for a long, long time.

"Well, then," he's saying, as I'm enjoying the reminiscence. "What was it you told me last week? The list of requirements you had for the guy you might be looking for, if you were actually looking?"

"You want me to list them now?"

"Yep. Go ahead!"

I try to clear my head, before beginning, "I want, if I was looking, a soul-mate, someone who understands me, who doesn't want heaps of space, but who loves holding me and is great at sex, with whom I can share life with equally and who possesses a passion for what he does. He has to be upbeat and able to see the positive in the negative and have the confidence to really live, not just exist."

"Did you learn it, parrot fashion?" my brother jibes.

"Stop interrupting! I'm on a roll," I shout louder as a toilet flushes, "It would be nice if he bought me presents for no reason and if he would show up just because he was missing me and stay the extra night, when he should have gone home. He's someone who will catch my tears and who owes me nothing, but mostly he's a guy who will love me for who I am."

There's a round of applause and I push the door open to see four girls in the bathroom.

"Right on, girl!" says one.

"Is he out there?" asks another. "Because if you don't want him, point him out to me. If you've got someone that fits those criteria, I wouldn't let him out of my sight!"

"I'm still here," my brother hollers, reminding me of the phone I'm still gripping to my ear. "Can you tick some of those boxes, because if so, that girl with the loud mouth is right. What's the problem? Get back out there and go get some more! Stop faffing around and let me get back to work!"

"Do you think?" I ask lamely.

"I think!" he replies forcefully. "Now go!" With that he hangs up.

"Okay, ladies," I say confidently, "please let me pass, I can't be sure he meets all my requirements yet, but I'm willing to give it a shot and find out!"

"Go get Prince Charming!" cries the louder girl, reaching out to pat me on the back.

"As long as it's not that fat, balding guy at the bar!" says another as they all giggle.

There is nothing else to do except submit. Yes, I've surpassed myself and I've been doing fine on my own, but deep down I know I function better with someone else helping to ground me. Adam seems sane. We've shared some fairly emotional conversations. I've seen positivism in his personality and his self-esteem seems on intact. What's to be lost? Physically, I'm thinking that we obviously click. He's an attractive guy, he tastes wonderful, and I'll take a gamble that the sex will be good.

I should have realised this earlier, but often opportunities only present themselves when you're ready.

I feel ready.

Striding forth, I leave the girls in the ladies. I pass the fat, balding guy at the bar – *hey I'm sure he'll suit someone!* – and make my way back to the table. Adam puts his hand out towards me and I grip it. He pulls me down next to him on the sofa. "Is everything okay?" he shouts for what feels like the tenth time tonight.

I just nod.

"Did you run away? Did I overstep the mark? Should I have waited longer?" He frowns, anxiously.

"No, its fine," I shout, grinning at him. "I just needed a moment."

He pulls me in closer. "Are you sure?" he asks, obviously still concerned.

"Yes," I watch his face relax. "I am very sure!"

And I do feel very sure. Sometimes you just have to shut your eyes and jump in. I'm grinning from ear to ear.

"Shall we go home?" he asks, still gripping my hand. "I'm not really up for a club."

"Yes, let's go home," I say.

The End

Acknowledgements:

My special gratitude to everyone who has read Betrayal, Malt Whisky, & A Toilet Brush in its various drafts, especially my beta readers Linda, Christina, Jennifer, Donna, Fern and Carolyn.

Sincere thanks also to my Consulting group, Jill Moffat, JoAnne Keltner, and Perri Wood, who looked at and critiqued cover designs and wording.

Fena, thank you for all the changes and alterations you made to the cover, only for us to decide on the original after all. Our interactions were always upbeat and your responses immediate, despite you living on the other side of the world. You're a star!

My appreciation to Caroline and Ian Wilson who proof-read my Scottish terms but mainly, oodles of "thank you"s to my superb, copy-editor Carolyn Pinard, who has helped me in so many ways; more than she'll know.

I would also like to mention Laura Pepper Wu at 30 Day Books for her wonderful on-line course, personal interactions, and to wish all my fellow pupils success in their ventures.

To someone, I remember fondly from my past, I'd like to say, 'Hi Johnee Miller, those were the days!'

Finally, I'd like to mention the special support I receive constantly from my family. You are my home, my life and my sanctuary and there are no words to express the enormity of my gratitude.

About the Author

Born in South East England, Ira has lived in Scotland and North Florida. She has always had a desire to write but got sidetracked scribing lyrics for a band and by a career in Alternative Health and Property Management.

Having time to take restock of her life due to an illness, Ira finally had no excuses left and began writing. She hasn't looked back since. Her favourite fridge magnet is "Whatever you want to do, dare to begin it."

Keep up to Date!

Links to Ira's latest publications, musings and life's events can be found at:

https://www.facebook.com/pages/Ira-Phillips-Author/156496251208404

Ira's next book might be: Reversing on the Motorway
Then again, she is apt to change her mind.

Would you like to write a Review?

Ira would love to hear from you and will appreciate your reviews of her work. Or email @ ira.phillips1@yahoo.com

Printed in Great Britain
by Amazon.co.uk, Ltd.,
Marston Gate.